Praise for *The Sunshine Years*:

'A bleak portrayal of Sydney-sider thirty-something digressives and nihilists. I liked its refreshing inconclusiveness and its sparse dialogue-driven dramatic arc, and its evocations of physicality.' **Will Self**

'A brilliant story by one of Britain's best young writers. Set in the bright, light, big city of modern Sydney, it is a passionate, stylish novel. The book tells the big new truths about relationships and is one of those books that shimmers with ideas and observations. Afsaneh Knight is a star.' **Andrew O'Hagan**

Praise for Afsaneh Knight's *Slaughterhouse Heart*:

'I was gripped . . . sharp and astringent, with great emotion.' **Margaret Forster**

'An extraordinary and moving story that intuitively exposes the emotions men hate having to face.' *Esquire*

'Knight's debut packs a steady and unrelenting series of punches. A book about love, but not sentimentality . . . and all the better for its lack of easy answers.' *Vogue*

'Afsaneh Knight handles a shifting narrative with dexterity . . . deft and promising.' *Spectator*

'This will have you tied to the sofa all weekend.' *Time Out*

'A promising young writer.' *The Times*

'It's been a while since a book made me gasp at the power and freshness of its prose. Afsaneh Knight's *Slaughterhouse Heart* did; this writer drips with talent.' *Melbourne Age*

www.transworldbooks.co.uk

Also by Afsaneh Knight

Slaughterhouse Heart

The Sunshine Years

Afsaneh Knight

Doubleday

LONDON · TORONTO · SYDNEY · AUCKLAND · JOHANNESBURG

TRANSWORLD PUBLISHERS
61–63 Uxbridge Road, London W5 5SA
A Random House Group Company
www.transworldbooks.co.uk

First published in Great Britain
in 2012 by Doubleday
an imprint of Transworld Publishers

A CIP catalogue record for this book
is available from the British Library.

ISBNs 9780385614450 (cased)
9780857521446 (tpb)

Addresses for Random House Group Ltd companies outside the UK
can be found at: www.randomhouse.co.uk
The Random House Group Ltd Reg. No. 954009

The Random House Group Limited supports the Forest Stewardship Council (FSC®),
the leading international forest-certification organization. Our books carrying the FSC
label are printed on FSC®-certified paper. FSC is the only forest-certification scheme
endorsed by the leading environmental organizations, including Greenpeace.
Our paper procurement policy can be found at
www.randomhouse. co.uk/environment

Typeset in 12/14.5pt Bembo by Falcon Oast Graphic Art Ltd.
Printed and bound in Great Britain by
Clays Limited, Bungay, Suffolk

2 4 6 8 10 9 7 5 3 1

For my sisters
India and Amaryllis

'Time passes. Listen. Time passes.'

from *Under Milk Wood*, by Dylan Thomas

1

Story had the feeling that something was coming to an end. A sort of best of times worst of times feeling. Like the sky was going to open up, a big hole, and snow would just come pouring out. Snow in Sydney.

Snow would fall on the jacarandas, so confidently in bloom. Snow would melt into the frothy coffees that sat on all those outdoor tables. Snow would land on the naked skin of Sydney on a Sunday, and would fizz and hiss for a hot moment before turning to water.

'Fuck, dude,' Story would say. 'Snow.'

Of course, on this ordinarily glorious November day, the sky will remain closed. But Story's strange feeling will persist. As it had done for a while, now; it had been dogging at Story's corners, like an indicator blinking, tick tick tick tock.

He wishes he had someone to tell about it. Apart from the cab driver, obviously.

'The Fish Market, please.'

'Pyrmont?'

'Yep.'

He couldn't even describe it to himself.

It wasn't a good feeling. Like a giant balloon was not

going to burst on the ground in front of him, and five hundred supermodels come out, going, you know, 'Hello Story, Hello Story, Hello Story.' It wasn't a feeling like that.

But it wasn't a bad feeling either. It wasn't like his phone was going to start buzzing and it would be his boss at the Reserve Bank – the only man in New South Wales to be completely, eerily white, blanched by the air-conditioning and soggy from the sandwiches – who was going to tell him he was fired. No. Not that kind of feeling.

It was just a feeling, of snow coming down. Of things coming to ends. Of walking into walls.

Who could understand that?

Not the cab driver.

Not Mac, who would likely say, 'You've lost me, mate.' Not JP, who would likely say, 'Pull yourself out of your own fucking arse, would you, Story?' Not Vincent Batty, who would likely grin that googlesome grin of his and say, 'I thought Aussie blokes weren't supposed to have feelings, hey mate.'

Kali, maybe, would understand. Kali would listen to him speak it out, anyway. And she'd like the idea of the snow – that would make her smile.

But Story wouldn't be telling Kali. Because Kali was his big sister and she had a husband and a kid, and the space for that kind of conversation is gone.

The Anzac Bridge has flurried past, and soon the cab pulls up outside the vast Fish Market car park. Story pays from inside, with a small tip. He'll be leaving a big tip on the way back, because, you know – fish in a car. This direction, though, no need to be excessive, as he sometimes was when drunk, peeling off ten-dollar bills in reeling gratitude for arriving home alive and compos mentis.

He walks from the taxi to the Fish Market entrance, and

car after car glides past, big white Holdens and stretched Subarus. They are enormous and they hum and they reflect the heat. Story feels foolish to be on his feet; puny, and embarrassed. And a thought comes to him with energy — why doesn't he own a car? Why does he take cabs every-where, as if he lives in New York? Why has it never occurred to him to buy a car?

He could afford one. Actually — he could afford many. Two. Three. Four might be pushing it. Might lead to cutbacks in other areas of lifestyle. But he reckons he could do three without much drama. Definitely two. So how come he doesn't even have one? His apartment has two dedicated spaces in the underground car park, specifically for him. And a lift, that would take him directly up to his floor, that would spill him out, practically from his car to his kitchen, like fucking Batman.

Story feels his heart lift and glitter with the thrill of a bona fide new project — if he wasn't cooking this afternoon, he would go to a car yard right now. Not to the Jaguar dealer-ship two streets away from him, nothing that flash. He needed to find himself a big, muscly, meaty thing with a long boot. Understated, all-Australian, but a little bit hip-hop. Like these cars thrumming and sliding past him now. He wants one of those. Except black — white was for Westies — and with tinted windows.

With the short-term distraction of his friends coming, and the long-term distraction of a car, Story feels the day turning.

He finds his fish at the third counter he visits, takes a ticket — number 087 — from the dispenser, and waits his turn.

'Could you keep your fucking voice down,' hisses the man in front of him, ticket 086, to the woman he's with, also ticket 086. A couple. As one. Single ticket. Not an un-attractive woman, either. Thin, a bit flat-chested, but Story quite likes that. Big sunglasses and drainpipe jeans.

'Keep my fucking voice down?' she says, not even looking up at the guy, just keeping on looking at the fish. 'Why, superstar? Are your fans out this morning? Have we got cameras following us? Is the whole fucking Fish Market just desperate to hear what we're saying? Get over yourself, you prick.'

'Calm down, for fuck's sake,' he says to her.

'I'm perfectly calm, you bullying fucking control freak. Fuck off.'

'You're a nightmare,' says the guy, shaking his head, his voice low. 'A fucking nightmare.'

'Too bad you're married to me, then. Just choose a *fucking fish*, will you?'

'No way. I'm not going to choose a fish. Whatever fish I choose will be wrong. You'll fucking nag me for the rest of the day for getting the wrong fish.'

'God, you're a fucking idiot. I don't *nag* you. I'm not your *mother*. You fucking bully me into coming here on a Sunday morning, just so I can get fucking fish juice all over my feet, and come out reeking of fish, and now that we're standing here you won't – *choose* – a fish.'

'Number eighty-six!' the fishmonger has shouted out.

'You're seriously not going to choose a fish?' she asks him. He folds his arms. Shakes his head. 'Prick,' she says, this time under her breath. Then she looks up at the fishmonger, smiles a bright smile. 'Four kilos of clams, please.'

'Four kilos of clams?' the husband questions.

'Vongole,' she says.

'*Four kilos?*'

12

'Yes, fucktard.'

Fucktard. That's a good word, Story thinks.

'You know what this is? We need to get you something to eat,' says the dude, the husband. The clams are handed over in two bags. 'There's a great calamari stand down there,' he says.

'Calamari? At eleven in the morning? You're telling me I have to eat *fish* for my breakfast?'

'I'm not telling you anything' – he is accepting his change – 'I'm saying we should get some breakfast.'

The woman pauses. A fertile little cloud rises in the air between the two, a happy Hiroshima, which Story cannot see.

'I want ricotta hotcakes,' she says.

'You want to go to Bill's?'

'*Yes*, I want to go to Bill's. You can have your fucking fish breakfast, and you can drop me at Bill's on the way home.'

'The clams are in ice. We can both have breakfast.'

'You're coming to Bill's? What if they don't have fish on the menu? What if you can't have fish on toast?' says the woman.

'I'll have eggs.'

'You can't have eggs. You said you wanted fish.'

She has put her arm through his. They are walking away.

Story understands not one pixel of what he has just seen, not one word of conversation just heard. He neither understands the intimacy, nor the violence.

'Number eighty-seven!' says the fish man.

'Yep!' says Story, looking up, handing over his single ticket, for his lone self, representing just him. 'That's me.'

That calamari sounded good. The calamari mentioned by the warring couple. Story does a circuit of the market, trying to find it. He completes his loop, ends up back at the counter where he bought his snappers, and then he sees it, immediately to his left. *King Calamari Café.* That's got to be it. There is a long-faced teenager with potholed skin, standing slouchy behind the bar, staring into the middle distance.

Story has the hollows of a morning after inside him. He goes to the boy, and orders one portion of salt and pepper calamari, and a diet coke. He watches the chef behind the boy in the small kitchen, and receives his calamari minutes later. The diet coke has been forgotten.

'And I asked for a diet coke, mate?'

The boy gets one from the fridge beside him.

Story opens the can and drinks. He squeezes the wedge of lemon over the calamari, and soon – after having to puff his cheeks out and take in air from the heat of it – feels it warm his mouth and his stomach.

'This calamari's really good,' Story says to the boy.

'Cool,' says the boy.

'How come it's so crispy?'

'I don't know,' says the boy. There is a pause. 'I can ask.'

A minute later he returns with the wisdom: 'Semmer-leaner, the chef says.'

'Right!' says Story. 'That makes sense.'

He wants to ask if the squid is just rolled in the semolina dry, or whether it is first dipped in egg, or egg white, or something. But having registered the fact that the boy is now gouging into the side of his thumb with his canines, Story stays quiet.

He finishes up his calamari in silence, the sound of crunching in his ears.

14

2

Mac was thinking about chocolate. Because it was his job.

He worked for Arnold's, Australia's favourite fancy biscuit manufacturer, as a Senior Researcher and Developer. Believe it or not, he was paid quite handsomely, and had a career trajectory that would, in years to come, trawl Deputy Research and Development Head, Research and Development Head, and Vice President (Research and Development) within its net.

This particular chocolate thought ran thus:

If it was reasonable to assume that it would take the average male (Av.M) around seventy seconds, and the average female (Av.F) around ninety-five seconds, to eat from start to finish (wrapper to trash), a 40 to 60 gram individual-portion, biscuit-based milk-chocolate bar, then you could further assume that the chocolate bar would be consumed not long after the Av.M or Av.F had left the shop from which they had bought the bar, i.e. before he (*he* now taken to be gender neutral) reached the bus stop or train station, his car, home, or place of work. I.e. he would most likely finish his chocolate bar on the street.

This was relevant in terms of the potential problems re: Satisfaction Arc (S.Arc).

Caramello Koalas were designed to be eaten in one or two swift bites, an indulgence so rapid it barely counted. Women, it had been shown, who deviated from their diets with a Caramello Koala or Freddo Frog, did not experience the normal extent of guilt expected from a Diet Break (DB), nor, generally speaking, ongoing disruption to their diets. This was due to the sheer smallness of the item. The success for an adult, therefore, in a Caramello Koala or Freddo Frog was, perversely, the very fact that they were eaten with such speed.

Boost, on the other hand, was a full-size chocolate bar. It, however, had medium-hard caramel as a primary ingredient, and therefore could take up to four times as long to eat as an average individual milk-chocolate bar. It was safe to suppose, even with research pending, that it was this extended consumption time that accounted for some large part of Boost's success. It was likely that the average consumer (Av.C) would still be eating a Boost when he arrived at the bus stop – perhaps even when on the bus! – or have to linger outside his place of work in order to finish it. Eating a Boost was a significant event, therefore. The decision to eat a Boost could cause a Domino Decision Effect (DDE) – *Do I finish eating the Boost outside the office and delay my return to my desk? Do I take the Boost into the office with me, perhaps inviting comments from my colleagues? Do I leave eating the last third of the Boost for later?* Boosts often blurred the boundaries of designated snack time, and duly graphed high on the S.Arc.

But a biscuit-based milk chocolate bar, like the one Arnold's was planning to launch next March – codenamed

Bar X, its first foray from the fancy biscuit market, midst much mystery, anticipation and pressure – hit the middle to lower time register, and so ran the possible problem of leaving the Av.C feeling unsatisfied – the chocolate bar would not even bridge two locations, it would be begun and ended on the street. It would be a Transient Eat (Tr.E), and that could be its major hurdle.

But that was the nature of the beast – Arnold's made biscuits. Their radical move into the terrain of the individual chocolate bar had to be an extension of their famous name in biscuits. It was a conversation, if you will, between biscuit and chocolate; the individual chocolate bar had, at its heart, a biscuit. Biscuit was the centre of the thing. Albeit an avant-garde re-reading of the Arnold's classic Golden Crunch – lighter, crunchier and more snappable – but biscuit nonetheless. There was no getting round the fact that Bar X would take no more than ninety-five seconds for the Av.C to eat.

A clear thing they had to do, to avoid an S.Arc disaster, was to up the Mouth Feel (MF). While this wouldn't add anything to the—

'Hey, Mac!'

Mac looks up to see the tall, thin form of his friend Vincent Batty, shouting from across the street. He looks like a relative of the Cat in the Hat, Vinnie, all arms and legs and a supple, gangling back. His eyes are large and pronouncedly round – they goggle with an opaque light. His mouth is smiles and the creases in his cheeks are expressive. He is a North Sydney Grammar boy, like the rest of them.

'Vincent Batty! Mate! How's it going?'

Vincent has crossed the street, and encircled Mac in a brief, hard hug. Mac comes out of it pushing his glasses up his nose.

'Oh, you know, Mac,' says Vinnie, smiling his full-lipped, symmetrical, smile, 'out and about on a Sunday. You were looking pretty focused there. Had your head down like you were curing cancer. Almost didn't know whether to stop you.'

'Ah, thinking about work.'

'Work!' says Vincent. 'Biscuits, eh. Not a cure for cancer.'

'No.'

'Biscuit-kind is lucky to have a man as dedicated as yourself.'

Mac laughs.

'You hung over?'

'No, why?'

Vincent nods at Mac's face. 'Specs,' he says.

'Oh. Just better for your eyes than wearing contacts all the time.'

'Right-o. You going over to Story's?'

'Yeah, yeah, on my way there now. The cricket'll be on already.'

'Fucken A it will. You want to grab a beer over the rest of the over? We can head to Story's in the break.'

'Sweet,' says Mac. 'Hey!' Mac taps Vinnie on the chest with the back of his hand. 'I got the invite, mate! So you're actually doing it?'

'Apparently. And you're going to be with me, mate, in a cravat and a pair of fucken pantaloons.'

'Yeah, right.'

'I'm being serious. Tree's got her heart set on these stripy knickerbocker-type things' – Vincent Batty is gesticulating with his fingers, making balloon shapes around his knees – 'for all the groomsmen. That's you, mate.'

Mac raises his eyebrows.

'You should count yourself lucky. She wants JP in a mankini and a top hat.'

'That's a pretty disturbing image,' laughs Mac.

Vincent grins, and they start walking. 'No going back now, mate,' he says.

3

The doorbell rings, and Story goes to the intercom.
  'Come up, dude,' he says.
  Two minutes later he opens the door to a tall man with wide shoulders, a head shaved number two, and fine bones, bones a little too fine for the size of his face. He wears a pair of gold–rimmed aviators. They shake hands, and Story taps JP on the outside of one arm, with the physical unease that has always puppeteered him.
  'G'day, mate,' says JP. He stands, his long feet in first position, like a ballet dancer, incongruous to the brawny rest of him.
  'How's it going, dude?' Story says, smiling and sounding congested. 'Hey, nice shades. Are they new?'
  'Ten dollars, Paddy's Markets.'
  'Ten dollars?'
  'Yep.'
  'Do you have any eyeballs left? I mean, dude, do you know where we live?'
  'Makes no fucking difference. The lenses are all the same.'
  'Those lenses are made from plastic, mate. In January, they'll melt.'

'What bollocks.' JP's face is twisted into anger, and were Story a stranger he would take offence. As it is, he's oblivious. JP goes on, 'These lenses are exactly the same as the lenses on your three hundred dollar sunnies. Difference is, you're a fashion victim.'

'Whatever, dude.' Story laughs. 'Do you want a vodka tonic?'

'Nah, I'm not drinking today. I'll just have a beer.'

JP scoops up a handful of smoked nuts from a bowl, and tips them bit by bit from his palm into his head. He doesn't comment on the spread on the kitchen counter, Story's usual effort: a dish of roasted figs and pine nuts, a tray of oysters with chilli and lemon oil; bowls of nuts and stuffed olives; an entire round of soft cheese.

'That thing reeks,' says JP, of the cheese.

'You want some?'

'No way.'

JP receives his beer, and takes it over to the large television. He flicks the TV on, and scans through the channels until he reaches the cricket. JP, received wisdom has it, is Story's closest friend.

The buzzer goes.

A few moments pass, and in comes Cannie – also, in a way, Story's closest friend. Although – different.

Cannie's been on the scene for ever. Story and she had become real mates at Sydney Uni, but she'd been around since they were kids – she went to Cammeray Girls', the sister school to North Sydney Grammar.

Christened Abigail Carlton-Terry, some young gun at Cammeray had taken Cannie's initials, AC-T, and put them in parallel to Australian Capital Territory – Canberra. 'Suits you,' said another, 'because you're fucking boring.' There'd been laughter at that, and the truth of it stung. But Canberra soon became Cannie, and its etymology thankfully forgotten. Cannie was now just – Cannie. It was even how she thought of herself.

She has brought flowers. She usually came with a bottle of white wine – the only person ever to bring anything except a box of beer – but, today, lilies.

'It smells amazing in here,' says Cannie, kissing Story on the cheek. 'As usual. What's in the oven?'

'There's a snapper cooking on the deck,' says Story.

'No, it's not fish. It smells like cake.'

'Oh, probably the figs.'

'God, Story, what's the point of ever eating out, when you can just come here?'

Cannie has walked across the large, modern room, over to the sofa, and bends down to give JP a kiss.

'Cannie, mate, Cannie. Hi.' JP stretches into an artificial, half-hearted yawn as he greets her.

'How's life?' says Cannie.

'Oh. Not too bad.' It occurs to him that he might stand up. But he's committed now – to sitting down. It's only Cannie.

JP stands twenty minutes later, for his own sake, when the cricketers have gone in for tea, and he is seeking refreshment. Cannie wishes he hadn't come this close just as her mouth was bulging so copiously with food. As he retrieves another bottle from the fridge, Cannie struggles with a whole fig fat in her mouth.

Cannie can go from almost schoolgirl fondness of JP, to smarting hatred, in a moment. She's never been able to quite get a grip on it, and she's never been able to quite fathom why – fathom what it is that JP does, that invokes her so.

22

'You got one of these, too, eh?' JP picks up a folded cream card from the counter, with a photo of a kissing couple on the front. Inside, in curly letters, it reads:

Mr Shawn B. Lercher and Mrs Edwina S. Lercher
Cordially request the great pleasure of your attendance
At the wedding of their daughter
Miss Teresa M. Lercher
to Mr Vincent P. F. Batty . . .

After venue, date and time, the dress code states that:

Ladies are cordially encouraged to wear hats or fascinators.

There is, of course, the inevitable, dedicated email address:

vincentandteresaswedding@hotmail.com

The well-defined part of JP that takes pleasure in the stupidity of others, bristles warmly.

'There are a lot of misters and misses in Tree's family,' he says, tossing the invitation back down as if it is a flyer, an ad for dry cleaning, a pizza menu.

Story giggles, then sniffs. 'Yep,' he says, 'and they're very *cordial.*'

JP laughs, a convincing, genuine laugh – in him, a rarity like a solar eclipse. 'Fuck,' says JP, shaking his head. 'You going to cordially wear a fascinator, Cannie?'

Cannie smiles thinly.

'They coming today?' JP asks.

'Not Tree. Just Vinnie. Tree's at some thirtieth birthday party.'

'Thirtieth? How old is Tree?' he asks.

'Early thirties,' says Cannie.

'I thought she was younger than that,' posits JP.

'She's thirty-three,' Cannie says, blandly. 'She was the year below me at school.'

'She seems a lot younger than you,' says JP, and burps silently into his cheeks.

The fish has been eaten. So too the rice, the noodles and the cucumber salad. They had all extolled. Apart from JP, who'd said, 'Actually, this is not bad.'

Really, Story should be saving the significant leftovers, putting everything in the fridge. But he's tired. Really tired. And tipsy. And he's up at ten to six tomorrow, as per usual. Plus, he's sorted the recycling, which is effort enough.

He scrapes all the food into the trash, fish heads, liquid and all, and takes the bag out to the communal bin, along with the heroically classified beer bottles, cartons and tins.

Then he sits at his table, on the edge of his long bench, and slumps, his back an almost perfect C. The cleaner is coming tomorrow, and she can deal with the rest of it.

He should have a shower, and he should call Mum, and he wants to do both. But he's not got the energy for either.

And sitting there, looking at the room, with the TV dead, and the voices gone, and the lights low, Story feels that feeling. That feeling of everything ending. Of everything moving away from him. Like if he reached his arm out, he couldn't quite touch any of it.

He looks at this apartment – in which he has lived for four years, which, an hour ago, was filled with his friends. It doesn't look like it's his.

The fridge starts up its chorus, the loud drone that it likes to effect for five minutes at a time. Busy, that fridge is, keeping the beer, the wine, the butter and the eggs cold.

The feeling can't be shook. It is there, juddering like the fridge, reprising itself, covering over the moments of hard quiet like dust.

4

They never got any easier, mornings. It'd been almost eight years, now, of needing to get to the same office at the same time, and still JP turned the alarm off and rolled over at least twice. Still he stood in the shower with eyes shut, thoughts melting down his face like candle wax, with the water and the steam. Despair thoughts. Gloom thoughts.

What was it about mornings? Why was he always so fucking tired? Why did he stand in the shower, five days out of seven, and hate himself? JP looked down, and there, settled comfortably on his stomach like a little loaf of bread – like a large, hair-covered hamburger bun – was a pouch of fat. A lard pie. That was reason enough, right there, for the self-hatred.

Forget the fact that he put on the same suits and shirts and ties every morning, sat on the same bus reading the same newspaper, so as to turn up at the same office. Forget the fact that this same office had, after seven years, still not promoted him. Forget the fact that he had become a lawyer in the first place out of fear, and spent his days providing himself with silent commentary on the pointlessness, corruption, and mediocrity of every bit of work he did. Forget the fact that he had only ever had one girlfriend in his entire life, for a total of two months. The rest — one-night stands and pick-ups, randoms and prostitutes.

Forget all of this, and focus only on the fat. On the loaf, the bun, the little cradle of ugliness. That, all by itself, was reason enough, this morning, to feel loathing of a gnawing and relentless kind. He was a gnawing and relentless kind of a guy, JP — it had happened along the way. He squirted a blue line of shower gel directly on to his stomach, and kneaded, with masochistic thoroughness, the soap around his skin.

JP doesn't remember the last time he had been excited by a woman. Dismissing, that is, the powerful lust he felt for most of them, most of the time. He wasn't talking about that — what Mac would call 'the Horn' — no, that was just the perpetual state of play. He meant the feeling of your face getting hot, the feeling of your heart being lifted up by a strong hand into your throat. The one-night stands — the randoms, the prostitutes — after it was done, and JP woke up with the sun pushing through the shutters, the things next to him in the bed were just awkward, fleshy and strange-smelling. He would always notice the fact that they had stubble in their armpits.

There had only been one exception, a crippling infatuation had intermittently since his teens. That one woman, he had been excited by. Amazed by, in fact. By her beauty. By her distinctness. By her fragility. And typically, fucking typically, she had been unattainable. Still was, in fact. Kali, his best mate's sister — and married, for good measure. She had decimated him, just by being in the same room, by smiling and saying, 'Hi JP,' and giving him a kiss on the cheek. *He remembered what she was wearing the first time he saw her.* Pathetic.

Anyhow, it was years ago, and it was a nonsense. He barely saw her. Maybe once every two years. If that.

JP looked at his paunch for a last, grim moment before wrapping a towel around himself. He went downstairs like this – his housemate, Tate, was still sleeping – switched on the coffee machine and poured himself a heaped bowl of cereal. Then, through the sliding doors and into the little back garden, where he stood bristling in the cool and eating his breakfast. Soon the day would be blistering under the heat, and this morning shiver would be a pleasant memory. It was forty degrees yesterday, likely to be forty-two today, a spring heatwave. The only good thing – the only – about these days of malign heat, were the evenings, when the sun was down and everybody spilled out on to the streets in relief and a baked sort of buzz. Yesterday, walking home, he had seen a girl sitting outside a bar with long, oiled legs, and he had stared at them, and then – so cooked was he by the humidity and the UV – he had actually looked up at her face.

The coffee machine droned out a thick, black espresso, and JP tipped it back into his mouth.

The day had begun.

It had been announced at the office. They had all received the email. Redvale were hiring a new guy. 'Welcoming' him, in fact. He was coming straight in as Partner. And this was the drumroll – wait for it – he was thirty-one.

His age hadn't been in the email. But this had:

Redvale are pleased to welcome Oliver Marchal to the firm as Partner and Deputy to Chris Stern in our Taxation department. Oliver comes to us from a distinguished career at Freshfields in London, where he served for three years as Associate, one year as Senior Associate and for the last year Of Counsel. We all look forward to having him with us from January 4th.

There was a rage somewhere deep, deep in JP's innards.

He typed the name into Google – '*Oliver Marchal*'.

And up the bastard popped. Over and over again. It seemed he was quite the talking head: *Financial Times*, *Investor's Chronicle*, even a mention in the *Economist*. A dream. JP had written three letters to the *Economist* over the years, and not one of them had been printed. Whereas this guy, this new Partner – Hail and Welcome! Oliver! Partner! – had a go-to quote, in an actual article. A journalist from the *Economist* had called him – met him for a coffee, for lunch – and had chased his opinion.

After fifteen minutes of solid Googling, JP was interrupted by a voice behind him.

'He's thirty-one, you know.'

He turned round. It was Karina, one of the department secretaries, handing him a fax numerous pages long. Why the fuck did people still send faxes?

'Who is?' said JP.

'Him,' said Karina, gesturing to JP's computer screen. 'The new guy. Oliver Marchal.' She said it 'March-ill'. JP had wondered about that, the pronunciation. 'And apparently,' Karina continued, 'he's really good-looking, too.' She smiled at JP, mercilessly, into his face. The room felt airless and heavy with computer waves, static hiss from the screens and hard drives, from all the machines.

'Dream on, Karina,' said JP, his head pulled back into his neck like a chicken's, his face coiled into a bad-smell look –

a default expression. She held out the fax to him and JP took it. 'Is that it?'

'Looks like it,' she said.

'Could you open a bloody window on your way out?'

'If you open the windows, darlin', the air-conditioning doesn't work. You should know that from your fifty years at that desk.' Karina's accent was a confident, extreme, un-tempered Queenslandic. Karina made no bones.

'Just open the window, would you?' JP was not being polite.

'Open it yourself.' Karina walked away. She is unbothered by JP, pays no more attention to him or his rudeness than she would a fly.

JP ran his palm over his five millimetres of hair, a velcro noise of rubbing. Fuck me, he could pull someone's guts through their throat, at this moment.

The bitch was right. He'd been sitting here, at this desk, since when? The beginning of time? Was there even a life before he came to work at Redvale?

There was school. A gap year interrailing around Europe and working in a pub in South London. University. Law school. Two months in Argentina followed by two years at a firm in Brisbane. And then – Redvale.

He'd been here nearly eight years. At this same desk. The only thing that had changed was the computer, when they upgraded the system a couple of years ago. And the tragic thing was that JP had actually been excited about that. He had experienced a little thrill as he walked through the floor and saw his new, pristine screen waiting on his desk.

Ticking ever closer to eight years at this desk, and the only thing he had to look forward to was another computer upgrade. Because he was never going to be made Partner. In a neon, nauseous flash, he realised it. Cruising close to thirty-seven years old, eight years as Associate – it was never going to happen. It'd been promised for three years now, that he was next in line, that they 'wanted to ensure his place in the future and the fabric of Redvale'. Carrick, his boss, had actually said that to him, as if he were reciting from some company manual.

And now, this new guy, this Pom, Oliver. With the un-pronounceable surname. A surname so uncertain that JP didn't even dare say it in his own head. Even the surname had him on the back foot! And he was straight in as Partner. Aged thirty-one.

Folk walking past JP would have thought nothing. They just would have seen his still back, still to the point of petrified, and his hands clasping the edge of the desk. They would have seen nothing. Whereas – JP was a bomb. An open crucible.

He stood up and walked, down the narrow corridor with windows along it, overlooking Macquarie Street. How easy it would be, with the side of his fist, to put a crack in each one.

Had he ever been anywhere but here? In this sealed, air-conditioned hive, a part of the furniture, doing work that would never change a thing in the world.

This was his life, and it was fucked. He wanted to crack windows. Crack heads together, as he knew he could. The fuckknuckles who inhabited this place, smug, stupid, laughing fuckers, he could smash them each one up against every window.

He walked straight past Sarah's desk, gave a single thud to Carrick's door and, without waiting, walked in.

Carrick had the receiver to his ear, registered his surprise with a lift of the eyebrows, and held JP off with an apologetic raise of his hand, to signal that he was on the phone. And then, a further signal to Sarah – who had come in to seize JP – that it was okay. He waved her away, and she disappeared back out to the secretary pool.

You fucking lying prick is what JP had wanted to say. *You lying prick.* It had been circling in his head, growing angrier and redder with each lap, and he had thought he would shout it into Carrick's face.

But he hadn't done so. Even though the rage was pushing against his skin, steaming out of his pores. He hadn't done so because of that hand gesture – Michael Carrick's raised palm – the innate gentility in it, the welcome. The fact that – beyond the surprise – Carrick had not objected to JP intruding into his office like a strung bull, that he had not taken issue at all.

Carrick ends his phone call with a businesslike 'Yes,' and then looks amicably at his employee.

JP is a missile with nothing to hit.

'JP,' says Carrick, as different in this moment in his dapper middle-age to JP as imaginable, 'you need to see me?'

JP shakes his head, his lips pressed together.

This fucking life.

'JP? What's happening?'

Carrick sits, his wall of legal books behind him, brown and red and like a shield. He is calm, open; as if he has all the time in the world.

'I've been an Associate for nearly eight years.' JP isn't shouting. He is not whispering either. Nor is he talking. His voice is rising in sharp dips and falls like far-off bullet spray. 'Eight fucking years. It's not working.'

There is no computer on the desk – what's happened to it? How does the fucker reply to emails? By magic?

'Right,' says Carrick, after a pause. 'I understand. You realise,' he goes on, 'that Oliver Marchal' – 'Marsh-al', not 'March-ill' – French, it sounds – 'is joining the Taxation department. We have space for Partners in Tax, JP – we even have need of them. It's a sector of our business where we're constantly being left with holes. You know, JP, better than anyone, that Corporate is a different th—'

'You don't need to give me this lecture again. I've heard it. From you. Plenty of fucking times.'

Where was his anger going? If only JP could hold on to it.

'Hugh Dempsey and Maggie Huang were both made Partners from Corporate.'

JP spots the computer – a slender, silver laptop – on one of the leather sofas near the window. So he replies to his emails with feet up, looking at the view. All right for some.

'Hugh Dempsey has been with us years longer than you, JP.'

'And Maggie?' counters JP. 'She'd been here, what, two years? And she's no older than me. You're trying to tell me that Maggie was more qualified than me to be Partner, after two years? Or maybe she just looks good on the Redvale literature.'

Carrick's eyes have widened, and JP can tell he has a hit. It gives him air to go on.

'I've sat here, putting in the hours, at the same fucking desk, for eight years. Every time we talk, you tell me the same thing: there's no opening for Partner. Corporate is over-crowded. I'm next in line. Unless, that is, another Asian chick

33

turns up, in which case – what? I'm fucked. I'm stuck doing donkey work for another five years.'

The phone has rung again, and Carrick briefly answers to tell Sarah he'll return the call. 'Sit down, JP,' he says, and his face has closed, has lost a little kindness. 'Maggie Huang was made Partner because, after eighteen months as Associate, she spearheaded the effort that brought in two million dollars' worth of new business from Telecom Australia. Maurice Docker didn't, and doesn't, want to work with anyone else. Since she's been Partner, she's brought us Brightmore as well, and has rebuilt their entire infrastructure for them. You know that, JP, you've worked with her on it. Maggie will be made a Senior Partner in time, and that will have absolutely nothing to do with her being an *Asian chick*, and everything to do with how she works for this company. And Oliver Marchal certainly isn't coming in to the company because he's an *Asian chick.*'

Carrick's tone is hard, and JP feels as if he's falling down a well.

'Don't fucking talk to me like I'm stupid,' says JP, his face screwed into his neck.

Carrick takes a decisive breath.

'JP. I'm going to ask you to take the rest of the day off. You need to get a grip. Go for a run. Do whatever it is you do. I've told you I think you'll make Partner, and I stand by that. But I'm not going to wave a magic wand and create a Partnership where there is none. Most lawyers only make Partner in their forties, or fifties, and even then it's only a few. I've said this to you before, but clearly you need to hear it again. The only way a Partnership will open up is if you perform, and when the opening is there.'

'You don't think I perform? Twelve hours a day, and I don't perform?'

Carrick has not seen JP in this rodeo mode before, as angry and ugly as a lowing steer. But it is not a surprise, and Carrick doesn't take it personally. 'Everyone here does twelve-hour days,' he says. 'Take the day off, and come and see me tomorrow.'

'Fuck this,' says JP. He walks out of Carrick's office. The walls are thin in this tin-pot place, and no doubt Sarah and her coven have heard every humiliating word.

He walks back to his desk, past the windows, and sits down in his chair, in a shamed, livid autopilot.

'Fuck this. Fuck this,' he says to himself, pushes his chair away from the desk, gets up, grabs his suit jacket and his case and walks to the lift.

It's a relief, when JP gets home, that Tate isn't in. Tate works backstage at the Sydney Opera House, which his daily life would suggest was the most louche employer in the city. Tate often enough came home when JP was showering for work, reeking of alcohol, and with a revolution of women, all surprisingly lithe and attractive for Opera House back-stage staff. As a result, JP barely saw him, which was fine. They had only ever crossed paths on one weekday before, when JP was flying to Perth on business and had come home in the early afternoon to pack. Tate was curled on the sofa like a cat, or a girl, watching Rugby League repeats and eating Turkish bread straight from the plastic wrapper.

The house is empty, this Wednesday afternoon – even Tate is at work. Everyone is at work. All cooped up inside, getting flabby and limp, while JP goes straight to the fridge. He burps, reaches for a bottle of Cascade, opens it, and takes it to the bathroom with him.

He had considered going straight to the pub near work. But much as JP had wanted to begin there, to suck a beer into him before he tackled the journey home, he didn't want to risk – not even the smallest risk – seeing anyone from Redvale. So, instead, he bought a beer from the bottle-o and drank it at the bus stop.

The shower is running. Off comes the suit and the cheap shirt. On go the T-shirt and the shorts. In goes the beer.

There will be no one to drink with JP today, as the sun burns down into the ocean, and the ultraviolet rubs his skin into thinness, and the drink softens his belly to mulch. He'll go alone.

His feet pushed angrily into thongs, JP takes the 333 to Bondi. He walks the small hill to the North Bondi RSL. The inside is dark and the stale alcohol smell ekes out from the bar with familiarity, and sincerity. JP signs his name in the visitor book.

Out on the deck, and there is the ocean. Huge, viciously reflecting the light. Surfers dangling in the waves like corks. A dense scattering of people on the beach: women with brash, gleaming bosoms, men with small swimmers and thick thighs. And, of course, tourists. Backpackers. The English: pigeon-chested and burnt.

Don't fucking talk to me like I'm stupid, he had said to Michael Carrick.

He hated that place. He hated himself for working there; that had started pretty early on. Redvale was one of the Big Six, and as such liked to think it was akin to a Magic Circle or White Shoe firm: bollocks. It was a medium, mediocre money-raker. They did the same old shit, for the same old people, and they did it no better or worse than any other Sydney law firm. Their staff were not hotshots and prodigies from around the legal globe, they were only – Maggie Huang included – the best that Australia had to offer. That is, the best of those who had not been able to go overseas and get a job at a Magic Circle or White Shoe firm.

Redvale was staffed by those who were not quite good enough to be really good. And that he, JP, could not even distinguish himself among such an undistinguished bunch, was reality hitting like a knee in the balls.

And what the fuck was the Pom, Oliver Marchal, doing leaving Freshfields for Redvale? What were they offering him that would make the greying office block on Macquarie Street, New South Wales, a better prospect than giving quotes to the *Economist* from the grandeur of Freshfields, in London?

The deck is nearly empty – it is a weekday in November – except for a woman sitting alone at a table, whose crossed leg has a ripple of cellulite running up her thigh and into her dress. She is in her fifties, and has a bikini on beneath her dress. She'd clearly come from the beach; she was still steaming from it; that heat haze that surrounds a person recently fried. She is drinking a glass of white wine.

And there are all the other women, lined higgledy-piggledy on the sand, a few obscured by sun tents, but most flat on their backs with the sun on top of them. They all look the same.

If there could just be one thing of beauty – only one small thing – that crossed his path today, JP could reconcile himself. He could carry the anger on, as he did most days of his life, he could peacefully put Oliver Marchal to rest. If he could notice just one thing, however small. It would make

this day, this destiny of drudgery, this fury and misery —
bearable.

The sun beats down on the splayed bodies. The sand gets
hot, and beers get lifted mechanically to the mouth. Hours
later, JP will make his way home, and he will unzip his fly
and piss against a quiet wall. There will be no beauty in any
of it.

5

Kali had transparent skin, like a butterfly. In some light, you could see the blood in her cheeks, fragile blue cobwebs.

Her mother used to say, while striping zinc down her nose and over her cheekbones, '*D'ou viens tu? D'une autre planète, je crois!*' And then, in later years when French no longer existed, 'Look at this beautiful skin! We found you under a bush, I reckon.'

Her brother, her father, her mother, all went a good, deep Australian brown in the summer, and in the winter were a rosy gold. But even at her most tanned, Kali had a whiteness underneath, as if her skin were tissue paper that you could just peel away, layer by layer.

She had her mum's nose, that was certain. And the upturn to her top lip came from her dad. And while she and Story looked not much alike, they had that curious family resemblance, that ties people to the same tree.

Her see-through skin, though, and her hair – who knows where they came from. A throwback to some great-great-grandmother who lived under the sea. Skin like water, and thin blond hair that looked like fluff in the mornings. She looked in the mirror in the quiet of the house, and saw all those capillaries whispering in her eyelids, and saw her scalp bright white through her hair, and she seemed to herself an alien creature, bald and withered like ET.

Her husband disagreed. 'Not bad for an old sheila,' Guy says to her, when they go out for the evening.

Today, as most days, the house is empty. Guy at work, Jacob at school. Kali is showered and dressed, in yoga trousers and a zipped hooded top. She is waiting for her cup of tea to cool.

After it has cooled, she will drink it. And after that, she will dry her hair with thickening mousse. And after that – she doesn't know. It is eleven now, and by the time she has done her tea and her hair, it will be eleven forty-five, and Jacob will be back from school by four. Four hours only, in this day.

There are things she should do.

Like sort though Jacob's wardrobe and take out all the clothes that are too small for him.

Like tidy the fridges, get rid of all the soft cucumbers and greening cheese.

Like sift the pile of mail that had built up, putting junk and envelopes in the recycling, and dealing with whatever remained.

But these things sit on the other side of a crevasse, and she can't make herself do any of them.

Christmas is looming; she could drive to Paddington and start her shopping. She could get a juice from Ossa on Oxford Street while she was there.

Or she could go to Cole's to buy some more fruit and bread. They were low on Rinse Aid.

Or she could do what she always wants to do but never

does, which is lie down on her side of the bed. Eyes closed while the sun breathes fire outside.

Kali has a sip of her tea. It is still fractionally too hot. The house is silent. Underwater silent. The long kitchen counter is Corian and soft, and has a cold, melting feeling when you lay your cheek on it. This is the way — a little more than a right angle — Kali would turn her head when she swam. Joel, her coach, used to laugh. She was the only swimmer in the history of swimmers, he said, who closed her eyes out of the water and opened them in. She'd been a real swimmer, Kali, swimming for the state of New South Wales. But then she stopped.

'How come?' Story had asked, at the time.

She'd pursed her lips in thought. 'I don't know,' she'd said. Then: 'It takes too much time.'

She'd swum through puberty, that monstrous time of her first periods, having to work out with urgency how to use tampons — as she could neither stop training for a week a month, nor could there be a trail of blood in the water.

And she'd swum through her Dad dying. Only three days she'd taken off training — the day he died, the day after he died, and the day of his funeral. She remembers returning to the water on the third day after his death. She swam some lengths with just her legs, keeping her arms stretched in front, holding on to a float. With her head in the water she imagined him pulling her along, his thumbs in her palms.

But then Kali just stopped. It was the walk to the pool more than anything else — the same walk, every day. She didn't want to see those paving stones any more.

Since then — since retiring in her second year at uni — she'd barely been in the water. She'd go into the ocean with

Guy, during the early years; he liked flirting with her in there. He'd dive under and tug at her bikini bottoms. He wasn't much of a swimmer; he always pulled left and his legs sank too deep, although she'd never tell him that. And she never truly missed it; there was nothing in the water for her that she couldn't find out.

Swimming was also doing nothing – as much doing nothing as sitting here with her head on the counter waiting for tea to cool. It was just moving your arms and moving your legs. Stopping yourself from drowning. That's what you do each day on land as you walk about your life – stop yourself from dying – that's what life is – continuing to not be dead.

It was only the view of other bodies that made the swimming worthwhile – other moving arms and other moving legs, flesh rippling like sheets and taking on ghostly dents and billows as if being pressed by an invisible thing. The other people in the water, as your head turned to the right, turned to the left, every three strokes – they were what made swimming at all real. The things you saw beneath.

Today, in the shower, water had got trapped in Kali's ear. She'd kept it in there, deliberately, careful to keep her head straight. She had been hearing through it for the past twenty minutes, sounds lopsided and blunt. Now, her head on its side on the counter, there is a suck and a pop inside her ear. She feels the water run out, hot.

The tea is cool now. Too cool. That enchanted moment of just right, that midnight within her mug – has passed without her.

★

'I'm not going to cancel a week-long business trip so that I can come to your *beautician*'s wedding.' Guy is sitting on the sofa, with one hand behind his head and one hand around a glass of beer. His eyes are on the television, and he looks annoyed, but only vaguely, only with the 10 per cent of himself that is engaged with his wife.

'She's not my beautician,' says Kali. 'She only does my nails.'

'Jesus, Crump, same thing, isn't it? Why's she inviting you to her wedding, anyway? I mean, crikey. She can't ask every person whose nails she does to her wedding, can she? It's a bit fucking weird.'

Kali feels a familiar, pink despair rise up her throat. She swallows it.

'I've told you this before. We spoke about it last night. She doesn't just do my nails. The man she's marrying is one of Story's closest friends. They were at school together.'

'You never told me that. Fuck! Great shot.' Guy is watching golf. Some Masters, some Open; Kali may as well be wearing a see-through dress, a ten-gallon hat and have rubber chickens stuck up her nostrils.

'I told you yesterday,' she says.

'Did you? No you didn't.' Still, Guy's eyes are on the screen.

'I did. Vincent Batty. I've known him since he was a kid.'

'How come I've never met him?'

'He's not a friend of mine, he's a friend of Story's.'

'You go, Crump – I'm not stopping *you* going. Go and have fun. But I don't know these people. I can't cancel a trip that's been planned for months, just to go to some wedding. I don't even know them. Hang on one second, I just want to watch that again.' Guy rewinds the putt.

'I'd like it if you came,' Kali says.

'You'll be right,' says Guy.

43

Kali doesn't respond, and after a minute Guy registers the silence, as he would a mosquito by his ear. He turns to look at her. 'I really can't cancel this trip,' he says — *slap* — mosquito dead between his palms. He turns his eyes away again.

Guy doesn't ever look, for more than a passing second, at Kali's face. He didn't look at her on their wedding day: she remembers watching his profile as he spoke his vows to the celebrant, as if he were marrying her — a squat, curly-haired lady of about fifty — rather than Kali. He didn't look at her when Jacob was born — all eyes were then raptured to the new, small, perfect person — hers too, to be fair, hers too. But neither did he look at her when he woke up in the morning or when he came home from work or when he spoke to her or when she spoke to him. His eyes were always somewhere else. Looking away. Looking inwards. Looking up, down, behind, across, anywhere but at Kali.

Kali hasn't ever wondered why that is — has never sat and thought about why Guy skirts her eyes as if she were a Medusa — all she knows is that her face feels unseen, surrounded by air — lonely.

There is only one time she remembers having Guy's eyes on her, a peculiar few minutes when they buzzed around hers with anxiety, and she — while noticing the forgotten fact of how speckled his irises were, Dalmatian-black dots in blue — had fought the urge to laugh.

'Why are you looking at me?' she'd said.

'I'm not—' he'd said, and then with some big word, the size of a boulder, stuck in his throat, he'd turned back to look at the doctor and put his hand on Kali's knee and said to her sideways, 'Are you all right?'

'Yeah,' she had said. 'I'm fine.'

44

She truly was. A1. Cruise control. Tickety-boo.

'There is absolutely no reason,' the obstetrician had been saying, 'that I can find for you not to be able to conceive naturally. You're perfectly fertile. There is nothing physiologically stopping you. Your eggs are in good condition. Your uterus, your ovaries − you've got everything there to conceive, and to carry a healthy pregnancy. And, Guy, as I've said, you have high-quality sperm. You should be a very good match.' He lifted his hands up in an apologetic shrug. 'This is what is called *Unexplained Infertility . . .*'

And as the consultant had continued to talk, Kali thought he seemed like a dog barking. A nice dog. A dog in a suit. But nonetheless a dog speaking dog language. Woof woof *path of the egg* woof woof, bow wow wow *optimum fertilisation* bow wow, ro ro ro *intrauterine insemination* ro ro a–roooooooo. And as Kali listened, indulgently but absently, to the noises, she became aware of Guy's eyes scanning her.

She had met them. Speckled − blue and black − strange.

What was he looking at her for? Was he trying to see the baby that's not there? Babytwo, that's what they called it. Babytwo to Jacob's Babyone.

She had wanted to laugh. Because it really was very funny. Dr Dog, trying his darndest to explain to her why it is that she won't conceive. Guy, looking at her as if she actually existed. And nobody thinking to ask her, this uterus on legs, why it was that *she* thought *she* was not getting pregnant. She may have known the answer − but nobody asked.

'So,' Guy had said, when they were alone together, 'it sounds like intrauterine fertilisation is the way to go.'

Kali hadn't said anything. She had looked painfully young to Guy in that moment − like a silent child somebody had found by the side of the road, wrapped in a towel. She was away on her own planet again, body and spirit pulled apart like meat from bone.

He had tried to make her laugh.

'I could grab the baster and we can give it a go now? What do you reckon, Crump? Up for it?'

Kali had given a dutiful, aimless smile.

Guy walked to the fridge, to find himself a beer.

'You want a drink?' he had asked her.

'No, thanks.'

'Glass of wine? Got some of that Yaapie stuff you like in here.'

Have a drink, Crump, Guy had wanted to say. *Have a couple, lighten up a bit.*

'We already,' Kali had said, standing up, 'have a baby, you know? He's beautiful and healthy, and that should be enough.'

Her eyes were dead again. She was talking from somewhere far away.

'What are you talking about?' Guy had said. 'You're saying you don't want another one?'

'No. I'm just saying we should be grateful for what we've got.'

'But we both want another one.' Guy was aware of the asperity in his voice, so added, 'Come on, Crump, the more the merrier. I thought we'd talked all of this through.'

Kali was leaning against the kitchen counter, her arms folded, looking ahead at nothing. Guy had felt suddenly afraid she might cry.

'Let's forget it, eh?' he said. 'We don't need to do anything now. Except have dinner. You hungry?'

Kali cleared her throat. 'I don't know,' she'd said.

Guy always boggled at this. How can a person not know

46

whether they're hungry? In his impatient moments, he says to her: *Come on, Kali, for fuck's sake. Are you hungry, or not?* But he was careful, then, and confused.

'Why don't I cook?' he had offered, wanting to take the pressure off her.

She had laughed at that, spontaneously.

'Eggs *à la* Guy?'

'You love my eggs.'

'Yep,' Kali had said, even though it wasn't true.

6

There was this bird, this myna bird, that had been coming to Cannie's window. Not round the other side, to her balcony — no, that would make too much sense, to come to where the flower pots are, and the sunshine, and the space for digging and hopping. To her bedroom window, which had nothing more than a small, barren ledge, was south-facing and had no light. It came day after day, to crap all over her windowsill, sit there in its own crap, and — seriously — tap with its beak on the glass. It was brazen — it'd stand outside, glassy eyes darting, and wouldn't fly off until Cannie was only three feet away, throwing imaginary stones.

'*Bloody Max*,' Cannie said, through her teeth, when this morning she saw a fresh spattering of green and white dung, still wet. She'd have to leave it until after work, when no doubt it would have solidified nicely, and she would have to plug away at it with a fish slice.

Dressed and tidy and in a close cloud of her grassy French perfume, Cannie takes the stairs down to the car park. She is on the third floor of four, part of a well-heeled and tranquil apartment block in Neutral Bay — itself a well-heeled and tranquil suburb north of the Harbour Bridge. Her neighbours tend to be older – married, divorced, or widowed. Maybe Max is choosing her, from the entire building, because he can smell the solitude, through those two little holes in his beak. She's not got anyone to divorce, nobody to die and leave her.

She gets into her car, a mid-sized Volkswagen, buckles up, and the radio turns on with the key, ABC Sydney, as she'd left it last evening. The car is neat, coins for parking hidden away in a drawer, service book and manual in the glove box. It smells as it did when new, no human odours or lingering scent of sandwiches.

Cannie begins the easy drive to St Leonard's, to Onestar, the company whose Marketing and PR department she heads. Onestar is not a glamorous company. It is not a slick city bank, or a cool Eastern Suburbs ad agency. It was the first telecommunications company in Australia, and it has remained, through privatisation and competition, the market leader. It is big, and male, and straightforward, and it rewards loyalty. Cannie has worked there since leaving university, and it would be no surprise if one day she became the first woman to run the whole place. And if, and when, she did, it would not be through killer heels and backstabbing, through hunger pangs of ambition – it would be through competence, and composure, and hard work.

This morning we're asking the question, says the jaunty voice of the radio DJ, *whether it is every woman's right to have a baby. It's all over the papers today, the latest piece of research from the School of Fertility at the University of—*

Cannie presses the radio off.

She has never been ambitious. She has never wanted to stick her head above the parapet, or dress in feathers, or flash her brain about. She has never even wanted to marry and

49

have babies at the allocated time. (Now.) She has, instead, wanted to do well, and feel certain, and Cannie felt grateful that in modern Australia you did not have to pioneer, or reach too far, to achieve a nice life. A successful life, with a job high up in a glass building, and a flat with views of the Harbour.

With this morning's snail mail, opened and sorted by Cannie's assistant, Tania, is a sealed envelope.

'I didn't open that one,' Tania says, ''cause it looked personal.'

It is the first of December, so the corporate Christmas cards have started trickling in – but this card is different. The envelope is written in a round, unsophisticated hand, and on the back is a picture of two small, entwined horseshoes. *Miss Abigail Carlton-Terry*, it says on the front, and, inside, it says – *Cannie.*

Mr Shawn B. Lercher and Mrs Edwina S. Lercher
Cordially request the great pleasure of your attendance
At the wedding of their daughter

. . .

Ladies are cordially encouraged to wear hats or fascinators.

So she has been included, at last. Picked for the netball team, invited to the sleepover, asked to dance.

On the front of the card is a black and white photograph of Vincent Batty and Teresa, kissing each other lightly on the lips. Tree's arms are slender and gym-toned, her dark hair in a sporty ponytail. She is as undramatically pretty as Cannie undramatically isn't.

Tree is a beautician at a small salon in the city, and Cannie runs one of the biggest departments of one of the biggest companies in Australia – but things don't change, and Tree remains easy, and preferred. Even though Tree is not a talker, with never much to say, and never much change to report – it is Cannie who is boring. Tree is not boring. She is simply – *sweet*. The dynamic is old, and stagnant, and Cannie, with a sense of unease and inflammation, realises that she is grateful for the invitation.

'Jesus *Christ*!'

Cannie leaps from her desk with atypical drama. It brings Tania scrambling in.

'Are you all right?'

Cannie's heart is beating, around her ears like hot bees.

'Yes, I'm fine,' she says. 'There was a bird . . .' Cannie is walking towards the window, concentrating on calm, 'that flew into the window.'

The noise of the bird bursting against the glass was like a stifled gunshot – an assassin with a silencer. But though the noise was deadened, Cannie had registered the collision with such force that it felt as if it must have made a crack in the heart of the building. And in a circle of events she cannot quite straighten, Cannie remembers for a moment the wings twisted and the beak wiped against the window, before the bird fell out of the air like an apple.

'Oh, my God,' says Tania, following Cannie. There is a scrape of blood, and something like mucus, at eye level.

Cannie walks close to the glass, her forehead almost touching, trying to see down to the pavement. She thinks she can see the corpse – small as a fingernail – below.

'It just flew right into the window?' Tania asks.

'Yes! At top speed. I think it's down there.'

'Do you want me to . . . go and see?'

Cannie looks at Tania, and wants to say, *Please, please go*

51

down, and pick it up, poor thing. Her heart is still dancing. But it would be too much to ask, from a professional relationship, to ask Tania to take on this act of God. And, regardless, the bird is dead. 'No,' Cannie says, 'you've got enough to do. Maybe ring Maintenance and let them know.'

'Sure,' says Tania. 'Are you all right, Abigail?'

'Just got a shock, is all,' says Cannie. 'Bit of a fright.' She laughs.

But once Tania has gone back to her desk, Cannie stays standing, horrified. Of all the windows, in all the buildings.

And what if that dead bird was Max? What if he had followed her here? What if Cannie went home and the shit had dried up never to be wet again, and Max never came back, because he was dead down there outside the Onestar door?

Cannie breathes out, and thinks she should have asked Tania for a coffee. She's going mad, today. Mad. Birds and weddings and blood on the glass. Max! A bird with a name.

She'll walk to the coffee machine herself. It'll do her good.

7

When he was busy, Story was fine. When his lunch breaks were social or spent working, when his evenings and weekends were full. With Christmas in less than four weeks, time is being filled up, sand pouring into it, filling up the jar. Christmas parties government and corporate, the Reserve Bank's own celebrations and commitments – the sand is rising past his knees, up above his waist – soon it will creep up his nostrils so that he cannot smell, and force him to shut his eyelids so that he cannot see, and soon it will pop and cork his ears so that he cannot hear – and that will be a relief.

Tonight, though, is a problem. Tonight Story has nothing to do, and the silence around him begins to hum. He looks at his screen. 19:32. Three naked hours until sleep.

– *G'day.*

– Mate. It's Story.

– *I know.*

– You up for a drink? Could meet you at the Five Kings.

– *No. I can't.*

– No worries.

JP is busy. Doing what, if not already drinking? Pounding

grim-faced round the streets of Sydney like a minotaur, sweating and gnashing, so that old ladies cross themselves and close their doors.

What was the point of this evening, if there was nothing in it? What was the point of just watching it pass? Out of the jar like sand. Hearing it hiss through the small hole with speed. What was the point of sitting at home, thoughts chewing round the outside of your brain like a lawnmower?

Story tries Vincent Batty, and goes straight to answerphone. So where the fuck is he? Probably in the basement of the Source Hotel, where he works, shagging some grateful chambermaid over the spare mattresses. Ak! Story shouldn't think like that. Vincent's nearly a married man. He had made his choice and left all that behind.

— *Hey mate, what's up.*

Mac is sounding happy.

— Hey, Mac. How are you, mate?

— *Pretty good. That was a stellar spread you put on last Sunday.*

— Oh, no worries.

Story is smiling to himself. This sounds hopeful.

— Listen, mate, I thought I'd head over to Paddo for a drink at the Five Kings.

— *What, now?*

— Yeah. I'm leaving work now.

— *Um. Look. Yeah . . . mate, I'm not sure I can make it.*

Mac's words have suddenly slowed down. He's um-ing, ah-ing.

— *Ah. I'm kind of . . .*

The phone goes silent for a moment, as if a hasty hand has muffled the receiver.

— *I'm kind of tied up, mate.*

Mac sounds shifty, and his voice has a teenage wobble that

54

betrays unauthorised amusement. He is trying not to laugh.

Whatever, Story thinks – whatever. Fucktard.

He's not going to make any more calls. He never calls, anyway. He doesn't know why he's calling now, like he's some *mother*, somebody's mother who still picks up the phone and dials. He'll send one text, and then go home. He can get take-out, buy some Christmas gifts online.

Cannie, he writes, *bailing on a work thing so free for –*

It's only Cannie. He doesn't need to lie. Story deletes and starts again.

Free for dinner if you fancy it?

Love to but cant comes the quick reply. *At a work thing. Silly season has started already! Cx*

Story used to assume, in moments like this, that it was just him, missing out. That everyone else was in the eye of their own peculiar storm, while he sat in his dinghy at the edge. But, today, looking at the straight lines of his mates, at their relentless, gentle, vulgarity – Story thinks, for the first time, that maybe life isn't happening to them, either. And it doesn't mean anything, that everyone is busy. It doesn't mean anything or show anything, and Story is not the only person on earth as he stands at the bus stop. See? It's not just him. There is a small colony of ants beside him, behind him, in front of him. Fingering their phones, all the women with that usual Sydney thing of good bodies and plain faces, except for possibly the one with the white laptop case, she had a face that could maybe be construed as pretty. And the men tippetty-tapping with thumbs, texting their life stories all about town, average as sandwiches, boring as soup. If something were to fall, down like Lucifer, from the thirty-storey rooftop next to them – limbs flailing – that'd show them.

There is no reason to dread it, a short evening at home.

55

Fuck knows Story's tired enough this time of year and could do with the respite.

But it's the walls of it all. The ceiling and the floor. The weirdness of the little things like rubber bands and shirt bones that he spots in drawers, as if this cardboard flat with the stainless-steel fridge and the expensive sound system and the big 1950s poster leaning against the wall is more than dress-up — as if it's actually some kind of home, and he's been in it, like a snail, moving his shit about and breathing air in and out and picking things up and putting them down and living.

The evening is still warm, as Story walks from the bus stop. Maybe it's the warmth that does it — makes his apartment feel like a tomb. Maybe if it was raining, and cold, and windy, then he wouldn't be standing on the street like a child outside school, looking for excuses. Maybe then his home would be his castle.

Story reaches for his phone once more, before he'll give up and go inside.

'Story!' His sister picks up.

'Hey! Kali.' He is pacing in front of the door to his building, one hand flipping through the keys in his pocket.

'How's it going?' she says, and her voice has her whole self in it — Story can picture her, as she's always been.

'Good,' Story lies. 'How are you?'

'I'm good,' she says, and she is lying, too. Between them, the space for truth gets smaller.

'How's Jacob?' Story asks, and Kali answers, and they talk the talk of strangers. Story can't tell her, now, that he called because he needed her — and because there is no reason. How can he tell her that in these past weeks he has grown afraid of his own shadow, like a puppy?

The best he can do is say, 'I'd like to come to dinner. Or just come round. See you guys.'

'That'd be great,' says Kali. 'Come for dinner.'

Story looks up, hope sudden and full of air, to scan the road for cabs. He wants to raise his hand, summon a taxi and go to his sister now. A lightness comes, and pushes the heaviness aside as if it had never been. Why had he been making such a fuss? He will go to Kali now, and everything will be okay.

'How about Monday?' Kali says. 'Guy should be home then, too. He'd like to see you.'

Pop. Monday. Story turns from the road, away from any chariot that might pass. 'Sure,' he says, without thinking.

'You can do Monday?' Kali confirms.

'Monday's good.'

The heaviness is back – it never left – and Story walks into his building. A thousand paper planes had flown towards him, and he had not managed to catch one.

He will open the door to the deck so that the dark air comes in, and order a butter chicken and a naan and peas and paneer and yoghurt. He will sit on the sofa with the television on and his computer on his lap, and his wallet nearby so he can buy things, and the remote nearby so he can change the view. And even with all that noise, all that food, all that radiation, he can hear every sound he makes, every breath drawing and every bone clicking, each sound a scraping in his ears. There is something watching him in the corner of the room, and it has no name, and Story has no name for it, either.

8

'Reckon you could stop perving at my sister?' says Story.

'Your sister's hot,' Mac says.

'Fuck off,' says Story.

'She's skinny, though, eh,' Stavvo continues, 'your sister. She's got small tits.'

'Fucking *shut up*,' Story says.

It is the usual Saturday routine, when there are no school teams to play for, or rugby games to watch. They sit in the sand at Manly, and get fish and chips before catching the bus back home at five. The buses are full of kids in bikinis and speedos; there is sand in small pools on the seats.

Stavvo keeps talking. 'Is that why she rugs up like a Paki?'

'What the fuck are you on about?' Story asks. 'She's not rugged up.'

'She's in old-lady swimmers.'

Kali is not wearing a bikini, that is what Stavvo means. She is wearing a black-and-white stripy one piece, with high-cut legs and a scooped-out back.

'You're a fucking cock,' Story says, looking away.

JP has been silent – he is lying on his towel, asleep. Cannie knows he is asleep, as the boys had been discussing what to pour on his head – seawater, sand, or the option of a specially purchased milkshake – and he had not stirred. His eyelids are hidden by mirrored sunglasses, and the middle of him by a pair of white-and-blue board shorts, but the rest of him lies prettily like a prince in a fairytale. A prince – still and perfect and strong, mouth softly shut. Snow White, a line of hair running up his navel. Cannie watches him. She hears the talk of the other boys through a curtain, as if there is thick cloth hanging between.

'. . . best tits of the day, no doubt—'

'. . . missed it, when was it on—'

'. . . she's a slapper, as well—'

Her awareness rests on JP's feet, tipping and drowsy, and how close they are to her own wakeful toes. She must not move, lest their feet brush together.

When she had arrived, he had looked cursorily at her bare body, and then disinterestedly away. If she took that personally, it was her own fault – there were racks of bodies along the beach, what did she expect? It was just a manner he had, a manner, which told you something about yourself you didn't want to know. She had deliberately not eaten today, to make sure her stomach was flat.

'Cannie, you coming?'

The girls are heading off, first to the kiosk, then back to their own spot further down the beach.

'Yep.' Cannie pushes herself up from the sand, and her knee grazes the edge of JP's foot. He darts away from her touch, like a snake.

Once the girls are out of earshot, Stavvo says, 'Christ, she's boring, that Cannie.'

Mac shrugs.

'She's not,' says Story. 'She's actually all right.'

'D'you fancy her, mate?' Stavvo grimaces.

'Nah!' says Story, "Course not! Just saying, she's actually got stuff to say.'

'You reckon?' says Stavvo, 'Like what? Hey! Mate!' He shoves JP with the heel of his foot. 'Wakey wakey!'

'Fuck off,' grumbles JP, leaning up on to his elbows and feeling the beginning of sunburn on his face. 'I need to get in the water.'

JP, as it happens, had not been sleeping. He had heard all the chatter, all the talk of ambushing him as he slept – but he had continued to pretend. Under the pretence of sleep, he had been watching Kali, through half-closed lashes. She had been sitting near the water line with a friend, one of those waterproof sun hats over her head. He had watched her, and watched her, and felt the heat bake and penetrate his body, down to his bones, that physical rapture of sun on skin. He had seen himself walk over to her, and put a hand on her delicate, naked back, and as she turned to smile at him, his stomach would burn with euphoric oil, live oil pouring inside him, and bring him back to his teenage self, lying on a towel with a tightening groin.

Kali had stood up, and was walking towards the sea. JP knew she was a swimmer, and wanted to see her enter the water. But as his eyes followed Kali, they were blocked, at the last minute, by the body of Cannie, sitting close and massive, stopping his view. All he could see was the outer edges of Cannie, where her swimsuit thickly met her skin. Kali, small in her distance, was hidden behind this human mountain. In the water like a fish – like a dolphin, a smooth thing without scales – but unseen by him. He could not lift his head to watch her, without exposing his wakefulness.

When Cannie got up and left, it was too late. His eyes could no longer find her. In the water or out, she was lost. And as he sat up on the sand, his love began to lose its purity – like ink released into water, the faces of his friends and the towels and the drinks and the facts of the beach began to encroach.

With a boogie board in one arm, JP walks to the water, intending to wash away the sun-smell and sweat, to stop the sunburn, to speed himself up a bit. And as he walks, here is Kali, hair wet, body drying, coming towards him, smiling politely as she passes, not a word.

He had to keep walking. How could he stop? Stop, and stand, feet dying in the sand, as if her passing had petrified him. He keeps walking. And he hears her talk to Story behind him: *I'm heading back, soon, Marian has a car, if you want a lift . . .*

And love was a crocodile, that ate you finger by finger, and what could you do but keep walking, keep walking, keep walking away.

9

The face wash in the shower had been put down wrong, again. By Guy – who else?

It was a fat, white tube, with an orange lid, and Guy had stood it up, lid down, on the soap shelf. As he always did.

So, of course, when Kali picked it up and unscrewed the top, a little gush of cold, gungy water dropped out and fell on her foot, from where it had collected in the hollows of the lid.

Kali washed her face and neck with the salty-tasting foam, and twisted the lid back on. She stuck the tube upside down – the thin, white edge of it pushed in between the slats of the shelf – so that the lid faced upwards, and the water couldn't collect.

Tomorrow, the forecast was that Kali would walk into the shower and find the face wash lid down once more, and, yet once more, would have to confront the old, cold, collected water.

It was not likely, after more than a month of this face wash warfare, that Guy had not noticed. He's not thick, much as he pretends to be. He's got to be doing it on purpose, putting it down on the shelf the wrong way. Best-case scenario –

because he thinks it's funny. Most likely scenario — so as, with couched hostility, to prove a point; to let Kali know, as she stepped into the shower and her day began, that he would not relent, or bend, or be considerate.

Way back — before the face wash — there had been: never taking a single empty bottle out of the shower, until there had been thirty of them — it looked like they were sprouting — and finally Kali couldn't cope any more.

There had been: damp towels slung over the shower glass, despite there being a heated rail, *right there*. Kali had over and over removed them, and then, one raging week, had pulled them down and left them to moulder on the floor.

And, back in the mists, before they had renovated their house, there had been: the sliding door to the shower, always leaving it open, never troubling to shut it, until Kali eventually slammed it with such force that a corner of the door had splintered.

The shower had become an arena, for Kali's anger. For her lost words.

Once, in the early hours of the morning — when Kali had been lying sleepless in their bed, Guy still not home from some business dinner — she pushed the covers off and strode to the bathroom, mute heat all over her, had taken Guy's shaving gel from the mirrored cupboard, and had squeezed it all, her thumb aching, down the shower drain. Then had put it back in the cupboard and felt breathless. She had felt cold, suddenly, and naked despite her pyjamas, and had gone back and pulled the doona safely around her again.

When Guy had got back over an hour later, steaming, breathing loudly, holding on to walls, only then had Kali been able to close her eyes and rest.

★

'Story's coming round,' Kali says. 'For dinner.'

Guy downs a glass of water. 'I didn't know that,' he says.

'It should be in your diary, I emailed it to Estella.'

'Well it's not. It doesn't matter much, does it? You prefer seeing him alone.'

Kali doesn't say anything.

'Where's Jakey?' Guy asks.

Jacob, Kali says in her head. *He's my son and I named him Jacob.*

'Soccer training.'

'Oh, right.' Guy walks past Kali to the stairs, and bumps her on the lips as he passes. Kali hates these hard pecks.

'What time'll you be back?' she says to him.

'Don't nag me, Crump.'

Kali has to breathe in.

'It's a business dinner. It'll finish when it finishes.'

She says nothing. Guy jogs upstairs.

She walks to the stove, where a pot of tomato sauce is simmering. She rarely cooks, these days, and at this moment she considers taking the pan in her two hands and tipping the sauce down the sink. What if the handles of the pan burnt into her palms, left crescent-moon barbecue marks? Would anyone, ever, notice? Only the mortician, as he turned her dead hands over in his. Or did morticians only exist on American television?

Tomato sauce used to be Story's favourite – whether it is or not any more, she doesn't know. But she was cooking it for him. And for Jacob, who'll be dropped back at seven thirty.

She looks at Guy's empty glass of water, drained on the countertop. She's not going to move it. Let it stay there for ever.

Kali opens the door smiles at Story; she puts her arms around his neck. She's the only person in the world, Kali, who makes Story want to be good.

'Do you still like tomato sauce?' she says to him.

'What, like with hot chips?'

'No. Real tomato sauce. With spaghetti.'

Story thinks. 'Yep, I reckon I do. I haven't had it for years, though.'

'You used to love it.'

'Did I? I suppose I did,' it dawns on him. 'Yeah, yeah, I remember. The tomato sauce at that place—'

'Ginello's.'

'Yeah, that's the one. Yeah, I *did* use to love that. With that Parmesan machine, d'you know what I mean? The one where you used to turn the handle and it grated the cheese.'

Kali nods. 'I used to have the carbonara.'

'Is that place still there?' Story refers to Kali, because she is the authority, the memory, on all of those things when they were children.

'No, it closed down ages ago. He divorced and had to sell up to pay the settlement. He'd been having an affair with that waitress with the curly hair.'

Story laughs. 'How the hell do you know this stuff, Kali?'

Kali shrugs. 'Dad. Ginello always used to come and talk to him after dessert. He'd go on for hours.'

Story is remembering. 'Fuck,' he says, 'I do remember that waitress. She was blond, right? And used to wear those sparkly tops.'

'Yep,' says Kali, 'and stilettos.'

'She was awesome,' recalls Story, fondly.

'Well, she was probably the reason Ginello's shut down.'

'Far out,' says Story, 'I can't believe I'd forgotten all this stuff. He used to bring us out those ice creams, with the sparklers in them, that Ginello dude.'

'Yes.' Kali is smiling gently. 'Chocolate bombs.'

'Hey,' Story asks, 'where are the menfolk?'

'Guy's at a work thing. He won't make it tonight.'

'Oh,' says Story, disappointed – he'd been looking forward to seeing Guy. As Story has described it before, when he first met Guy, he had thought, *Who the fuck is this dude? Seriously*, he'd said to JP, *like I thought, who is this fuckwit?* But it turned out that underneath the off-putting, butch saltiness – underneath the volume – was intelligence, and enthusiasm, and clarity. And Story loved watching Guy with his sister. He loved watching how Guy protected her.

Kali had always had something exposed about her. When she opened the door and put her arms up to you, it felt like you had to hold her just right, like she might slip and fall away if you didn't hug her tight enough, but might evaporate if you hugged her too hard. In certain lights she was like an angel – although the only person he had ever said that to was Mum. They had looked over to where Kali was sitting in the sun, and Mum had replied, her head slightly to one side, 'Yes, that's right.' Then she had woken up a bit, and had rubbed Story's hair and said, 'And you, too, you're my little angel, too.'

But it was different, Story had known that. Kali, sitting over there: it looked like the sun had moved just to shine over her. The rest of them walked in and out of light, but Kali was pursued by it.

And Guy looked after her. With his means-business,

66

wolfish look and his unprocessed laugh. His ability to bring her down to earth.

'Hey, Mum.' Jacob walks in the front door, a rangy eleven-year-old with blond hair, darker than his mother's, round his eyes. He's carrying a kit bag in one hand and dusty boots in the other, and so without a hand free has to blow his hair out of his face. It falls back over his eyes immediately. He lifts the arm carrying the boots, and attempts to sweep the hair back with his forearm. 'Hey, Uncle Story.'

'Jake, Jake, my mate!' Story says, excitedly. He gets up and goes to the boy, grinning, and pats him on the back. When Story finds himself wanting to touch someone, wanting to make contact, his physical composure declines – further. His body seems to quiver slightly, as if it can neither convincingly contain the desire, nor be simple and reach out. 'How's it going, dude?'

'Yeah, I'm all right. Pretty hungry, but. Hey, Mum,' he says again, as he walks past his mother sitting on the sofa, and leans down to kiss her on the cheek.

'Hello, Babyone,' she says, briefly taking and holding his hand as he past. Even though she hadn't missed him – he'd only been gone since the school day began, that morning – it's always a relief to have him home again. She feels it bodily, as if a strap has been removed from around her chest. 'Dinner'll be ready in ten minutes.'

'I'm just going to dump my stuff in the laundry,' Jacob says as he walks away.

'Good boy,' says Kali.

'Is Dad here?' Jacob calls.

'No.' Kali has to summon energy to say anything else. She inhales. 'He's at a work thing. Are you going to have a shower?'

'Yep.'

Story always notices, every time he sees his nephew, just how strong his accent is. His Australian. Like Guy's.

'Okay,' says Kali. 'Try to be quick.'

'Yeah, yeah,' says Jacob, loping up the stairs. 'I'm starving, anyway.'

Story watches him go. 'Is Jacob going to be, like, seven feet tall?'

'Maybe. I don't know where he'd get it from, though. Guy's only five eleven. He might just stop growing at thirteen, like I did.'

'Did you not grow after thirteen?'

'Not much.'

Story looks up to the ceiling. 'Yeah,' he says, 'I guess not. It's different for boys and girls, though, isn't it? Don't girls finish growing earlier? I went on growing until the end of uni. I was shorter than you until Year 11, basically.'

'Peanut.' Kali smiles – she really smiles this time, you can see her teeth.

'Peanut,' Story agrees, and laughs.

Kali had called him this when they were children, when they were teenagers, when Story had been small and solid and brown. Story was still small and solid and brown – at best ten centimetres higher than his sister – but somehow, not a Peanut any more. Just Story. She'd stopped thinking of him as Peanut – when? Yes. When he went to Sydney Uni. And, deliberately, Kali had only ever called him Peanut at home – she knew what damage it could do if it got to the classroom.

Nobody, looking at these two sitting on the white sofa, would doubt they were related – and yet they share none of their details. One blond and fine and slender, fluid and pale. The other dark and thick and robust, physical and viscous. Down to their eyelashes, they are different. Story's shoulders slope into his shirt, whereas Kali's sit square. Her nail beds are short, whereas his travel pinkly to the end of his fingers.

'Oh, hey,' says Kali. 'Have you thought any more about Christmas?'

'Ah, not really,' replies Story.

Kali says nothing, remains as she is, and Story feels he has to continue with his words. Her silences do that.

'It's about getting the time off. And it's just so hot in Byron.'

Kali looks wordlessly at him.

'I was thinking, can't Mum and Derek come here for Christmas?' he appeals.

'It's hot everywhere, Story,' Kali says, simply.

'I know, but it's hotter in Byron. Your feet bloody burn when you try to walk on the beach.'

'That happens here, too.'

'I know, but you know what I mean. It's oppressive.'

'They can't come here,' says Kali. 'If it was just Mum and Derek, that'd be fine. But with the girls as well,' Kali means their stepsisters, Derek's daughters, 'and probably whatever boyfriends they've got at the moment—'

The truth is, there had been talk with Mac of going to the Whitsundays for the New Year, and if they were to do that, it would take all Story's holiday. But sitting here, thinking about it, with his sister next to him – of course he'd go to Byron for Christmas. What else would he do?

'Look,' he says. 'I reckon it shouldn't be a problem taking the time off. I'll confirm it with the office tomorrow.'

Kali sighs, as if she has been holding air in, and can only

now breathe out. She unfolds her legs from underneath her, and gets up to put the spaghetti on.

As they sit down to eat, Kali says, 'You're going to Vincent Batty's wedding, right?'

'Er, yeah,' says Story. 'I'm a groomsman.'

'I didn't know that,' says Kali, 'although of course you would be.'

It occurs to Story, that he has not spoken to his sister for a while.

'Who's *Vincent Batty*?' says Jacob, looking struck.

'Vincent? He's a mate of mine. From school.'

'Vincent,' Jacob verifies, 'or Vincent Batty?'

'Er, both. I guess I think of him as Vincent Batty. But his name's Vincent.'

'Batty's, like, his surname?'

'Yep.'

Jacob raises an eyebrow and looks entertained. Story smiles.

'So you call him *Vincent Batty*, his whole name, to his face?'

'Yeah,' says Story, 'sometimes. Sometimes just Vincent.'

'I've got a mate like that at school. Lucas Giddy. You know, who we call by his whole name. Never, just, like – Luke. *Lucas Giddy.*'

'Really?' says Story, thinking about it. 'I guess there's always one. Something to do with the rhythm of it.'

'And the surname,' says Jacob.

'There is that.' Jacob is getting to the age where he can hold a conversation; it's pleasing. Story turns to his sister again. 'Has Tree been talking about it? The wedding? You still see her, right? For your . . . stuff.'

'For my nails. I've seen her for years, now. They've invited me. To the wedding. And Guy.'

Story is surprised, although he doesn't know why. After all, Kali knows them both well – as she said, Tree has done her nails for years. And Vincent used to come to their house a lot when his parents were divorcing. Kali would look after him, in that unspoken, implicit way of hers. She'd stay by the fridge after getting a juice, and talk to him, about music, or surf, or school, or whatever. He'd been fifteen then, and had had a soft spot for Kali since.

'Cool,' says Story. 'I didn't know. I didn't know you were invited. Are you going to go?'

'I am.'

'Not Guy?'

'He's away. On business.'

Story nods. 'Cool, well, it's cool you're coming.'

'You don't think it's weird?'

'What?'

'That they've invited me.'

'No! Why. Do you?'

'No,' says Kali. 'I thought it was lovely. Until Guy said it was weird.'

'Nah, it's cool. I'll be there, handing you your thing – your programme – in a really bad suit.'

Kali laughs.

'This is great,' Story says of the spaghetti, after his second mouthful. He reaches for the bowl of grated Parmesan, and dusts another spoonful over.

'It's all–right,' shrugs Kali; she draws the words out.

'Nah, it's really good, Mum,' says Jacob.

'We should've got your Uncle Story to cook – he's the chef.'

Jacob stops, mid-forkful, and looks at her quizzically. 'You're a really good cook, Mum.'

'Everyone thinks their mum is a good cook,' says Kali.

'No they don't,' Jacob says. He's talking with his mouth full, but Kali lets it go. 'Zacko's always complaining about his mother's food. He says it's disgusting. And it is as well.'

Story giggles.

'It can't be actually *disgusting*,' says Kali.

'It is! When I was round his house she made this fish stuff, which was, like, fish, with this white sauce all round it. Like, cheese sauce.'

'Fish? With cheese?' Story is startled.

'Yeah,' says Jacob, 'like this white sauce. And then this rice, which was all stuck together, like glue. We both had to put heaps of sauce all over it, otherwise we couldn't have eaten it. And it gave me this really bad stomach ache.'

'Far out,' says Story, with depth. The fish and the cheese thing is affecting him.

'Well, Zacko has to eat it all the time. I'm amazed he's not in hospital.' Jacob's eyes go wide, in feeling.

Kali and Story both laugh.

'You're a really good cook, Mum. Even when you just cook, like, stirfry. All my mates like your food.'

'D'you reckon?' says Kali.

'Yep.' Jacob, having inhaled his helping, is already taking seconds. 'They all eat loads when they come round.'

'Really?' says Kali. 'I don't even cook.'

Jacob looks at his mum like she's mad. 'What are you talking about?' he says. 'You cook all the time.'

Kali furrows her brow at the table. Then looks up.

Story's crown is down, towards his plate, the shape of his dark head a familiar thing. Jacob, with his thin, handsome hands, is ladling cheese from the bowl to his plate. She looks at them and thinks – that they are all she needs, these two.

10

Every morning, JP waits until he is sitting on the bus before he turns his BlackBerry on. It is a line he has taken: a stance. 'Nobody needs a BlackBerry,' he wants the platform to say, 'unless you're the fucking prime minister.'

This morning he sits by the window as the bus shudders away, and turns his BlackBerry on to find: an email from the *Sydney Morning Herald*; and a text message from his credit-card company, detailing his balance.

There is a feeling, something akin to shame, at the lack of professional traffic.

JP turns to his browser, to read the morning's news. The headlines are still being dominated by a Rugby League sex scandal. Same old story, different names attached.

The annoying thing about the *Herald* website is that you can't post comments. JP navigates to a different newspaper, and clicks on the link to the same story. With his BlackBerry close to his face and his thumbs working, he writes:

Is anyone in the press or the NRL brave enough to tell the truth about this? If a woman takes her clothes off and offers her body to a group of men how, by any interpretation is it their fault if they accept her advances?

He scrolls back to correct his commas.

Miss P was a groupie, drunk and desperate to have sex with one or all of the Brisbane TigerSharks. After having spread her legs for all of them, and now realising that not one of them is going to call, send flowers, or get down on one knee, she's crying rape. She may well 'feel dirty' now, but she only has her own spread legs to blame. All the angry women out there: can you take a deep breath and explain to me how this is anybody's fault but Miss P's?

In the *Name* field, he types, *Sydney Solip*.

The bus has swelled JP out on to the pavement, and as he walks into the foyer of his office building, his BlackBerry goes. Ting ting.

JP is one of four hundred-odd recipients of this email, and the subject line is *Redvale Week*. He scrolls through it at speed. *A collegiate approach to developing client relationships. Students get a taste for life at Redvale.* The final item is the Corporate Triathlon, this year in aid of some children's charity. The company is entering mixed teams, whose raised sponsorship it will match. Go, Redvale.

He bins the email, and as he exits the lift he sees Carrick walking towards him. Carrick is with John Fleet, a Senior Partner – the company figurehead, an unlikely, uncouth guy with a wide middle, graceless and abrupt, but astute. Another, much younger man is with them, who has no tie, and yellow hair. Yellow, not blond, and five centimetres longer than it should be.

Before they clash, Carrick stops, extends his hand. 'Morning JP, good weekend?' he says.

JP takes it, shakes it. 'All right.'

'John, you know JP,' Carrick gestures, John Fleet nods, with his hands in his pockets, and says, 'Morning', 'and this' – Carrick puts a hand on the yellow man's back – 'is Oliver Marchal. He's joining us in Tax.' JP feels himself nodding, mechanically, a flood rising in his throat. 'Oliver,' says Carrick, 'this is JP Fry, who's on my team in Corporate.'

JP finds himself shaking hands.

'Great to meet you,' says an accent so English it might as well be playing croquet.

'I thought you weren't starting 'til January,' says JP, betraying himself in so many ways.

'I'm not,' says the accent, genially – *great shot, what!* 'How did you know that?'

Nobody says anything. Oliver is smiling.

'*Redvale Week*,' JP says, growls almost. He hates himself.

'Your fame precedes you, I'm afraid,' says Carrick.

'Ah,' says Oliver Marchal, '*Redvale Week*.' There is something conspiratorial in the way he is looking at JP, which JP doesn't welcome. 'I was just having a look at today's. *Redvale Week* is on the money; I'm not starting until January. Just being given the guided tour.'

The guided tour. Which until this moment – until Oliver Marchal set his chirpy, cut-glass English feet on the decrepit, ocker carpet of Redvale – had never existed.

No such red carpet for JP when he arrived. But then – he was just a shitkicker. And this guy was . . . What was he? Fucking royalty. Two of the firm's most senior partners personally showing this yellow, bleating fuckwit around.

'Entering the triathlon, JP?' Carrick puts a hand on JP's

shoulder, and JP prickles away from the patronage, he can't help it.

'I don't know,' says JP. 'I hadn't thought about it.'

'Oliver?' barks John Fleet, rocking his bulk backwards and forwards on his heels. 'How about you?'

Oliver laughs; there is an easiness about him that ups JP's hackles.

'It'd kill me,' Oliver says. 'You'd be able to spot the weedy, white Pom a mile away. How about you, John, are you going to go for the burn?'

'HAH!' says Fleet; it is the closest JP has ever seen him to laughing. 'Go for the burn! It'd take more than you asking.' Then he looks to the lift. 'Let's move. I've got a meeting to get to.'

'Good to meet you, JP,' says Oliver, and puts his hand out. His shake is firm.

'Yeah,' says JP. 'All right.'

Bzzzzzzzzzz. BREEP BREEP!

JP's BlackBerry trings, momentarily before the same email chimes on to the computer screen.

To open on the PC, or the BlackBerry? Decisions, decisions.

JP pulls up his inbox. He raises his eyebrows at the sender: David Ostent. Tintin.

fellas,

[the email begins]

the winds are blowing and i'm gonna be touching down sydneyside on Thursday for a pre-Xmas squizz. heading back to wellington on monday. would be good to catch up over a schooner or two.

77

over and out, tintin

ps Vinnie – thanks for the wedding invite, I'll be there with my dancing shoes

What's he doing in New Zealand? JP thinks, before going back to the article he had commented on earlier. With a satisfied rush in his chest, he sees that his post has gathered a lot of responses. Illiterate, most of them. And by women – fat, lonely, angry, the types who had nothing better to do than sit at home at their computers foaming at the mouth. After finishing the last response, JP immediately clicks on *Leave Comment*.

Calm down, ladies!

Debra D. – it is in no way unlawful for multiple men to have sex with a woman, as long as the woman consents to sex, and is of legal age.

JoAnn – it is not up to government to step in and redefine the law according to public opinion. The Australian media are not a law-making entity; they are, at best, shit-stirrers, and, at worst, a lynch mob.

Miss P can't cry rape in retrospect – she said yes at the time, and saying after the event that she's changed her mind does not constitute rape.

If she didn't want to be plugged by five different men, she should have kept her clothes on and stayed out of their beds. There's no legal recompense for being a slapper.

He reads over his paragraph quickly, and decides to change 'be plugged by' to 'have sex with'. Just as he clicks on Post Comment, his inbox dings, this time followed shortly by his BlackBerry.

It's a reply from Story, to Tintin's message.

Beach house hotel, friday night? Be good to catch up.

Friday night. That'd work.

Tintin's been off the radar for a while – last heard he was in Los Angeles, trying to peddle his script. He left Sydney with great hooting and tooting, having agents and producers lined up, and a red carpet from LAX all the way to Hollywood Boulevard. So the story went. But then – no word.

When they were teenagers together it had been annoying – Tintin's desperation to be different. He told lies, as if he believed them. One morning break, they were standing in the sun by the corner of one of the outdoor courts, a usual spot.

'Hey,' Tintin had said, 'did you guys know that Robert de Niro's in town?'

'Everyone knows Robert de Niro's in town. It's all over the fucking news,' said Mac.

'Bobby de Niro,' said Vincent Batty, in a Mafioso accent.

Tintin had leant against the mesh fence. 'He's a lot smaller than I thought he would be,' he'd said.

'How the fuck do you know?' barked JP.

'You been stalking Robert de Niro, Tintin?'

'Yeah.' Story was laughing. 'Been sleeping outside his hotel, have you?'

'Nah mate.' Tintin had been serious, looking at the floor. 'Nah. I just randomly ran into him.'

'What the fuck are you talking about?'

'Mate.' Tintin had been a picture of calm vacuity. 'I was just walking home off the bus, up Summerhill Road, when he pulled up in a car.'

'Bullshit!' said JP. 'You're making this up.'

79

'Robert de Niro,' said Vincent, 'pulled up next to you on Summerhill Road.'

'Yep,' said Tintin. 'Well, he didn't get out of the car, or anything, I spoke to him through the back window.'

'Yesterday,' repeated Story, just to get it straight, 'you got off the bus, and Robert de Niro pulled over in a car.'

'Yeah,' said Tintin, smiling lightly, 'it was weird.'

'Too fucking right,' Vincent had said, in a tone that made them all laugh.

'I want to hear this,' goaded Stavvo, these days married with kids, and living up in the Northern Beaches. 'Go on, mate. What happened?'

'Well, he just asked my name—'

'What did you say?' barged Mac. 'MC Arse Bandit?'

'I told him David,' continued Tintin, entirely unaffected by his friends' laughter. He wanted to get this tale out — he has had it in him since yesterday afternoon, imagining and walking home from the bus stop, eating his way through a packet of Tim Tams he got at the corner. 'He'd just seen me on the street, I guess. He asked me if I'd go to a casting today.'

Story had started giggling breathily through closed teeth. The laugh was so genuine, so delighted, that it travelled up into Story's nose, and he considered having to put his face in his hands. 'That,' he had said to Tintin, snorting, 'is the most ridiculous thing I've ever heard.' Story could not control himself. He had started to choke.

Sitting at his Redvale desk nearly twenty-five years later, JP remembers the moment. He remembers Story's incapacitating laughter, which they all caught — their abdomens ached with it, and their heads rang. It's not something, that whole-body, abandoned laughter, that he has had much use for in adult life.

JP remembers Vincent Batty's peppering of questions, each one asked with an expression at once dry and affectionate—

So, Tintin, mate, what do you reckon Robert de Niro was doing on Summerhill Road on a Tuesday afternoon? Maybe he was on a scenic tour of Sydney's northern suburbs, in between press appearances . . .

JP thinks he might remind Tintin of it this Friday — he wonders if he will still stick to his story. Or will claim to have forgotten. Or whether he will, really, have forgotten.

The things that had made Tintin annoying back then — the fictions, earnestly told, the grand plans, the belief that he was a prince in his own fairytale — he had grown into. Now, the times Tintin roll-up-rolled-up, he brought the wind in with him. He seemed to be, with all his high falutin' — free. He seemed to be as he was back then: undimmed.

And, by relief, sitting on his shadow side, JP felt trapped. Untravelled. And old.

I'll be there after work.

JP presses *Send*, and as the email whooshes across town, and away across the Tasman, another email simultaneously arrives. The two noises collide with each other, and the computer gives a brief, cacophonous burp, a sound of clanging and feedback and data buzz. JP raises his eyebrows.

It is a moment, in the day.

11

Cannie is at the car yard, with Story, listening to him chatter while she thinks about Tree and Vincent's wedding invitation.

'Mitsubishis are subversive, you know, I reckon,' Story is saying. 'Like, not as nouveau pretentious as Subarus. But not as, you know, shit-boring as a Holden or a Ford.'

So Cannie's invitation had come late – significantly later than everybody else's. When JP had made a joke, at Story's house, about all the misters and misses on the invitation, about the fascinators, Cannie had kept her face still, embarrassed to let it be known that nothing had yet landed on her doormat. She had been curious to look at the invitation, size it up and judge, see where the service and party were being held – but she had let it lie where JP flipped it, not wanting to show her exclusion. Now, having finally received her own curlicued card, Cannie wonders if she had been on the reserve list, included only when a first-choice guest had vacated a space by turning the invitation down.

'Like, I'm not a tradesman, you know? I shouldn't be allowed to drive a Ford,' Story says. He is laughing at himself, though at what level Cannie has begun to wonder. He's

always been unsteady, only at peace when he has approval –
but the teenage vocabulary and the silliness have become less
of a joke, and seem now just to be the way that Story speaks.
Those folds of empathy and sweetness that Cannie used to
rely on, show themselves less often.

'Although those trucks are quite cool. Like, the real trucks,
with the space for tools in the back.'

'You're not buying a truck,' Cannie says.

'Nah,' agrees Story. 'Like some Bra Boy dickhead. I've
decided on my station wagon.'

'How long d'you reckon that guy's going to be?'

They were waiting for the salesman to return, a thin man
with a bald head and the sleeves of his suit shirt rolled up to
the elbow. Every time he bent down to demonstrate the
interior of a car his red tie dangled. Tempting to snip it off,
if one had a pair of scissors handy. He was bringing out the
keys for a test drive.

'You getting bored?' Story asks.

'I *am* slightly over it,' says Cannie. The sun seemed huge
today. It was beginning to hurt the top of her head.

'You wanna go to the Parkside, and I'll meet you there?'

'No, it's cool, I'll wait. I'll go inside.'

'You don't want to come for the test drive?'

'Ah. Can't say I'm that bothered.'

'I'll show you a good time?' Story smiles.

Cannie smiles back. He's a mate, Story. Underneath all that
straw.

This part of Sydney, south of Surry Hills, is flat and hard
and windless, and the heat swells like an ulcer. As Cannie
walks into the showroom, the air-conditioning registers –
her skin has a moment of effervescence, a shiver of joy.

'Would you like a glass of water?' the girl at reception asks.

'I'm all right,' says Cannie. 'I'll just sit here and wait.'

'You're not going with your partner for the test drive?'

'Ha!' Cannie's amusement bursts through her fatigue. 'We're not together.' She should get a T-shirt printed up.

'Oh, I'm sorry,' says the girl.

'No, it's all right. Don't be.'

The girl smiles at this, and Cannie feels immediately disloyal.

'Are you sure I can't get you a water? Anything else? Cup of tea? Or I can get you a coke from the machine, if you like?'

Cannie has a paranoid moment of wondering whether the girl feels sorry for her. Whether the offers of drinks have a pitying, downward tone to them.

'No, honestly, I'm all right. Thanks.'

The girl behind the desk is young, and her skin is yet perfect. The wrinkles wait under the top layers – they have not pushed up, like grass, on to her forehead, around her eyes. Those sculptural Australian lines, where the sun chisels in deep; lines into which make-up gets grooved, in little flesh-coloured deposits. There isn't a woman in Australia whom the sun doesn't mark, in some way. This girl, too, thinks Cannie. It will leave its paw prints on her, too.

As she sits on the padded leather bench by the magazine rack – lined with identical, glossy Mitsubishi brochures – Cannie supposes that if she was a second-choice guest at Vincent and Tree's wedding, it was fair enough. She and Tree had never been close at school; they were in different years. And her place in Tree and Vincent's life has been established through the group – she would never see them by herself. Whereas Story, Mac, JP – they were all going to be grooms-men. They are part of Vincent's circle.

84

Through the glass, the sky is gigantic and thick blue, and empty but for the sun. Just the sun and the earth. Nothing else in the universe. It was a paradise, this city, all those golden cars low down on the horizon, and up there the sun burning. Only sometimes, in the rain, did it lose its dazzle; but soon the sun came out again and zinged and chipped at the edges of everything. Sydney had not got too big for its boots yet – not yet, not yet – and Cannie felt proud of that. It wore its beauty lightly, and did not – whatever anyone from anywhere else said – commit that Australian sin of trying too hard. Sydney rolled from car yard to sky without pretension – it looked after its people with sand, and coffee, and rarely the sound of a beeping horn. There was a confident peace, here – Sydneysiders weren't constantly trying to get somewhere else, climb over the wall, as they were in the rest of the world. *Poor Man's LA*, Story liked to say – but he didn't believe it. He just enjoyed saying it, as it made his world feel big. But Sydney was big – you only had to look up to know it. *Poor Man's LA*, but Cannie could picture Story happy as Noddy driving around in his tinted wagon.

'How long,' Story was saying to the salesman, who sat strapped in next to him like they were husband and wife, 'would an order take?'

'Usually four weeks, Story, but I'd do whatever it takes to get it ready for you in three, max. You'd have it in the first week of January, Story.'

'It's worth doing, then.'

'Absolutely. Then you'll have exactly the car you want, down to the buttons, Story. Christmas present for yourself, Story! If you're spending money on a brand-new car, you want it just how you want it. Foo! Don't mind if I do!' Two girls were standing on a corner, holding pails, collecting money for a charity. One wore a baseball cap; the other had yellow hair tied up on top of her head. They both wore shorts and small bikini tops. 'Reckon they'll be doing all right today!'

'Yeah, no doubt,' Story says.

Growing up in Sydney, being a teenage boy, had been something of a painful heaven. In that – everybody was mostly naked. The beaches, particularly in the Eastern Suburbs, but also everywhere else, were made up of boobs. A great democracy of boobs.

Quite early, behind the armour of a pair of sunglasses, Story became a specialist on nipples. On their size, their colour, their position on the breast. When he was thirteen, he could have half an hour of mucking about on the beach without much thought on anything, and then a pair would emerge from the water, wet and stiff, and there would be an excruciating squeezing between his legs, alongside his expert analysis.

And wherever you went, there was a girl nearby, a topless girl doing cartwheels. She was always there, on every beach, doing gymnastics, without her bikini top on, occasionally flicking her eyes over. More often than not laughing with a friend, or a boyfriend. She had her nuances. Sometimes she was attempting amateur martial arts. Sometimes she was playfully throwing sand at her companions, and then running and bouncing away. But whatever the subtle variegations, there she was, the Cartwheel Girl, on every summer beach in Sydney. Her adolescent bosoms separately perfect, open, unaware.

Teenage years, and Story and his compadres would lay their towels nearby and say, flatly and hormonally, 'Fuck. She's hot.' They said it again and again, every Saturday, at North

Narrabeen or Manly or Dee Why, at each of the spreading, stretching, laughing, cartwheeling girls. It was their own personal peep show. No furtiveness or pocket money required. It was there, beating to the pulse of their puberty, there for the ogling, laying itself bare on every beach in the city. The awesome, unfettered equality of nakedness in Australia.

But it had been a while ago, now, that Story had discovered, hunkered into the sand with the business pages, that the boobs no longer worked. In fact, at times, they got on his nerves. These rows and rows of tits, stripping women of their mystery, becoming like steaks in the sun. They began to look almost ugly. Like dangling faces.

Seeing a naked girl eating chips on the beach – even though it had been the landscape of his young life, even though so many of the Cammeray girls had done it, their chests nudging into the cones of fried potato – somehow now looked actively, decisively, *un*attractive.

Mac wouldn't agree. Vincent Batty certainly wouldn't agree – there's nothing he loved more than a day in the sand, *narking at udders*, as he liked to say, jutting his chin out and wiggling his fingers as if he was having a feel. JP wouldn't agree either.

Fuck, who knows. Story just felt like the years of display had left him dry. And so, while he saw the two schoolgirls with their tits like eggs in heat, holding their tins and doing good deeds, and while he saw why – *obviously*, he saw why – his Mitsubishi friend was having a moment, he didn't share it. He didn't feel the need to watch them in his mirrors as he drove past.

'You go down to Coogee at all, Story?' the salesman asks, gesturing with one thumb in the direction of the beach.

'Nah, not really.'

'You should give it a whirl, Story. The chicks've really gone up a notch. You know, you'd just go there for the surf, really. The chicks'd all be covered up in wetsuits, surfer chicks. You still get them, but. But all the other chicks've really raised their game.' He smiles and exhales at the thought of it. 'Like those two girls back there – like, *prime*, you know, Story? The Coogee chicks are up to the quality of Bondi, now. Some seriously hot bodies, mate.'

Back in the showroom, as Story is filling in his paperwork and parting with his deposit, the happy salesman stands, swinging on his heels and swiftly balling and flattening one hand against the other in an unfathomably fast way – the kind of thing you practised alone as a teenager, so as to bring out with nonchalance in public.

'So,' the salesman says to Cannie, 'what have you got planned for the rest of the day?'

She wants to be wearing that T-shirt, with an arrow pointing to Story: *We're Just Friends*.

'Ah, nothing much.'

'Heading to the beach?' The salesman smiles.

'The beach?' Cannie repeats. 'No.'

'Aw,' he says, the confidence of this killer sale ringing about him, still rocking and doing that thing with his hands. 'On a day like today what else you gonna do?'

Cannie smiles emptily. She thinks of the constellations of freckles and moles on her shoulders, and how little she enjoys wearing a swimsuit, these days. She used to bare her skin like everybody else – but in recent years, as the galaxies have spread over her back, and her legs have got thicker – she prefers not to. And the years of corporate work have made it worse, of course – her skin underneath her long sleeves and black tights is white, and spongy.

She used not to think about it, but now it is with unease that Cannie notices the pageantry of Sydney's brown flesh. Bodies droop from faces as if they are clothes on hangers. Everybody watching everybody else with mouths slightly open. Had she ever worn her body like that? Had she ever stood on the sand like that? With that smug, coaxing expression on her face? No. Not. She knows not. The only person to see her skin, these days, is Max. The myna bird. Who sits on the ledge with his head at an angle, watching while Cannie pulls her tights up on the other side of the glass.

They finally leave the car yard, walking to the main road to find a cab. Story is coasting and wordy from his new purchase.

'. . . don't know when I'm ever going to drive it!' he says.

'You'll drive it,' she says. 'It's amazing how quickly you come to depend on a car, when you didn't before.'

On the wall to the left of them is an inexpertly sprayed graffiti. It says, *I might be drunk, but you're ugly.*

Story laughs as they pass it by.

12

Sitting in the Beach Road Hotel, with only Vincent Batty and Tree yet arrived, Mac supposes Tree hasn't changed since they were kids. Same pretty face, with eyes, nose and mouth all arranged easily. Same thick, brown hair. Same clothes on the moderate side of trendy, showing a welcome and measured amount of trim figure – although she wasn't in the league of some girls, of some girls you see, like on Fashion TV. Or like Alessia. At work. Who was so slender she stood with a stoop, like a model. Who was just – full on hot.

Anyway, Tree's hot. She and Vincent Batty make an odd couple, physically. Tree definitely pretty, and Vincent with the body of a plank, big lips, gappy teeth and eyeballs so extensively round that you can see them in profile, full of white, like boiled eggs. Even though – don't get me wrong – Vincent is one of the most awesome blokes you could meet – you'd think she could've done better for herself. Although, actually, it makes sense, Mac reckons, in that Tree is just a beautician. Not a high flyer like – like – Alessia. And not even something like an actress.

And Vincent could make anyone laugh. Even their stoniest

teachers at Grammar. He made all the girls laugh, all the boys laugh, and at fifteen started DJing at parties, which was high up on the respect scale. That's around when he got together with Tree. And now – getting married.

'Hey, I got the invite,' Mac said, giving Tree a kiss on the cheek.

'Aw, cool!' says Tree.

'I don't need to reply, do I? I mean, you know I'm coming, right?'

'You're a groomsman, Mac! You better be coming!'

Mac laughs. 'I'll be there,' he says, 'in my top hat.'

'Oh,' says Tree. 'Has Vinnie not spoken to you guys about the clothes yet? What you'll be wearing?'

'Ah, kind of.'

'Tk. He's so disorganised!' Tree flicks him a look, softly reprimanding. 'There's gonna be a list at Ferrall's Boutique Hire in Chatswood Mall – do you know it?'

'Um—'

'You just have to go along and they'll size you up and everything – but it's all chosen. But we're not having hats for the groomsmen. Mum and I want all the ladies in hats, but not the men. I hope you don't mind.'

'I don't have a top hat, Tree. I was just being – look, it's cool. I'll wear what I'm told! D'you want another drink? I'm going to the bar.'

Vincent Batty nudges Mac on the shoulder with his. It's probably an optical illusion, but his schooner looks massive. More like a pint. 'You trying to get my woman drunk, Mac?' he says. Vincent's heart has always been in his music, a cheerful, bubblegum house that he spins under the name Vince McQueen. Five years ago, he had taken a day job as assistant concierge at a slick new hotel, and these mornings he wakes up and finds himself to be the assistant manager of the whole bloody place. He feels fraudulent when he meets people, introducing himself as a DJ. Because he's not. He looks in the mirror on Monday, and sees: Vincent Batty, Assistant Manager, Source Hotel, Woolloomooloo.

'Easy, tiger. How about you? Want another?' Mac asks.

'Seriously, mate,' Vincent says to Mac, 'watch out. When Tree's drunk she gets vicious. Goes for the eyes, don't you, babe?'

Tree smiles and makes a face.

Mac goes to the bar and, as he does, JP and then Story arrive. Story asks with a slightly nervous laugh, 'Is Tintin actually coming?' He has always felt awkward arriving into groups, being watched; even if he's known the group since childhood.

'He texted to say he'll be here by half seven,' says Vincent. 'In fact,' Vincent clears his throat for comic effect, 'he said: "we".'

'*We*,' says JP, and frowns.

'*We*, eh?' Mac echoes. 'D'we reckon Tin's got a woman?'

'Could well be,' says Vincent. 'Unless that's how he refers to himself, these days.'

'Who d'you reckon she is, then?'

'A trapeze artist,' says Vincent.

Story laughs. 'Yeah,' he says. 'Exactly, dude.'

Vincent Batty's hit the nail – Tintin always showboated women whom he thought had a USP.

'Hey, fuck,' says Mac. 'There he is.'

The large portion of conversation stops, apart from Tree, who is saying to Vincent with melodious crossness, 'The bubbles always make me burp, you know that. You don't have to make fun of me.'

As Tintin, in a black baseball cap, walks through the crowded room hand in hand with a woman, a ripple forms before them. Eyes brush up and remain, staring, for some moments too long. Eyebrows bounce in surprise. And while the buzz of the room continues unbroken, and everybody remains where they sit – there is nonetheless a current, a tacit parting of the waters, as the couple progress. She's – not what you normally see – in a bar – like this – or in Sydney, for that matter.

Mac raises a hand high, waves and smiles. Tintin smiles back, does a salute with two fingers.

'G'day, fellas, long time no see.'

Hugs, pats, shaking hands, smiles.

The woman, who has been standing back, is wearing silver rings on her hands, and a flimsy blue top. Her skirt comes above the knee, and is a tight, blue tartan.

Far out, thinks Story. *She has incredibly long arms.*

'Hey, everybody,' Tintin grins, putting an arm around and pulling her closer, 'this is Pinyata.'

The woman gives a little wave, coy, and says, 'Hi, good to meet you.'

And here's a thing – her voice – it is not at all what you'd expect. Is she putting it on? No – it's her voice. Her actual voice.

It is a cartoon voice, a cartoon of a girl. Sugary and pink and sticky, as if she is about to flutter into giggles at any minute.

And, on top of that, it is – *very* – Australian. Not that there's any reason for her voice *not* to be Australian. And not that there's any reason for it not to be Baby Girl. It's just . . . unexpected.

Not that there's any reason for it to be unexpected.

It's just that, you know, that's not how you'd've picked it. Although, there's no reason why not.

Her arms – her arms – her arms are – really – long.

As Pinyata is introduced around the gang, Tree says –

'Oh, my goodness, aren't you tall! How tall are you?'

– and Story, in time with his nervous slug of gin and tonic, feels a gulp of warmth for Tree, for saying it like it is. Tree is a girl, and she is harmless, so she can say things.

'Oh,' says Pinyata, her smile open and her voice like bubblegum – pink, glittery, fairy foo-foo bubblegum – 'I'm about six foot one.'

'Oh, wow!' says Tree. 'Although, you know, you look way taller than that.'

Story doesn't know why he feels so displaced, so uneasy. Or why he feels so grateful to Tree, simply for speaking without art. It can't just be because – he feels short – can it?

Pinyata giggles. 'It's the shoes!' she says, gesturing down to a pair of red sandals with thick, square heels. 'In these I'm about six five.'

She has big feet, thinks Story, looking at the stout, red high heels. *Her feet are bigger than mine.*

'Aw, good on you!' says Tree, as if Pinyata, by wearing heels, is overcoming some disability.

JP, in a good mood and trying to be friendly, says by way of introduction, 'I didn't catch your name.'

Story feels a rush of goodwill for JP. For JP and for Tree. He likes them both very much, and he wants another drink.

'Pinyata,' says Pinyata. 'Oh,' she says, 'and I'm sorry, you're JD? There are so many of you, even though Davey's told me who you all are, I've got to get my head round it!'

'Piñata?' checks JP.

Pinyata nods and smiles.

'*JP*, Yaya,' Tintin says to Pinyata, 'not *JD*. Short for John Pierre.'

'John Pee-ah!' says Pinyata. 'JP, I've got it, right, I've got it. Silly me! Heehee!'

His body forgetting itself in alcohol, JP was pleased, in his rusty way, at having these old faces around. Tintin was talking about Wellington, his new ground. He was describing it as a shimmering little Bohemia, and Mac chimed in with, 'It's a fucking shithole.'

'Ah, lest I forget I'm talking to a fucking JAFA,' Tintin says.

'Tautology, mate,' says Mac.

'What?'

'*A Fucking JAFA* is tautology. A JAFA, yeah? Is *Just Another Fucking Aucklander*. So a *Fucking* Just Another *Fucking* Aucklander is tautology.'

'Allow myself to introduce myself,' says Story, sniggering.

'Beside which,' says Mac, 'I only lived in Auckland for six months, mate. Hardly a native. Shit,' he says, looking at Pinyata. 'Sorry. I didn't mean anything by that.'

'Oh, fuck, mate,' says Tintin, 'it's too late for this. You know who you sound like, Mac?' he says, perking up. 'Mr Thornton.'

'Mr Thornton!' says JP, with gravitas.

'Yeah!' Story laughs. 'He's right, you know. You do sound like Thorno.'

Mr Thornton. He had been their English teacher for two years at North Sydney Grammar, and for one year their form tutor. He was old-fashioned and foul-mouthed and he genuinely – in a way that would make him grind his teeth and hold on tight to tables as if he were sinking – loved Irish literature. He talked of the affinity between Australians and Irish, and would make them learn thick passages of verse and text off by heart. They once spent two hours straight learning 'Bog Queen', and Mr Thornton tested them on it for weeks. In the middle of a class, without warning, he'd say, 'Fry! Bog Queen!' And JP would have to stand and start reciting. Then, 'Batty! Take over!' And Vincent would have to stand up mid-line and begin. Few of them ever forgot the words. JP still, in the shower, or making a sandwich, found himself casually muttering, *And I rose from the dark, Hacked bone, skull-ware. Hacked bone. Hacked bone-bone-bone-bone-bone*, as he searched on the shelves of the fridge for some cheese to slice.

Mr Thornton had never really taken an interest in any one of them personally, but he would write comments in the margins of your essays that made it feel like he knew you. *You*, he had written in red biro next to an under-lined paragraph of JP's, *are one of the last Romantics, John Pierre!*

At the end of their last class with him, he had said, cheerfully,

'See you, boys. May the road rise up to meet you.'

It had felt like a blessing. And for JP it held the hope of his youth within it, that breezy goodbye.

Tintin has assumed a serious expression, and is holding his beer a foot away from his chest. 'My heart would brim with dreams about the times!' he begins, in a loud, ricocheting Irish attempt, 'When we bent down among the fading coals! And talked of the dark folk' – here he raises his glass to Pinyata, who looks delighted – 'who live in souls!' He takes a swig of his beer. 'William Butler Yeats,' he says. '1893.'

'Of passionate men,' says JP, finishing the line that Tintin cut short, 'like bats in the dead trees.'

No one hears him.

'What the fuck accent is that, dude!' Story is saying. 'Pirate?'

'William Butler Yeats,' says Tintin, looking pleased, '1893.'

Looking at them now, JP sees the boys he used to sit next to in class. Same as they ever were. All around him.

'Do you want to say that again, mate?' Mac is asking Tintin. 'William Butler Yeats, 1893? Just in case we didn't hear the first two times?'

Tintin laughs, and as he does he removes his baseball cap, for a few seconds. He scratches the back of his head vigorously, and then replaces the hat, pulling the peak down low before pushing it up slightly.

And that's what did it – those seconds as Tintin with insouciance lifted a hat from a head; those seconds drove the night into a wall. They took every bird of comfort that had been humming around JP's head, and broke their little necks.

Under the hat, on the head, like a scar or an open wound, there were ten centimetres of dry scalp, where Tintin's hair had been.

JP blinks rapidly, as if he could flush the reality from his eyes. Unconsciously, he puts his hand to his own hard buzz cut. It is still there.

But the quiff that had given Tintin his name when they were fourteen – a plume of pale brown – and that in later years had become a long, surfie fringe – was gone. Tinny was losing his hair. He was half bald. Twenty years had compressed into one second, with a single push of the concertina.

And suddenly it felt like each body in there, in that heaving, writhing, sodden room, was a pillar of dust.

★

As they stand on the street outside the Beach House Hotel, the ocean occurs to Story in an upsurge. It's funny that it is right there. Simply background noise, you never notice it – and yet, there it is, loud as an orchestra, full of sharks and broken boats. Story's head is pressed with the sound of the sea.

Tintin and Pinyata are taking their leave, with a promise to 'See you tools at the buck's night.'

'And the *wedding*, silly!' Pinyata chirps.

'Sorry I didn't put your name on the invite,' Tree says, mentally totting how her numbers stacked up with this unexpected plus one. 'I didn't know about you.'

'Have a good Christmas!' says Story.

'Yeah, have a good one.'

Tintin and Pinyata walk away, holding hands.

'See you at the wedding,' Mac says, distractedly, thumbs punching into his phone.

'What are you doing, dude?' says Story. Mac doesn't answer. 'Naish, dude!' Story shouts.

Mac looks up. 'I'm texting,' he says.

'You drunk dialling, mate?' Story asks.

'Yep.'

'Who?'

'Gimme a second!' Mac says, looking at his screen again. 'A girl from work.'

'Fuck, seriously?' giggles Story. 'A biscuit chick?'

'Madame le Biscuit,' says Vincent.

'Imagine getting drunk-dialled by this fuckwit in the middle of the night,' Story goes on.

'By the looks of it,' says Vincent, 'he's texting her *War and Peace*, as well.'

JP is standing in silence, looking back at the pub. He doesn't give a shit about any of this noise – Story crapping on like some fat Chihuahua, as usual.

'Who is this chick?' says Story. 'You propositioning a stranger – like, some random chick at work – in the middle of the night?'

'She's not a stranger,' says Mac, finally pressing Send and looking up. 'We're friends.'

'Friends,' says Vincent.

Mac grins at them both. He puts his phone back in the pocket of his jeans.

'What?' says Story. 'Fuck buddies?'

'Nah,' says Mac, still smiling. 'Not that.'

'Well,' says Story, 'good luck, mate. Good luck. I'm pretty fucking hungry, you know.' Story wants to get away from the sound of the ocean.

'I could eat,' Vincent says.

'We could go to Barbecue Palace,' Story offers non-chalantly, never investing too much enthusiasm in a suggestion, lest it get shot down.

'Genius, mate!' says Vincent Batty.

'Vinnie, we've got to go home,' says Tree, squeezing his arm. He turns to his fiancée, as if only now remembering she existed.

'I tell you what,' Story says, 'Tintin's a wanker, right, but he gives good chat. Like, good blah blah blah. And that's what it's all about.'

'What,' says Vincent, 'like the hokey cokey?'

Story ignores him. 'He seems pretty happy with his chick, as well,' he says.

'Wouldn't you be?' says Mac.

Story is thrown. 'What do you mean?' He found Pinyata

kind of – irritating. Kind of foolish, with all her giggling. But he's worried that if he says anything – it'll come out sounding like he's prejudiced in some way. Like he's racist. Or heightist.

'Well,' says Vincent, 'I thought she was . . . cool. She's got some legs on her, too.'

'Too right,' says Mac.

'Her legs were okay,' say Story.

'Story, her legs were up to the roof,' says Vinnie. 'They were the same size as you.'

'No, they weren't,' says Story, hiccoughing loudly. 'I notice these things. Her legs weren't that long at all.' Staring Mac down, Story goes on, 'She's just *tall*, dude. She's got *tall* legs. But, proportionally, they're not long at all. And she's not got small ankles, either.'

'*Small ankles?*' Mac looks incredulous, and then laughs. 'Are you living in 1850 or something, mate?'

'I got an eye for detail.' Story hiccoughs again.

'Yeah, mate,' says Mac. 'You're a connoisseur.'

'She's a writer,' says Vincent, 'a scriptwriter. It's a bloody lot more exciting than what most people do.'

'She's a writer, is that right?' says Mac, lightly interested.

JP, who has been standing inside his own shadow, stops dead. 'She's not a fucking writer,' he says. His words are like rocks.

The others stop also, and turn to JP.

Mac feels his phone go. He takes it out of his pocket and turns his back slightly.

'She is, mate, she told me about her script,' says Vincent.

Coming down the road is a cab with its light on. Story steps to the kerb. 'Taxi!' he shouts. 'Hey! Taxi!' Swish, swish, swish, the fucking sea.

'She's not a fucking writer, mate,' spits JP, 'she's a wannabe.'

Vincent looks puzzled.

'You know what she fucking is?' JP goes on, 'She's dark, and she's a fucking giant. That's it.'

'*Dark?*' hoots Mac, looking up from his phone.

'Yeah.'

'You might as well say *exotic*, mate, or *dusky*.'

'What the fuck's your problem?'

'No problem, bro'. I just thought she was black.' Mac can't help himself. He starts laughing. 'But, it's cool. No doubt she is a dark, dusky, coloured, exotic and classy sheila, too.'

'Fuck you, you fucking cock,' JP says.

Mac looks surprised.

'You think you're so fucking superior? What, 'cause you're in charge of making biscuits for the nation? Without you, there'd be a biscuit crisis? You're a fucking inbred, mate, like everyone else in this city.'

'Fucking hell, fair go, JP—'

JP doesn't allow Mac's interruption; he's loaded. 'There you are, lecturing me on being PC, like I'm some fucking redneck, when you're the one, you're the fucking pathetic fuck, saying that dipshit woman is *cool*, just because she's *black*. *Black*, right? Am I saying it right? Black, and a fucking giant – that's enough for you, mate, is it? You going to stare at her like everybody else in that shithole? She was a fucking moron – so desperate to be *kooky*, it's pathetic, talks like she's a fucking five-year-old – and, what? You and Vinnie are crapping on like that makes her special? Story's right. She's just some random. Who happens to be fucking dark. *Black*, mate, *black*. Tall! Black! That's fucking it! Every fucking dick-rag on the planet has written a *script*.' JP says the word as if it is a rat dangling at the end of his fist, he has come to the kernel of his business. 'She hasn't done a fucking thing, mate. She and Tintin are perfect for each other. They can stay in Wellington, everybody staring at her, fucking tadpoles in a fucking small-town puddle, blowing smoke up each other's arses for the rest of their lives.'

The cab has pulled over. Story stands by it on the road. 'Guys!' he calls them over, 'taxi!'

'We're going the other way,' Tree says firmly, Vincent's hand in one of hers and looking away from JP.

'Sorry, mate,' shrugs Vincent Batty. 'Under orders.'

Mac, who has just received a text, looks up from his phone, trying to limit a smile. JP's fumes and thunder have slid right off him, oil and water. He goes round road side of the taxi, and gets in.

Story hasn't yet shut his door. 'Are you coming, dude, or what?' he says to JP.

JP stands where he stopped, in his suit and shirt, tie in his pocket. He looks at the taxi, and the carelessness inside it.

'Fuck this,' he says. He turns, and starts walking.

Story twists the key in the lock of his apartment door. That's always the test of how drunk he really is — and, tonight, he passes with flying colours. He gets the key in first time. He does not have to lean against the wall; he stands, erect, a soldier and a proud man. Story watches the key, as if it is the only thing in the world, slide into the lock, a little miracle. Perfection — *key in lock*.

He walks inside and pushes the lights on, then dims them low. The cleaner has been today, and so the place looks pretty nifty. There's no mess. The surfaces are all empty, the kitchen is radiant with bleach, and through in his bedroom his bed will be a precise square of fresh sheets.

He walks to the fridge, and looks inside. With Vincent marshalled home by Tree, JP stomped off in a strop, and Mac gone to screw some chick from the office, there were no takers for Barbecue Palace, after all; Story's hungry. The fridge holds: a box of eggs, tomatoes, spinach, beer, wine, cheese, bread, milk, a pot of fresh pesto from Mancini's. He aims for the pesto.

He rips the stale edge from a remnant of baguette, discards it, opens up the remaining bread with his thumbs, and spoons in the pesto. He stands, in his kitchen, with a halo of crumbs around him on the counter, and eats.

It's a good fucking feeling, this. Warm inside, warm outside: just right. Like Sydney was being heated from below, warmth coming up from the pavements. Just drunk enough. A clean flat. Food and comfort.

Story felt happy like a fat, cosy cat.

And he thinks to himself, in this moment of blurred satiation, that his life is really pretty fucking good. That he has spent the night with friends, laughing. Feeling the laughter in the muscles of his face and underneath his lungs.

Those feelings – that feeling – of things ending, that had been fluxing and winking from corners – seem now like a neurosis. Story, with bread pushing into his mouth and wine pushing against his stomach, feels so content, feels himself such a chieftain of this Sydney night – that he cannot remember the feeling that had bothered him so, as having been real.

The anxiety, the inexplicable sense of mourning, the confusion that had been growling at his ankles so persistently – he feels free of.

As the last of the bread goes into his mouth, Story reckons

he could do with some light relief. He wakes his laptop up from its sleep, and, making sure all his other applications are closed down, opens up his browser and types into the box, *pornxxxchange.com*. He has the hiccoughs again, from eating too fast.

On to the screen appear row after row of small squares, a grid of little thumbnails. Above each is a brief description: *Pussy popping lesbian orgasms*; *18YO amateur starts with 1 ends up with 6*; *MILF gets cream-pied*.

Story moves his mouse over one of the squares, and clicks – within seconds a movie is breaking on his monitor: a naked woman is lying face-down on a bed, with her arse in the air. Her face is turned towards Story. A topless man, in jeans, kneels behind her, and is pulling, and pushing, with rage, a large black dildo in and out of her. Her eyes are closed and her mouth is open and noises are coming out of it. Story wonders if Vincent still does this, when Tree's not at home – because it's different, isn't it?

Story quickly pushes himself up to standing – before anything else, he realises he has to go and pee.

He goes to his bathroom, undoes his suit trousers (which he has been wearing since six twenty this morning – yesterday morning, it is now) and sits on the loo seat, as he often does when he is tired or drunk. He leans his elbow on one thigh, and leans his head in one hand as he pees.

He closes his eyes as he waits for the last pints of the night's booze to pass, closes his eyes, and thinks of the woman on the computer. Thinks of where the dildo is actually going, and casually reckons he'd like to see a close-up.

He closes his eyes, and thinks of Mac, getting out of the cab at Taylor Square with a huge grin on his face.

He closes his eyes, and with eyes closed, and mouth part-ing – he falls asleep.

Story is like that, peacefully, for nearly an hour. A feat of unconscious balance, like a commuter standing and sleeping on a Tokyo train. But then, as if the weight of his head has suddenly increased with whatever's inside it, his palm can no longer support his skull, and his head goes hurtling towards his knees, his arm goes splaying out to one side.

Story jerks awake in an undignified muddle. He opens his eyes wide, and feels a waking panic at where he is, and when. He grunts when he sees himself dangling into the pan, and stands – his bottom sucks away from the seat uncomfortably. The skin where he has been sitting is a troubled red.

He takes off his shoes, socks, trousers and underpants from around his ankles as quickly as he can, and leaves them where they fall on the bathroom floor.

Story walks through to the living room – all the lights are on, and his laptop is sleeping open on the table. He touches the keyboard, to call up the time, and there, underneath the resolute judgement of 04:17, is *pornxxxchange.com*.

The video has run its course while Story has been asleep with his trousers down and, written over the still image of the woman with her face in the mattress are the words, *Watch Again?*

Story bats the screen with a flick of his hand; it thumps shut.

Blinds open, lights on, Story stands in his bare legs and work shirt, with a green glob of pesto spreading oil on the collar.

He stands, and he sways slightly on his naked feet, and he feels slightly afraid.

The whole flat — lit up with artificial light, with the dark, empty world outside — seems so vacant and so silent, so lonely, that Story doesn't know how much longer he can stay alive within it. He doesn't know from where it's come, but there is water crowding behind his lids. He rubs his eyes with his fingers.

This is a place he knows. He tells himself that. *This is his home.*

There is his rug and there is his lamp, silver and arched from a shop in Double Bay. There is his wallet on the kitchen counter, with credit cards within that testify: this is him.

There is his stack of old CDs, there is his table made from a single tree. There is his phone up by the kitchen wall, his landline; it rarely rings. There is his fruit bowl made of glass, with a jumble of things inside: pens, phone charger, painkillers. There is his barbecue out on the deck. There is his issue of *wallpaper** magazine. There is his laptop with a naked woman crawling inside.

It all frightens him. It is as if he has never touched these things before. He doesn't even recognise his own hands.

And again it is here, the feeling that Story cannot understand, even while it rings like tinnitus in his ears. The feeling of everything being over. The feeling of silence, of a thick dust, like snow, having covered everything.

Story turns off the lights and makes sure his front door is locked. He walks to his bed, and pulls down the clean, white doona. As he gets into bed in his work shirt, the silence in his room becomes like white noise, and Story says to himself, that when he wakes it will be morning. It will be morning, soon.

13

Story had never really known whether he liked her or not. She did this thing, this funny thing when she spoke – like she took really deep breaths in the middle of sentences, almost gasping. It was quite noticeable. That is to say – you couldn't miss it. *Hhhhaaarr*, like that, inhaling. Like the noise somebody makes when they're dying. Like she was desperate for air.

They were together for long enough that he ceased to notice. Except for when they were in a room with new people, people they didn't know – then it became like a strobe: *we went to see it on Friday – hhhhhaarr – night, but that was before – hhhhaarr – we met up with the – hhhhaarrr – others.* Story would become prickly and self-conscious, and would distance himself from her. He'd try not to stand too close. He wouldn't touch her.

He found her attractive, in that she was a woman with a woman's body and a woman's mouth. She wouldn't have sex with him – just his luck, the only girl at Cedars High not to spread – and at times it made him feel frantic. But on the plus side, it was one less thing to worry about – to worry about himself and how good he was and whether he was doing what he was supposed to be doing – and in her defence she was always giving him blowjobs whenever there was the use of a semi-private space, a bedroom with a dodgy lock or the back of a family car.

She'd been easy to be with, too, Kath. She was always content, smiling, happy to go along with whatever. (Except sex.) She laughed at his jokes – *ha ha* – *hhharrrr* – *ha* – genuinely, and with her eyes. She ate a lot of chicken. As long as they were somewhere where she could have chicken, she was all right. And she loved movies. They went to a lot of movies.

But, still, Story didn't know at the time what he felt for her – whether he felt anything. When they had first kissed – Kath and him, both sixteen years old – Story's thought was not on the kiss itself, on what the colliding of lips was doing to his body – but rather what his mates would think of her. Whether they'd rate her. Whether they'd give him some respect for it, think she was sexy in some way small or big; or whether they'd take the piss out of him for getting together with a dog.

As it happened, they accepted her pretty readily, although there weren't the congratulatory nudges and winks Story had hoped for. Just hellos and nods and inoffensive dis-interest, and that was that. But Story was always wondering. Whether they talked about the breathing behind his back. Or the gap between her front teeth. Or the fact that her tits were quite big. He wished they had said something about how hot she was – then he'd have the freedom to believe it himself.

Mum had liked her; she had also asked whether Kath had asthma, and Story had said no, that was just a thing she did. She'd come over for dinner quite a bit, and she and Kali would chat, and it always struck Story how different they looked, Kath and Kali. They'd been nice, those dinners. He remembers the first time they were sitting on the sofa and he with creaky trepidation put his hand on her leg. Neither Kali nor Mum commented or laughed or whispered, and that was the door to a time of peace, girlfriend comfortable within family. When they'd split up, Mum had said how sorry she was, and to 'give Kath my love'. Story passed on the love. It was all very civilised, especially for seventeen-year-olds. Other relationships around him were igniting like tinder, or smashing against rocks; intense, serious teenage affairs, floating on hot air. But Story and Kath were altogether calm and noncommittal. They never declared undying love, or spoke of their future in fairytale terms. Kath would say, *Love you*, at the end of a phone conversation; but that didn't count, did it.

Story wonders now, with nearly twenty years' hindsight, whether he had, in fact, without knowing it, loved her. Whether she had been the one he loved. Remembering – they'd had quite a lovely time together. It had been warm and alive, having another body next to yours to bear witness to the day. Had they stayed together, like Vincent and Tree, they, too, would probably be getting married now. What a strange, strange thought. To have been with someone so long – to have been with someone for ever – used only to them – to their shapes, their sounds, their footprints. Imagine if she were known to him, still. Maybe Tree and Vincent had got it right – and the rest of them – wrong.

The Cedar High girls finished at three fifteen and Grammar finished at three thirty. Kath got the bus over and often was there at the gates, in that low, afternoon sun. It felt the day was just beginning – a second waking, a second morning, two days in one. They took the bus to Balmoral, and sat with their feet in the sand, giving the inevitable *G'day* and nod to other uniformed faces that passed. They shared earphones and mouthed silently to songs with their toes buried. Story remembers it being hot there, no shade, in their school clothes. Kath sometimes took her skirt off so she was just in her underwear and white shirt, and the sand would stick to her legs.

Other days they'd walk to the mall and have coffees and sandwiches. Story often hankered after a strawberry milk-shake, but never ordered one with Kath there – always a grown-up cappuccino. As well as chicken paninis, there were these berry friands from this particular place that she liked, and Story once bought her a bag of them. Kath seemed amazed by that, like this small paper bag had a tsunami inside it rather than a few cakes. She took it as an act of romance, when, of course, Story would've done it for anyone.

Looking back on it, they were happy. As happy as Story had been with anyone since. But how could they not be? He would come walking around the school gates and there she'd be with a kink in her hair from where her ponytail had been all day and the light was rolling down the streets like logs. People were beautiful, then, before the dawn of wrinkles and thick stubble and enlarged pores – the Sydney sunshine was made for young skin that didn't need forgiveness – faces lit from within like jack-o-lanterns. Kath was no exception. She didn't have acne and she didn't have a moustache and so the rolling light stuck like honey and drew a corona around her.

Just sitting somewhere was enough, feeling hot within your bones, and with something to consume. Nothing loomed or towered; Sydney's old buildings were small and introspective and the same colour as the ground, and the new ones were mild and nondescript. No tall trees, no ugly colours. Everything, here, the right size. No spires reaching up to touch God's beard; low ceilings, the right height for a man. God was in the sunshine, in the air-conditioning, in the big, white cars. Everyone, here, wants the same thing – a happy life. And so there were no arguments. No arguments in restaurants or on street corners, like you saw on the television in New York, no arguments in parks or outside pubs, like you saw in those old, grey cities in Europe. Too easy; it was all, too, easy.

Sydney doesn't mind if you just love her for her blond hair. She is a puppy, delighted to please. Who needs an old soul, anyway? Enough of that up north, with the crocs and the mozzies and the hard, red floor. If you can't be happy in Sydney, you can't be happy anywhere. Sydney put joy in the water and forgetfulness in the sand, and as long as you drank water and stood on sand, happiness would curl up and stick like heat from a campfire. A hormonal happiness, full of vitamin D and phosphor, it overrode sadness of any other kind.

And, Story thinks, he may have loved Kath, in that way. In that way of low trees and pretty colours. Of warm within your bones. Of hormones and vitamins and sand. He questioned it then, because he didn't know what was to come after. Because how was he to know that there was not to be anything more? The sunshine years rolled on.

14

Story stands in the cubicle, in front of the mirror. There he is. Hello. In a dress suit that is digging in at the waist and pushing his stomach down below the waistband – it looks like he is wearing one of those inflatable rubber rings. The jacket is too big, as if he is a child in hand–me–downs.

It's bollocks what the woman had said.

'We can mix and match the jacket and trousers,' she'd insisted, in a resolute manner that suggested she had been working here her entire life, 'so that they fit perfectly. We don't want baggy trousers or short jackets!'

She'd whisked items out of her back room with an invulnerable confidence that they would be exactly right.

'How are we getting on in there?' she says, from beyond the curtain.

'Good,' says Story. 'I'll be another couple of minutes.'

'Everything fitting nicely?'

'Yeah, I'll just be a minute.'

'Shall I come in and take a look?'

'No,' says Story – for God's sake, *no* – 'I'm all right.'

Story never wants to come out. He wants to stay in here until the world has turned to dust outside. He strips off the

112

suit with speed, fighting the urge to roll it up into a ball and trample on it. Scratchy, cheap suit worn by — how many other men? Hundreds. Each rubbing their hairy, white behinds into the seat of it, sweating their way through weddings, parties, charity dinners.

What will he say to the woman?

What will he say to Tree, moreover?

She had sent an email, to all the groomsmen. The instructions were clear. Black tux, grey shirt, grey bow tie, all picked out and waiting to be sized and paid for at Ferrall's Boutique Hire. Story stands in his cubicle, miserable in his work shirt, socks and underpants. How long can he stay in here, before the saleswoman comes calling through the curtain again?

Story has, at home, in his wardrobe, four suits that used to be his dad's. None of them fit him, or ever will, unless he had one of those height-extension operations that he read about Sumo wrestlers getting, pads of fat inserted into their skulls. And even that wouldn't work, Story reflects, morosely. He'd then be in an ill-fitting suit, with a head like Frankenstein. Cuban heels did nothing either — he'd tried. Weren't all sons supposed to be taller than their father? Wasn't that, like, some immutable, Darwinian *fact*?

He has his dad's ties, though, and he wears those. They are beautiful. It took him a while to come to terms with them — after Dad died, when Story was slap in the middle of his teens, he was too embarrassed. He wanted ties like the other boys — block colours, navies and burgundies, with stripes or small dots. Dad's ties were intricate, full of tiny men in boats or endless small rabbits, and in old tapestry colours, terracottas and pale greens. He had Dad's bow tie, too, thick and made of textured silk.

113

But he couldn't even wear that to the wedding. Instead he had to rent the grey, shiny one that Tree had decreed.

He'd first worn one of Dad's ties to a St Andrew's dinner – his college at Sydney Uni.

'I like your tie,' Cannie had said to him, and, thinking about it, that was probably when Story and she became friends – definite friends, rather than two nearby cogs in their local, teenage machine.

Vincent and Stavvo were the only ones not to go to uni; Mac had gone to Melbourne. Story, JP and Cannie had all got places at Sydney. It was nice having them there, as lodestars.

JP had been into his rugby. He'd played for the Sydney University Seconds, which was a pretty big deal. He'd drunk, and often ended up in a shadow at the end of the bar, talking without a smile to some girl, who he'd then go off and shag. It had never occurred to Story to look whether it was the same girl, or different girls. Either way – that was JP's spot in the zoo. The end of the bar. JP had been offered a place studying law, without thinking too much about it. His parents were proud, that was certain – they embraced the figures like beloved friends: 'Top *4 per cent* of the state,' his mother would say; 'only *nineteen others* in his year,' said Dad.

Cannie – worked hard, and never looked any different to Story. It was like she dressed in the same clothes every day. She wore flesh-coloured bras. Story knew that because they flatted together in their second year and they'd be on the line in the yard, drying like big flaps of skin. She'd had a boyfriend, then. Story had never quite believed in him, because Cannie seemed so unexcited – the bras hanging up outside were still solid beige. They held hands and everything, but she appeared unchanged by it – which, even to Story's tongue-tied understanding of human relationships, seemed wrong. Or maybe that was just Cannie? She came alive in moments of quiet, on her own. Story remembers walking with her to JP's birthday party at a bar in Newtown, and he realised she was wearing a dress he hadn't seen before, which skimmed about her as if she had lost her heaviness. She was wearing lipstick, too. 'Hey,' Story had asked, 'is Nick coming to the bar?' No, Cannie had said, No, he's not. So the new dress and the make-up weren't for Cannie's boyfriend; it was no surprise to Story when they broke up, without drama, a year later.

And Story – how had he been? Well, that is when he had started cooking. In their shared kitchen, unused much except for tea and toast. He'd started with Thai and Vietnamese, from a book called *Complete Asian Cookery*. He bought himself a wok, which he kept oiled and up on a high shelf, in case one of the others did something stupid with it. He'd go to Paddy's Markets and study the different types of noodle, white, slippery and two dollars a pack. He liked it there, a break from Sydney Uni, as if he were a man from somewhere else, doing something else, alone.

It felt to Story those years at uni, as he got drunk and went to lectures and took flight in pak choi and fish sauce, that he *was* alone. That love was happening next to him, bombs falling from great heights – or not even bombs – grapefruits, watermelons, packets of noodles – dropped from ten-storey windows, so that they became deadly. He kept sidestepping and jumping, trying to stand underneath – but they missed him every time.

Story couldn't feel it. He thought he might love a girl, until she looked back at him, and then the promise disappeared. Even Cannie's indifferent Nick had *something* to him. And Vincent Batty and Tree, who were on a break then, and seeing other people – when they were in a room together, at a party or pub, Story could see the blistered mess between them, that showed where love had been.

'Your standards are too high, mate,' said Mac one night, back from Melbourne in the holidays, 'that's your problem. As long as they're not fat, what does it matter? What about that American chick? The one you said did the hand jobs? She was all right.'

Story shrugged. 'Yeah. Just didn't want her staying over, you know. Didn't want her staying with me.'

'Shit, mate! They don't have to move in! Look at JP, he just fucks and moves on.'

Sex was good. It was fine. It was just there had been no girl so far who had really rocked up in bed. They made the right noises, and moved about a bit – but Story felt that all the impetus came from him, and that felt embarrassing. It felt like he was holding the keys to a car he didn't know how to drive.

And, you know what? He *had* a suit. A black-tie suit. Why the fuck did he need to rent one?

Story comes out of the cubicle feeling brave. He has smoothed the suit out and is carrying it over one arm.

The saleswoman's eyebrows are high in an expectant arch. 'How d'you get on with the tuxedo? I have the shirt and bow tie here for you to try—'

She lifts them towards Story, who doesn't take them. He, in turn, takes the trousers and jacket in his hand and lifts them towards her. It is a stand-off.

'You know,' he says, hearing his own weakness, and telling himself not to buckle, 'um, I've already got a suit. That I can wear to the wedding.'

'This is a tuxedo,' explains the lady. 'It's not the same as a regular suit, even if they're both black.'

'I know,' says Story. 'I've got a tuxedo at home.'

'Oh. I see,' she says. 'Well, if the Bride and Mother of the Bride are happy with that, then it's just the shirt and bow tie.'

'Um, yeah,' says Story. As she has taken the suit from him, she has put the shirt and tie in his hand. Story wants to drop them, next to him on the carpet. Who rents shirts, anyway?

'Do you sell shirts and ties? I mean, could I buy these, new ones of these, instead of renting them?'

'*Yes.*' The lady is happy, she is back on side. 'Certainly, we do. I could see whether we could order these particular ones in for you?'

'That'd be great,' says Story. This is his window. Of escape.

He gives her his phone number, and collar measurement.

'Would you like to try the shirt on, for size?'

No. I'd rather eat a turd. 'It should be fine.'

Story leaves the shop with the grim picture of himself, JP and Mac lined up next to each other in their matching suits like backing singers.

How to broach this with Tree? Surely she can't mind him wearing his own tux? And his plan is – a plan which is causing a pocket of hope to grow inside him – to find a shirt – another grey shirt, from a nice shop. Not from here. A not-shiny shirt. It will be an afternoon's – possibly a whole day's – activity. Cannie might come. They could have lunch in between.

If he were to get married, would he want all this stuff? Hired suits and ladies in hats and receptions at golf clubs? He reckons not. Maybe Mum and all her Om Shanti crap had sunk in, after all. Maybe he'd want to get married somewhere outside, or at home – old home, that is. Waruda Street. And if he were — ever — to get married, Story cannot imagine a single face he'd want next to him. Not Kath, from Cedars High. Not Pippa, one of the interns at the Reserve Bank. Not the actress from *Fridays With Joe*. Nobody.

Story thinks of his sister's wedding, at the Botanic Gardens. Guy in an open-necked shirt, and Kali in a dress so understated it looked like she was just popping out for a coffee. Except for the dip in the back where her blades showed and you could imagine two feathered wings sprouting out.

No doubt Vincent Batty would be all trussed up in the blackest of black tie, and Tree would be a vision in some clinging, dragging dress. She'd look pretty; Vincent would look scared; it would be lovely, and moving, and bittersweet, as weddings were.

Story puts his sunglasses on — new, gradated Ray-Bans; it had felt good buying them — and holds on to the thought of his new shirt, holds on tight, as if it were a buoy that could keep him afloat; as if it could drown out the memory of standing in that cubicle, looking at himself in disbelief, a stranger in a mirror, a reflected foreigner, a guest in his own life.

15

When they were kids in Kirribilli, Mum always felt sorry for the runts at the garden centre, and so, once again, they had a Christmas tree with branches on only one side – the others were stunted and worn away. The whole thing was uneven and shonky and pathetic, and every time Story or Kali hung a bauble on it, needles would plunge to the floor like diving birds.

They did it proud, though. She overdid the lights, Mum – so many that they were practically strung on top of one another – and they all did their best to hang multicoloured balls from every available point. The poor tree sagged in happiness, that it had been rescued and turned into such an extravagant, festive bonfire.

'You see,' says Mum, 'how nice it looks?'

'That's because you can't see the actual tree,' replies Story.

He and his mother had a version of this dialogue every year.

'Why would you even feel sorry for a *tree*, Mum? If nobody bought it, they'd just recycle it. Turn it into paper or something.'

'No, they'd burn it,' she says.

'So what?' says Story.

'So I'd rather it was here, looking nice like that.'

Mum's name was Florence, when she was high on compassion Dad called her Nightingale – and, no doubt, it was endearing, Mum's instinct to love everything. But at times it also felt indiscriminate. Like Mum had the same tenderness for the pitiful tree as she did for Story, her actual, alive, gave-birth-to son.

That Christmas Day – the year he had been given his own camera by his parents; it had felt like stepping over a threshold – the phone rang in the early evening, a time that suggested it was Mum's family in France.

'Hello?' Story heard Mum answering expectantly, in her French voice – 'Allo? And then Australian again: 'Vincent? Merry Christmas. Are you having a nice day? Yes, of course he is, I'll just get him.'

Story comes to the phone.

'Vincent Batty, mate. Jingle bells.'

'Yeah, mate, and to you. You right?'

'Pretty good. Heaps too much food, but.'

'Yeah, right. You busy?'

'Busy?' says Story. 'Not really. Just at home, you know. Doing the Christmas thing.'

Vincent is silent on the other end of the line.

'Hello?' says Story.

'G'day,' says Vincent.

'You all right, Vinnie?'

'I'm right. I was just wondering if you were busy. 'Cause if you weren't busy, I'd come round. Come and say g'day.'

Story's generosity has, whenever the moment is ripe, always put on a rubber ring and jumped right in.

''Course,' he says. 'That'd be cool. You coming round now?'

'Yeah, I reckon.'

'Are, um, things kicking off at home, mate?'

'Oh, you know,' says Vinnie, his voice sounding dull, 'same old, same old.'

Mum's only objection to Vincent's visit was that she had 'nothing to give him'.

'Don't worry 'bout it, Mum. He'll have nothing for you, either.'

'Yes, but I am the grown-up. Poor boy.'

'He's all right. His mum and dad will just've been fighting, you know.'

Mum went upstairs to find a gift for Vinnie from in among her drawers, and Dad – his last Christmas on earth, although nobody knew that, then – went to the stereo.

'You know what this means,' he says. 'We're going to have to put the Christmas music back on.'

Story rolls his eyes.

Dad, elegant and restrained, and in possession of one of those genteel Australian accents that was virtually English, had always been a nifty mover. It had put Story off dancing himself, his father's ease at it. No matter even if Story pulled out a suave and magnetic rumba, he'd still feel inferior.

'Dance with my daughter?' Dad asks Kali, who has been sitting with her legs tucked underneath her on the sofa.

'Oh, *God*,' says Story, 'we're doing the Partridge family.'

Kali gets up, and puts her hand on her father's shoulder. 'Is Vincent all right?' she asks Story, as Dad scoots her backwards and forwards on the carpet, humming through his nose. She goes along with the steps without thinking.

'Not really sure,' says Story. 'He sounded pretty down.'

'Are they having Christmas all together? I thought his dad had moved out.'

'Not yet. Think the new place he found fell through.'

'What about his little brother? Is he there, too?'

'Paulie? Dunno. Reckon.'

'Is he coming round as well?'

As Kali talks to her brother, Dad watches her. They say she doesn't look like any of them, but, her face moving now, he sees himself there. It gives him pleasure. He is dancing with her, and she is talking to Story, and he watches her. The glass doors and windows are all open, the hot air is coming in and the Opera House is lit up red and green, barely visibly in the day's sharp sun. As the song finishes, she stands, her arms now loose and down, and continues to talk, as if she hadn't been aware of either dancing or stopping. Her father supposes she is so used to it by now, having been skimmed through dances since she was a toddler, that she no longer notices. He strokes her cheek.

'Sorry,' Kali realises. 'Did I not dance?'

'You did, you did,' says Dad.

When Vincent rings the doorbell, Jessye Norman is singing Christmas, and Florence has come back downstairs with a prettily wrapped package for him.

'Oh,' he says, when she gives it to him, with a *Merry Christmas, Vincent*. He looks at it in bafflement, as if she has just put a dead animal in his hands. The breadth of his misery is clear.

'Come in,' she says.

'G'day, mate,' says Story, pressing into an unwieldy hug, with an arm trapped in between them. 'Deck the halls, eh.'

'Yeah,' says Vincent.

Dad gives Vincent a warm, Yule-type handshake, and Kali smiles from where she stands in the kitchen doorway.

They are all casually dressed – in T-shirts and shorts, Mum in a loose, knee-length dress and Dad in a shirt open at the neck. But Vincent has clearly been smart today. He is in suit trousers and a shirt buttoned right up.

'Open it later,' says Mum.

'Cheers,' says Vincent. 'Hope you don't mind me coming round. Mac's up at MacMasters.'

'It's good to have you here, Vincent,' says Dad.

Vincent Batty's parents had been divorcing for a while now. Of all the couples to take an axe to themselves, they were the most unlikely – Presbyterians, strict and unexciting, they didn't question much. You'd assume they'd plod unimaginatively together towards their grave. And yet, by Vincent's description, they were existing in a current of elaborate rage, hating and spitting more violently each day.

Vincent would make his friends laugh, relaying with comic drama the insults thrown and mimicking grunts and puffs and high-pitched hostilities. *They stop when Paulie or me come in the room. As if we couldn't hear them when we were standing right outside. Coupla twats.*

But none of that buoyancy now. He stands in his church suit, skinny and long and droopy as seaweed.

Vincent accepts a plate of food from Florence. He eats the turkey but leaves the chestnut stuffing to one side, and eats the soft bread. He and Story go and sit in the garden; a breeze is coming in, although the heat is still thick. Kali comes down to see them.

'It's nice you're here,' she says to him.

'Really?' says Vincent.

'Where's your brother? He could've come over as well.'

'Nah. Didn't want to. Got his own mates. He's in his room

asleep, I reckon. Sleeps all the time at the moment. Only way to avoid the 'rentals.'

'Your Dad's still at home?' Kali asks.

'Yeah. Wish he'd fuck off, though,' says Vincent. 'Reckon he's only still at home 'cause his girlfriend won't have him.'

Story looks surprised.

'He's got a girlfriend?' asks Kali, calmly.

'Yeah. That's how all this shit kicked off. Don't blame him, but. Mum's gotten ugly.' Vincent looks up at Kali's serene, open face. There is pain over him, but he shakes it off and grins. 'She's where I get my looks from,' he says.

Story laughs.

'Vincent!' scolds Kali. 'In which case she can't be bad, because I think you're good-looking.'

'Yeah, right,' says Vincent. 'I look like a bloody muppet. Don't mind, though. At least I don't have Mum's face. I mean her expression. Like her whole mouth always going down-wards like one of those really ugly fish.'

Kali looks disapproving, while Story smiles.

'I saw on the TV,' said Vincent, 'on this programme, 'bout how your face changes when you're middle-aged; it becomes permanently like the expressions you've been making your whole life? Like when you were a kid and somebody said, *Don't pull that face or the wind might change and you'll be stuck like that for ever.* Well, it's true. And my mum's got a face like a slapped arse, because she's been making it her whole life. At least I don't look like that.'

'Of course you don't,' says Kali, smiling a little but keep-ing her sincerity, 'and I bet your mum doesn't either.'

Does, mouths Vincent, and Story laughs.

'I wish you weren't having such a bad time. I wish it could be better,' says Kali.

Vincent looks at her, his mate's big sister, whom he hadn't much engaged with until these last few months, when he hung about in her kitchen a lot, rather being anywhere but at home. She said good things. She answered questions you hadn't asked, but wanted to. She said things that took the wind out of your sails, and let you just sit still for a bit.

There is silence for a while. Vincent looks down at the dry grass, and listens to the quiet. He can hear the Harbour water. Rich folks out on their boats; you could see them from the upstairs.

'It's a good spot you got here,' he says to them both.

They were rich, Story's family, Vincent supposed. But it didn't matter and it wasn't like they were rich like the flash gits on the boats. Just a bit richer than Vinnie and the rest of them.

'You know,' said Vincent, into the quiet, 'what my mum did today? I saw her. She was in the kitchen this morning, doing the lunch stuff, and she was just crying.' He looks up, with a face of confusion, as if his mother's crying was the most inexplicable and strange thing imaginable. 'Like, just crying. And sniffing, and stuff. She's been so nasty to Dad – ever since she found out – and now she's suddenly all sad. And even when I left the kitchen I knew she was just in there, crying, still, you know? As she went about her business, chopping, you know, and crying.'

Story doesn't know what to say. He feels out of his depth. Kali listens. Gives the silence to Vincent to fill.

'And I hear Dad say to her, *Stop your frigging waterworks, Mel.*'

Kali flinches.

'Like, who says that,' Vincent goes on, '*frigging?* What kind of cock actually says the word *frigging?*'

125

He sighs and looks around, notices for the first time that the Opera House is lit up for Christmas.

'They've done the Opera House Christmas colours! That's cool.' He looks back down at the grass. 'Have they always done that?'

Kali shakes her head.

Vincent returns to his narrative. 'Then we're sitting eating lunch, right, and Mum's sitting there staring, not saying anything, and Dad's trying to talk to us like he gives a shit, and Mum suddenly says, like a total freak, she looks at Dad and says, *I've pissed on your turkey*.'

'What the fuck?' says Story.

'Seriously, mate. And Dad goes, right, *Come again, Mel?* And Mum starts crying and she says, *I pissed on your turkey*.'

'Jesus Christ,' says Story. 'Seriously? Did she piss on your turkey, too?'

'Just Dad's,' says Vincent.

'Then what?'

'Then Dad goes, *Get out of here, boys, get out of here, get out*. And Paulie and I get up and go. Pretty fucken chuffed to be out of there, to be honest.'

'That's fucking crazy,' says Story.

'Too right. They're both fucken window-lickers.'

'Was everything all right, when you left?' Kali asks, her forehead tuckered with concern.

'Same old, same old,' Vincent says. 'Paulie sleeping. Mum and Dad had a bit of a slanging match. And you know the thing,' says Vincent, brightening, 'that gets me? Is how the fuck did she *actually* piss on his turkey? I mean, she's not got a dick. She can't just whip it out and have a little tinkle over his plate, can she?'

Story starts giggling. Kali smiles and frowns simultaneously.

'Like, how did she *do* it? Kali? Would she have pissed into a jug, or something, and then poured it over? Or got his plate and squatted over it?' Vincent stands up to demonstrate, crouching horribly in mimicry.

Kali looks, and Vincent, catching her eye, laughs. She comes over, and puts her arms around him.

'What's that for?' asks Vincent, as surprised by her light arms as by an electric shock. She pats him on the back, as if her hands are feathers, and Vincent feels embarrassed at all his swearing and gesticulating.

'It's horrible,' says Kali, 'all of it. No matter how funny you can make it sound. You must be feeling terrible,' says Kali, 'with what your parents are doing to you.'

Vincent breathes out of his mouth. 'My fault,' he says, 'for being such a dickhead.'

'Don't *you* be crazy,' says Kali. 'It's not your fault. It's not your fault at all.'

Soon after, Kali walks back up to the house. Vincent, watching her go, says, 'Your sister's awesome.'

'Er, yeah,' says Story, not used to receiving simple approval from his friends.

'But, just so you know, mate, I don't fancy her.'

'Thanks for sharing that, mate. She's three years older than you, anyhow, you know. So you'd be a bit of a freak if you did.'

'Mate, that chick in that new movie who gets her tits out and has sex — what's her name?'

'The one in *Backflip*?'

'Yeah. I fancy the fuck off of her, and she's about ten years older than me.'

'Different,' says Story.

'Not really,' says Vincent. 'Anyway, the others all do.'

127

'What? Fancy my sister?'

'Mac reckons she's hot.'

'Give it up, mate.'

'And JP's fucken obsessed with her.'

'What are you talking about? He is not. He barely knows her.'

'He looks at her like she's a fucken pussy sandwich.'

Vincent mimes grotesquely with his mouth and hands.

'Mate. Fucking seriously. I'm going to fucking kick you out.'

'Back to the loony bin.' Vincent starts laughing, deep, from his stomach. 'Sorry, mate,' he says. 'Bit out of order, eh?'

Story raises an eyebrow, and then, seeing his friend resemble the self he normally is — the happy one, the free one, the one without a stoop and a hangdog look — Story smiles, too, and thinks no more of it.

16

Twenty years later, Kali walks into her mother's house in Byron Bay, and, as usual, recognises nothing.

She knows it – she knows all of it – from the rough decade her mother and Derek have been here. The poky hall, coated with framed van Gogh posters, and 'local art', which opens on to the big living room, light-filled and panoramically gawking across at the sea. *I couldn't live without it*, her mother says, with Derek's tubular, dry-skinned arm over her little shoulders. *The sea and the sky are home for me, now*. It is as if Derek's arms are covered in translucent snakeskin.

The dining table – their childhood dining table, its dark legs just visible – is covered with a lilac and yellow tie-dye cloth. In the middle of the low, carved coffee table is an *artwork*, a wood sculpture of a dolphin, with a star on its fore-head, leaping over a rainbow. She and Guy had become hysterical over it, when it first appeared – it had been Derek's sixtieth-birthday gift to her mother. 'I tell you what,' Guy had said to Kali, when they were in the safety of their room (not that he ever modulated his voice), 'that man's a fuckin' genius.'

Kali knows the whole house, could navigate it with eyes

closed; but she recognises none of it. Even the displayed photos of Kali and Story as children, taken by their father's living hand – hit empty space. Kali looks at them with complete absence. None of it is hers.

Jacob, of course, feels easy ownership of the place. These are his grandparents, as far as he's concerned, and this is their home; he first came here when he was three months old. He never knew Kali's father.

So he goes straight to the spare room he calls his, and puts his stuff on the floor. He opens the fridge and helps himself. He has sometimes fallen asleep on Mum and Derek's bed. It is his place, but not Kali's, and that feels strange.

If you had known the house on Waruda Street, Kali thought to Jacob, *you couldn't feel at home here.* But she doesn't say it; of course she doesn't. She never talks about that house, not even with Story; never even with Guy. By staying silent, she keeps it safe.

Kali doesn't even recognise the Christmas tree. As usual, it has no lights – 'because global warming is turning Australia into a desert as it is,' says Derek. 'We don't need to make it any worse in the name of Christmas. In the name of Christ's Mass!' He says everything, Derek, with a great, white, shark of a smile, teeth dominating. Teeth that look veneered, but, her mother swears, aren't.

Australia is a desert already, says Kali in her head. *Australia has always been a desert.*

If she said it out loud, then Derek would go into his spiel: 'Do you know what scientists call us? They call us, they call Australia: the Dead Zone. *THE DEAD ZONE*,' he says again, for drama. 'Because within two hundred years – in the lifetime of your grandchildren, Jacob' – Jacob looks up from his British soccer magazine – 'there'll be nothing left here.

The lot of it: gone. No water left. How about that?' Derek looks exultant. 'The climate in this country will be so hostile, nothing'll be able to survive. That's what we've done to our planet.'

Then, thinks Kali, *what difference would a string of fairy lights make? If we're screwed, we might as well have a decent Christmas tree.*

This year the tree is studded with sprigs of kangaroo paws, and the usual disparate collection of baubles: a hippo in a red hat, some kind of glittery shoe.

Florence comes and puts her arm round her daughter's waist. 'Sammie and Coral are going to come round later to see you,' she says.

'That's nice,' says Kali.

'Although it's you they're really wanting to see, ChouChou,' she says to Jacob. Florence's endearments are the only part of her that remain French. Her accent on every other word, her face, her food, her habits, her husband, her life – are Australian. Every year, more Australian; saltwater and sun. Kali had a dream, once, that she was tracing her fingers in the lines of her mother's face, and out of the soft wrinkles kept falling little sprinkles of sand. Australian sand.

'Don't they want to come tomorrow, when Guy is here?' Kali asks. She knows it's a long shot.

'No, no – they are coming on Christmas Eve, once you are all here, and on Christmas Day as well, of course. They'll see a lot of everybody. They live so close. They were excited to see you as soon as you arrived. And Sammie has a special surprise for you,' Florence says to Jacob.

'What special surprise?' Jacob asks.

'A-ha! You're just going to have to wait and find out.'

Jacob makes a frustrated noise. His grandmother laughs.

Kali suspects, with empathy for her son, that the special surprise will not be soccer- or lolly-related. And, early that evening, when Samphire – Sammie – turns up with her sister, Coral, Kali's suspicions are met.

The ceiling fans are doing their best overhead – no air-conditioning here, on environmental grounds. *How much,* thinks Kali, *do those forever rattling fans use in electricity?* No air-conditioning, despite the heat garroting you from morning until night. Just the windows and the doors all open, the wind chimes giving an occasional, sweaty burp when a breeze sashays past. When Jacob was a baby, Kali used to go and sit in the foyer of the bank, on Jonson Street, for ten minutes' release. The sweat would dry like a shell over her, and life would seem momentarily manageable. Then, when she walked back out through the automatic doors, Jacob ahead, in the pushchair, the heat would switch into her face again like a hairdryer.

Jacob is wearing a basketball kit, airtex shorts and vest, with a number 15 on the front and back, his arms and legs skinny and bare. He has found an old visor of his grand-mother's, with a transparent, red peak, which he has pulled down low over his eyes; he is experimenting with seeing everything through the red.

He has taken the special surprise well, particularly con-sidering that Sammie had asked him to be a 'Flower Boy'. Not even a Ring Bearer. A Flower Boy. Might as well ask him to put on a tutu and tiara and be a ballerina.

But he had been quite relaxed about it, and even, it seemed, pleased.

'Cool,' he'd said, and given Sammie a hug. 'What do I have to actually, like, do?'

'Well, we're still deciding that ourselves,' says Sammie,

tucking artfully feral blond hair behind both ears, with both hands. 'It's gonna be cool, though,' she says, 'you know? It's gonna be beautiful. We're not gonna do anything stuffy or traditional, so you don't have to worry. It's just gonna be a great, big day of our love.' She looks at Jacob, and smiles.

'And I was hoping,' Sammie goes on, turning her body slightly towards Kali, 'that your mum will be a part of that, too.'

Kali feels her face solidifying. She feels watched.

'Kali,' proposes Samphire, 'will you be my bridesmaid?'

Kali is silent.

'Along with Coral, and Jeanine,' Sammie says.

Kali can see that Derek has moved his hand to her mother's knee, in sentimentality. She can see that her mother is close to tears.

Kali feels like she wants to cry, too. But for other, smothering reasons.

'Well, of course.' She clears her throat, her face still immobile. 'I'd be honoured.'

At least she spoke.

Sammie immediately lunges across the sofa and presses Kali into a hug. Kali's chin is thrust up over Sammie's shoulder, and her neck backwards. She strokes Sammie on the back once or twice, and it occurs to her that despite – well – everything – she *is* fond of her stepsisters.

'Isn't that beautiful?' says Derek, as if Kali and Sammie are exhibits.

'Can I get a hug, too?' Coral asks. 'I'm Chief Bridesmaid.'

Kali wonders what she must look like, engulfed by her two matching stepsisters; an anaemic priss, encircled by these jangling, smiling, surfer dollybirds. Bracelets and silver and tassles and little tattoos, lean muscles and round breasts. Even their smell is unfamiliar to her. They smell, strongly, of something else – of another people, of another place. Of another family.

The love in the room reaches its zenith when Derek says to Florence, who is now crying, 'Look at this room full of my gorgeous girls. It makes me just wanna howl at the moon.'

Kali had texted Guy to announce her stepsister's nuptials, and Guy had responded, *Pass my congrats*. That had pleased Kali – Guy's lack of interest.

'Guy says congratulations,' she said to Sammie.

Then she had texted him again, *I have to be a bridesmaid.* Five minutes later, her phone beeped: *Christ.*

Guy was underwhelmed and cynical, and on this subject Kali sees that she and her husband have an understanding. A rare, bright wavelength among all the fog. So when, that night, lightning strikes – Kali calls him, a speed dial as rusty as an old, dead door.

'Hey, hey,' he picks up, 'how're things Chez Flo?'

A ray through the cloud, his voice on the line sounds safe, and Kali begins to cry.

'Hello?' says Guy.

Kali can't stop.

'Kali?' he says. 'Shit. Are you crying?'

She nods. She can't manage anything else. She can hear his office phone going in the background – he's still at work.

'Estella!' Guy yells. 'Axe the call! Kali, are you okay?' Guy is worried; it makes his voice rough. 'What's happened? Is Jacob okay?'

'Yes,' swallows Kali. 'Yes, everybody's fine.'

'What's happened?' asks Guy, insistent.

'I just' – Kali breathes, closes her eyes, breathes again – 'I just hate it here.' Without volition, the tears start again. Kali looks for something to wipe her face with.

'Oh, fuck,' says Guy. He relaxes into his chair, and shakes his head. 'I say this to you, every year. *Let's not go.* You know that, right? That I say it to you, every year.'

'It's not about that!' Kali manages to shout while keeping her voice low. 'I'm not crying because I don't want to be here!'

Guy bellows through his office door, 'Estella!' Kali can picture his big lungs working. 'No more calls! I'm on the mobile!' Then, to Kali, 'Look, fuck, Crump, what's happening? What's happened?'

Kali takes a breath in. She could remain silent – it would be easier. She could just stay quiet and tell him it didn't matter and put the phone down.

'Mum's wedding dress.' Kali can feel her sinuses filling with liquid again. She breathes out through tight lips, to staunch the water.

'What did you say?' asks Guy.

'You've got to listen to me, Guy.'

'I'm listening! Don't make this about me. I'm listening, I just can't hear what you're saying.'

'Samphire's wedding. Can you hear me?'

'Yes, Crump.' Guy's voice is tense, but balanced. 'I can hear you. Samphire's wedding.'

'She wants' – grief chokes its way into Kali's voice, and she stumbles back towards tears – 'to wear Mum's wedding dress. Her wedding dress, that she wore to marry Dad. Not the fucking dress Mum wore to marry Sammie's own fucking father, but the dress that she wore to marry *my* dad.'

'What?' says Guy. It takes him a moment – first of intense

relief, that it is nothing more serious, and that Kali is actually speaking – speaking and swearing, no less – then of surprise, then of irritation. 'Why the fuck would she want to do that?'

'I have no idea. And I've got Mum there, just sitting there like, like, like a doll, saying it's the most beautiful thing, and that she can't think of anything that would make her happier.'

Guy leans back in his chair. The night is outside his window, and his whole office is empty outside his closed door, but for Estella.

'And you know what she wants to do with it, what Sammie wants to do?' Kali says, feeling like her heart, her head, her sanity are splitting open. 'She wants to cut it up. She's going to cut up Mum's wedding dress, and make it into some – revolting – tacky – beach dress.'

'Christ,' says Guy. 'And your mum is happy with that?'

'She's ecstatic. She says it'll breathe new life into it.'

The sigh down the line is rich, with years of exasperation. 'This is so fucking typical,' Guy says.

'It makes me feel sick,' says Kali. 'I feel sick.'

'Why would she want to take her dress, only to cut it up?' Guy asks. 'If she's going to cut it up, why not just get a new dress?'

Kali can't say anything. She wishes her nose would stop running.

'Tell her she fucking can't,' Guy says, as if he's decided it.

'Mum's already told her she can.'

Guy can feel his jaw hardening; it creates a little arc of pain in his right molars, where the enamel is thin. 'Those girls are fucking retarded. You've got to talk to your mum.'

'I'm not going to talk to Mum.'

'Why not?'

'Because she's their mum, now, more than she is mine.'
The truth of it is like being pushed from behind.

Kali's abiding memory of her father, was the back of his head.

In his narrow study, his small, heavy desk sat in front of a window which looked squarely into the jaws of the Opera House. Into the black mouths of those six white fins.

He would sit at that desk, his head framed by the window, his back to the door, and the door always open. It never occurred to Kali, until he died and she grew up, to marvel at how he ever managed to focus on anything, with the door open like that, in the middle of the house, someone forever walking past, stomping on the stairs.

And his head was always down, never up towards the view. It was not Dad who used to look out at the Opera House – but rather the Opera House that used to look over the water to him.

When Kali was quite small, it seemed as though the Opera House, particularly at night, was about to munch through the water, shaving boats off either side, until it reached number 33 Waruda Street, and bite her father's study from the rest of the building in one swoop – chomp walls and desk and Dad in one go, before retreating back to its Point, leaving a hole in their house. It looked, at times, as if it was only biding its time until it came for its feast.

She knows now that it meant no such harm – that great Sydney shark was only watching him, intrigued. It would gleam and trill and turn its scales to flash at him, but that man, sitting at his desk, was incorruptible. He would not move. And so – it went on watching him, daily, in wonder, the only man in its reach not to look up and be dwarfed.

Did it grieve when he died? When, one day, he did not

come with crown low to sit behind the window? And neither the next day. Nor the next.

Did the Opera House, with all that music tiny in its belly, all those people inside like ants in the dark – did it rear up and grieve for Kali's father, whom it had watched across the water for so long?

One day, about two months after Dad died, Kali came down the stairs and his study door was shut. It had never been shut before.

She stopped, instantly, and with an apprehensive, cold wash, thought that maybe something terrible had happened, so terrible that Dad had found the handle and closed the door.

Then, with sodden, bewildered shame, Kali remembered that, of course – of course nothing terrible had happened. Of course Dad hadn't shut the door. Of course he wouldn't at any moment be opening the door and walking out, to say goodbye. Because he'd left already.

Story looked nonplussed.

'Yeah,' says Guy, taking a long drain from his glass of buck's fizz, his mouth wide around the edge of the glass, 'so she was a bit wobbly for a bit there.'

'Hang on.' Story never feels completely relaxed with Guy, perhaps because he likes him so much. 'You got to rewind there a second, dude. You're saying Kali was upset because of . . . why?'

'Sammie's going to wear your mum's wedding dress.' By way of clarification, Guy simply repeats exactly what he has just said, before burping calmly. 'She's going to cut it up into something new. Some wedding bikini! Who the fuck knows? Kali's not pleased. Like I said, she was pretty unhappy.'

Story stands there, goggling at the facts and trying to sew them up. His brain works like clear water at the bank, but now – sludge. Mum's wedding dress – he remembers it – a deep, knee-length blue – Sammie's wedding – why would Kali be upset?

Then the stone rolls away.

To his embarrassment, Story feels dizzy. He holds on tighter to his glass, as if the weightless flute could be an anchor.

'She's going to wear Mum's *wedding dress*, you mean,' Story says. 'Her proper one. The white one. The one she wore with Dad.'

'Yeah, yeah, sorry, mate, I meant to say that – did I not say that? Can't keep up with all the weddings. That's Kali's problem – that it's your mum's old dress.'

'That's why Kali's upset.'

'Ye-ap; she's better now. I keep telling her she's got to talk to your mum, but she's clammed up, as usual. Won't do it. I'll fucking talk to her, if Kali won't.'

'Don't do that.' Story says it quickly, definitely, almost without breath.

This is not something that Story often feels. That is: angry. Angry is something that crouches low in him, rarely rises.

In this room, they are surrounded by people. 'Family friends'. Family friends swarming, in here, on the deck, out on the grass. A Christmas 'tradition'. Not a face from their child-hood in Sydney. Byron hippies. The new brigade, that came in with Derek, fifteen years ago. Their children. Some grand-children. Coral and Sammie's friends. *The Girls*, as Mum calls them, her platoon of female friends, all brown and wrinkly with bleeding lipstick and long teeth. Through the generations, tie-dyed. Each one in ownership of a dolphin artwork.

Mum had always been a little like that, of course. Hence — their names; hence Story and Kali. Hence — the wall hangings in Waruda Street, covered in elephants and tiny mirrors. Hence the embarrassing couscous and dhals they were fed as children, rather than the burgers and snags you got round mates' houses.

But it had been an enthusiasm rather than a defining way of life. There had been something honest about it, animated and real. And, alongside, Mum had remained: French. She had remained herself.

But now, with Derek, she had slipped into the unthinking, undefined, unclever. She had lost her accent. She had lost her edges. And the hyperbole of it, the same shallow vocabulary applied to everything, as if Mum had only five adjectives in her dictionary.

In this illuminated moment, it occurs to Story that, one day soon, Mum will have been married to Derek longer than she had been married to Dad. He holds on to his glass, tight.

'I'll talk to her,' Story says to Guy. He clears his throat. 'To Kali, I mean.'

'Yeah, well, she's calmed down, now. Although you don't look too happy, mate.'

Story looks up at Guy, and realises he has to shake himself off. 'I'm all right,' he says, takes out his painter's knife, and smears on a smile.

It is one in the morning, the odd light still glimmers down to the water, the odd Christmas string, but the ocean beyond is black.

The heart of the party have left, gone home to sleep their woozy, humid sleeps, leaving only their debris behind — empty and half-empty glasses, scrunched napkins, a few cigarette butts in the garden, bunches of flowers and bottles of fizz, a ribbon-tied Christmas cake, a wrapped-up present or two.

Florence is making cheese on toast for the remaining few – only family now, plus Becky and Bernie Cleary. She cuts the bread into fingers, and lines the fingers up on a plate.

'They seem like good people,' says Becky to Florence, sitting on a stool in the kitchen, 'his parents.'

Becky is a dear friend, she adopted Florence immediately when Florence had come to Byron Bay from Sydney. Becky is short, and solid, and neat. Neat little teeth, neat cap of hair, neat blue eyes. In her time she had been known for her athleticism, she had been a hockey player; and you could still see it, even through the roundness and the neatness and the small, frameless spectacles.

'Oh,' says Florence, pleasantly tipsy on the wine and orange juice, feeling young, feeling happy at all those known faces who had been filling her house – she would think about the mess later – 'they are *so nice*. And they love Sammie, you know, *so much*.'

'Did you know – oh, don't mind if I do' – Becky accepts a cheese-toast finger, 'that I thought his name was actually Dando! I didn't realise he was a Daniel.'

They are both smiling, 'Me too, at the beginning,' says Florence. 'Well, that is how he was introduced to me. *This is Dando*, Sammie said. I just thought it was one of those Australian names.'

'He's a good-looking boy, too' – Becky takes an understated bite – 'with those lovely broad shoulders.' She wiggles her shoulders forward and raises her eyebrows, and Florence laughs. 'Oh, I can't wait,' Becky continues, with animation, 'to see Sammie in her dress! She is going to be the most gorgeous bride, isn't she?'

Florence nods.

'They are the most gorgeous-looking girls, those two,' says Becky.

'Stunning,' agrees Florence.

Story has walked to the kitchen counter. He had come determined to find hummus, but the substitute sight of cheese on toast is not upsetting.

'Hello, darl,' says Becky, putting a friendly arm around his back as he comes to the counter and picks a cheese finger, 'we were just talking about your sisters.' Mum mixed mustard and cream cheese into the grated Cheddar; her cheese on toast was, frankly, superior.

'What, Kali?' he says, on the tail end of a gulp. Story's face suddenly falls, furrows. 'There's no mustard in this,' he says to his mother. 'It's just cheese.'

'No, the girls,' says Becky. 'Sammie – the bride!'

'Do you want some mustard with it?' Florence asks.

He shakes his head, doesn't look at his mother; finishes off the finger.

'Oh yes,' Story echoes, 'the bride.'

Would it be churlish to point out that The Bride was not his sister?

'We were saying,' says Becky, 'how gorgeous she's going to look.'

There is a crack of laughter from across in the living room, and Story turns to see.

'Something sounds funny!' says Becky.

Derek is laughing – of course he is. His face is permanently ready; Story imagines it poised in toothy smile even in sleep; for Derek it's only a question of emitting the noise. Derek could just say, deadpan, 'Ha, ha, ha,' and it would appear as if he was frenzied with laughter.

Laughing also are Willy and Jane, Dando's parents, along with Dando and Sammie. Bernie, Becky's husband, is laughing silently, his mouth wide open and his face red. Kali is within the group, smiling wanly. She looks very thin, Story realises, and so much more beautiful than everyone else. Like a thin cat surrounded by a fat raft of koalas.

Guy must have gone to bed.

Story's younger stepsister, Coral, and her boyfriend, Tommo, are sitting at one end of the sofa; Tommo's arm is dangling to the floor with a bottle of beer at the end of it, and Coral is tucked into his legs. They've been talking to Alex, Dando's younger brother, who sits at the other end of the sofa in a bright white, ironed shirt.

As Story looks over, Coral is in the middle of a wide, unabashed yawn.

'D'you want me to take this over?' Story asks his mother, picking up the plate of cheese on toast.

'Yes, Coco. Give one to Kali, I don't think she's eaten much. I'll make some more.'

Story's arrival with the dish of food is greeted with much trumpetry and appreciation, except for Kali, who says simply like concrete, 'No thanks.' Story looks at her, her slightly weighted eyes and benign expression, and reckons she's drunk, a bit. The others: no question. Pissed as farts.

'This is awesome, Flo!' Dando shouts over.

'There's more coming!' is the reply, and Florence and Becky giggle to each other over the kitchen counter.

'Oh, hey!' Coral reaches up from the sofa. 'Can I get some of that?'

'Would you like some?' Story offers the plate to Dando's crispy-collared brother, Alex Oxy Ultra White.

'Er,' he says, examining the plate in an unimpressed way that reminds Story of his friend JP, 'yeah, all right.'

'What was funny?' Story asks.

'Well,' says Derek, a big fish in this here pond, smiling enough to split his face, 'we were, ah, applying the rules of Dando's nickname to the rest of his family. So we came up with Aldo, for Alex here.' Derek reaches down and gives Alex's shoulder a cordial shake. Alex looks irritated. 'Jando for the good Mrs Doak, and then' – the group titters, Bernie lets out a woof of laughter, Kali remains glazed – 'Willy would be WILDO! It may as well' – radical mirth is returning to the party, and Derek is struggling to stay calm – 'be DILDO!'

'Sammie and Dando could have a baby called Dylan,' suggests Story. He sees Kali's smile sharpen.

It takes the rest of them a moment, a prolonged moment, to do the sums. Then laughter breaks out again.

'Aw,' says Coral to Tommo with sincerity, 'I love the name Dylan. Don't you?'

'All right, all right!' says Willy Doak jovially. 'You lot can talk, with all *your* names!'

'Oh but they're byooo-tiful,' says Jane Doak. 'I just love 'em. I'd love to have an unusual name like all of you – but I'm stuck with plain old Jane!'

She turns to Kali, and puts a floppy hand on her arm; Kali clears her throat in response. 'Now, Sammie told me about your name,' says Jane, 'but I've gone and forgotten again. Can you tell me what it means, darling? I know it's not Kylie! I know that much! I get told off for that by both my sons!'

Kali's mouth is open, but before the words have time

to hit the air and find their sound, Derek takes the floor.

'*Kali*,' he says, instructively, rocking on his heels with his hands behind his back. 'K-A-L-I, the Hindu goddess of destruction.'

'Goodness me,' says Jane. 'That's right. I remember now. I remember thinking when Sammie told me, *What a pessimistic name!* You're not a bit like that, though, darling, are you? I'm sure you're lovely.'

'She's the goddess of time, really,' says Kali, 'and change. Death comes with that, but that's not really the point.'

She's had to say this, versions of this, so many fucking times in her life, surely she'd have the spiel down by now? Surely she'd know how to say it without apologising?

In one obtuse, dismissing swipe Jane says, 'Oh, I love it. And we'd never heard of the name Samphire before, had we?'

'No, no,' says Willy, 'I hadn't the first clue when I heard it!'

'It's a plant,' says Sammie – her cheeks are pink with wine, her smile glows, her tank top stops just short of her skirt, she is just the picture of common or garden Byron prettiness – 'which grows by the water.'

'Beautiful,' says Jane.

Dando kisses Sammie on the side of her head.

'You may know it,' says Story, a little more loudly than he had intended, 'as *GLASSWORT*.'

'What did you say?' asks Sammie.

'*GLASSWORT*,' says Story, looking at her. He says it again, '*Glasswort*. The general name for samphire is *glasswort*.'

'Glasswort?' says Sammie, incredulity over her face. 'How come I've never heard of that?'

Story shrugs. Looks disinterested.

'It's a fact,' he says.

'How do you know that?' Sammie asks.

'I remember learning about it in biology. At school.'

Not true. A total lie. Story had Googled it at work one day, as Christmas and the flight to Byron Bay were looming. 'Google it,' he says.

'Glasswort's not my name, anyway. It's Samphire.'

'Yep,' says Story, nodding in agreement, nodding in full sympathy.

'It's a plant,' Sammie says, 'which grows in Europe.'

'In bogs,' says Story, before taking a resolute sip of his iced water. He opens his mouth wide so that an ice cube tips in. He crunches.

'It does not grow in bogs, you freak,' says Sammie. Dando is laughing, as is Alex; it annoys her.

'Google it,' says Story.

Google it, Story reasons, is sort of like the acceptable version of *Fuck you*; it's going to become his catchphrase, for sure.

It has been one of the things — one on a list — that Kali ongoingly hates: the way her and her brother's names are lumped together with Samphire and Coral's. As if Kali, a tantric goddess, was at all the same as a bog plant. As if their names, given to them in thought and romance by their parents, somehow allied them with these two surf bunnies, named in ignorance by their stoner mother, Derek's first wife, and the shitwit Derek himself.

In St Vincent's Hospital, Florence gave birth to her babies, and together she and her husband named them. They were a family. Years later, up the coast in the numbing heat, Derek and his wife sprouted their two, completely unrelated, strangers — and yet, somehow, they are supposed to be a tribe. No blood, no heart, no name in common — and yet, yet again, they are being told that they are a tribe, this time by plain old Jane Doak, telling them all how *unusual* their names are.

In this moment Kali accepts that she is, in fact: drunk. *Per se*: drunk. *Ipse dixit*: drunk. *Quod erat demonstrandum*: drunk. And being as she is: drunk, the rage has dissolved to hilarity, and she is fighting, quite hard, and with flaring nostrils, the laughter that agitates inside her. She must not, whatever she does, she must not catch Story's eye. It's all over if she catches his eye.

'Samphire,' asserts Derek – he understands humour as much as the next man, but this is just silly, he's got to display some strength here, some disapproval – 'grows near the water. Just as coral' – he looks over to his other lovely daughter with patriarchal pride – 'grows *in* the water.'

'I see what you've done there,' says Story.

Bernie Cleary gives a little, *heheh*.

'But it's interesting actually,' Story goes on, 'because did you know that *coral*, as well as being the marine-exoskeletons that we all know and love, and as well as' – Story emits a little hiccough, a cross between a hiccough and a burp – 'obviously' – he gestures indifferently to his stepsister, 'the person on the couch, is also the name for the unfertilised eggs of a lobster?' Story clears his throat. 'Or a crab.

'Lobster egg,' he says, to elucidate. And then: 'Crab egg. The eggs of lobsters' – hiccough – 'and crabs.'

Derek gives an angry laugh. He knows he's being aggressed, but he can't pinpoint how. All he can do is pretend to be in on the joke.

'You've gone crazy, boy!' Derek says through his thick smile. 'You're just playing silly buggers!'

'Far out,' says Dando. 'You're telling me that coral is actually, like, eggs?'

Story looks up at his sister, as he hears her laughing. Her lips are trembling and her eyes look full of water; she is holding herself in. This small laugh she had allowed out of the pressure cooker, because it felt acceptable to appear entertained by Dando's stupidity. The other laughs, pushing along with the alcohol against her eyeballs, she couldn't let escape; they were laughs that came from somewhere pink, and disobedient – had she allowed those laughs out, within seconds she would have been rolling on the floor, howling with laughter, tears hammering down her face, unable to stop.

'No, dude,' says Story, reassured, somehow, by his sister's smile, 'they're two different things. There are different types of coral. There's coral—'

'Are you talking about me?' Coral, through the padding around her brain, the gristle and juice, had heard her name being called in a far-off land.

'No,' says Story.

'He's just playing silly buggers,' says Derek.

'I'm imparting biological fact, here, actually,' says Story, before turning back to Dando. 'Coral is the name for a couple of different things. Firstly, for *coral*, like you get in a coral reef, the hard stuff, the little underwater trees – you with me? Then, secondly, coral is the name for lobster or crab *eggs*. Technically, lobster or crab eggs that have not been fertilised.'

'Oh,' says Dando, 'I getcha. I was gonna say, far out if that ocean stuff is eggs.'

'For real,' says Story. 'Google it.'

Coral has turned back to Tommo. 'I don't know what they're on about,' she has said to him. 'Do you want another beer? I could do with some water.'

'Now tell me, Story, how do you know all of this?' says

Bernie Cleary with notably precise diction, as if he is speaking the words in their perfect form.

'School,' says Story, trying to keep conviction in his voice.

'And you remember all of that from school, in such detail? Impressive. Maybe you missed your calling there, Story, you should've been a marine biologist.'

Sly old bastard. Mum had always said he was smart, ran some electrics company or something, but Story hadn't believed it until now.

'Yes,' pipes Jane, 'it's fascinating! I wish I had a brain for all of that stuff. In one ear, out the other, with me!' It was clearly her mode, to cheerfully decry herself. Her husband has lolled asleep in the dining chair that he had pulled up.

'I reckon you're making it all up, anyway,' says Sammie, as Florence infiltrates the group with a fresh plate of cheese on toast; there is general munificent declaration at her arrival, amongst which Story says, once more, 'Google it.' He thinks about adding, 'bitch,' on the end, gangster-style, but is dissuaded from that by his mother talking over him.

'With mustard,' she says, joshing him on the arm with her shoulder, 'and Philadelphia.'

Story looks at the plate his mother is holding out to him on her palm, like a waiter.

'I'm all right actually, thanks, Mum,' he says.

'Have one,' Florence says.

'No. Thanks,' Story answers.

Kali watches this small, painful exchange between her mother and brother. And, looking at Story, she sees that he has done all this talking for her – the underscored jokes, the disguised assaults. Risking the dislike or the hostility of others as he has been – it is not like him. He knows about the dress, he must do, and he has done this for Kali.

'You're a one to talk, anyway,' says Sammie. '*Your* name is the weirdest of the lot.'

'Well,' says Story, 'it's better than being called Narrative, don't you reckon?'

This gets a laugh, a large laugh — Jane will repeat it to her husband Willy once he has woken — Story is permitting the room to guffaw in the open at what they had whispered on behind their hands.

Florence is tutting, screwing a corner of her mouth a little, and shaking her head with benign frustration.

'Or Anecdote,' says Story.

'Anecdote!' says Dando, laughing a big, exposed *HUH*. '*That's cool.*'

17

Christmas had been: Christmas. It had been fine.

Christmas had been: Veuve Cliquot in the morning, *French Champagne* as his mother called it. She waited, throughout the year, for a friend to bring a bottle of the good stuff, and when on birthday or Australia Day they did, she'd squirrel it under the stairs for Christmas.

'Would you like a glass of Verve, darling?' she'd ask her son – you could hear the R in it – and then, 'Good for you,' when he assented, as if accepting a drink was akin to agreeing to climb Everest. She said it with encouragement and approval alive in her voice, *Good for you*, as if her son has gone through so much, just to get himself to this point, to this day, when he could with a yawn and a 'Yeah, all right' accept alcohol from his mother.

Christmas had been: going round to the Lessiters' down the road, for oysters and more fizz at midday – this time a quite good Aussie vintage. They were pristine in that house. Only a few minutes' drive away, but another, glassier, world of neatness and pale carpets. *A very Merry Christmas to you, JP! Where's your brother?* And Debs Lessiter now married and expecting, with her dark hair dyed a convincing, choppy blond.

'John Pierre is going to be a groomsman, at a friend's wedding,' Mum had said. 'John Pierre? Aren't you, darling?' As if his being a hanger-on at third-party nuptials could compete with Debs's wedding ring and swollen stomach.

'Yeah,' says JP. 'So what, Mum?'

'So. I'm just *saying*,' says Mrs Fry through her teeth. 'It's just conversation, isn't it? These are old friends, and they'd like to know. Wouldn't you, Philip?'

'Of course!' smiles Philip Lessiter. 'Whose wedding is it? An old friend?'

Fuck. As if it mattered.

Christmas had been: presents in the afternoon. A book and a calendar of Sydney skylines. 'Look!' said his mother. 'The view for January is just like the view from your bedroom!' This to make him believe the gift was a thoughtful one. A giant, special-edition Toblerone from his dad.

JP gave them a recipe book, a short-sleeved shirt and a blue scarf. He had a Cormac McCarthy for Piers, whenever it was Piers was due to turn up.

'Have you got anything for Emmy?' Mum asks. Emmy was Piers's girlfriend of two years.

'No,' says JP.

'Oh,' says Mum. 'Right.'

There is a long enough pause, while JP is ignoring and his mother is waiting.

'Well,' says Mum, 'would you like to give her this soap that I've got for her?'

'No, Mum.'

Another pause. 'Because I've got her something else as well, I've got her a lovely T-shirt from Morgan's, you know, that really trendy shop in the Plaza? I can just give her that.'

JP is not listening.

'John Pierre?'

'Yep.'

'Would you like to give Emmy the soap?'

'No, Mum.'

Piers and Emmy turn up at five, after lunch with Emmy's family. They are cheerful.

'Merry Christmas, dickhead,' Piers says.

JP smiles as he pats his younger brother on the back. 'Ah, you're a tool,' he says. 'Hi, Emmy.'

'Merry Christmas, JP,' Emmy says; she is in a red summer dress.

'Yeah, Merry Christmas.' JP is drunk enough to smell her, to notice her smell as they kiss on the cheek.

'These are for you, Rosie.' Emmy hands a bunch of sunflowers to Mrs Fry. 'From Mum and Dad's garden.'

'Oh how gorgeous!' she says mournfully, as if the flowers were a *great shame*. 'You shouldn't have done that!'

'They're from Mum and Dad, really,' Emmy says.

'Oh, that's so kind of them! They must've taken all the sunflowers out of their garden! They shouldn't have done that.'

'No,' says Emmy, 'they've got loads.'

'Have you drongos had a good day?' Piers says, hugging his father.

'Been all right,' says JP.

When Mrs Fry returns from the kitchen, where she has been groping through the deathly heat and the roasting mists for a vase, she sees Piers elbowing his elder brother in the side and laughing. 'What are you doing to your brother?' she says. 'Are you drunk, Piers?'

'Not half as drunk as you, Mother, I'll bet.'

JP laughs out loud.

'Honestly! I really don't think that's very nice. That's a disgraceful thing to say.'

Piers journeys over and puts his arm around her. 'Cheer up, Mum,' he says.

Christmas had been: carving the turkey. Dad basted and roasted, but JP carved; that transfer of duty had happened when JP was nineteen, and in his first year at Sydney Uni. Nobody ever really said why; Mum had just asked him to do it. A week before Christmas Dad would still go down to the mall, where there was a knife guy outside the deli on the ground floor, and get the knife sharpened.

Over the meal, with Emmy at an empty plate – they had only finished eating an hour and a half ago at her parents' house – and Piers with his modestly filled, Mrs Fry says, 'That's a nice watch.'

JP looks over. On his brother's left wrist is a black and silver Tag Heuer.

'Is that real?' he asks.

'Of course it's real! It is my Christmas present, from my beautiful girlfriend.' Piers grins at Emmy, with turkey in his cheek.

'No!' says Mrs Fry.

'Let's have a look,' says JP.

'Get a load of that,' says Piers with his mouth full, turning his wrist in front of his brother. 'Done pretty well for myself, eh?'

'You're a tool,' says JP.

'Well!' says Mrs Fry. 'I wouldn't complain, Piers! I wouldn't complain.' And then she lets out a laugh, a shocked, sad laugh.

'Is that a real Tag?' JP asks Emmy.

Emmy, on close examination, looks a little uncomfortable. 'I wouldn't get him a fake for Christmas,' she says.

'Right,' says JP. 'Right.'

Christmas had been: falling asleep on the couch at 9 p.m., to be woken by Piers balancing a gift on his head.

'Fuck off,' JP says, irritably, batting the package away.

'Mate!' Piers laughs. 'That's your Christmas present!'

'What the fuck are you doing putting it on my head?' JP registers the bag in one hand. 'Are you leaving?'

'Yep,' says Piers. 'Having a Christmas drink with some mates down in Paddo. You want to come?'

'No, mate,' says JP, sleepily cantankerous, and now in a knee jerk annoyed by Piers's exit. 'No.'

'Well, Merry Christmas, Bro.'

'Yeah, Merry Christmas, JP,' says Emmy.

Christmas had been: Mum saying, 'I'm surprised he came here at all, when they've got Emmy's parents in Rose Bay.'

'Now, Rosie,' says her husband.

'I'm just saying,' she says. 'I'm just saying, Ray. They probably have a far better time over there than they do with us. There's nothing wrong with that. Nothing special over here.'

Christmas had been: Christmas.

It was New Year, New Year's morning, actually, that had provided the unexpected moment of joy.

JP had ended up, at a Bondi pub, talking to a girl, and going home with her. She lived in an apartment on Bronte Beach, high up and basic, a 1970s modern box, with a heart-breaking view over the ocean.

They had spoken, the night before, as equals. JP had liked her. She was attractive.

They had sex, and JP had enjoyed it; he had not hated himself. He had not hated her.

In the early morning, JP had woken up, and it had woken her. They had sex again. Afterwards, at about seven thirty, JP

155

had showered and dressed and said thanks. Goodbye. She, still in bed, gave him her number.

With his hair wet and only the shadow of drink about him – no real hangover – JP stood on the empty Bronte pavement, all souls but a very few still inside, and felt the New Year sun breaking on him. All the cars were parked. None of the cafés were open. The beach, apart from one solitary, hard-core jogger, was empty.

This city, this city of millions – belonged to him.

No cabs, and – probably – no buses. JP thought, and looked at the beach. He decided to walk.

Halfway up the hill from Bronte, with his heart pumping oxygen, and the sun shining yellow, JP felt a feeling of emptiness within and without. Were you to ask him, at that moment, what he thought of himself – at that moment, at that moment only – he might reply, that he didn't think he was that much of a cunt, after all.

18

'He's completely fucking plastered,' she was saying to her friend. 'I thought he was going to chunder in my mouth.'

They were sixteen, somebody's parents were away for New Year, and had left their offspring home alone – a first, momentous act of trust. The doors had duly been thrown open to the North Shore high school network. About three hundred teenagers, including JP, Mac, Story and Cannie, were in the garden, the house and the garage, cigarettes were being put out on the floor, booze spilled on to sofas and appliances, and all beds being used for sex. The host of the party – a boy from St Botolph's – was out of it and panicking, and from his place on the floor imploring his friends to *call the fuckin' police, pleeeease, call the police.* A neighbour eventually did but, in the meantime, Cannie stands and watches the two girls go down the stairs. They are pretty, in the transitory, insubstantial way that most youth is.

''Scuse me,' says Cannie, shoving her way to the bedroom that the first girl has just left. JP is sitting on the edge of the bed, his shorts and underpants pulled down to show his pubic hair and the beginning of his penis.

'Shit,' says Cannie, seeing him. A boy and girl have come into the room after her. 'No,' says Cannie to them, 'I'm using it in here. Get out, please. Get out, please. I was waiting to use it in here. It's my turn.' She physically pushes them towards the door.

'Calm down!' says the girl, giggling. Her friend's hands are down the back of her jeans.

Cannie locks the door behind them.

'JP? Shit. JP? Are you all right?'

JP looks blindly up at her.

'Yeah,' he says.

'You've got to pull your shorts up.'

He looks down slowly, dumbly, at his uncovered groin, then at Cannie again.

'Fuck off,' he says. 'What do you want?'

He is remembering the girl he has just had underneath him, who had nice tits, and now is gone.

Cannie doesn't know what to say.

'Got any water?' he asks her. She shakes her head. 'Fuck,' he says. 'Full of fucking slappers, this place.' His words are sliding into one another like oil, his eyes are filmed — he's completely gone, Cannie realises. She should just leave. 'All of 'em got fat legs,' he slurs, 'like all 'a girls at Cedars.'

'I'll help you downstairs,' says Cannie.

JP doesn't hear. He sits where he is, his torso dowsing around in small circles. His eyes close and every few moments he jerks to, and says: 'Fuck'. He looks sick.

Cannie watches him. She cannot help but look at his groin, soft and intimate and exposed.

There is a banging at the door.

'We're busy!' Cannie shouts. 'Go away!'

'What's going on?' JP asks, bolting awake. 'Fuck!' He

stands, tugs his shorts up and falls back to sitting again on the bed. 'Got any water?' he asks again.

'No,' says Cannie. 'There's water downstairs. I'll help you down, if you like.'

'Why?' says JP.

'To get water,' says Cannie.

'Right,' he says.

JP's hair was longer, then. Short back and sides – but it stuck up several centimetres from his scalp. His nose was fine and pinched, and his lips sculpted. Cannie had, before, imagined kissing them, with a painful ache – that dilating, contracting desire of the untouched to be touched. She had imagined it happening at a party like this – in a room like this – but not with JP stupefied like this. She sits down on the bed near him.

'Did that chick go?' he asks Cannie.

'Um, I don't know.'

It occurs to Cannie all the things she could do, to keep him with her. In another lifetime, she could climb on top of him and lift her top off and kiss him, like a girl in a film.

'I'll help you up,' she says, and shuffles next to him. 'Put your arm over my shoulder.'

'What the fuck are you doing?' JP asks.

'I'll help you downstairs. Put your arm around me.'

JP slings his arm on to Cannie's back, then drops it back down again. He turns to her – a sticky, extended moment – and then, in his slow blizzard, fleshes his mouth on to hers.

There is a firework in Cannie's heart –

This is the moment –

This is the moment she has wanted – everything inside it –

JP pulls away with an expression of confusion and disgust; at himself – but Cannie takes it to be for her.

'I don't need your fucking help,' he says. 'I can walk. I'm not a fucking cripple.'

He lurches to standing, while Cannie sits in the trail of her moment. All given and broken in one round second.

JP is trying to open the door.

'The door won't fucking open!' He bangs on it. 'Hey! Open the fucking door!' he shouts to the people outside.

Cannie sits. They're going to break the door, and she doesn't care.

JP rattles the lock, and finally pushes the door open.

''Bout fucking time, mate,' says a boy outside. The boy comes in with his girl. They are holding hands.

'Come on!' he says to Cannie. 'Can you rack off? You've had your fun.'

19

Back in Sydney, Christmas over, the New Year come, Kali is taking down cards. In amongst them, on the shelves, are framed photos – she and Guy on their wedding day; Jacob newly born; on the doorstep on his first day of school. Kali picks one up, and looks at it – Guy with his arm around Kali's shoulder, Kali with her hand on Jacob's chest, Jacob with his head resting against his father; a circle; linked. With the picture between her fingers, Kali feels confused – had it really been so? Had they really been so happy?

No. No they hadn't.

She remembers the picture being taken, however many years ago it was, now. Jacob can't have been more than eight. Standing on her mother's deck, with Guy's arm slung across her like a dead animal, teeth bared at the lens. Earlier that day, on the plane up to Byron, Kali had sat with Jacob between her and Guy, a totem, a talisman to protect her from her husband, from whom she felt separated in coruscating misery.

She had tried, at first, as she always did. Tried to stab through the sports pages and reach him, bring him close. As the plane took off from Sydney and hit the sky, she had said,

'I hope Sammie and Coral won't be there the entire time.'

Guy had not responded.

'Guy. *Guy?*'

He looked up from the newspaper with a jerk, eyes wide, as if he has just woken up.

'Yep,' he said, breathing in.

'Did you hear what I said?'

'Sorry, Crump, no. What was it?'

'I was saying that I hope Sammie and Coral aren't around the entire time. I hope we get some time just to ourselves.'

Guy had looked at Kali, blankly, and said, 'They'll be right,' before turning his face back to the article, eyes scanning for the paragraph just left.

This had been nothing new. This was, in fact, their daily domestic dynamic – Kali prodding for intimacy, and Guy remaining fixed inside himself. But, at that moment, with the roar of the engine around her, that aeroplane thunder, Kali had felt like the most silent person in the world. She felt incandescent with silence, and – as Guy turned the page of his broadsheet with chapping and crackling, and folded it in two – Kali felt close to crazy with it.

She was surrounded by noise, of every colour. The drinks trolley at the top of the aisle, rattling and clinking. The permanent whish of the air-conditioning, the pipes and wires bristling around this aluminium tunnel. Talk, clearing-of-throats, the locking and unlocking and folding and unfolding of the loo doors. It was a jungle noise, verdant and lawless, and Kali had sat within it like a white fist, like a piece of plutonium, radiating silence, shining silence, the most silent, silent person on earth.

'I can't do this any more,' Kali had said, out loud.

Nobody heard.

Jacob, bless him, had his head bent to his computer game; Guy remained set on his newspaper.

It was then, somewhere over New South Wales, silence worming into her as if she were wet earth, that Kali decided to stop speaking. To stop nudging, urging, talking at Guy's wall. To stop, always, beginning the conversation. Because — if she did not begin the conversation, then there was no conversation. Then there was only silence. And that would be their space now, silence would be the space between them — no more words to warm the air. Because if he really — really — had nothing in his heart to say to her — then what good were words anyway.

Sometimes, somehow, despite it all, there were still good moments. Like this Christmas just past, when Kali had found out about her mother's wedding dress, and she had, out of desperation, called Guy at work. And he had listened. Hadn't told her she was being an idiot. He had engaged. Hadn't dissolved away into whatever was in front of him on his desk, on his computer screen, on his BlackBerry.

And Kali had felt such a live relief, from the solitude, from the silence, that when he had arrived in Byron the next day, she had put her arms around his neck. 'That's nice, Kali,' he had said, still holding his suitcase with one hand, and putting the other on her back.

And even though Kali knew that these moments would not last — that Guy would cut her hope back down with a matter-of-fact slap — yet she could not help herself. Her heart would rise so high in her chest that her toes would lift off the ground, and, floating like that, she would look at her husband and want to be near him, regardless that she knew she was walking towards a blind drop. Her heart, in a rupture of oxygen, would uncurl, would crack out of its eggshell like an old dodo, surprised and delighted to find itself back in the light.

That night, a fortnight ago, she had woken in the early hours, feeling hot, and had sought out Guy's body, sleeping and stale, like she was seeking water. She put her head on the side of his chest, and an arm around his middle, and, with her head at that bad angle and her other arm turning dead, she lay, not wanting to move, eyes closed, feeling found.

The following day she had spoken to him about Jacob's Christmas present, and they had talked conspiratorially about Florence's ever more expansive Australianness – 'She's almost as Aussie as the bloody Queen,' Guy had said, and Kali had laughed. And as the guests started arriving for the party on Christmas Eve, Kali – with Story newly arrived from Sydney and in her corner, and Guy beside her – felt solid enough to accept a glass of buck's fizz, and then a second. And she found herself feeling easy enough to stay standing and present until one in the morning, peaceful and tipsy. In years past, Kali had felt an irritated resentment at her mother and Derek's blithe insistence (in the name of 'tradition', which made Kali's motor stall) on throwing their party on Christmas Eve – Christmas itself was hijacked by it, everybody woke up late, tired, under par. But this year, for the first time, with fizzy wine around her like an aura, and her words released from their ark, Kali actually thought it was quite nice. Fun. At the least, festive.

She smiles as the last people are leaving. *Merry Christmas, Merry Christmas*, at Coral, Sammie and their entourage, including a bombastically hiccoughing Alex Oxy Ultra White. At Becky and Bernie Cleary, Becky who says to her, 'You eat up all of those treats tomorrow, darl,' kissing one cheek and squeezing one arm; 'Get some meat on you, and

164

you give a kiss to that gorgeous husband of yours, will you?'

In the kitchen, Florence has begun the clear-up, an annual, extraordinary Mary Poppins display, in which thirty minutes transformed the house, deck and garden back to their pre-party state. Story is helping, tipping splinters of crisps and dregs of wine into the compost bin with a jaunty flick of the wrist and a roguish look on his face. Kali pats him on the bottom as she walks past. She feels suddenly tired.

She goes to her mother and kisses her on the head. 'Do you mind if I go to bed?' she asks.

'No!' Florence suspends her busy-ness for a moment, holding her hands in their yellow rubber gloves away from her body as if they are wings. 'Go to bed! Goodnight, Kali-Kali, you have a good sleep.'

And Kali says, all in the same moment, something that she has not said for years, which is, '*Joyeux Noël*, Mum.'

Florence captures a breath, only a small one. '*Joyeux Noël, petite bougie*,' a childhood name; '*Dors bien*,' and Kali feels a hand on her cheek, and thinks, *Mum has taken off a rubber glove, for me.*

Her mother's voice, speaking in French, is a flag in the ground. It is a recovery, a grenade thrown against Derek, and all those parts of Florence he had claimed, and all those parts he had thrown away.

'No need to rush and get up tomorrow,' Florence says, as Kali leaves the room. 'Have a lie-in.'

'No chance of that with Jacob! He'll be up with the sun.'

'Send him to me,' says Florence.

Walking to their room, feeling sure and serene, Kali, with wry affection, anticipates finding Guy spread like a starfish on the bed, face down, lights glaring, asleep. She has already entered the warm impatience with which she will rouse and scold him and get him to move.

165

But she arrives at the door, and the room is dark – and empty. Kali turns the light on. No Guy. Her heart scoops, low then high. *He is in the garden*, Kali thinks. He has got himself a whisky, and he is in the garden with a cigar. She can picture him, drunk and content, picking pieces of tobacco from his lips. Kali folds her arms, and walks back out, at speed, through the house, round the deck, and down.

No Guy.

In front of the TV? In with Jacob? Bathroom?

No. No.

No.

Kali in agitation opens the front door. She takes a few steps outside.

'Guy?' she calls, quietly.

The street is dead. All lights off, doors locked, eyes closed.

Kali closes the front door as silently as she can. She walks back to their room, her mobile phone is on the bedside table. She picks it up, holds down 2, *Calling Guy*.

For one poisonously hopeful second, Kali can hear his ringtone only in her ear – and then, like a rake, Guy's phone begins to vibrate on the chest of drawers.

Kali calling.

Kali, standing so still she could turn to stone, wants to rip his phone apart with her hands. She wants to smash it against the wall, against her head.

Instead, she puts both phones back down. Switches them off.

A few years ago, she would have waited. Sat, shuddering and desperate and frantic on the edge of the mattress, and, when Guy finally arrived back, she would sob, and Guy would say something like, 'Jesus, get a grip, Crump,' and then she would hear herself shouting.

Not any more, though.

Kali walks to the bathroom and brushes her teeth. Walks back to the bedroom, takes her clothes off and, smelling the sweat on herself that has started to seep, and with her mouth dry, she puts on her pyjamas and gets into bed. Pulls the sheet around her shoulders. Lies, unmoving, eyes open behind her lids, something small inside her writhing and pushing perspiration out through her pores – who knows, if it is her heart, or her soul.

Two hours later, Guy comes in. He lets his clothes drop on the floor, and lies on the mattress. He does not touch her. The smell of his drink is ripe on him; he has been feeding himself. Within seconds, his breath slows and loudens, and he is asleep.

And in the morning, Christmas Day, Kali says nothing – and neither does Guy.

20

'Her name's not *Kylie*. It's *Kali*. K, A, L, I.'

JP has just come out from the boys' loo, outside the North Sydney Grammar dining hall. He is fourteen.

'It's no big deal,' says Kali, feeling conspicuous, yet smiling at JP, this kid who has just risen to defend her name with a pressed scowl.

JP receives her smile and feels his bones heat up.

'I know that, drongo,' says the girl who has been mis-pronouncing. 'Who are you, anyways?'

Gloria, the girl, had always pronounced 'Kali' as 'Kylie', and Kali had not ever known how to correct her. Words like that – *nos*, *nots* and *don'ts* – could never form in Kali's mouth; they were too brutal. JP had done it for her.

'He's a mate of my little brother's,' Kali explains.

The girl, Gloria, looks over him with irritated disregard. 'You coming in, Karls?'

'Yeah, in just a minute.'

Gloria is dressed up, in tight leggings and a leather jacket, red lipstick and black eyes – she has just been a Jet in the Cammeray Girls' and North Sydney Grammar production of *West Side Story*. It had been their final night, and cast and crew, students and staff, were all having a celebration in the North Sydney Grammar hall. There was music, sandwiches, and no alcohol, although a reliable quota had snuck transparent spirits in with their backpacks.

JP had been a non-speaking, barely singing Shark; he just hung around the back of the stage hating himself while simultaneously fantasising about doing more. He had already washed away the eyeliner he had been required to wear, the smudged remnants of which hooded his lids. He was still in costume: folded-up jeans, a black T-shirt and a rolled bandana tied around one bicep.

'That *is* how you spell it, right?' he says.

'Yeah,' she says, 'thanks,' and JP is not sure what she is thanking him for. He looks at his hands, as if he might find something inside them.

'Doesn't it bother you, everybody calling you Kylie?'

'I'm used to it,' Kali says.

'Yeah, but it's not your name.'

'I know.'

He's an odd boy, this one, but Kali's never minded him. Three years younger than her, he's already taller – approaching six feet, and with the thickness of a man. There is hair underneath the skin of his face, and smoothed along his forearms.

Kali is in jeans and a singlet, her bra straps thinly visible, and a sweatshirt tied around her waist. She has been stage-managing. Un-made-up and clear, the air seems to be moving towards her in streams, as if she is the white heart of a thunderstorm.

'It does bother me,' she admits.

'Yeah,' says JP. 'You should say something. When people get it wrong.'

Kali's eyes move to JP's, and meet them. He dies, his first death. His first skin shrugs off him, a dry scarf falling to the floor.

'I don't like −' says Kali, flicking her eyes away '− it sounds rude − correcting people all the time, you know?'

'You shouldn't mind that,' says JP. 'It's your name.'

'Maybe,' says Kali. And she smiles at him.

I'll look after you. That's what JP wants to say, then and there − outside the dunnies in a hallway of North Sydney Grammar. But even at fourteen, his self-critic is honed. *I'm fourteen years old*, he whispers to himself, angrily. *I'm a fucking child. I've got nothing for her.* His rugby boots and his posters and his books and his new denim jacket, all in a pile at her feet.

'Did you enjoy it, tonight?' Kali asks.

'What?' says JP.

'The show.'

'Was all right.'

'It was the best night, by far.'

'Yeah,' says JP. 'No mistakes.'

'No,' says Kali.

He moves his eyes up to her face, and then away again, up, then away, her details coming to him like a jigsaw. The chin, the nose, the hair loose by her ear. To piece it together would take one, long look, which he has not the hope for.

'Are you and Story going to be in the same class again together next year?'

'Yeah,' says JP. 'Mr Thornton.'

'Is he supposed to be okay?'

JP nods, shrugs. 'Not too bad. He swears a lot, they say.'

Kali smiles again, rays of light through the corners of her

mouth. 'Oh, yes, that one,' she says. 'He'll have you reciting poetry.'

'You know him?'

'Some friends have had him.'

Friends, thinks JP – *boys*. Older *boys*.

'Don't mind poetry,' says JP.

'Me neither,' says Kali.

JP is in fear, of this moment ending. He has kissed three girls before, but he would give them up and their remembered flesh, he would start again for one touch of this mouth – bright, beautiful, high as a bird.

'Although I'm not much good at studying it,' Kali says. 'I'm more maths. Science. I like reading it, though, when it makes sense.'

'We did T. S. Eliot last term,' says JP.

'*Cats?*' says Kali.

'Yeah,' says JP.

'And other stuff, right?'

From his glances at her face, JP can see that Kali is smiling, almost laughing – at herself, he thinks. He finds himself smiling, too.

'I better head back in,' says Kali.

'Yeah,' says JP.

'Take care,' she says.

And JP cannot remember what his last word was, as he watched with released hunger her back, as it moved away.

21

Story hates his flat. Hates it so much that he wishes he could roll it up like a canvas and set fire to it like a cigarette.

But where else would he live? He has an aesthete's eye (obviously) and finding this flat was the culmination of six months' hard – nay, obsessive – searching. Where could be better? Unless he got his jaw around a sandstone terrace in Paddington, with wrought-iron balconies and all that. Then he'd have to buy. And that would be too much like a home. He doesn't want a home. He has a home. Home is Waruda Street, with Kali in her bedroom across the corridor, Mum humming somewhere hum hum like a hummingbird, and Dad's head and shoulders bent down to his study desk.

And this flat is where it's at, dude. Where it's fucking *at*. And if he can't be happy here, where can he be happy? He lives in the heart of Sydney. There are women. There is sunshine warm as a burst blister; sea and sky. Great food. Great mates. Awesome wine. Shit-hot A1 job. Frickin' gangsta-mobile on its customised way from the car factory. Life is cheap, and Story's got a fat wallet, and where the fuck else could he be happy, if not here, in paradise?

And, Christ, where would he actually rather be? Back in Byron at Derek's, with the clammy sheets and the shitty tree and all the inane talk of Sammie's wedding? She had been talking, seriously, of having it on the beach and riding up to the ceremony on a white horse, like the most gigantic dickhead in the world.

'But where would you get *on* the horse, Sammie?' he had asked her.

'What do you mean? I don't know.'

'I mean, you're just going to get on the horse at one point of the beach, right? Just get on it, for the purposes of getting off it a few metres further down?'

'I don't know what you *mean*,' Sammie had said, again.

'It's okay.' Story had given in. 'You want to ride up on a horse, like a princess in a fairytale. I get it.'

'Exactly!' Sammie had smiled. 'But like a surfer princess! A one-of-a-kind *Byron Bay* princess!'

'Do they hire out this horse especially for weddings?' Story had asked.

'Yes,' Sammie had affirmed.

Story had spent his whole life trying to be liked, by everybody. But since the wedding-dress thing, he had decided he didn't give a shit what Derek's lot thought. Let them hate him. It was like a door had opened inside him, and all these bats had come flying out. Better out than in, as Derek himself had belched over dinner.

And, as Story had spoken to Sammie, he had felt Kali quicken next to him, and that had felt good. They were together again. In that sense, Story supposes he would rather be there, in Byron, feeling his merry dislike and with the shadows of his old, lost family in the corners.

Besides, it had been Christmas. With Kali and Guy and

Jacob. And Mum. The outline of her. Somebody who looked like her, but didn't talk like her any more. It was better than nothing.

What next? What is there now, to carry him through the slow drip of rain, drop by drop, into his bottle? There is Vincent Batty's wedding. There is the sourcing of a grey bow tie, and – yes! – the buying of a wedding present. Story's not going to bloody buy them salad tongs or butter knives or towel sets from their list. So that'll take some hours, spread over evenings, of thought and research, and at least a day of actual shopping. And, presumably, there's going to be a buck's night, too. That's got to happen quite soon, if the wedding is only five weeks away.

Story opens up his online diary, the new calendar for the New Year. Vincent and Tree's wedding is already in there. And then, what else? What other social pulley to draw his imagination from February to December? He would like to see Stavvo. He'll organise that. And at some point Sammie will ride up on her white horse, in Mum's dress. That will arouse the schedule nicely.

And, there's this email. That Story has been ignoring since yesterday.

Please forgive the unsolicited email.

And not from a penis enlargement firm, a person offering free money, or an African businessman with funds in Ghana, half of which he'd like to share with you. Actually, thinking about it – perhaps from all three – in that the email is from Goldman Sachs, in London.

The Goldman Sachs bloke would like to meet with Story when he is in Sydney next week, assess the size of him, and put out a tentative poach. The usual deal, which Story has got before from some of the other shysters – Deutsche Bank,

174

Merrill Lynch, JBWere. Story's not been interested before, and he's not interested now, but, were he to meet with this guy, it would be another lodestone in the month, something to fetch his thoughts away from this flat, with its shrinking walls; this diary, with its empty pages; this tick tock tick tock of a bomb hidden in the corner.

22

From: Paul Batty
Subject: VINNIE'S BUCKS NIGHT!!!
Date: 15 December 11:23:25
To: 'Naish MacIntyre', 'John Pierre Fry', 'David Ostent' [and 21 more]
Cc: Vincent Batty

Dear Bucks – hope you've all recovered from Xmas and new year, coz this is going to be a big one!!!!!!!!
Gentlemen as you all know my big brother Vinnie is getting married in February and its up to us to send him off in style!!
We wanted a weekend in Las Vegas – Sin City boys! But Teresa put the cuffs on that one. So Vinnie's got one last night of freedom – Australia Day!!! January 26th. Lets make it a big one boys. Let me know which of you can make it.

Plan of attack:
11am Harbour Ferrython, Ritchie Truss running the sweep-

stake at Ritchie.truss@sourcesydney.com.au – the winner gets bought free drinks by the rest of us for the rest of the day!!! Stakes are high lads!!

12pm Australia Day Barbie at the Icebergs RSL Bondi

2pm Bondi to Bronte pub crawl!! Stopping at tamarama Surf Club, the Marine Inn and the Surf lounge Bronte. Bring your swimmers.

7pm surf and turf and more beer at the Windsor Inn (where Vin had some happy years!!)

10pm Blue Room with VINCE MCQUEEN ON THE DECKS!!! The Blue Room have laid on free entry and a round of free cocktails – cheers boys!!

Midnight Dexy's Gentlemens Club. We got a private room booked and a private performance from 'THE TWINS'!!

Depending on numbers will be about $250 each. I'll do the tally when I hear from you all.

Cheers. Build up your drinking arms Its going to be A BIG ONE!!!!!!

Paulie

Paul Batty was a less beanpoley version of his brother, paler hair, but the same boogly eyes and big, red Rolling Stones lips. He was a – flooring salesman? A kitchen salesman? Some kind of fixtures and fittings salesman. After a cursory check of his calendar, Mac emails back – *Bring it on – sounds epic. Good work Paulie. Count me in. Mac.*

Paul is Vincent's Best Man. Mac always thinks it's a bit odd to have your brother as your Best Man – your brother is your brother, you know? He's already got a title. Your best mate should be your Best Man. But then Mac only has sisters, so he's no expert.

If Vincent hadn't chosen his brother, who would it have been? Most likely, Mac. And if Mac got married, who would be his Best Man? He would have said Vincent, for sure. But there was always that question, you see, of reciprocation. Mac didn't feel he could ask Vincent any more, now that Vincent hadn't asked him.

Fuck. Enough. *Basta basta*, as he'd heard Alessia say.

Three messages had come through since he started on Paul Batty's email, all responses to this morning's meeting, no doubt. It had been mooted to take an efficient hour, and turned into a two-hour marathon, a debate on whether to and how to establish Bar X as a market *Dunker* from the offset.

KitKat had a whole subsidiary stealth-marketing strategy based on the subculture of consumers who used certain individual-portion chocolate bars to dunk into tea or coffee, as opposed to biscuits. It was, in fact, an ongoing joke in the biscuit, confectionary and sweet-snack world – *Which came first, the chocolate-shelled biscuit, or the biscuit-centred chocolate bar?* Someone had shouted, in response to this, during the meeting this morning: *The cup of tea came first!* And although this was obviously a joke – a good one, which rightly went down very well – Mac had actually thought about it and believed it most likely to be true. The 1990s move from basic biscuits as the traditional Dunker of choice to the luxury, thick-shelled biscuit (such as the Arnold's Chocolate Duchess), alongside the biscuit- or wafer-based chocolate bar (with KitKat riding high as the undisputed king), was most probably consumer-led.

The nineties saw an upward luxury trajectory among office Dunkers, moving on from the plain biscuits, such as arrowroot, wheatmeal and gingernut, up through the mid-range indulgent, such as sandwich biscuits, basic chocolate and luxury butter, right to the high-end chocolate biscuit, those with a minimum 4-millimetre chocolate covering or a feature layer such as caramel or praline. And, of course, the KitKat.

Arnold's Bar X could be the first individual chocolate bar, with its indisputable biscuit heritage, to give KitKat a serious run for its money as a Dunker. Certainly, establishing Bar X as a Dunker would have to be done via stealth marketing – no direct advertising – for example, beginning by supplying Bar X directly to offices, in a way similar to that done, very successfully, by Krispy Kreme. There was no question in Mac's mind as to what side he was on – it would be senseless – a wasted opportunity – if Bar X wasn't put across as a Dunker from the word go. But, frustratingly, there had been dissenting voices in the meeting, and the discussion was ongoing.

Mac was going to have to send an email, cogent and unrushed, laying out his argument. He had half an hour until he was due at the next meeting, and reckoned that would be enough time. *Basta* time – or did *basta* not work like that?

He reads through the emails already received. One, from a peer in Marketing, lays down a good path for him to follow:

Indirect marketing takes time to penetrate. If we do decide to go for the establishment of Bar X as a Dunker, I as a marketer would strongly suggest we begin the process now. As Alessia pointed out in the meeting, if we are to go forward with this, time and personnel need to be allocated asap with all the relevant departments. While we are all stretched with this launch, I confidently believe that Marketing can find the time to do this.

Mac smiles to himself – he cannot help it – *Alessia*.

Ever practical. Ever able to cut through the waffle and the crap and get to the engine of it. Even in a room full of her seniors – not afraid to speak up.

They'd been sleeping together for about four months, now, and Mac still couldn't quite believe it. She was the hottest woman in the whole office, tall and willowy and with hair so straight it looked like it'd been ironed – women like that didn't normally find their way into the biscuit kingdom, over the custard-cream drawbridge and inside the shortbread walls. *And* she was still in her twenties.

The day after it'd first happened, Mac had been standing talking to a colleague when she'd walked past and smiled at them both.

'Fuck, you'd do her, no two ways about it, eh?' the colleague said. And Mac wanted to say, *I did, I did, I did do her, mate*, but for some reason he kept quiet, even though she was far and away the hottest woman he'd ever slept with and the kudos gained by telling of their carnal relations would be *huge*.

Something inside him felt wordless. And soon, after he and Alessia had been together a few more times, he found himself bristling like a cat whenever a comment was made about her, and bristling more when he heard it implied that she'd got her job thanks to a pretty face and an uncle high up in the company. *Have you not noticed*, he wanted to say, *how good she is? How she delivers, every time, whatever is needed?* But he doesn't. Mac keeps quiet. Puts his hands in his pockets. Because Alessia, his junior researcher, was fast becoming precious to him, and he did not want to break this or even bend this, this thing with her, whatever it was. He did not want to show it to anybody, lest their looking destroy it, like a ghost turning to dust in the daylight.

'Hey, Naish,' says a colleague at the opposite desk, 'you're not pulling any punches here, mate.'

The email. He supposes he'd worded it pretty strongly.

'You reckon?' says Mac.

'Yeah, mate. Pretty powerful stuff. Pretty convincing. If this doesn't convince them we need to go Dunker, nothing will.'

Mac wondered what Alessia would think of his email. She'd like it, he hopes. She'd always made a point of mentioning his stronger emails, she'd talk to him about them with a brightness in her eyes that showed she cared about her work, too.

'I didn't know you wore glasses,' she had said, one recent morning after.

Mac had felt awkward. He was only in them because he had no choice. Yesterday's contact lenses were dried and shrivelled on his bedside table, he had no spares within reach, and he had to put his spectacles on to get to the bathroom without walking into a wall. They were ancient glasses, as well, oval-shaped and a thin line of tortoiseshell around the lenses. Deeply unflattering.

'I hardly ever do,' said Mac.

'They look really good on you,' Alessia had said. 'They really suit you.'

'Are you taking the piss?'

'No, baby! They do! You look handsome.'

'They're about fifteen years old. They're like the glasses an old lady would wear.'

Alessia laughed. 'I like a man in old-lady glasses,' she'd said.

Mac thinks to himself – pleased with the email he has just sent, and off with his laptop to his twelve o'clock – that he might take a look at getting some new ones. Besides anything else, it wasn't a good idea to wear contacts all the time.

Late this Christmas Day just gone, drunk and tired, Mac had texted her — *Merry Xmas beautiful girl.*

Walking past the meeting room now, he sees her through the glass — Alessia, with her head down to a stapled file of papers. It wasn't just him — it wasn't just Mac — it wasn't *subjective* — she really was beautiful.

23

January the fourth. The Advent. That yellow-headed tool, sitting behind an office wall at thirty-one years old. The knowledge that the fuckwit was in the building made JP warp.

JP had, on and off since their brief meeting, tormented himself with Oliver Marchal. He had Googled him, exhaustively. Done image searches, searched through the Freshfields website, had an active alert should any new information be published. What he wanted to find – he didn't know. But with each tiny discovery, his insides gurgled with poison.

Thanks to all the Googling, the thing that was bothering JP at this moment was the search box on his PC – were anyone to type an 'O' into it, it helpfully dropped down all the 'O' searches that he had previously made. Which included: *Oliver Marchal, Oliver Marchal Freshfields, Oliver Marchal Freshfields London, Oliver Marchal lawyer, Oliver Marchal solicitor, Oliver Marchal tax law, Oliver Marchal taxation, Oliver Marchal tax solicitor, Oliver Marchal taxation solicitor, Oliver Marchal The Economist, Oliver Marchal Investor's Chronicle, Oliver Marchal London, Oliver Marchal Redvale,*

Oliver Marchal London Sydney, *Oliver Marchal partner*, *Oliver Marchal bio*, *Oliver Marchal biog*, *Oliver Marchal university*, *Oliver Marchal solicitor university*, *Oliver Marchal solicitor school*, *Oliver Marchal Winchester College*, *Oliver Marchal Old Wykeham*, and *Oliver Marchal hate* – to list a portion.

Was there any way to delete the search history from Google?

JP types it into the box: *delete old searches from Google*.

But no time now – the office phone tones –

'JP Fry,' he says.

Down one floor in Tax, Oliver has been getting to know everybody.

'Hello,' he has said, in his convinced English way. Some liked it, some did not.

Now he is behind the closed door of Chris Stern's office – Chris Stern who currently runs Tax, who is sixty-eight years old, has big, loose ears, like a Ganesh, a combed covering of white hair, and not a scrap of fat on him.

'You're only men in the department,' Oliver says, blandly.

Chris Stern frowns. 'No, no,' he says, 'we've got plenty of girls. All the PAs. Sheena, and that girl Sarah, and there's my Belinda. We get those interns in, in the holidays.'

There is not a whiff of humour here. Just the same primitive straightforwardness with which Chris Stern jogs barefoot down Palm Beach and back, every Friday night, Saturday, Sunday and Monday mornings. Chris does not question himself.

'Oh, yes, of course,' says Oliver. He had been introduced briefly to the two sand-blond interns that were here until their term started in February. Bona fide law students. But – a type. 'I meant in the legal team.'

Chris is still frowning. 'I suppose,' he says, 'we shysters are all blokes. But, Christ knows, there are plenty of women everywhere else in Redvale.'

Oliver nods.

'Never really thought about why we don't get women in Tax. They go for the glamour, I suppose, don't they?'

'Well,' Oliver says, 'I know Peter and Sullivan look like they've been doing a good job on Queens Dairy, so far. How long have they both been here?'

'Oh, crikey,' says Chris, surprised by the question but not bothered, 'a while, both. 'Bout five years. Maybe more. Sullo's been here a bit longer. When you've been here since birth, Oliver, like me, they all seem the same.'

Oliver smiles. He won't push for department bios, just now. 'And you're happy with your team?'

Chris has both his hands planted on the armrests of his chair. He is bouncing in it, almost imperceptibly. 'It works,' he said. 'It all works. Everyone knows what they got to do, and they do it.' After a pause, he adds, 'There's no room for bludgers in Tax, *you* know that.'

Oliver raises his eyebrows, in agreement, turns his mouth down, nods again. 'Well,' he says, 'I'm going to work on Queens Dairy, as we said. Anything else, though, you need me on – let me know.'

'You know,' says Chris Stern, smiling a sunless smile, 'if old Michael Queen were alive, he'd be having none of this.'

Oliver looks at Chris quizzically.

'Ah,' Chris says, 'he was a decent old bloke. But a bugger to work for. He basically didn't want us to do our job. Just wanted his profit and loss filled out, and that was it. His Dairy accountant would collate everything, and we'd just check it over – he didn't actually need us at all. Every time we came to him, told him about a break that he was entitled to, he'd refuse to listen. *No ducking and diving*, he'd say. The *government* wanted to give him this money, and *he* didn't want it! Thought we were all mongrels, trying to tie his company up in clever tricks. It was a punch-up, just trying to give him what was legally his.'

Oliver laughs.

'Some Pommy bastard up to tricks with his beloved cheese! Ssss–puh!' Chris makes his laughter noise.

'It's honest work!' says Oliver.

'Preaching to the converted, mate. Although even this lot, Micko Queen and David Greville – have you met them yet?'

'No, tomorrow,' says Oliver, 'but I know them on the phone.'

'Well, even this lot you're going to have a hard time convincing to stump up for a war you might lose, son.'

This prompts Olly into life – his face engages with a flicker, 'Oh, no, no, no, no, no,' he says, standing up and offering his hand, 'this is just law, Chris. No winning or losing about it.'

'Hm-hh!' says Chris, his handshake pure sinew. 'Let's wait and see.'

'Chicken-schnitzel wrap.'

'Sure thing. Toasted?'

'Yep. And a flat white.'

'Sure thing. Anything else?'

JP hands over a ten-dollar note, and two two-dollar coins. He pockets his change.

'That'll be ready to collect at the other end of the counter, thanks,' says the girl, in her snug white T-shirt and black apron. JP sees this girl often, three times a week every week, and yet it has not occurred to him that he might be friendly.

JP walks over to the collection point; he knows the drill. He sees over the counter his wrap being made, the avocado being spread on to the tortilla, mayo, sweet chilli sauce, and then schnitzel being sliced diagonally and placed on top. Unless someone else is waiting for the same thing?

He looks economically around the room to reckon whether anybody else has the chicken-schnitzel look about them. And – fuck. Two behind him in the queue – the figjam fucker himself – Oliver Marchal.

JP's head is hot. With heart beating and jaw tense, he wills his sandwich to be ready before Oliver Marchal moves to this end of the counter. He considers commanding over the bar that the wrap not be toasted, that it be handed to him as is. But then, Oliver Marchal might hear his voice. He considers silently leaving, without his lunch.

'Flat white?' says a voice.

JP looks up, takes the coffee. Says, uncharacteristically aware of his volume, 'And I'm waiting for a wrap?'

'On its way,' says the young guy.

JP takes a sip, straight out of the card coffee cup.

This is not the normal routine.

Normally, JP takes a white plastic lid from the stack, and seals it around the top of the cup. Normally, he waits for his sandwich and then finds a quiet table to settle at, outside if possible. Normally, he takes his first sip of coffee only once his sandwich is finished, and the coffee is a little less than lukewarm.

But at this moment, his body trying to distract itself from panic, he takes a sip directly from the hot, open cup.

And as Oliver Marchal pays for his lunch and takes

instruction to wait at the end of the counter, his eyes for a moment blankly meet JP's. JP looks down, angrily.

'Chicken-schnitzel wrap!'

'Yeah.'

'JP!'

It took a moment, but Oliver Marchal has now recognised.

'Oliver Marchal,' he says, smiling openly, offering his hand. 'We met before Christmas. At Redvale.'

'G'day,' says JP. He has had to put his sandwich back down on the counter to shake hands. He is not smiling.

'Happy New Year,' says Oliver.

'Yep,' says JP. He picks up his wrap again, crackling in white greaseproof paper.

'You know – oh, excuse me' – Oliver has moved aside, a woman has edged past to pick up her order – 'the coffee in this city is a complete revelation.'

JP nods perfunctorily.

'Did you have a good Christmas?' Oliver asks.

'Was all right.'

'Did you take much time off?'

'No.'

Looking at him, he's not exactly like JP had remembered. He's not that short. Not as short as he looks. And his face is – browner. But his hair is still a flashy yellow. And although it's clearly been cut recently, there's a lot of it. He looks like a chick – a chicken, that is. Thick, feathery yellow. Almost like his head is covered in yellow fur.

JP takes another swig of his coffee. Still no lid.

'Are you working on anything particular?' Oliver Marchal asks.

JP thinks of the last two days at the office. January 2nd,

when only a ghost staff was in. He spent most of the short day surfing the internet and leaving comments underneath articles. The *Huffington Post. News.com.au.* The *New Yorker. Harper's. Planetrugby.com.* At one point he fell asleep at his desk, with his chin on his chest.

'Nothing new. Most offices aren't fully back up for another couple of days, anyway.' JP could feel the warmth of his sandwich in his hand. He squeezed it slightly.

Oliver nods. 'School holidays, right? This is your long break.'

'Yeah,' says JP. Then he takes a dive: 'Quiet time for you to start.'

Oliver raises his eyebrows a little. 'Well,' he says, pausing for a moment – he'd make a shit barrister, JP thinks, 'I've got a lot on for now getting to know the department and the clients.'

'Carrot and ginger!'

'That's me,' says Oliver, and takes the juice. It already has a lid on and a straw in.

JP frowns dispassionately, a shrug with his mouth. He wants to ask: *What have they given you? How much of the company have they given you?* And as he stands there with his chicken-schnitzel wrap getting cold in his fist, he feels a churning near his heart. He wants to ask the question, and he wants Oliver to answer that they've not given him much. That they've given him nothing to speak of.

But he doesn't ask the question, and Oliver doesn't answer, so JP cannot forgive.

Instead JP says, 'Isn't it going to be a struggle, just getting to know Australian tax law?'

Oliver laughs, a small, easy *heh*. 'Well,' he says, 'no doubt the finer points will present themselves.'

'Spinach cannelloni!'

Oliver leans in and takes the box. 'I suppose I need a fork,' he says, and takes a step towards JP, reaches round him to the tubs of wooden cutlery. They almost touch. So close that JP can hear Oliver's BlackBerry vibrating somewhere inside his suit. 'Were you eating here, or going back to the office?'

'Uh, here,' says JP.

Oliver has, in practically one suck, finished his juice, and he tosses the empty container into the big, aluminium bin.

'Well, would you mind if I joined you for ten minutes? As long as you don't mind having to watch me wolf my food. I've got a meeting at two.'

JP looks at Oliver. Doesn't say anything.

Oliver walks a few steps to an empty table, and puts his lunch down on it. As JP walks after him, he has the uneasy feeling that he is *following*. Like a dog. He sits down, and pulls the white paper halfway down his sandwich. He takes a large bite.

'Who've you worked with most, in Tax?' Oliver asks JP, blithely, before ladling up a mouthful of warm cannelloni.

'Tax?' asks JP, food still in a corner of his mouth. He swallows. Why does he feel edgy? 'I've had contact with most of the Tax guys. Kris Greco, mostly, I've worked with. And Stern. Chris Stern always oversees.'

'You have clients in common, you and Kris Greco?'

JP frowns. 'Telecom Australia. Middle Freight. Gould's' – JP slugs from his coffee – 'the pharmacy chain.'

Like Queens Dairy, all, by the sound of it, good, long-standing Aussie companies. 'Who are your biggest Asian clients?' Oliver asks, before taking another bite of cannelloni.

'What, mine personally?'

'You. Your department's.'

190

'WHY Media, I suppose,' says JP, moving a sip of coffee around his mouth to clean the schnitzel out.

Oliver is drawing blanks. He cuts another slice from his cannelloni with the side of his fork, aware that he hasn't much time. 'Y Media? Like, the letter Y?'

'W – H – Y,' says JP.

'Who are they?'

'They've been around for a while. They print Chinese-language newspapers in Sydney and Melbourne.'

'They're based here?'

'Yeah. Sydney.'

Oliver nods. He is scraping the remains of his lunch into one, final forkful. 'Any clients based in Asia?'

JP looks directly at Oliver for a moment. Since finishing his sandwich, with only a centimetre of coffee for company, he has been feeling awkward. Oliver Marchal has a lightness around him, as if everything is asked out of nothing more than sunny curiosity. JP feels uncomfortable with it, as if he is sitting in the rain. He shifts in his chair.

'I may be working with M&A to pitch for a client whose head office is in Japan. If we got it, that'd be my biggest work with Asia. The biggest Asian clients at Redvale are with Energy and Resources.'

'I've not met any of E&R, yet,' Oliver says. He wants a client list. Department by department. 'Listen, mate' – he wipes his mouth, scrunching the paper napkin into his empty container, and sticking out a hand – 'I'm heading back. Great to see you again.'

'Yeah,' says JP. He has finished his lunch, too. But short of suggesting they walk back to the office together, holding hands, all he can do is remain.

He watches Oliver as he strides away. Sitting, feeling jittery and angry with himself, JP waits until Oliver is out of sight before he stands, and walks up the shallow hill towards Redvale. The soles of his shoes land in those footprints, left a few minutes before.

24

Since seeing Tintin before Christmas, Story has occasionally had Stavvo on his mind. Stavvo, another old mate from Grammar, who was meant to meet them at the Beach House Hotel, but didn't turn up. Tintin had gone up to Avalon to visit him the day after – Story had felt a bit injured by that, childish as it may be.

He hadn't seen him for over a year, he realises.

Finally, after some tense contemplation, Story had sent an email.

Stavvo mate,
    Happy New Year, hope you had a good Crimbo. Hope alls well.
    It was a shame not to see you when tintin was about in december. It's been a long time mate. Can you come round for a drink and a bite with Cher and kids Sunday 7th?
    Story

Story remembers, with precision, the night they all had together after Stavvo's first kid was born, to wet the baby's head. They'd got him ratted at the Clock Hotel, and had cigars out on the street. Stav had had a glow on him, a smile on him, the whole night.

'It's just un–fuckin'–believable,' he kept on saying, with an escalating slur. 'Un-fuckin'-believable.'

Good on you, mate, they'd said, and had made toasts to the little one, and to Stavvo being a dad.

As they'd put him in a cab home – this was a couple of years before he moved up to the Northern Beaches – he'd said in a lurch, *I'm gonna do right by my girls. I'm gonna do right.*

That'd stuck in Story's head, for some reason.

Even after he moved to Avalon, Story saw a bit of him. They'd meet for the odd drink after work, and Stavvo would turn up at group events.

But then – he just went off the radar. No more evening drinks. Putting in appearances at only the most far-between parties.

An email had come back before the morning was out.

It would be better if you came up to us in Avalon. Lunch Sunday 7th. Stav.

Typical Stavvo. Same as his phone manner – no pleasantries, no chitchat. Bald. On the phone you got the feeling he hated you – *Yep. Okay. Bye.* Spoken in a deathly monotone – at least by email he just seemed terse. And yet in person – easy. Fast to smile, fast to laugh.

Story accepts the invitation. He has no choice. He could not reasonably say, *I don't want to come to your house* – which was the truth of it. He had wanted Stavvo and Cher to come to him. *That's* what he had wanted. He would've looked forward to it. He would've made a ricotta and sweet onion pasta bake for the kids – he'd already planned that before he sent the email. He'd planned it down to putting the chopped parsley in individual side bowls instead of through the dish, so that the kids didn't have issues with green bits. He'd learnt about green bits through bitter experience with Jacob.

He'd even thought about buying in some toys to keep them happy.

But, as it is, he finds himself with a bumpy heart in the back of a taxi, a taxi that from the Eastern Suburbs to Avalon will cost him a hundred dollars. He holds in one hand a bag from a toy shop near work. He'd been inside, eyeing various fire engines and small, crocheted dresses, for a few minutes, when the salesgirl approached him:

'Are you looking for anything in particular?'

Story cleared his throat. 'Coupla things for a coupla small kids.'

'Boys or girls?'

'Um, a boy and a girl, I think. I'm not actually sure. They're a friend's kids. I haven't seen them for a while.'

In point of fact, he'd never seen them. Well – he'd seen the first baby, when it was really tiny. That was a girl. He was basically certain that that one was a girl. But the second one, Story just can't remember. He recalls receiving the text from Stavvo, one of those birth circulars, you know – *Born at 4.37 this morning, 3.31 kilos, big feet! Beautiful and healthy. Mum did brilliantly* – or similar. But he can't bring to mind exactly what it said. Whether it was a girl baby or a boy baby. You got those messages, had a small moment of warmth, and sent back a generic *Congratulations mate, love to you all* sort of thing.

'What ages are they?'

Story, feeling under pressure, feeling exposed, frantically tries to piece together how long ago Stavvo had his kids.

'The older one is . . . about . . . four. And the younger one is about one or two.'

He was then directed to toys that 'would be suitable for a little boy or girl', and had chosen a wooden tray of fruit and vegetables which were held together with velcro – you sliced through them with a little knife; they were actually quite cool – and a soft, grey rabbit with a round tummy and long ears.

'Rabbits are a great unisex item,' said the salesgirl, 'boys and girls both really engage with them.'

After an hour through slow traffic, Stavvo opens the door to Story in shorts and a white shirt, and with a bottle of beer in his hand.

'G'day, mate,' he says, smiling broadly. They shake hands and then lean into a hug.

'It's really good to see you, dude,' says Story. He hands Stavvo a bottle of champagne.

'Bubbles. Nice. You never been here before, eh?' Stavvo asks.

'No, no, not here, mate.'

'Come through, the girls are in the garden.'

Story walks through the house, which has wooden floors and big, modern paintings on the walls, through the kitchen, which has covered bowls of food out, clearly mid-preparation, and into a large garden.

Cher walks forward, she is wearing sandals and shorts and a small, white singlet, and is clearly pregnant. 'Hello Story,' she says, kissing him on the cheek.

'Hey, Cher, you're ah – another one on the way, wow—'

'Girls? Can you say hello to Story?'

'Hello,' says the older girl, looking at him with gravity from under her sunhat.

196

'You're called Story,' says the younger one.

'I am, that's right.' Story is feeling nervous. 'Nice to meet you.'

'Alice, and Lucy,' reminds Stavvo, pointing to each with the butt of his beer bottle, assuming mildly that Story might not remember.

'The girls have been quite interested in your name,' says Cher. 'We've been talking about it.'

Story pushes a smile on to his face; he is feeling scrutinised by these two unforgiving little goddesses. On top of which, he feels anxious that the gifts he has brought are much too young for either of them. The little one, Lucy, is definitely no younger than three.

'I don't know anybody called Story,' says the older girl, Alice.

'We've got story *books*,' says Lucy.

'Well,' says Story, still taking everything in − the grass, the big sun umbrella, the relative good taste of it all − 'that's what my mum named me after. She named me after story books.'

'That's weird,' says Alice.

'Remember, Alice,' says her mother, 'we were saying that there's a little girl called Alice in a book? And that you've got the same name as her?'

'She's a little girl, though,' reasons Alice.

'Mate,' Stavvo is standing next to Story, 'can I get you a drink? Beer? Wine?'

'Ah, you know, a glass of water would be good for now.'

'Heavy night?'

'Not too bad. Um. Just was a bit, ha ha, you know, stuffy in the cab. I'll have a water first, and a glass of wine in a bit.'

'No worries.' Stavvo heads into the kitchen.

197

'You took a cab all the way up here, from the city?' Cher asks. 'That must've cost a bit.'

Story's face is still tense with his smile. 'I've got something for the kids,' he says.

'Ah, that was sweet of you, Story,' says Cher. 'You didn't have to do that.'

'Um, this is for you—' Story holds the bag out to the older one.

'What do you say, girls?'

'Thank you.' Alice takes the bag. 'Come here, Lool,' she commands her younger sister. 'Say *thank you.*'

They pull the toys out of the bag and begin to tear off the gift wrap.

'I hope I've got the right kinda things,' says Story to Cher.

Cher touches him on the arm. 'I'm sure they'll be great. You didn't have to bring anything.'

She's nice, Cher. That's something Story often forgets. She may be no nonsense and have the legs of a wrestler but, regardless, she's nice.

'What's all this then?' says Stavvo with energy as he comes from the house and hands Story a glass of water. He offers him a tortilla chip from a terracotta bowl. 'I thought we'd had Christmas already!'

'It's a rabbit!' says Alice, her eyes enlivening, losing their guard.

'A *rabbit!*' says Stavvo, with enthusiasm. 'How about that!' He nudges Story. 'You shouldn't've done that, mate.'

'I've got loads of rabbits,' Alice informs Story, soberly.

'Oh, really?' he replies, his fears confirmed.

'She loves them,' says Cher. 'She collects them.'

'But I haven't got this one,' Alice goes on. 'This one is a

really good one because he's got a *really firm stomach*.' Alice squeezes the rabbit purposefully.

Relief floods, and Story laughs.

'Good one, mate,' says Stavvo. 'You're in.'

Stavvo has a beast of a machine, on which he's barbecued a leg of lamb. Cher has made salads, proper salads with toasted nuts and roasted vegetables and shaved cheese. She's marinated berries and served them with ice cream.

They've made an effort, and Story appreciates it.

After the shyness, and then an initial flurry of interest in the new person, the little girls are now doing their own thing, and Cher is inside clearing up. Stavvo and Story are sitting at the table under the large parasol, the January heat holding them close. Story has been drinking white wine, and it glows in his head and chest.

'It's a nice place you got here,' says Story, meaning it. 'You know what I was thinking?' Story is feeling intimate enough with Stavvo to speak his mind. 'I couldn't understand why you'd be up here all the time, never come into the city. But now I'm here, I can see it's pretty sweet, dude. I can see why you wouldn't go far.'

Stavvo laughs. 'Mate,' he says, taking a swig from the mouth of his bottle, 'I'm in the city every day. I work there, remember? Haven't got much choice.'

Story had forgotten that, too. He'd had it in his head that, as he didn't see Stavvo any more, Stavvo must be up here twenty-four seven.

'Yeah, yeah, of course,' says Story. 'You still at PIS?'

Pacific Indian Shipping. Stavvo must've been there for ten years, now. A decade.

'Still with 'em. They treat me nice. Kiss on the cheek before bed, and all of that.'

Story laughs. 'I know what you're saying. The Reserve Bank seems to like having me around, too.'

'You must nearly be running the place by now, eh, Story?'

Story can feel his wine heating up in his hand; he leans forward and puts it on the table. 'Not quite.'

'So, you haven't sold out to the wanker bankers yet? I bet you're still getting offers.'

Story shrugs, pretends indifference – for some reason, even in private, he ignores this recurrent topic within his life – 'Yeah, well. They come knocking every now and then.'

'Not tempted?'

'Not yet.'

'I see,' says Stavvo, smiling, looking at Story askance.

'You're still in Logistics?' Story changes the subject.

Stavvo nods, in the middle of a sip. 'Yep, that and moving more into general management.'

'Lool!' a fine, angry voice peals across the garden, 'that's not how you do it!'

'Alice!' shouts Stavvo. 'What's going on?'

'She's not playing it right, Dad!'

'That's because she's younger than you!' Stavvo doesn't move from where he sits, just lungs it to where his daughters are playing. 'You got to explain to her, remember? Luce! Let your sister explain to you!'

Cher's voice calls from inside the house. 'Terry! Are you watching them? Is everything all right?'

'Everything's fine. You going to play nicely, Allie?'

There is no answer. All has gone quiet.

Story laughs. 'Fuck, mate,' he says.

'What?'

'Ah' – the wine is colouring everything golden – 'it's funny. You got two kids.'

To Story, Stavvo is exactly the same. The same candid simplicity. The same lack of sartorial style – a uniform of shorts and shirts thrown on without thought. The same bonnet of black curls that had earned him his nickname at North Sydney Grammar: *Hey Stavros! Are you Greek or something? With hair like that, you fucking should be.*

And yet, in a matter of minutes, he's sitting here with a shipping career and a house in Avalon and two kids playing in the garden and another on the way. Un-fuckin'-believable.

'Had 'em for a while, mate! Alice is starting school in a few weeks.'

'School.' Story shakes his head, and bats away a sluggish fly. 'Far out.' It's a whole other life. 'It feels like I haven't seen you for years, mate,' he says.

Stavvo burps. 'I've been here.'

'Yeah,' Story says, casually, 'but you're never around.'

Stavvo looks at Story for an extended moment. 'I'm around,' he says.

'Nah, Stavvo, you know what I mean. You've gone bush, mate.' Story laughs. 'I mean,' he concedes, 'I know you got kids, now.'

'And a wife,' says Stavvo.

'Yeah, yeah.' Story looks conspiratorially at his friend. 'And a wife.' JP has said it about Stavvo more than once: he's under the thumb.

Stavvo drains his beer and brings the bottle down heavily on the table – *bang*. In that moment, as the bottle bumps, Story realises for the first time that he can hear, sitting here, the sound of the sea.

'That is the ocean I can hear, right?'

'Story, mate,' Stavvo is talking with steady candour, 'I'm not going to keep coming out for beers when my wife's not invited.'

The sea whispers. Hard lights have been turned on. Story feels suddenly sober.

'How do you mean?' he asks.

'Mate, what I said. Fuck, I drank that beer too fast. Got air in my chest. If *every* time, Cher's not invited, then I'm not going to come.'

'Stavvo, seriously?'

Stav looks easily at Story, and nods.

'But obviously Cher's invited!' says Story.

'She hasn't been. Not to much.'

'Dude, if I occasionally ask you out for a beer with the boys—'

'Drinks with the boys is one thing. But whenever I come along Mac's there with one of his randoms, and Cannie comes along, and Vincent Batty shows up with Tree — but just not Cher.'

'But, mate, mate, you should just bring her along!' says Story. He feels a rising panic, like the harder he thinks, the less he can find the words.

Stavvo remains peaceful. 'Just easier not to come,' he says. 'Haven't got the time, anyway. And we've got kids, you know. Can't just go drinking every Friday night. You'll get it when you throw in the towel and settle down, mate.'

Story had not seen this coming. He can't reconcile it — with the Stavvo he's always known. This is the guy who, on his own buck's party, took off all his clothes, boarded a boat of girls in bikinis nearby and ran naked through them before jumping back into the sea again. He'd done it unprompted, and had had everybody in hysterics – *Don't know how you managed that without getting a boner*, someone had said.

This is the guy who used to rate passing women on the ABC: Arse, Boobs and Cunt. This is the guy who had shouted out to a parading chick at the cricket, *I can see where the axe got you, sweetheart!*

And now he's saying that he won't come out if his wife's not invited.

Thinking about it, in between beats of panic, Story accepts – that Stavvo is right. Tree's just Tree. Cannie's Cannie. Mac and the latest backpacker are taken for granted. But Cher – well, she was Stavvo's *wife*. It made it all different.

'Stavvo, I feel . . . I'm . . . shit. I'm sorry if you think that we didn't want Cher there. It's just . . . ah, fuck. I can see it now. I can see how it must've seemed.'

'Hey, don't worry about it. I'm not fussed. It's a different life, now. I like to go on the occasional binge, blow off steam, as much as anyone. But, the rest of it – I'm just not up for it. More trouble than it's worth.'

This plain statement comes towards Story like a helix. Like he is looking into an indecipherable black bag of DNA. He feels overwhelmed. He reaches for his wine glass, wet with condensation.

'I'm coming to Vincent Batty's buck's, though. Sounds like that'll be a fucking bender.'

'Done!' Cher comes out of the house with a satisfied smile. 'You all right, girls?' She gets no answer from her daughters. Patting her husband on his shoulder, she asks, 'What are they doing over there?'

'No idea, babycakes,' says Stavvo.

'Well, as long as they're not killing themselves. I'm going to sit here with a glass of wine for a bit.'

'Onya,' says Stavvo, and as she sits down next to him, he puts a lazy arm round the back of her chair.

Story hears the sea. He hears the sea.

25

She can't poison him, although it has occurred to her. Another bird, some harmless sparrow, might land and eat it, and then she'd have that on her conscience. Besides, she doesn't want to kill Max. She doesn't want another dead bird in her life, to add to the one that stonewalled into her office window before Christmas.

But Cannie does want Max gone.

She is not a late riser, but on Sunday mornings Cannie likes to stay in bed. On Saturday evenings, the night before, she collects the newspaper articles she has found interesting, from the day's supplements and magazines, and puts them in an indulgent stack on her bedside table. When she wakes on Sunday, there they are, next to her water, her lip balm and her hair tie, ready to go. She keeps a packet of baby wipes, also, to clean her hands if they get too black from the ink. Her sheets are pale blue, and marks show up easily on them.

Cannie sits up in bed, arranges pillows behind her, ties her hair in a bun on top of her head – no prizes for style on a Sunday morning – and with the satisfied comfort that she is alone, nobody to see her unwashed, unbrushed, bladder half full – she reaches for the cord to raise the blind.

And – clatter, flutter, flail – there he is. Max. Momentarily spooked by the raising of the blind, but not so much that he flies away – only enough to make him skitter his wings and hop backwards twice.

Bloody Max. Bloody bird.

'Chaa! Get away!' Cannie flaps.

Max is wary. He jumps another step back, his head on one side. What is she doing, his friend beyond the glass?

'Get away!' Cannie shouts.

Max lifts his dark wings, up behind him like an angel, but doesn't move.

Cannie rears up, shedding bedclothes on to the floor, her pyjamas creased. She bangs on the window with the side of her fist.

'Get away! Get away! Get away!'

Max makes that terrible sound, shrill and fearful, and scrambles off into the sky.

Cannie is left standing, the smell of sleep crumpling around her. Her teeth feel dirty, and she needs to pee, and she no longer wants to read the papers in bed. That – has been spoilt. And she feels angry – shaken – and she doesn't know why. Why is it that Max disturbs her so? She has never been a bird lover, fine – but neither has she cared one way or the other. Yet Max – incenses her. Sees her trembling and unsteady by her bedroom window. It will remain shut, today, despite the heat.

Cannie goes to the bathroom, and looks in the mirror. It is not flattering, her hair scraped away from her face in a bobble, making her face look fat; and her bosoms unshaped in her vest. But that is the whole point – of Sundays, of having the papers ready by the bed, of living in this flat, which is not overlooked, and is soft and comfortable in exactly the way Cannie had wanted. The whole point is that nobody is watching; that she is alone; that here Cannie can live peacefully with herself as she is.

Except now, she has a visitor. His eyes moving, little heart pumping, a warm container of life, spreading shit on her window sill, ferreting his beak into the spokes of his feathers, watching her, watching, watching.

He has to go.

Once she is showered, and dressed, and feeling stronger, Cannie makes herself tea and switches on the computer. She is having an early dinner with Story tonight, so she will try not to eat until then.

Getting rid of birds, she types into the search box. The answer comes straight away – the internet tells her she needs an owl. Plastic or ceramic, to look through her window and scare Max away.

Owl scarecrow.

Within a minute, Cannie has ordered an inflatable owl from a garden centre, to be delivered to Onestar, to avoid the collection trek to the post office.

Is Max really that stupid, though, that he will fall for a plastic bird? Yes, he bloody is, Cannie tells herself – he's a bird. A *bird*.

26

Story is sitting with Cannie at the Mochi Rooms, in Surry Hills. They have met for dinner, and both have bulbous, frost-yellow glasses of wine in front of them.

Story looks forward to seeing Cannie, in a way he doesn't any of his other friends. She appreciates the food they eat. They talk about different places, beyond Sydney, beyond the Pacific. She laughs at him and asks him questions and can drink a bottle of wine and not be drunk. They always chat, chat, chat – and that's what it's all about, after all.

'You're really thinking about it?' Cannie asks. 'I mean, seriously?'

'Yeah, well. Not really. Maybe. I don't know. I've got to talk to them.'

'But you've talked to them already.'

'I've got to go to London, and talk to them.'

'Do you think you will?'

Story puffs out air through closed lips. 'I dunno. I think so. In a coupla weeks.'

Cannie sips from her glass, and looks down. Story can see the line of scalp where her hair parts into a few millimetres of dark roots.

'It's interesting,' Story goes on, 'what they're offering.'

Cannie frowns a little. 'It sounds it.'

'But I just don't know yet whether it really is what it says it is, or whether it's just another Goldman Sachs front, a bit of sociological lip service to make up for all their fuckin' skimming.'

'And if you took the job, you wouldn't also be doing all that fuckin' scamming?'

Cannie has heard *skimming* as *scamming*. Story lets it be.

'I'd never be a — a banker. They wouldn't offer me that — not at this stage, anyway. It's the same old analysis that I do at the Reserve Bank. Writing. Telling the bankers how to make their money, in the case of Goldman's. But that's only a small part of what they're offering me—'

'So, this International Markets Institute, they work with the British government?' Cannie asks.

'No, not exactly. They currently advise several committees within a few governments, including the British government.'

'What do Goldman Sachs get out of it?'

Story laughs. She's smart, Cannie. He knows it, but he often forgets until she reminds him.

'Good question.'

'What are they really offering you? Because at the Reserve Bank, you're doing really well, aren't you?'

'I'm doing all right. Yeah, pretty well.'

'It's only a matter of time, at the Reserve Bank, though, isn't it? Before you're really up there. What I'm saying is, would you really risk all of that for Goldman Sachs?'

'It's not really a risk,' says Story, 'if what they're offering me is just as good. Or better. I mean, not money-wise. Money-wise, obviously they're offering me a lot more.' He can't resist — 'Three and a half times more, plus stock and bonuses.' Cannie's eyebrows go up. 'But I mean in terms of career. In terms of what I'm doing and where it's going. I need to check it out. But it sounds serious. They certainly make it sound like the bomb' — Story reverts to a little light gangster-speak: 'You feeling me?'

'You'd be out of government, though.'

'Yeah, but that doesn't matter. I'm not really in government anyway.'

There is a silence. Cannie thinks of the times she has heard Story refer to himself as *in government*.

'So,' says Cannie, 'you're thinking about it.'

'Maybe. Anyway,' says Story, turning a corner, a shine suddenly entering his eyes, 'the whole point of this was telling you what happened *after* I met with the dude from Goldman Sachs!'

'Prawn betel leaves.' The waiter slips a rectangular plate, with three green triangles on it, into the middle of the table.

Usually, Story would prioritise the food. Usually, at this moment, he would be itching underneath a casual demeanour, unsatisfied, until he had a parcel of prawn in his mouth. But today — not so. The betel leaves loiter on their porcelain.

Story's whole being is animated. He shifts in his chair.

'I had my first threesome,' he says.

Cannie's focus sharpens. She is amazed that Story has just said this. Amazed that he has said this — *to her*. Amazed, in fact, that he has said it at all.

Cannie had grown up with three younger brothers, and in among all their rites of passage, the bodily fluids, ejaculations, the mucky, smutty, hormonal aggression — she'd never heard this. She'd never heard anything *said* with this manner.

'Did you,' says Cannie.

'Seriously, dude.' Story is beaming. 'It was unbelievable. Seriously, you know, it's the way of the future. Like, I'm never having sex with just one woman again!'

Cannie understands this is meant as a joke, and finds a fragile smile.

'Who were they?' she says, taking a glug from her glass, and registering the untouched betel leaves.

'They were these two chicks,' Story begins, sensing a muted response from Cannie, but so carried on his own wave that he crashes over it, 'who I met at Clooney's. You know Clooney's? Where I was meeting Nick Tucker from Goldman's. After he'd left, these two unbelievably hot chicks came and sat at my table.'

Story wonders whether he should tell her – it would make her laugh – about their names. The Kylies. But he swiftly decides no – Cannie is from a solid Hunter's Hill family, her father is a property developer and has parties at the Royal Sydney Golf Club. In this great, classless society, telling Cannie about Kyleigh and Kailee would identify them as a certain sort of person – as downmarket. He would struggle, from then on, to convince Cannie of their lustre, of any of their sex appeal, of their created, garish beauty.

Cannie listens in silence. *Unbelievably hot*. She can picture them. She feels her feet – boots sensible as chimney stacks – underneath the table.

'Like, *unbelievably hot*. We got chatting' – Story is rocking his shoulders back and forward a little, in the rhythm of his own joyful fable – 'we drank Moët et Chandon together. And one thing led to another, and they came back to mine. They *asked* if they could come back to mine.'

'What did they want from you?' asks Cannie matter-of-factly, impartially suspicious.

The question knocks Story from his cloud.

'What do you mean, *What did they want from me?*' he says in a din. 'They wanted *me!*'

Story, whose responses to things are tranquil, whose pace is measured, has exploded almost before Cannie has finished her sentence. He is looking puffed and stunned.

They wanted me.

She looks at him, her dear old friend. A touchstone and a relief among the other Grammar boys – when they were kids, she would make her way to him, and only then, when chatting together, could she look at JP, JP and the others, and feel relaxed.

He has always been: plump, short, with matt, soft skin, like silk. He is the same now. For all the tailored shirts and Mowett Ette Shone Don, as unglamorous as ever. His face rounder, his middle spongier, and with a dark five o'clock shadow under the perfect, baby skin.

They wanted me.

Tummy pressing roundly against his shirt, a sheen of sweat on his forehead.

'Sorry, Story,' says Cannie, trying to sound light, as if placating a child. 'I didn't mean anything.'

'Well, you know? What do you think they wanted! They were hot. You know, seriously fucking hot. They wanted me.'

27

Nominally an informal drink, the meeting with the bloke from Goldman Sachs had within it the tendrils of a job offer. This time not just the usual economic and equity research chatter, but something else called the International Markets Institute. The words *government, lawmakers* and *World Health Organization* kept entering the fray. Also the phrases *stock options* and *relocation package*.

'You need to come and see us in London,' said the guy.

And instead of the usual vague mooing noises, Story found himself replying, 'I could do that.'

'When?'

The guy had bought unbelievably good wine from the bar, and Story had been impressed by the class of it. No champagne and strippers, none of that. A bottle of red, Australian.

They shook hands goodbye and, with gold in his gut and London in his head, Story sat back down again in the low chair.

Thinking about it, in earnest, Story felt as if he was pulling a curtain aside and looking into another world.

'Are these seats taken?'

Story looked up. 'No,' he said.

'Do you mind if we sit here?'

'No, no. No problem.'

The two women sat. They shimmered like snakes, sun-golden and Sydney-sexy, torsos on display, blond hair blow-dried straight over their shoulders. One of them wore a glittery singlet, cut out at the sides so that you could see the shape of her breasts, the bottom edge of them. Each woman held a flute of champagne. Manicured nails with white tips.

They had been there for a minute or two, and Story was preparing himself to get up and leave, when one of them asked, 'Do you mind me asking what your name is?'

Story was surprised.

'My name? Uh, my name's Story.'

'Story? What, like, how d'you mean?'

'S – T – O – R – Y. Ah, Story.'

'*Story*. That is such a cool name. Like, seriously. I've never heard anything like that. That's so cool.'

'Yeah, that's really original,' said the other one. She had fuller lips, and a rounder, more basic face than her friend, who was sharp-looking, and made-up.

'I'm Kylie,' said the first one, offering a hand.

Story shakes it, aware of her grip being loose in his. Her skin was warm.

'Kylie, nice to meet you.' Story cleared his throat.

'She's also Kylie,' she said, smiling.

'Yeah,' said the one with the softer face, with the mesmeric breasts curving into her top, 'but it's spelt differently. I'm K – A – I – L – E – E, and she's K – Y – L – I – E – G – H.'

'You always get that wrong!' The pointy one's face stretched with an undeveloped giggle. 'K –Y – L – E – I – G – H. Kyleigh. And she's K – A – I – L – E – E, Kailee.'

214

'That's what I said, isn't it?' said Kailee.

'Well,' smiled Story, 'nice to meet you both. Kyleigh. And Kailee. Good to meet you.'

'And you. Thanks *so much* for letting us sit here.'

It went from there.

As Story's surprise and confusion mellowed into acceptance, he bought a bottle of champagne from the bar, and then another, and they were drunk and Kyleigh put her hand on Story's thigh. And as her hand remained there, one of her fingers moving softly, Story got drunker and put his arm behind her, down around her hips.

At that moment, Kailee says, 'Hey, guys, how about a line? Story, you got anything, babe?'

'Nah, sorry,' says Story. 'I mean, you know, I don't carry it any more. Just say no, right?'

The Kylies curdle with laughter.

Having looked up at Kailee, Story cannot help but stare at the visible semicircles of her breasts, casually blaring at him. He knows he has looked for too long, and forces his eyes away, hoping that Kyleigh hadn't spotted the leering, involuntary as it was.

He wonders what's going to happen now – with Kyleigh's hand confidently creeping up his thigh, and his hand tentatively on the first curve of her bottom, it's clear that Kailee will soon be the third wheel.

At that moment, Kailee stands and reaches over the table to the bottle of champagne. Her singlet gapes, her breasts hang, gently pointing outwards, the entire, tanned, flat front of her visible. Story cannot help but look: he looks. A man at the bar looks, too. He nudges his friend, and they both: look. *Fuck*, says the man at the bar to his friend, *look at the tits on that*.

And the lips, says his friend, *they'd suck the chrome off a tow bar.*

Kailee walks round the table and sits next to Story, to pour champagne into his and Kyleigh's glasses.

Story worries again, blurrily, if his gawking at Kailee will have offended Kyleigh, if it will cause her to retract her advances. But then, Kailee says, 'Well, what d'you reckon we take the party somewhere else, then?'

And, smiling unabashed into Story's face, she leans in and licks him on the lips.

Story, for a moment that lasts a lifetime, is dazed — as the wet of Kailee's spit lingers on his mouth, Kyleigh's hand presses ever harder into his thigh.

'Can we go back to your place?' asks Kyleigh.

It had got to be, like, one of the best moments of Story's life.

In his bedroom, the lights are dimmed down low, and Story's iPod is jacking out music. There are three champagne glasses, filled at various levels with Mandarin vodka, champagne and lemon juice — an inspired cocktail that Story dreamt up as the party started.

There is an ashtray, filled with dead butts, a piece of used chewing gum that gleams like a small, wet foetus, and a lit cigarette smoking on the edge.

Story is standing, laughing like a sweaty, indecorous Buddha, naked but for the tie around his neck, and a some-what feeble erection.

Pulling him around the room by the tie — backwards and forwards in drunken, stumbling lines — is Kyleigh, who is giggling, and is naked from the waist down. Her legs are short, but slim, and the hair of her crotch is trimmed into the shape of a neat little heart.

Kailee, on the bed, says, 'Wooh! Wooh!' as Story is yanked

forwards and backwards by his tie. She sits cross-legged, chewing gum, which has in it the grey juice of cigarette tar and alcohol. She is naked, but for a pair of underpants. Occasionally, with boozy absent-mindedness, she looks down at her pubis and squeezes with two fingers at an ingrown hair – at close quarters her skin is crowded with small black dots. Her back curves as she sits, and her middle concertinas into a few tiny rolls of flesh.

'Bring him to the bed, Kyleigh!' she says. 'Come on, baby, come to bed!'

Story grins as he is led on his rope. As he approaches, Kailee, in her pants, moves the ashtray from on top of the duvet to the floor. She leans back on her arms and sticks her legs in the air.

'Take my knickers off!' she yells. 'Go on! My knickers! My *panties!*'

Kyleigh, who has been hauling Story around, gets on to the bed, still holding his tie. Story splutters as the tie wrings his throat, and he stumbles against the mattress. As he does, he sees a blurry, greeny tattoo on the back of Kyleigh's neck, and another on her ankle.

You see that? Even at a moment like this – ambrosial, intoxicated – Story is all about the detail – *see?*

The tie is pulled, he coughs, and his face lands against the bare legs of one of the girls. As the grains of his hair and pores of his cheek lie against the naked, female skin, a desire runs through Story's body – consuming him and surrounding him:

Fuck – the desire is loud, and large – *if only the guys were here now, watching me now.*

The twins! The twins at the buck's night. At Vinnie's buck's. There were going to be twins. That would be Story's

217

chance to say it – to tell them all: *Forget this shit*, he could say, *this* watching, *you need the touching. You need the real thing, dudes. Two at a time, eh, JP, eh, Mac, eh, Stavvo, eh, Vinnie?* And then he could tell 'em. About this fucking circus, this fucking breaker, this fermented breath and gluey hair, pulling him under now.

28

If JP's dad had been a journalist, a novelist, a biographer, instead of a small-time solicitor, JP would have a column in a newspaper by now. The only reason he didn't is that he wasn't part of the club – journalists' kids and publishers' god-children – who got shoehorned in to a writer's job straight out of uni.

The article he's just finished reading is a piece of shit. Weak, predictable and totally lacking in any kind of style. The subject of the article is provocative – wheelchair access to lapdancing clubs – and yet the writer manages to strip it of all interest. JP types the byline into Google – there is no immediate biographical information – no Wikipedia entry – but there is a small string of recent articles for the same newspaper. Daddy is the editor, no doubt.

JP treads his well-worn path to the readers' comments underneath the article.

So this is news? This kind of voyeuristic 'tit'tle-tattle should write itself, but it looks like Ainsley Brookes can hardly hold a pen. Where did he learn his craft? On the school newspaper? It's bad enough a grown-up newspaper publishing such an obviously titillating article under the guise of pleasing the PC brigade, but the quality of the writing is so poor *[JP deletes* poor *and replaces it with]* risible, that it is not even worthy of the gutter press.

He signs underneath: *Sydney Solip.*

When JP was a kid, he hadn't always wanted to be a writer. First, he'd wanted to be a rugby player. He was good, but he gradually realised, with his dad shouting from the sideline, that he wasn't good enough ever to play for Australia.

'You should have run with it, JP!' Dad would say after the game. 'What's the point of kicking it straight back to the other side?'

He wasn't good enough to play Super Rugby either, or even captain any school team. He made it through to the Firsts at Grammar, though.

'Missed opportunity, JP,' Dad said. 'You could have won it there. Lazy eye.'

And he made it through to the Seconds at Sydney Uni. He supposes he might have made it up to the Firsts had he pushed and pushed and trained every day – but he couldn't be fucked with it. He was never going to get that much better, in the long term.

JP goes back to check the webpage. No response to his comment, yet.

He'd thought about writing for the school magazine. But it was a group of kids he didn't know, and he never did anything about it. It was a shit magazine, anyway – smug and self-conscious and nerdy. When a boy in his year was made editor – the same boy who was called on to play improbably good saxophone in all the school concerts and plays – JP felt scornful and angry. He went home that afternoon and his mum asked him how he was in the same way she did every day and took his backpack from him as if he were a princeling and asked him if he was thirsty, and JP realised that neither of his parents, beyond the rugby, knew even minutely what his interests were. In what slice of muddy ground his heart lay.

They wouldn't know of or guess his disappointment at not being made editor of the school magazine, even though he hadn't applied to be and had never even written an article for it. They wouldn't know that he liked writing, and now the rugby pipedream was over he wanted to be a writer of some kind. All Mum ever spoke about, with gummy eyes, was how handsome he was, and how smart, and why didn't he grow his hair a bit longer it was such a beautiful colour and nobody ever got to see it. All Dad cared about was his rugby playing, inferior as it was – Dad clutching at the straws of his own vicarious passion.

And when his grades at uni meant he could apply to study law, he just plodded on into it, feeling the blaze of his mother's jubilant expectation that he would be a better lawyer than his father. Which, of course, he would – that wouldn't be hard. At the same time, JP had also got the prospectus and forms for the University of Sydney Journalism postgrad – but he never did anything with them. He felt embarrassed by them, in fact, as one would by a stash of porn.

Somebody has posted a reply.

Dear Sydney Solip, I like and admire Ainsley Brookes' work, including this article. It's balanced, respectful and doesn't go for the obvious route of sensationalism. I think using a lapdancing club as the example to demonstrate wheelchair inaccessibility is original and humorous. I don't believe it was meant to offend. I'm surprised you have reacted so strongly! Anne Duffy.

JP's excitement heats immediately, fat in a pan. He clicks on *reply*.

Humorous? Original? Maybe if you've been reading a lawn-mower manual. It is the usual predictable, patronising crap – stick a nice, juicy disability in and you can get away with a load of bad research and journalism, and stick some naked women in and you'll pull in the readers no matter how bad the article. I've reacted strongly because I find it obnoxious that my dollar pays for such transparent, taste-less attention-seeking, masquerading as (very poor quality) journalism. Sydney Solip.

When JP was working at a law firm in Brisbane – his first ever job – he sent a short story into the *New Yorker*. For a month he didn't get a response. After six weeks he called. The unfamiliar, movie-sounding female voice said, 'Was the manuscript unsolicited?'

'Er – yes.'

'Did it come via an agent, or did you send it direct to us yourself?'

'I sent it,' said JP. 'Not through my agent.'

'I'm afraid, sir,' said the voice, 'we're unable to read unsolicited manuscripts, unless they come via an agent known to the *New Yorker*.'

'So you don't read anything anyone sends to you?'

'We do, sir, as I said, if the manuscript comes via an agent known to the *New Yorker*.'

'Right,' said JP. 'Right. So what will happen to it, now?'

'To your manuscript? It will be returned to you, sir, with a cover letter explaining in more detail what I have just told you now.'

'Go fuck yourself,' JP said, once he had put the phone down. He thought of a line in his short story — *She doesn't know, and she will never know, and there is something noble in that* — and he thought of that line shoved back into an envelope unread and back into a mail sack in the stomach of a plane, and the thought felt painful.

After a sprinkling of further humiliations with the same story, JP sent off an article about Brisbane public transport to the *Courier Mail*, and received an email from the newspaper the same day saying they'd like to run it in Saturday's paper.

JP had felt — somewhere hot and alive inside him — that this could be the beginning.

He returns to the comments page, to see that *Anne Duffy* has not yet replied. But, with satisfaction, JP sees that his post has stirred up quite a storm.

There are three replies already posted, and, JP suspects, more in the wings. The most recent reads:

Being confined to a wheelchair herself, what further research do you reckon Ainsley Brookes needs to do? As for attention-seeking – Ms Brookes does not even refer to her own disability in the article. I don't know how much more low key she could have been. I've always been an admirer of hers, and this article didn't disappoint. It turned many Australian ideas of equality on their head, and I say good on you Ainsley.

So she's a she. And she is a chick in a wheelchair – JP gets it, now. Most of the posters are women – the sisterhood are out in force, beating at the blokes with their unshaven sticks.

So she's in a wheelchair? Just because she can't use her legs doesn't mean she can use her fingers. No matter which way you look at it, Ainsley Brookes can't write for sh**, and her being disabled doesn't change that. The sooner we drop the PC stick and start rewarding talent for what it is, the sooner our newspapers will actually be readable.

He hits *post reply* with only the most hasty re-read, and thinks to himself he's going to look Ainsley Brookes up properly – do the research that she didn't! – and then he can nail her in his next post. He feels exhilarated.

That article of his, in the *Courier Mail*, on Brisbane's public transport – had turned out not to be the beginning. JP had had one further article accepted after that – a foundation of hope – after which brick after brick of rejection. It became over the years JP's dirty little secret, that he continued to email out articles, which were published at a hit rate of one in twenty. He knew they were good; he knew it was the editors – jumped-up little journalism grads – who had not a bone of literate understanding. His umbrage grew with his body of unpublished work.

Ainsley Brookes. Google.

On the fourth page of results is the Wikipedia page JP hadn't got to first time round. There is a photo of Ainsley Brookes, lissome and smiling, accepting some award while standing on her own two, long legs. No wheelchair in sight. *Fucking idiots*, thinks JP, he's going to have a field day.

The entry reads:

Ainsley Brookes (née Haughton) is an award-winning British journalist who has been a Foreign Correspondent for *The Times* (UK) and Special Correspondent for the BBC, and now works as a freelance journalist in Sydney, Australia.

Educated at Cambridge University, where she studied Arabic and Persian, Brookes began her career in journalism as a newsroom journalist at *The Times*. After a year, she was appointed *The Times*' Cairo correspondent, during which time she was nominated for the Lorenzo Natali Journalism Prize. Brookes left *The Times* to work for the BBC as their Baghdad Correspondent, and two years later was appointed the BBC's correspondent in Kabul, during which time she was nominated for and won the Bayeux Calvados Award for War Correspondents, Television.

While reporting on the ground with the British Army in Kabul, Brookes sustained an injury from a mortar attack and subsequently lost the use of both her legs.

After her injury, Brookes returned to work for the BBC for a period of six months as a presenter on the BBC News Channel. Brookes left the BBC after marrying her long-term partner, historian Daniel Brookes. The couple relocated to Sydney, Australia.

Brookes now lives and works in Australia as a freelance journalist.

JP sits for some minutes, staring at the photo of the leggy British blonde in the high heels. He does not know what he is feeling.

He types *Ainsley Haughton* into the search field — and there she is. Page after page of article and reference. Her mortar attack clearly documented in the press.

With a new name and a new husband and a new wheel-chair and a new life in Sydney, her work is unrecognisable — JP cannot be blamed for judging her crappy article on wheelchair access. I mean, for fuck's sake. What the fuck is she doing? After all that? After a life in Cairo and Baghdad and Kabul? What the fuck is she doing under a sheet in Sydney writing this kind of crap, as if she's dead? JP blames her, Ainsley Brookes, Ainsley Haughton, vigorously, for her life choices, and for misleading him into his alley of anger.

He has done nothing wrong.

It's other people who are the pricks.

He shuts down the article and its comments page. The replies to his *legs don't work, fingers don't work* crack must be mounting up. He couldn't read them, without his heart getting stuck quacking like a duck in his mouth.

'Smug English prick,' JP says to himself, as he sees Oliver pass, smiling as if there is a joke in the air that only he can smell. There they were, having a fucking sandwich together a couple of days ago — *Mind if I join you?* — and now he walks past, hair glowing like a fucking road sign, as if JP were in-visible. Oliver doesn't even notice him, worker ant that he is, sitting at some random desk in the colony.

Oliver walking past has been the final taunt in a day full of blisters. The final rage in a day, like most others, full of rages. But it comes second (yes! Even the obsession that is Oliver Marchal with his road-sign hair comes second today. And even Ainsley Brookes) to a booby trap that arrived in his inbox twenty minutes before.

Re: Laos adventure
Dear JP
Thank you for sending your article sorry it's taken me a while to get back to you. However, while I enjoyed reading it and you write well I think it's not right for us. Writing the opening in the format of a conversation is confusing and it's a bit over complicated for the travel+adventure section.

If you have another travel experience that you are able to write more simply about I'd be interested in having a look.

Best wishes
Kate

Kate Renton
Editor – travel+adventure

Upon receiving it, JP's heart had retched up and hit the roof of his head. It had remained there, beating a distraught drum for a few seconds, before shame took over and JP with a sense of exigency dropped the email into his trash folder. He swallows his heart back down into his chest – it takes several gulps – he wants to pretend the email never came. He wants to hide it.

Even though there is nobody to hide it from.

Anger and humiliation wrestle, and JP is unable to think about anything else.

He could do with a drink. A drink would help. A Molotov cocktail with a whisky chaser.

JP takes the email out of the trash, and reinstates it in his inbox.

Writing the opening in the format of a conversation is confusing and it's a bit over complicated for the travel+adventure section.

How is it that some bitch who doesn't even do punctuation is the editor of a newspaper section?

Over complicated.

What part, exactly, was over-fucking-complicated? Confusing? *Confusing?*

JP remembers the little thrill he had felt, sending that article off. The smile, small teeth in a rare show, as he read it back to himself – he thought it was good. It *was* good. It had grace. It had morals. *In Laos*, he had written, *you are forced take a step back from the overconsumption that masquerades as Western life experience. Here, in the unforgiving heat of the local market, the unctuous roll calls of designer lifestyle that we are used to suddenly seem like the smoke and mirrors that they really are.*

Those lines were *good*. They had taken work, and they had rung from him, like bells.

And then, Oliver Marchal had walked past, a smirking prince, and JP's heart was back up in his skull again, and he feels shame, of an eviscerating kind. The email goes back in the trash. In another life, he would send his fist through his computer screen.

29

They were all decent enough blokes, Vinnie's mates: co-workers from the Source Hotel; guys from his days behind the bar at the Windsor Inn; musos – DJ mates and this one, gelled club promoter; cousins and brother; and then them – all the North Sydney boys. Stavvo had a pass out from the wife for the afternoon, and Tintin had flown in from Wellington. Being a dick, and an attention seeker, he'd brought Pinyata – still in the picture, some kind of personal best for Tinny – to the Ferrython, an Australia Day institution. JP was glad he hadn't gone along to that, to see her with her coloured shoes and puff of hair, giggling and garnering stares. And what a prick, Tinny, bringing her along in the first place. JP is surprised that he didn't go the whole hog and bring her here, as well, loudly saying, *She's black, you know, black, my girlfriend is black*, and then wheezing into some feminist exposition on the patriarchy, buck's nights, and a woman's right to play a part in them. As if Pinyata's coming to the Ferrython made her Emmeline Pankhurst.

'I couldn't fucking believe it, mate,' Tintin is saying now, to the group around him, his face four beers to the wind. '*Blacking up*, in the twenty-first century. And not even on some redneck cable channel – on prime-time television!'

'Give it a rest, mate,' says Mac. 'Not you, too. We're all sick of it. It was just a bit a fun.'

'Mac! Even ignoring the fact that it's completely fucking racist, it just makes the rest of the world think that we're a country of bloody rednecks.'

'The rest of the world doesn't give a shit, mate,' JP swipes. He agrees with Tintin, but won't say it.

'No other country in the world would allow it,' Tintin goes on. How long, thinks JP, before he brings his girlfriend up, and the shade – the colour – of her skin. He'll cast her as Rosa Parks this time. 'Seriously, mate, we're the only ones.'

'Bro, you ain't seen nothing!' says Mac. 'You're talking about fancy Sydney racism. Go to Queensland, or – what was the name of that place in Western Australia – Kalgoorlie! In Kalgoorlie, they probably have *Abo Mondays*, where any-one appearing on television *has* to be blacked up, it's part of the rules. A bit of blacking up on prime-time telly, and jiv-ing about to the Jackson Five, is *nothing*, mate.'

They all stand outside in the rigid heat, on an area of poolside deck roped off for them. There are swimmers, burn-ing in the light as they do their laps, and the beach beyond is full. Boats are out on the water, and there are garlands of Australian flags hung mugger around the place. The smell and smoke of grilling meat is swelling in the air, hanging in the heat as if it is too heavy to rise. Vincent Batty, JP notes, has just been made to drink three schooners back to back by his Windsor Inn mates – he's going to be a mess before long. As for JP – he's happy to be here. The beer and heat and meat and friends and promise of water to come are a good, sensory forgetfulness. He's got his swimmers and a small towel tucked into a back pocket. Fuck knows what will have become of them by the end of the day.

This pool is where JP has been training for the Corporate Triathlon — he had put his name down after the Christmas break — and after two weeks he can already do forty lengths here, no drama. He goes for the odd swim at Boy Charlton after work — but it is the Icebergs that he is beginning to know intimately. He knows the lines and marks of the pool bottom as if they are the lines and marks of his kitchen floor. He has begun to recognise some of the regulars by the underwater view of their legs. Arriving here, beginning the routine of showing his pass, lockering his stuff and showering before going to the water — is a release, a contract with the one part of himself that feels peace. The few times there has been a summer surge — a sea wave breaks the pool wall and hits the water — it has felt like a blessing, a divination of a personal kind. JP stands here next to it now, his water — with these men, with beer and sun and no hat to protect him — and feels that his claim to the Iceberg's pool is a secret, known to him alone. He feels all right.

A group of their party has started singing, in rich accents, 'Advance, Australia Fair'. It is a strident and unabashed rendition, and some civilians beyond the ropes are joining in, in the spirit of the day. JP thinks he might begin in baritone.

As he comes in on *Our home is girt by sea*, his chin pressed into his chest, JP notices an imprecisely familiar figure coming out of the water — a man, neat, and blond — very. The man's head is turned towards the buck's party — most people's are — and as the man dries himself with his towel, he continues to watch. JP keeps looking at him, keeps singing — *Our land abounds in nature's gifts, of beauty rich and rare.*

The man, whom JP has remained aimlessly watching, suddenly waves, and begins to jog over. *In joyful strains then let us sing* – JP is trying a harmony – the man is almost at them, and JP dawns that the man – yellow-haired and smiling and not a crumb of fat on him – is coming for him.

Advance – Austray – lia – Fair!

There is a round of applause, including from Oliver Marchal.

'JP,' he says, from the other side of the rope, 'I didn't know you were a singer. How are you?'

JP takes, thunderstruck, the offered hand. He feels something, in his brow, but he doesn't know what.

'I'm on a buck's party,' he says.

'Buck's? Stag?' Oliver is very slightly out of breath.

'I'm a groomsman,' says JP. 'At my mate's wedding.' As if that somehow makes it okay.

'A groomsman? You – muck out the stables?'

'No. A groomsman is like—'

'An usher,' smiles Oliver.

JP is po-faced. Behind him, they've started up a round of 'We Come from a Land Down Under' – *Can't you hear, can't you hear the thunder?* A few are providing a superb, echoing falsetto over the top.

Oliver laughs. JP doesn't. 'Oh, happy Australia Day!' Oliver says.

'Thanks,' says JP, 'I . . .' Then he stops. He doesn't know what to say.

'See you on Monday.'

Oliver takes himself away to the changing rooms, and JP turns around, feeling as if he is a tree just felled. Feeling the phantom of Oliver's hand still in his.

'Who was that?' asks Story.

'Bloke from work.'

'He looks familiar.'

'Does he?'

'Yeah,' says Story. 'No. Maybe not. He looks like a lot of Aussie men, I guess.'

JP doesn't want to betray Oliver, by telling on him that he is a Pom. He cannot understand himself at this moment, his shame, or the beating of his heart. He takes a drag from his beer. His loyalties are in a ball, like fishing wire.

'It's not about who you marry,' says JP, 'it's just about marrying someone. It's about getting married.'

'Yeah, but they love each other. It's obvious they do.' Story and JP are on the corner, outside the Blue Room, waiting for the others to emerge. They only have one more stop on their timetable, Dexy's, the strip club, to which they can walk from here. JP, while drunk, has deliberately not annihilated himself tonight – the triathlon has pitched camp at the back of his skull. And Story is a vet, he's boozy and tired, but on his feet.

'You hang around anyone for long enough, you love them,' says JP. 'People love their pets, mate.'

'Dude, you're saying Vinnie loves Tree like a *pet*? For fuck's sake, Japes – you're not happy for them?'

'Yeah, I'm happy for them. Good on 'em.'

'But you don't reckon he loves her.'

'I didn't say that, mate. I'm saying it doesn't matter whether he does or not. Marriage is just what you do.'

'You're talking bollocks, dude. You don't marry someone just like that. You marry someone because you love 'em.'

'That's all fucking fairytale. It's Hollywood. You marry someone because they're there, and they're decent, and because human beings get married. And I certainly don't reckon Vincent Batty and Tree are star-crossed lovers, if that's what you're saying.'

'Dude, you're one in a million – you're a groomsman at his fucking wedding.'

'Mate, listen! I'm not saying anything unusual here! Good on 'em for getting married. They've been together for long enough. I'm not saying it's a bad thing – it's just what everybody fucking does – you hit your thirties, it's what you *do*. Job, flat, wedding, kids. That's *life*, isn't it?'

The word *life* comes out as hail – it has a hardness around it.

'Have you ever been in love with anyone, JP?'

'Have I! What about you? I get to hear all about your sleazy threesomes, but don't hear you yacking about love much, Story.'

'It wasn't sleazy!'

'I don't really want to know, mate, to tell you the truth. But the point is, I don't see you climbing up balconies proposing much.'

Story is hurt by the lack of impression his threesome has made. Even though he's used to it. He once spent months, in secret, learning how to shuffle cards like a casino dealer – and then when he casually pulled out the skill in public, nobody gave a shit.

'What's with the Romeo and Juliet tonight, JP?'

'Seriously – love and marriage in *your* immediate plans?'

'Not immediate. But yeah.'

JP is slowed down by Story's answer. 'Really?'

'Well, of course! I don't plan on spending my whole bloody life alone.' *Alone.* Story hears the word as if someone else had said it.

JP thinks of a moment earlier in the day, when he walked

into the water of Bronte beach. As he'd gone under and sins past and sins to come had been washed away, he thought he would go home. He'd had enough of this Australia Day, of Vinnie's great send-off, and he wanted to train tomorrow. But, of course, he came back on land, walked apathetically with the rest of them to the next pub – and stayed. He regrets it – still being here – hanging on with his hands to the razor train of this conversation.

'Why aren't you with someone, then?' JP confronts, his tone now grumpy.

'Shit, dude. I'm only thirty-five!'

'Only thirty-five!' JP's face contorts into bullying amusement. 'Nothing *only* about it, mate. If you were a sportsman you'd be retiring about now. Thirty-five's old.'

'No it's not.'

'You're delusional.'

Vincent Batty spills down the steps of the Blue Room, with more bucks clattering at his back.

'Hey, Vinnie,' fires JP, 'tell me again why you're getting married now?'

Vincent Batty is drunk, and everything looks too big for him, his belt buckle, his shoes, his eyes in his head. 'Sold my soul already, JP, my friend. Thought I might as well admit defeat and go for it.'

'Hey, Vincent,' Stavvo is saying, 'did you see that scientists have discovered a food that turns off 90 per cent of a woman's sex drive?'

'Yeah, what's that?'

'Wedding cake!'

'Ha ha!' Vincent is spooling slightly.

'That true, Stav?' Story says.

235

'Yep. Thrill of the chase, eh? But it's probably men just as much. I got nearly three kids, though, mate – not doing too badly.'

'So you've had sex at least three times since your wedding,' Story says.

'Sounds about right.' Stavvo grins. 'Hey, are we going in, or what?'

'Paulie's just sorting it on the door.'

'This is the bit I've been waiting for. Fuck the rest of it.'

While Vincent's brother gives names at the reception of the lapdancing club, the men – down to a group of fifteen – swarm on the pavement. They are humming with alcohol, emitting a pack smell of booze and sweat and fatigue.

Mac is standing a few feet apart, texting.

'You bothering some chick again?' Story asks.

Mac finishes his text before looking up. 'Yeah,' he smiles. 'I'm going to meet her.'

'What – now?'

'In half an hour. I'll come in for a bit first – paid for it. Might as well.'

Vincent, who has been listening with heavy eyelids and a sick look about him, starts wandering away.

'Vinnie! Mate! Vincent Batty! Where are you going?' Stavvo goes after him.

He shakes his head. 'I'm right. Just gonna call Tree.'

'Tree?' Stavvo laughs. 'Don't be daft, mate.'

'Just wanna check she's . . .' He trails off.

'She's still alive, mate.'

Vincent looks as skinny and long and goofy as he ever has. He looks sad, too, JP thinks.

'Vincent,' says JP, 'do you want me to take you home?'

'Yeah,' says Vincent, gagging a bit as he speaks. 'I do. Go home. I want to.'

'Don't be a dick, JP,' says Stavvo. 'It's his fucking buck's, mate – he's got his life to stay at home. Come on, Vinnie.' Stav takes him by the arm, and leads him back towards the red light.

'Stav,' says JP, 'he's over it. He can barely stand up.'

'Better call her,' says Vincent.

'Bollocks,' says Stavvo, taking Vincent's phone from him and putting it in his own pocket. 'Gentlemen – this is the bit we've paid a fucking fortune for – Vinnie can't go home. There are two fucking girls in there, all lubed up and ready to sit on this young man's face. At the very least, I'm watching, mate. Come on, Vinnie, we're all going in now.'

Do you want your wife here now, Stavvo? Story wants to say. *You pissed off she wasn't included tonight?* Story remembers Stavvo's two daughters; the one who collects bunnies. He looks at Stav, and looks at Vincent. Vincent seems distressed, and concentrated, and Story thinks that in this moment Vinnie might prove himself a king.

Then Vinnie grins. 'You're a fucken weaponhead,' he slurs to Stavvo.

'Try not to look like you're about to pass out,' Stav replies. 'Just until we're inside.' And Vincent Batty is guided through the herd, man of the moment – king of something else.

JP and Story remain separate, as their group filters into the club.

'You going in?' asks Story.

'No, I'm heading off.'

JP is disappointed by Vincent, too – but not so much that he cares. He could do with a woman, to have a go at for a bit. But not like this. He doesn't like to be watched by other men as he titillates himself.

Story stands, deciding whether to go in. He's been here before – boozed and lacklustre in King's Cross.

'I'll go in,' Story says, the decision easy either way – the decision too easy to take. 'I'll go in and say my goodbyes.'

30

He should go home and sleep – that way he'd stand a chance of training tomorrow. But he won't. JP will do what is simplest when he is in this state, which was to stay on Darlinghurst Road and nod at a bouncer and plummet into a lightless, air-conditioned strip club that smells of farts and cheap freshener, and feel himself released like a fish back into water. Alone and clean, while the others made their lust rancid, showing it in front of each other.

As he walks, slowly, round the block, waiting for Vinnie's bucks to have disappeared into their own place, JP thinks of that girl from New Year's Eve. They'd spoken a couple of times on the phone – they'd even had dinner.

But she'd turned up to the dinner in a dress – like a full-on, slinky cocktail dress – to a casual place on Victoria Road, with her cleavage bare. It had all been a bit desperate.

When she'd told him about her job, in arts PR, he'd said, 'PR. Isn't that what you do if you're not smart enough to get into advertising?'

At the end of dinner they had split the bill and JP had said, 'It's over-rated, this place.'

That had been that.

JP has completed his loop. The crowd outside Dexy's has gone – Vincent Batty and his mates have slooped inside. JP can go to his own place, three doors down, unobserved. As he makes to the entrance, he thinks of Kali.

It's a surprise. It always is. When she appears in front of him, still, after all this time gone by. JP hadn't seen her for a couple of years, and he wondered if she would look the same, the same whiteness and blondness and thinness. Or if some weight had settled on to her – she would be, what? Nearly forty now? – and pressed away some of the inexplicable purity and quietness she had always seemed to walk with.

It wasn't painful to think about her any more, which was something. There'd been *some* evolution since he was sixteen.

And her husband – what was his name? (Who was JP kidding. He knew his name. His name was Guy. He was a massively rich construction bloke.)

JP is at the door of the club, and he lets Kali pass away, back into the air. He does not hold on to her – he stopped that a long time ago. He used to, at the height of his teenage infatuation, imagine with all his contorted, crumpled might what it would be like to have her against him, lying in his bed against him, exactly as things were – his socks and pants and books on the floor, a damp towel slung over the back of his chair, his rucksack open, rugby boots outside the door. He imagined what it would be like to have her there, in his childhood bedroom, in his teenage bed, all thin skin and fine hair. He used to imagine so intently that he'd end up digging his nails into his palms and banging the back of his head slowly against the wall.

And as for the date with the girl from New Year's Eve – fuck it. She had been far too solid, far more solid than he had

240

remembered. All body. All flesh and muscle and bone, in that desperate dress.

He had considered, at one point during dinner, making a go of it so that he could go back to her place and have sex with her; but he had with speed decided no. He would have the smell of her on him, and he would taste in her mouth the food they had just been eating.

Better this way — this was the club he knew best, where they had small rooms in a warren out the back, by the dressing rooms, where the protocol for sex was simple and JP was a known customer. If he was after someone specific, he might have to wait until a girl was off shift, but apart from that it was easy — $100, done. The girls were naked already, so all they had to do was spread their legs, at most remove a g-string.

And when he thought about these intercourses in the outside world (zombies from the night before did sometimes creep into the daylight) — at home alone in his room, walking from the bus stop to the office — he thought that possibly the girls sometimes enjoyed it. He was not such a fool to believe that they lusted after him or would voluntarily, without payment, do it. But when he was inside them, they oftentimes seemed to like it enough. He was gentlemanly, after all, no rudeness or brutality, no kinkiness, and also well-endowed, things being relative. He imagined it as rather like his own attitude to soup — he never wanted it, never ordered it off a menu, never looked forward to it; but once he was actually eating it, it was more often than not quite nice.

There is always a moment, at the entrance, before the bouncer steps aside.

'Mate,' he says definitely to JP, as acceptance, and takes one step back, his hands remaining locked together in front of his groin.

JP nods, and walks into the colourless, gaseous dark, down a few steps and to the bar. There are two women on stage rubbing their bare crotches against the same pole – he has caught the end of a show.

'A Cascade and a Chivas Regal on ice,' JP says to the barman, who, like all the men in this place, is fully dressed. There is a woman, naked but for knickers, high-heeled sandals, and a face shiny with make-up, sitting on a bar stool – careful to perch at the edge, so that her bottom does not splay.

'Oh, hey,' she says to JP, recognising him, 'how you going?' She shifts on the stool.

'All right,' says JP. 'How are you? Want a drink?'

'A white-wine spritzer,' she says directly to the barman. 'Not too bad, thanks,' she says to JP.

She is as pretty – or as not pretty – as any of the girls here: plain, guttural sexiness, a scattering around the room of Eastern European sharp lines, blue eyes and small noses; but no beauty. Bodies, bodies everywhere; no faces. But women had that advantage – they could take their every face, and work magic with eyebrows and paint and hair extensions. As long as they had the body, JP reckoned. The body had to be the real deal.

JP's eyes flit around the room as he talks to her, scanning in the details of the other women. He might go and sit near the stage for a bit.

'You been out tonight?' she asks him.

'Buck's night.' He won't tell her that they are all a hundred metres away, three walls to the left. 'Where are you from, again?'

'Dunedin,' says the girl.

She was an actress, JP remembers that from another late-night-early-morning encounter. Except, by the rules he had applied to Pinyata, she wasn't an actress – she was a stripper. Who wished she was an actress even though she clearly wasn't.

But the rules applied to Pinyata don't apply in here. There is space, in this windowless laboratory – in which he, JP, has the confidence of a white coat – for a little more kindness. He is the zookeeper, and he can afford to be kind.

'Do you want to sit at a table?' JP asks.

'Sure,' she says. And the two of them walk, with their drinks.

What would his mother say? What would Rosie Fry say if she saw her son here, as he drinks and looks up at a stranger on stage, fingering her own breasts? If she saw her son in his blue T-shirt, the top tuft of his chest hair just visible, sitting with a girl whose nakedness spread from her shoulders to her arms, her back down to her thighs, and up again round to her chest?

Rosie Fry would not, in fact, be that surprised. Because she has asked herself, at times, what it is that JP does to *cope*. Seeing as he is a man. And seeing as he has no girlfriend. Has had no girlfriend, to her knowledge, ever. She may even blame herself for all this – for having loved her eldest son far more than she could ever love his father.

The fact remains that JP is not so different from many others in this city, where women are what women are, and women are the joke, the kernel of the joke. And the facts remain that JP lives his life, pays his share of the rent and buys cheese and bread from the minimarket at Five Ways, goes to work on the bus and drinks beer, trades in bodies on a Friday night, trades in bodies not his own, wakes up, these days jogs with the seedling of the Corporate Triathlon in his shoes, hates himself at moments, repulses himself at others, usually exists with manageable rage, and mostly does not contemplate that life could be any different.

31

Well, um, cheers for that Paulie. After that, I reckon this might be the shortest marriage in history.

Laughter.

Could somebody lock the doors while Tree's still in here, please?

Laughter.

Anyway, look, I've got some notes here, and I'm going to read from them.

Uh, Teresa and I, have been together for nineteen years, now —

Disbelief.

Yep, seriously. Nineteen years. On and off.

Laughter.

But ever since I first saw Tree, when I was sixteen and she was fifteen —

Cradle-snatcher!

Yeah, mate, all right! Anyway, even back then, I knew she was the one for me.

Aaaah.

And she's just as beautiful now, as she was then. Even more beautiful. You look amazing, babe.

Aaaah.

Now, not many people know this, but when I first met Tree, she was actually going out with someone else.

Oooo!

Yes, it's true, it's true. A bloke called Mike Liddle. Remember him, babe? Well, let me remind you.

Laughter.

He was an absolute dickhead from St Botolph's.

Laughter.

He was also a shit-hot half-back, weighed about a hundred and ten kilos. And the problem was that Teresa here, my lovely wife, didn't remember to tell me that she was going out with him. So imagine my surprise, when strolling along Curl Curl Beach one Saturday with my mates, just having a chat, you know, chilling out, minding my own business – imagine my surprise when I was attacked from behind by this brick shithouse and three of his brick shithouse mates.

Naturally surprised, to be taken so unawares and thus brutally—

Laughter.

I said to the fellow, between being punched in the head – 'What the bloody eff are you doing, mate?'

To which he replied, 'You ever eff-ing touch my girl again, I'll eff-ing pull your dick up through your throat.'

Yes. Well.

It wasn't just me who took a Class A pounding that day, it was two of my groomsmen, JP and Stavvo over there. Cheers, fellas. And another of my groomsmen, one David Ostent, aka Tintin – can everyone see Tintin? There he is! Give us a wave, Tinny! Well, Tintin ran away, didn't you, mate? Remember that, Tinny? Remember running for cover like a girl?

Laughter.

Ah, no hard feelings. Well, after that, my mates, as you can imagine, told me in, er, fruity terms, to have nothing more to do with the sheila. With Teresa here. Problem was, I was hook, line and sinker for her by then. Like I said, babe, I knew straight off you were the one for me.

Aaaaah.

And, as luck would have it, the same day I got a call from Tree, telling me she'd dumped the dickhead, and asked if we could meet up for a milkshake. And it was a bloody good thing, too, as I don't think I could've managed without her.

Aaaaah.

She's been changing my colostomy bag ever since, haven't you, babe?

Laughter.

And, you know, yesterday, while I was finishing up this speech, I thought it might be a decent idea to do a bit of Googling – you know, look up the Botolph's loser, Mike Liddle, who pasted me and broke my mate's nose.

Pause.

Turns out he's head of CitiBank Australia. Seriously. So, um, you made the right choice there, babe.

Laughter.

Anyway, the rest is history. And it's been nineteen years.

And when you've been together for this long, you learn all the good things about each other, and the worst things about each other, too, you know?

Pause.

Laughter.

The burping. The farting. The snoring. The drinking. The eating with your mouth open.

Those are all Teresa's bad bits, and, as for me . . .

Laughter.

No, only joking. Tree only snores when she's had too much to drink, don't you, babe? And she only ever farts after curry.

Laughter.

And, as for me – well. I burp pretty much all the time. I fart. I snore. I drink too much and behave like a wanker. I eat with my mouth open, and I have been known to fall asleep on my plate – when there's food still on it. Yeah, I know. Not the best look. Ravioli up one side of my face. I behave like a bit of a child at times, and I can be a right moody bastard when it's the time of the month.

Tree puts up with a lot, and she stands by me anyway. And I can't thank you enough for that, babe.

Aaaah.

As I said before, I'm a very lucky man. And, apart from the farting and all –

Laughter.

– I reckon there isn't a bad thing about you, babe. You're kind, and thoughtful, and generous, and gorgeous, and I'm just so lucky to have you.

Aaaah.

Um, and before I get too soppy, I want to thank all of you tools.

Laughter.

Everybody here, for being here today. If you can judge a man by his mates, then I'm doing all right. You're a bunch a dossers and numbnuts, but you're great mates, and thank you all.

Thank you, Paulie, for destroying my marriage in the first hour, mate.

Laughter.

And, seriously, for being the best brother I could ask for. You throw a great buck's party – it's a shame it's only happening once. I'll do the same for you, one day, mate.

Thanks Mum and Dad, for putting up with me for so long.

Laughter.

And the biggest thank-you ever to Edwina and Shawn, for throwing us such an awesome party today. You guys have always been very generous with me, and I promise you I'm going to do my very best to look after your daughter.

Aaaah.

I've been so nervous about this speech today, that I haven't even had a drink. So time to get drunk, now!

Laughter.

And, uh, to help with that, I just want to make a little toast –

– um, to my beautiful wife.

Cheers.

You're stuck with me now, babe, there's nowhere to run. And I couldn't be happier. You've made me a very happy man.

So –

Here's to her indoors, Mrs Teresa Batty!

32

The surprise of the day has been Mac. Not the fact that since university he has avoided wearing his spectacles at any social occasion, yet here he is, at a wedding, being photographed, wearing a box-fresh, black, rectangular pair. No, forget the glasses. The surprise is that Mac is not only here with his glasses, but here with an entire, other person – a rabbit in a hat, in the form of a woman. Who has been introduced to them all, with baffling casualness, as Alessia. Alessia, in turn, has greeted them all with a relaxed smile, as if it is perfectly normal that she exists.

Mac and Alessia stand together, and her whole body angles towards his. She wears a navy-blue dress, cinched in at a small waist, has rod-straight hair and a noticeably pretty face. At moments throughout the day the two, plainly, without any bustle, kiss each other on the lips. Mac strokes her hip with his thumb. She has a light hand on his knee. It is inexplicable.

The only way JP knows how to tackle it, when he and Mac have a moment alone together during the drinks reception, is to say, 'You're looking like crap, mate.'

'Me?' says Mac, looking surprised, and then smiling.

'Suppose I am. It's pretty full on at work. Haven't been getting much sleep.'

'You've been working nights?'

'Yep.'

'What on?' JP's face has gathered into disbelief, all the skin rucking in towards his nose. It's not like Mac is Oliver Marchal – he researches biscuits, for fuck's sake.

'Our new product launch,' says Mac.

'A new biscuit,' says JP, sardonic.

Mac shakes his head, gathers his mouth to one side.

'What, then?' JP, with naturalness, looks irritated.

'It was in the papers yesterday' – Mac appears to be looking relieved – 'so I can talk about it. We're launching a chocolate bar.'

'A chocolate bar.'

'Yep.' Mac smiles. Now that JP is looking for it – yes, Mac does truly look crap. And tired. There are greyish creases under his eyes.

'What, like a KitKat or something?'

Mac nods. 'Yep, exactly. But not a multi-part bar like the KitKat – you know, it doesn't break up into four? Or even two. It's a single bar. Based on – or around, I should say – the Golden Crunch biscuit.'

'Hmm.' JP considers this. 'But what part of it is hard work? Is it the marketing, and design and stuff?'

'No – well, yes – but that's not what I've been working on. Although I am involved in all of that, too.'

'So what's been keeping you up nights?'

Mac's forehead rises, he takes a deep breath in, and then sighs it out. 'Shit,' he says, 'everything. Creating the bar, from scratch.'

'How d'you mean? You're not the chef.'

Mac pushes his glasses up his nose, even though they're not slipping. He's not quite used to them. 'The ingredients – the texture, the taste . . . the entire bar – is dictated, and refined, by what we determine will succeed in the market-place.'

'What d'you mean, *we*?' says JP.

Mac smiles. JP will never believe anybody in the world does anything worthwhile.

'I mean us. Me. And the rest of the research team.'

'What,' says JP, 'so you go, "People like chocolate, put some chocolate in it," and then they do.'

'Nah, mate. Are you really asking? We're at a wedding, Japes. You want to spend this time hearing about my work?'

'Why not?' JP shrugs. *Amaze me*, he thinks.

'Well,' says Mac, breathing in, 'the central success of this bar will lie in the fact that it is recognisably an Arnold's biscuit product, and so recognised pretty instantly by the entire population, right? Everybody knows what a Golden Crunch is. And yet – it has to distinguish itself completely as a chocolate bar and *not* a biscuit. It's a bit of a tightrope. So – the two layers of Golden Crunch at the centre need to *taste* exactly as they do out of the biscuit packet, but they need a different texture.

'A),' says Mac, still smiling, but more sparsely the more involved he becomes, 'They need to be thinner, each layer a max of four millimetres, so while on first bite you recognise the Golden Crunch taste, you don't at the same time think you're eating a biscuit. And, B) the texture needs to be lighter, and more porous, so that when the consumer is biting through the chocolate to the biscuit some of the chocolate is carried by the teeth into the biscuit experience – and through the other side. It has to be a whole product –

the chocolate and the biscuit need to work together in your mouth.'

Mac pauses for a moment before continuing: 'This bar's position in the market' – earnestness is loosening his smile even further – 'has to bridge three established points – which I won't go into now, because it's too much jargon for a wedding reception. But one of our issues has been – right up until the last minute – successfully coalescing the time frame needed to eat the bar with what we call the Satisfaction Arc – the sense of fulfilment the consumer experiences both during and after eating it. It's the *after* bit that is the most crucial – how long the experience of eating the bar carries on into the consumer's day. And getting that balance is all about the minutiae of the oil content, cocoa content and soy lecithin content, and – without completely rethinking the entire project and adding caramel to the bar, which was out of the question, and would be cheating – it proved to be a bit of a chemical, algebraic nightmare. But we got there – just!' Mac smiles again. 'That's the tip of my iceberg. All the other big stuff, though – the creation of a new retail infra-structure – you probably know, Arnold's main outlets are supermarkets, which isn't the case with an individual choco-late bar – is another department. That, I can't lay any claim to, mate.'

JP is astounded – by the fact that Mac has just used the words *coalescing* and *algebraic*, and also by the fact that Mac doesn't, as assumed, sit at a desk all day picking his nose and eating custard creams. 'Right,' he says. 'I get it.'

'Sorry, mate,' says Mac, drinking from his flute. 'I didn't mean to go off on one. Got tunnel vision.'

'It's interesting,' says JP, with seriousness.

Mac laughs. 'Really?'

'Although, actually, does any of it actually matter? Won't a bloke basically buy a bar of chocolate because it tastes good?'

'Yes, he will,' says Mac.

'Then your job's pointless.'

Mac smiles, his eyes looking shiny through his glasses. 'Keeps me in beer,' he says.

Mac is never precious about himself. JP's always liked that in him. 'And in biscuits,' JP says, his face soft.

'Are you fucking joking!' Mac animates. 'It's impossible to get a biscuit anywhere round our office! Arnold's are completely paranoid about any of their employees suing them for getting fat – they've been instructed by you blokes. They're constantly shoving fruit down us. Meetings – we get bloody berries and mango and crap like that. You got a cup of tea, you're desperate for a biscuit – no fucking way.'

JP laughs. 'Makes sense,' he says. 'Do you have to sign a waiver?'

'What, in case we get fat on biscuits? Not yet.'

'KitKats, right?' says JP.

Mac nods.

'Or Mars Bars.' JP is rubbing one flat palm against his chest – he is relaxed. 'When they were launched however many years ago, there was no market research or, what did you call it – Satisfaction . . . Gradient?'

'Arc.'

'Right!' JP snorts. 'There was no *science*. No chocolate-bar *science*. But KitKats and Mars Bars were made and they succeeded. Because they tasted good. And the chocolate bars that didn't succeed, because they tasted bad – failed. Your new chocolate bar? It'll either succeed or fail, and it won't have fuck all to do with your research.'

Even Mac – placid as a goldfish – would normally take small issue with this. Having already allowed, with good nature, his career to be called pointless, it is now being rubbed in like salt. And – in ignorance.

But such is the joy on his skin, running in a ribbon over to Alessia, shining like a shield and a strength – so far into his organs has the happiness penetrated – that he, genuinely – doesn't care.

'Maybe,' he says, weighing up how long it would take, and with what little dividend, to convince JP of the validity of his type of sociology, 'maybe not. You've got to remember that KitKats and Mars Bars were launched into a virtually empty marketplace. Consumers today are overwhelmed with choice. Along your lines, though,' Mac says, his tone lifting, compassionately trying to find a strand of conversation with more concord, 'Alessia is really good at calling exactly that – at determining what needs further research and what doesn't. What is essential to Arnold's, and what is – like you said, mate – pointless. You know, I get tunnel vision. Whereas she can really take a step back and call a blind alley a blind alley.'

'Alessia? That chick?' JP looks like a well of horror has just yawned in front of him.

'Yeah, mate,' says Mac, beaming.

'*She*,' says JP, his face still coiled, 'works for *Arnold's Biscuits*?'

'Didn't you know that?'

'No. How could I know that? I've never met her before. She's a complete random.'

'Mate, I thought I said I was seeing a chick from work? Maybe I didn't. I thought I did.'

The currents in JP's head are short-circuiting – all the

broken wires are sparking and fizzing at their tips, a light show.

'Maybe you did,' JP says, his voice flat. He drains his glass. There is a silence, into which Mac radiates.

'She's that chick,' JP monotones, remembering, 'you said you were rooting.'

'Fuck. Is that what I said?' says Mac, looking nervously over to where Alessia talks to Story.

JP ignores him. 'What, so how long has she worked there?'

'Not long. 'Bout a year.'

'So you've been sleeping with her for a year?'

'No, mate,' Mac lowers his voice. 'No. We first got together about, ah, six months ago, although, obviously, when she first started, I thought she was hot—'

'Yes,' JP concurs, on instinct.

'But I didn't reckon she was, you know, interested. We've only been seeing each other seriously, like – you know what I mean – for a couple of months.'

JP looks at Mac. There is something of an age gap, five years, maybe more, between the two – between Mac and – Alessia.

'Are you her boss?' JP says.

'Yep.'

'Well then, mate – doesn't take a rocket scientist.'

The junior researcher, screwing her boss – it is a joke Alessia and Mac have already shared, and owned. So, once again, Mac is in whole armour. He laughs. 'Whatever, mate,' he says. 'We told our boss last week, and he's cool with it.'

JP wants to ask the question – *Are you serious, then? Are you serious about this woman?* – but he does not know how to form the words, in his mouth or in his heart. And, anyway – Mac's face is answer enough. He is – covered; in joy; in

256

certainty; in somebody else. And he's brought her to Vinnie's wedding, for fuck's sake. JP feels as if he is looking at his friend through the wrong end of a telescope, as if Mac has been, in a single second, pulled back at speed, and now looks back at him from a kilometre's distance. It is like he has put on a hat, and gloves, and a coat, and his extremities are no longer visible. He looks like a man in a bowler hat from a Victorian photograph, substantial, yet far away.

There is a moment, here, where JP could decide to let this space mutate into alienation. Certainly, his nature leads him that way. But, instead, he says, with mouth curving down and disinterested tone,

'Right. Good onya, mate.'

The tables are named after Vincent and Tree's favourite movies, and Story is at *The Godfather Part II*. He has been in silence now for about five minutes. Seriously, dude. Five minutes. He cuts edges off the inedible beans with the side of his fork, and pretends to eat them, just so that he doesn't have to sit there, silent and immobile, like a weirdo.

On his left is an old auntie of Vincent's, who comes from rural New South Wales, and she and Story seem to be having different conversations when they attempt to talk to one other.

So do you and Vincent work at the hotel together?

No, ah, no, I work for the Reserve Bank of Australia.

So, you're not a friend of Vincent's?

Yes. I am. I'm one of Vincent's groomsmen. He and I were at school together.

How do you know, Teresa, then?

Well, er, because she and Vinnie are together.

She looks nice in her dress, doesn't she?

257

She looks great. I've known Teresa since we were at school, as well, though.

I hardly know her, though, she's never said much to me. They all say she's a nice girl.

Conversations which Story struggles to follow. Thankfully, he and the auntie have now reached an impasse. They have given up.

On his right is a girl, a friend of Tree's, whom he talks to with even more difficulty than the difficult old auntie.

The trouble is, the girl — Miranda — laughing with the neighbour on her other side — is — how would you say it? Stunning. Clear and vivid and quick to smile. She introduced herself, and those few small words from her mouth grew and clung like pondweed, until they filled the room, covered over everything, crept and bred into Story's mouth, until he couldn't speak, couldn't defend himself from even the dust in the air.

What was he to do, in this bog, in this cloud? As slow as mud, and as stupid. All he can do is look at her, look at her — and then try, with all his density, to look away — to not look — to not look at her as she sits, here, beside him.

She has a strong English accent. Her hair is an indescribable colour, a mixture of brown and auburn, like a leaf. And during their one conversation so far, Story cast himself as the dotty aunt.

So, erm, how do you know Vincent and Teresa?

I work with Teresa. How about you?

Doing, um, nail-painting, right? Manicures?

Yes. That, and other things. All beauty treatments. Are you a friend of Vincent's?

Tree once said to me she wanted to open up her own salon. Uh. I remember her saying that.

Did she? She's never said that to me. I think we'd all like to do that, one day – be your own boss. What do you do?

Vincent and I were at school together. That's how I know them.

It was excruciating. Story is aware of his own dullness, strangeness, and three steps behind. But he is powerless to stop it. Sitting next to Miranda, Story feels that he has a lamp in his face, a policeman's torch, and in its blinding light his whole self is wrong – his shirt, his shoes, his feet inside them. He wants to hide himself, and sit up straight, and somehow be better.

He feels ugly. Because she is so lovely.

And because he can see himself at this one moment, through the alcohol and the constructed social personality – he can see himself as he must seem to her – can see himself as he is; as he really is.

'Did you really run off,' Pinyata asks, 'when Vincent was being beaten up?'

'No, Yaya!' Tintin protests. 'Of course not! You know me, don't you? You know me by now.' He has taken both her hands, and is looking into her eyes. 'You know I wouldn't do something like that. Vinnie was just going for a cheap laugh.'

'Tintin,' says Mac, smiling fondly, 'don't tell porkies.'

'Mac, due respect, mate.' Tintin is irritated. 'You weren't even there.'

'True. But I saw you guys the next day. Vincent could barely walk. Stavvo had two black eyes, and JP's nose was wiped half across his face. But you were looking pretty dapper – not a scratch on you. And the others *said* you did a runner.'

'Don't listen to him, Pinyata. He's just winding us up.'

'Tinny, I understand if you're ashamed. You don't want

your woman thinking you're a coward.' Mac stops to laugh. 'But it was years ago. Get over it. I'm sure, today, you'd stay and fight like a man.'

'Bullshit, Mac. Bullshit. I didn't go anywhere and I'm no bloody coward.' Tree banned the donning of any chapeaus by the groomsmen, so Tintin's thinning hair is there for all to see. Has he been colouring in his scalp, with *pen*? Surely not. Surely not even Tinny.

'Hey, Stav!' Mac calls. 'Stav! Can I borrow you, mate?'

Stavvo walks over, his perennial, natural saunter, from where he had been standing with his wife and two other guests.

'Yep,' he says.

'Did Tintin, or did Tintin not, run away like a girl when you blokes were lynched on Curl Curl?'

'He did,' confirms Stav. ''Course he did. Vincent said it all in his speech. It was a pretty bloody good speech, I reckoned.'

Pinyata cleaves to the change of subject. 'Oh, it was gorgeous,' she says, 'when he said he couldn't manage without her! That was so lovely.'

'How long you two over here for?' Stavvo asks, marvelling at how Australian and girly Pinyata sounds, while looking so big and foreign. To Stav, she looks different to just your usual darkie. She looks like one of those tribal leader types. A chieftain. With her huge hair and her height. 'You've been here since the buck's, right?' To Stavvo's surprise, his wife, Cher, doesn't seem to find her foreignness noteworthy. All Cher said about Pinyata is that she is wearing a white, strapless dress, as if she was at her own wedding. *It takes a certain type of woman to do that*, Cher said.

'Yeah,' says Tintin, still affronted, but also relieved at the topic change. 'We're here until the middle of next week—'

'What have you been up to?' Stavvo asks. 'You should've come round.'

'Ah, mate,' says Tintin, 'we woulda loved to. But we been so tired with the film, and everything – we've just been going flat out – like sitting up all night – that this is such a good break for us. We've just been lying on the beach, doing nothing, eh?'

'Yeah,' giggles Pinyata. 'It's been *amazing*!'

'Not like *you* need to work on your tan!' says Stavvo, smiling, to her.

'No!' Pinyata laughs, her life experience having trained her to complicity.

Tintin beams.

She is here alone. He is certain of that now. There is no one to dance with her, except Story, who has trundled her once around the floor while she laughed at him. But now she sits on a bench outside, and watches the dancers sweating and pumping their arms through the glass doors. One leg is crossed over the other.

JP is drunk, thank God. A good drunk, a drunk that feels helpful.

'G'day,' JP says. 'It's JP. Story's mate.'

'I know who you are, JP!' Kali smiles, and stands up.

She kisses him on one cheek.

'You're not dancing,' says JP.

'Neither are you.'

'Ha! No. Your – husband's not here.'

'No, he's not.' If Guy was here, he'd be pissed and up for it and forcing her to dance with him, telling her all the while that she had to *relax*, that her dancing was *uptight*, that she had to just *let go*, and she would stiffen and stiffen until she walked away from him to be safe on her own. He'd reprimand her for that, too. It is a relief to be without him. 'He's in South America. Some new oil refinery.'

'Oh, he's a – a –'

'Builder. Industrial buildings. Factories. Refineries. Mines.'

'That's right. How's business?'

Kali smiles. Shrugs. She still has that absence – the feeling that part of her is evaporated, somewhere else.

'How are you, JP?'

She looks even smaller than before, a willow lost inside her loose trousers. She has taken her jacket off, and wears a grey silk vest. Her arms are pale and smooth and fine, elbows big and knuckly at their centre.

'Not too bad. I'm all right.'

'How's your work? Law, isn't it?'

'Yes.' Her husband is in South America building multi-million-pound steel empires, and he is here. Same desk. Same computer. Same dead end as ever. 'Not too bad. Law's law, you know. And, in my bit of it, nothing much changes.'

'What's your bit of it?'

'Corporate.'

She is about to fly away. JP knows it. The tables around them are mostly empty – the dance floor is full, and there is a group around the bar. But Kali is not likely to join either the dancers or the drinkers, so she will fly away. JP has nothing with which to catch her. Only his hands.

'How come you're here?' JP asks. 'Story didn't say you'd be here.'

'I've always had a soft spot for Vincent,' Kali says. 'He used to come round to our house a lot, when we were kids. And Tree has done my nails for years.' Kali wiggles her fingers, and laughs. 'I see her every two weeks. You become friends, after a while.'

'That makes sense. I just. You know. It was a rude question. I didn't mean it to sound like that. You're just so – other, you know? I'm not used to seeing you as part of my mates. I mean – you're not.'

'Other?' Kali echoes.

'Er, different. You know? You're my mate's big sister.'

'Am I? Still? Even though we're adults now?'

JP looks at Kali, who lightly looks back at him. She is – a punch in the heart. His head smashed against a wall.

She is older, yes. But it shows in frailty, rather than age. As if life had slowly pressed the colour out of her. If anything, it has made her more beautiful.

He looks away. If she moves he will catch her. Catch her in his hands and force her to remain. He will crush her in his hands like a butterfly. He wouldn't care if he killed her.

'Well, that's probably when I know you from. Back then. Not like we see a lot of each other now,' he says.

'No. It's nice to see you, though.'

She sounds like she is about to leave. *Nice to see you. Goodbye.* JP panics – he tosses words out, as a net. As a bomb in front of her. The road is smoking, she cannot pass.

'I remember you swimming,' he throws, 'when you used to swim.'

Kali looks surprised, says nothing.

'I saw you swim, you know. At the University Championships.' JP is talking fast. 'You came second.'

'Yes! That'd be right,' Kali says.

'Come on! Second is bloody good! I couldn't swim like you did.'

'I really wasn't that good.'

'You were.'

'You're funny,' says Kali. 'You sound like my dad.' She pauses, while her own words settle on her. 'Anyone can swim decently if they have the training.'

'That's bullshit,' says JP. 'Even if everybody had the training you did, I can tell you nobody in this room could swim like you did. Some people are just naturals.'

'You're really kind,' Kali says.

'Why did you stop?'

Kali looks at JP, her eyebrows up. He is fierce and sensitive and just as he always was. She is in empty space here, with him. She thinks she can talk, and no harm will come.

'I felt sad,' she says.

Kali has never said this before — she hadn't even known if it was true until this moment. There is a blanket in the air, a low ozone above them.

'When you swam?'

'Yes. Pathetic, isn't it?'

'No,' says JP.

'It is, though. To give up all that. Give up all that training — because you *feel sad*.'

'No, it's not. I understand. Swimming is sad.'

Kali laughs. 'You're making fun of me,' she smiles.

'I'm not! I promise I'm not. I'm just saying — I find swimming sad, too. And I'm not even a swimmer — like you.'

'The ocean's all right. But it's too big. You can't swim cleanly in there.'

'Too much else,' agrees JP.

'Yes.'

They look at each other.

'Did you use to think when you trained?' JP asks.

'Yes.'

'After a while, when you get into a rhythm, you start thinking, don't you?' He remembers her, accepting silver, her face sad like a moth, and he wishes he could have died right then. Then they wouldn't be here, now, separate.

'Yes,' says Kali. She is looking at JP's face. At his flat bones and small features.

'Do you smoke, or something?' JP asks.

'No. Why? Are you after a cigarette?'

'No. I just saw you were sitting out here, by yourself. Thought you might be smoking.'

'I don't smoke. Just came outside to be outside. I love it when it's warm like this, at night. I have to go soon, anyway.'

The wine and beer swill and sing to each other in JP's head – they ask questions. The beer is saying to the wine, *Do you know he has wanted her for twenty years?* And the wine replies, replies to the beer, *Tell her. Tell her then.*

But JP says nothing. Because he may be a Rumpelstiltskin, a witch, a troll under a bridge – but unlike the rest of these fuckers he does know what love is. He knows it is a tinder-box. He knows it is the open sea. He knows that it is silent – that it has no words.

Cannie had agonised over wearing a flower in her hair.

She was not the kind of woman to carry off a showy bloom tucked into curls – there was nothing flamenco about her – her hair was textureless and mid-blond – and that after two hours in the salon. But nonetheless she wanted a flower, today. She had bought her dress after seeing it in a magazine, and in the magazine the model had a flower in her hair, and the model had looked gorgeous.

Cannie had had her eyebrows done, her hair cut and styled, she had a new dress, and had spent time on her make-up. She wanted the flower in her hair, even if it would look silly, even if it wouldn't suit her. A red rose, the size of her fist, petals like boats.

She had thought she might follow JP, when she saw him wandering outside, his trousers two inches too short and showing the gamut of his socks, looking clear, and untroubled, and as handsome as he has ever been. She might have a cigarette with him, if that's what he was doing – once, twice a year, she fancied it, when it was a warm night and she felt nimble and liquid.

But for some reason Cannie stops when she sees JP talking to Story's sister, who has been sitting outside on a bench. For some reason Cannie stops as she stands, and watches them. JP is looking at Kali's face. Which is not beautiful, Cannie thinks – too pallid and feathery for that. But with a translucent quality that makes you stare – she understands why JP looks at her as he does. Ethereal, like an imagined light. The light you saw when you died! She was thinner, too, thinner than she used to be. Really very thin – her bare arms were about half the size of Cannie's. It made her look younger than when she was a teenager – as young as a child. And JP next to her looked like a Goliath. JP is looking at Kali, in a way that Cannie can't hold – it petrifies her. Cannie cannot take her eyes off them, and she cannot move.

With a panic she does not understand, Cannie scans around for Kali's husband. Where is he? Is Kali here alone? Why is she talking to JP alone, without her husband here?

'Your flower's fallen out!' says a voice behind Cannie. It is one of the Cammeray girls she knows vaguely, from Tree's year, all with terrible, vulgar feathers perched like pigeons on novel parts of their heads.

266

'Sorry?' says Cannie, turning around and putting her hand to her head.

'Your flower!'

The girl – the woman, as she is now – reaches behind Cannie and with a twisting prickle of pulled hair releases Cannie's rose.

'See?'

She holds it in her hand, bedraggled and starved, for Cannie to witness.

Cannie takes the rose from her, petals falling as she does.

'Thanks,' Cannie says.

'No worries. You going out for a ciggie?'

'No,' says Cannie.

Petals are falling from the centre at the slightest touch.

'Excuse me,' says Cannie, and presses her way to the loo, to throw the ugly, dead thing away. How stupid – how stupid and sentimental and drunk she is – that a spoiled flower is making her cry.

'Story,' Vincent says – it is late, there is a small group of them left, now – 'do you know why I love you?' His arm is resting routinely on Tree's shoulders.

'You're on my hair, Vinnie,' she says to him. He moves his arm.

'Er, because you're drunk?'

'No, *not* because I'm drunk. My drunkenness may be a . . . fact, but it does not involve my love for you.'

Miranda laughs.

'I love you,' Vincent Batty continues, 'because you are the only straight man in Australia to drink through a straw. You always have been. And you always will be. And I love you for it. *You*,' says Vincent, on a roll, 'are a fucken maverick, my friend. You are fearless. And I drink to your health.' He takes a slosh from the full glass.

Tree is laughing now, and even Story is smiling.

'Hey, what are you even drinking, mate?'

'Fizzy pop, dude,' says Story. 'Fizzy pop.'

'What, some kind of shandy? Some kind of straw shandy?'

'Southern Comfort and ginger ale. It's genius, dude. Seriously. Way of the fucking future.'

'Southern Comfort!' pipes Tree, excitedly, as if suddenly recognising a long-lost friend. 'Southern Comfort and lemonade! We used to drink that when we were kids! It was really good. I don't know why we stopped, actually. I haven't had it for *ages*.'

'You stopped drinking it because you turned thirteen, babe,' Vincent Batty says.

Miranda laughs – again. She can't help it when Vincent talks. 'Did you guys all go to school together?'

Story realises that she is addressing him. 'Yeah.' He clears his throat. 'Well. We did. Some of us. Me, um, Vincent Batty, obviously, and, er, JP and Mac. And Stavvo. You've met them, right?'

'It's really lovely all of you from school are still friends.' That contained, bordered English accent.

'Oh, yeah, well, yeah.' He coughs. 'Do you have old friends, like, from school?'

'Not really,' says Miranda. 'We moved around, when I was a kid. So I never really had friends from one place.'

'Yeah, no,' says Story. 'That must be, ah—'

'You're a banker?'

'No. Not really. I mean, sort of. I work for the Reserve Bank. Of Australia. The English equivalent is, uh – the Reserve Bank . . . of . . . I mean, the Bank of England.'

'Oh, I see.'

Motherfuck. Even with alcohol coming out of his ears like cartoon steam, Story knows he's being the most boring, fucking boring fuck in the history of fucking boredom. Miranda had been laughing, she had been *laughing*, they had all been *laughing*, and putting aside Story's knotted stomach, they had been having *fun*. And then by some majestic accident they appear to be talking to each other alone, and Story just fucking *kills* any fun that had been there – like, clubs it over the head until it's dead on the floor. They're talking to each other like they're old people at some family barbecue, as if not a single drop had passed their lips. The sheer, fucking inept boringness of him has sobered them both up. He's kryptonite. Fucking kryptonite.

And why? Why? *Why?* Story was normally the first to laugh. The first to say, *Lighten up, dude.*

He could still save it; change the wind; say to her, *Have you ever been in love before?* Or *Have you ever been to the Bayswater Brasserie?* Or, that old ice-breaker, *Do you fancy a line?* Although, he senses, that might not go down so well. How the fuck do you talk to someone when you want to disappear and be reborn as another man?

'I'm moving to London, though,' Story bluffs, 'to do a—'

'Hi.' A friend of Miranda's has come over, and directs this perfunctory greeting at Story.

'Hi,' he says back. But she has turned to Miranda already.

'I'm getting a taxi home, Mirry. Are you coming?'

Miranda turns to Story. 'Looks like I'm going,' she says. 'It was nice to meet you.'

'Good to meet you.' That is what he should have said to her two hours ago. Fucktard.

'You too.'

Miranda gives Story a kiss on the cheek, and walks away.

Story stands, alone, and from some corner of his consciousness he watches Miranda say goodbye to Tree and Vincent, with a comfortable arm around their shoulders.

Then, she is leaving the room, she is walking out into the night, and Story is thinking to himself, *Is she as young as she looks?* And he is thinking to himself that suddenly the drink is catching up with him – is it the drink, or is it something else? And he is thinking to himself that out there she is in a taxi and a driver is driving them back to wherever it is they live. And he is in the centre of this spinning, gurning room, and it is – it is – it is as if while the room whirls faster around him, everything inside his vortex has become still. The stillness, again.

33

Story is in a taxi. He has opened the cab window and leans his face towards the moving air, like a dog on a hot day, ears flapping in the current.

As long as his eyes are open, he feels okay. He can focus, on the trees, on the pavements. When they speed past the occasional person, Story reels a little – it is better to concentrate on the bricks and mortar.

They are close to home; Story feels for his keys in his pocket. There is Rice Bowl on the corner, now shut up. There is the tapestry showroom with the gigantic oyster shell in the window. There is the Jaguar yard, glossy, dead cars reflecting the streetlamps. And there – is something new. A piece of graffiti, large white letters painted the length of the corner wall:

I'm so high I could eat a star

Blink, and you've missed it. The taxi has moved past.
Story turns his head back, but he can no longer see it.
Blood rushes to Story's head, and he feels like he might be sick. He doesn't want to forget, the words he has just seen.

He opens his eyes, as if they have matchsticks propping them – and breathes.

Finally, he is at the door to his building. He presses the fob to the pad, and the familiar buzz receives him. As the lift goes up, he leans his head against the wall. In the kitchen, he grips the sink, before pouring himself a glass of water, then another, then another.

What a fucking idiot! *The Reserve Bank . . . of England.* What a fucking, fucking idiot. Story closes his eyes, as if he might disappear along with the room. His balance starts to rumble; he opens them again.

He has been in denial about it for a while, but as Story concentrates on staying upright, he admits to himself that he can no longer get away with drinking like this. When he was a teenager, he didn't actually know what a hangover was. He would say, *Fuck, I'm so hung over,* just because that's what you said. But, actually, even after a cheap wine and gin binge, he'd wake up after twelve hours' sleep feeling like a flower, clean and soft and ready for a croque monsieur.

In his twenties, the hangovers began, and, ironically, he now no longer wanted to say he was hung over. He wanted to stay quiet. Analgesics entered his life, along with coffee. And once or twice a hangover verged on blood poisoning, and he found himself lying on his side in bed, unable to move.

But these days – *fuck.* A night of drinking like tonight would decimate him until Monday. His body would feel creaky and angry and disrupted, he would have diarrhoea for a day, and his emotions would crawl on a wheel of meek horror. He'd heard Mac say it before, *I can't drink any more, mate, it kills me,* but Story had drolly put that down to Mac being a wanker. And as each of his own excesses washed up with a weekend of dreadfulness, he'd encourage himself to believe that he was sick. That he had a cold. A virus. A case of mild food poisoning.

But, with honesty smacking itself wee wee wee all the way home, there's no getting away from it – his body just can't take it any more. His body is just a little . . . bit . . . too . . . old.

Which is weird, because he's only thirty-five.

The graffiti that spun him round like a boxer comes back.

I'm so high I could eat a star.

He wishes he could show it to her. To that girl. Miranda.

Story feels a hollow, roiling envy of whoever it was that wrote those words with their big, white brush. Envy of a person who had ever felt that way, who had ever had such a high, up in the sky with their mouth wide open.

His highs had never taken him there. Drugs had taken him as far as brief, blissful harmonies, drumbeats, lordships of small alleyways. But never to anywhere so other that you could curl yourself out of your skin and fly, all muscle, to bite holes out of the sky.

What could take you there? If not a pill or a powder, then what?

Life had taken him to the highs of the Reserve Bank of Australia, Sydney, and now was pushing him towards the International Markets Institute, London. It had taken him to champagne and holidays and a threesome with two Westie slappers with big pores and ingrown hairs, who, it turned out, had stolen his credit card and defrauded him of nearly seven thousand dollars. It had taken him to Dexy's Gentleman's Club, to watch an old friend be humiliated and aroused like a roped-up dog, and then, a week later, to Cammeray Golf Club, to watch that old friend put a ring on his highschool sweetheart.

273

'Fuck,' Story says out loud, and then shakes his head, as if trying to spray something away from himself.

He had waved Vincent Batty and Teresa off in a taxi, and Christ knows he wishes them well.

I'm so high I could eat a star.

Life brought him to the Cammeray Golf Club, to *The Godfather Part II*, to sit next to her.

Her face is beautiful. Not just one of these bodies that conned you into thinking they were something more than legs and arms and organs and plucked hair.

And all he is – is a man. No archangel, fallen from somewhere greater, sucking stars.

If she were here, the strange, silent sediment could blow off everything, and all could be as it was before. Maybe she could do that.

Story can picture her coming home with him, laughing, and getting into his bed. The image is so vivid, so inflamed, that Story opens his eyes wide, his lids stretching far enough for his eyeballs to fall out on to the floor and land with a splat, to stare back up at him. He opens and opens and opens his eyes, and he feels – terrified.

Terrified like when he was a virgin schoolboy and the thought of being with a girl was more frightening than the thought of being without one. When his first successful kiss was like a plummet into icy water.

He wants to leave this flat. He wishes he could have left the wedding and gone somewhere else, never here. Here, there is too much old. Old clothes; older than him. Too much waiting, for a thing to happen. Too much pretending, that life was the rainbow you had expected.

The room is still. Story has in his hand a talisman, in the shape of that English girl, Tree's friend, the beautician, with

long fingers like a Madonna and autumn-brown hair growing out of her temples.

He is frightened of her, of Miranda, but it is an enchanted
type of fear – Story keeps her held, in his hand. If he left, she
might come with him. He goes from the kitchen to the bedroom, from wood to carpet, through the small corridor. His
face is apprehensive, as if he were walking the plank.

34

Cannie is sitting on a bench in the Camperdown Memorial Park in Newtown. Behind the bench is a wall, monumental sandstone, covered in graffiti, and behind the wall is the heavy net of trees that shades the Camperdown Cemetery. She's lived in Sydney all her life, Cannie, and yet has never been in there. Why would she? There's been no reason. Its last dead were buried a hundred years ago. Convicts and shipwreck victims and lieutenant-governors; a strange, distant dead that have no claim on today's sun-tanned city, flat whites, yum cha, pleasure boats.

There are probably more dead under where she sits. The whole park used to be the graveyard, she knows that much. All those bodies are likely still oozing beneath her, their roof thudding from the dog walkers and joggers, and from the bands and litter and kissing students when the Newtown Festival sets up. Could they have guessed, when on their feet and alive, that this gold-rush harbour, full of hot, open sky and sticky trees, would ever become what it is now, glossy and urban and flirtatious?

There will be brides under there, too. Like Tree, pretty in their dresses. Dead, as if they never lived.

Cannie had tried, at the wedding, to imagine herself in white, with her arms showing. It didn't come easily. Neither the thought of the signature – your name, and life, and self – tied up in ink to somebody else's. Why do it? Why share yourself like that?

She looks at her feet. She has stretched them out so they rest on a bald patch of grass. Next to them are her shoes – mid-high, sensible heels that she has worn to pretty much every wedding for the last five years. They have the bobbles and nubs of her feet within them, even empty like this – the bulb of her big toe has made a mound in the suede, and there are splayed-out pockets where her feet are at their widest. With the ghosts of her feet still within them, the suede is thinning in patches, and the heels too low ever to be glamorous, they look to Cannie like the shoes of a scullery maid – like the shoes of some poor girl buried in the grave-yard at her back. Her mauve polish, self-applied, is chipping around the top of her toenails.

Cannie is wearing yesterday's clothes, minus the nude tights. Her calves could do with the sun. Despite the high summer, they are dough-pale, and uniformly covered with a budding stubble. She is wearing the black and red floral dress she bought especially for the wedding, and a silvery shawl that matches the colour of her shoes.

There is only one dog walker in the whole park, wearing shades although the sun has not cracked. It is that warm, grey light, chasing the last of the night. The other benches along the wall are as yet empty. No one to judge her in her party clothes from the night before, to make smirking assumptions that would all be correct.

Cannie has walked to this bench, at slow pace, down two roads and across another, from a student house where she has

277

just slept with a stranger. A stranger called Ben, who is in his second year at Sydney Uni, studying architecture. Only five more years left, as he had said to her, smiling. He had been gauche, and funny, and skinny, and luminously, invincibly young – fifteen years younger than her; technically (and mind-bogglingly) young enough to be her son. He had taken her home to his tatty, shared terrace, to his crumpled room and unmade bed, and at no moment had she wavered, at no moment did she regret the moment before. As Cannie sits here in the air, on her bench, in the dawn, she smiles at the fresh memory.

'Hey,' he had said to her, 'what happened to your flower?'

And she had been so surprised, that this young man had been looking at her, had noticed her enough to see the flower in her hair, and noticed her again now to see that it was gone – noticed her, and continued to notice her – that she looked at him blankly, without defence. He, along with the alcohol, had chivvied her to dance, and she'd learnt that he paid his way through uni by valet parking at the Source Hotel, where Vincent worked.

'B-list guest,' he'd said to Cannie. 'Only got the late call in when no one else could come.'

That had made Cannie laugh, the baldness of it. 'Me too,' she'd said.

Later, when Tree and Vincent had waved a woozy good-bye in their foamed taxi, and Cannie had gathered her shawl from the back of a chair and was making to call a cab, she felt a squeeze under her elbow.

'I'm meeting some mates at a bar,' he said. 'There's a band playing. D'you wanna come along?'

Cannie in her sensible heels. Cannie in her 70-denier tights. Cannie with her fringe and her trunk and her rectangular face, her daily disposable contact lenses and her apartment in Neutral Bay.

To say it was out of character would be understatement. But Cannie went along to the heaving bar with the band on stage – the kind of place that she didn't like, that was alien and ill fitting as a fig leaf – and yet felt completely at ease. And when at two in the morning and feeling lead tired she reckoned she needed to get home, he'd asked if she'd like to come to his instead.

It had been a surprise, that question –

'D'you fancy coming back to mine?'

And that unmistakable smile of proposition around his lips.

But the surprise had landed soft like a scarf, and it only took Cannie a moment – a small moment – to say, *why not?*

She didn't care what the others in the bar thought of her – this corporate woman in wedding clothes, years older than anybody else. She didn't care what they must have looked like together, as he put his hand up her dress as she climbed the stairs ahead of him. She didn't care if his dick were livid with the insides of a million other girls, if his bed had the moult of other long hairs all over its sheets. She didn't even care if he was doing this for a bet.

Cannie didn't care because it was her choice. Some passing note in this architect boy – whom she would contentedly never see again – had played a simple tune to her, and she had let herself out of her own skin for long enough to sing along.

They'd had sex twice – two and a half times if you counted one failed attempt in between – and Cannie hadn't slept. She'd lain awake in his bed, dense with tiredness but alive with something else, looking at the dark shapes of his room and at his narrow back. About half the size of JP's, Cannie mused. Her hand lay over his small, sleeping shoulders, idly picking at his skin.

The room seemed familiar. The thin, ungenerous curtains, too small for their window. The desk, with a dirty plate, a mug, a glass or two. The laptop on the floor. Clothes in corners and draped over surfaces. A couple of stacks of books. iPod speakers. An empty bottle of champagne on a top shelf, kept from some special occasion – so things mattered to him. She liked him for that.

Cannie had never lived like this at uni, but many of her friends had. This could be then. For all the time she felt had passed, this could be fifteen years ago. She could creep along the horrible old carpet to the bathroom, and look in the mirror, and this could be then. Fifteen years erased. The reflection would be thinner, lineless and clear of all the knowledge that has flooded the time between. Tree and Vincent would not be married – far from it. Tree would be at beauty school and Vinnie would be shagging one of the barmaids from the pub where he worked. Mac would be at uni in Melbourne, learning how to use contact lenses, spraying saline into those little pots, placing his invisible, superhero sight safely next to his bed. Story would be bored, already, and learning to cook with that giant wok of his. JP – would be where? Playing rugby. Trying to pull. Smiling as unexpectedly as a whale breaking the surface of the water. Who knows. And Cannie – she would be asleep, alone, with no lines yet on her face.

Tell any one of them, then – those fifteen years ago when this student house and one-night stand was theirs – that in time to come they would all be in Sunday best at Vincent Batty and Tree's wedding, at the Cammeray Golf Club, wearing dickie bows and pashminas, eating dry chicken and wet vegetables, raising their glasses in hollow toasts – and not one of them would have credited it. Except Cannie. She saw it all coming. She also saw JP look at Kali, as they stood outside by the glass doors – but that, she was not ready to admit to herself, yet.

The sun is opening like an egg. Cannie can feel its first gobbets of warmth, obdurate and pure. She should go home. Summon the energy from somewhere extraordinary and walk to King Street to find a cab. She considers for a moment walking barefooted, so as not to have to enter again her scullery shoes. But, no – her character has not changed entirely from a few hours of joy, as this past night has been. She nudges back into her shoes; her feet are themselves, once more.

35

JP had watched Kali leave the wedding. She had kissed Story on the cheek, before she walked away. The two people JP loved best, he reckoned. Even though Story was an A-type tosser.

JP, along with Stavvo, was among the last to leave.

'Where to now?' JP had said.

'Home, mate.' Stavvo was swinging on his heels, eyebrows up and face stuck in a smile. 'Got wifey waiting.'

Probably better that way. Better to be alone, JP thought.

He walked, and all he could think is that the last twenty years had been smoke. They didn't exist. The last moment in his life had been that day at Story's house in Kirribilli, when he had first seen her. In jeans, and a short T-shirt that showed a few millimetres of her narrow stomach.

'Hi,' she'd said, and those two letters had fanned around JP's gullet and crushed the heart out of him. It gasped up, out of this throat, and lay there croaking on the floor.

And then – today. Seeing her bare arms and expensive clothes, and feeling her politeness like cold air in his face. No time in between that first time, and today. No years of touching other girls and sitting behind his desk at Redvale, no moving house or throwing up or running with a rugby ball. Nothing but smoke.

Had she stepped close to him, for a moment in their conversation? Had the hairs of her arm touched his sleeve?

Married to another man, as successful and rich as JP is not. With a son. He, JP, was just her brother's mate. She, Kali, was just polite.

Had he kissed her, as they spoke by the bench, and had she moved away, and said no – then his life would have been over. The next twenty years, and the next, would be without gravity or weather. As it is – unkissed, untried – she lived on, in the cavity of his skull, and he lived, too, in a next-door vault.

JP has come to Taylor Square, to an old crematorium that is now a twenty-four-hour bar. He sits on a stool, and drinks. He has taken his bow tie off, and his hired jacket has fallen to the floor, which he doesn't notice.

Vincent and Tree. As inspiring together as toast. But good on them for doing it, for being together, for having a go. JP'd acquitted himself of his duties well. He'd posed for photo after photo, smiling with his teeth, standing in line-ups, holding Tree's feet as she lay across the groomsmen. All the required stuff.

Another wedding, everybody buying into the specialness. Saying, *Doesn't she look gorgeous in her dress?* JP wearing the suit and talking the talk and pleased at the craic of it, in one part – but, in another, thinking only of her. His heart slowly accepting her presence – evolving to the surprise of it; growing legs and walking out of the sea.

JP's head is bowed. He wishes he could run, now. Or get on his bike to the pool, and swim. He can't be a better man inside, but the outside can improve.

He stands up, and the stool somehow clatters down behind him. JP drops to the floor, like his strings have been cut.

'I'm all right,' he says, reaching for the edge of the bar and trying to tug himself up.

The bouncer has come over from the door, takes him by one arm and pulls him to standing. 'Time to go home, mate,' he says.

'All right. I'm all right,' says JP.

He is being navigated to the street — it is not an unpleasant feeling, to relinquish control for this moment, like a skater, being pushed along the ice by your partner. As the doorman deposits him, JP feels for the ground once more.

'Just need to sit down for a second, mate,' he says.

'Not here, you don't,' says the bouncer.

'Fair enough, you dickhead.'

JP laughs to himself, and on his hands and knees crawls towards the other side of the square, where he can rest his back against a wall. His jacket, with the bow tie in the pocket, relics of another man, remain inside the bar, on the floor, lost to JP for ever. No time has passed, at all.

36

She'd come to swim where there was no rip. A place to float. She should be swimming in the pool – the pool is what she knew. In the pool there were no currents to pull at your empty muscles. No sharks.

But, in the pool, everybody swam in straight lines, like ants carrying leaves. And as you become an ant – as JP had said – you start to think.

Kali remembers that silver medal, so soon after Dad had died. She hadn't known that JP was there. She had thought that no one was there. Not Mum, not Story – it was too soon. There was too much to do at the house. With Dad's will. With the letters and the flowers and the clothes in the cupboards that no longer had a body to lie with.

She had thought she was alone, that day. And yet it turns out, years later – that she wasn't. That JP had been there, watching her. Strange, for a memory to be rewritten, by somebody else.

And now, after their conversation at the wedding, here she is, in a black one-piece dug out from the back of a drawer, floating on her back. She opens her eyes occasionally to check she hasn't drifted too far, turns to her front and swims back towards the shore. The tide here is so gentle the waves feel like nothing more than speed bumps, little belches of water underneath.

'The fountain of youth.'

That's what Dad had called the ocean.

As a child Kali had been happy on the beach. Obviously she had. Everybody had. They were all in Nippers and they all went up north to Avoca for holidays. All the kids had lean calves from playing cricket in sand, boys and girls together. They all had blond skullcaps and dark shoulders and they all squinted with bare eyes at the scouring light. You existed outside, with sand in your creases, wearing whatever T-shirts and shorts were nearest and clean. Food on the beach, grilled on one of the communal barbecues, adults eating in the shade of trees, kids sitting unmindful in the midday heat. On holiday, you'd use the ocean to clean yourself and rinse off during the day – forgetting the sticky crust it left on you. That taut salt shell became like a second skin.

It was as her teens became her twenties, and going to the beach became a choice rather than a routine, that Kali found herself staying away. There was a cut-throat feeling to the Sydney shoreline, a primitive chaos to the way you marked your territory and spread your feathers, the way you came and went in packs and herds and growing and splintering numbers. Besides, she was training, then, and her place was the pool. Which had a beginning and an end, not this great, vast middle that was the ocean.

Here, in the salt, you could swim and swim, and when would you turn back? Where were the edges? What if you swam and didn't stop? Whether that feeling – of the fearsome endlessness – came from the ocean or from her own insides, she doesn't know.

A swimming pool contained you and gave you edges. A swimming pool gave you targets and laps and a big clock up on the wall. A swimming pool gave you a hard floor; your feet found it.

If she floated –

If she held her nerve and didn't look back –

Then she could die on the water. Join the other dead that must line the ocean floor. It might be a good way to die – getting cold. Or getting eaten. Or slowly burning; no water; under the sun. Sinking.

But – Kali can't sink. She knows that. If she emptied herself of oxygen and tied a cannon to her ankles, she'd still pop back up like a balloon – Jacob is her helium, and her lungs are full of him. She carries within her every tooth that has pushed through his gums, and fallen, and grown again; every hair that has pushed through his scalp, and fallen, and grown again. Jacob pulls her to life's surface, no matter how she falls.

Kali glides with the water, light as cellophane, and thinks of Jacob. She thinks of Guy. And, strangely, she thinks once more of JP. It is odd that the man at Vincent and Tree's wedding, who looked straight at her, and spoke with that unexpected grace, is the same man as the gruff teenager staring at the floor.

She rolls on to her stomach and slices her arms through the water, swimming a fast thirty metres before turning again to her back. Her body has not forgotten the strength it used to have, or the tracks in the water it used to travel.

Who was watching her now? She had thought she was alone that time, so long ago, when JP was in fact there. Who was watching her now?

'Dad,' Kali whispers, to herself, a sound as soft as cotton with the water in her ears.

She clears her throat.

'Dad,' she says again. Loud.

Careful, now, not to cry – not to lose another day to sadness. She has been sad for too long. Ever since Dad died and his memory disappeared like birds at gunshot, and you doubted your sanity, sometimes, wondering whether he had ever actually been alive. *Say his name*, she wanted to say, every Christmas, every gathering, when Mum stood there smiling as if he had never been. But Mum stopped saying his name – and they all did – even while his toothbrush was still in its glass; frightened of what they'd lost, the extent of it. Silence had come down like pitch, and they pretended, the three of them, that they had, not one of them, noticed the tar raining from the sky.

And it suited Kali, was the problem. The grief camouflaged easily, alongside her natural quietness, and still-ness; its grey edges trimmed her silver wings. But it confused her, too. It left her uncertain of any feeling that lived along-side it. How could she see any colours for what they were, if they all came through a grey filter?

Kali closes her eyes.

There was this family legend, of Kali, on the beach aged three. They were on holiday in Queensland, and the narrative went that Kali was paddling in the water. Mum was heavily pregnant with Story, and sat a few metres back, on the sand, while Dad erected a parasol over her. Kali had started splash-ing at something with her foot, and laughing – *Take a photo, quick; look, how adorable!*

As Dad retrieved the camera from the beach bag, Mum saw Kali lean down and lift the thing she had been kicking out of the water. At first she thought it was a carrier bag – a long, clear piece of plastic. But then, with horror, Florence realised that her daughter was lifting, like Salome holding the hair of St John, the translucent body of a jellyfish.

There had been screams, and Dad had, apparently, run and torn the jellyfish from her, thrown it far into the sea, before lifting his daughter brusquely out of the water. Kali had cried, in incomprehension, and had been swiftly taken to the hospital, where she was declared free from any sting or damage.

Mum, retelling, described it as a miracle. And Dad would laugh, and look at Kali in that way he sometimes looked at her, with his eyes shining, and he would say – *There is some-thing about you, Kali*, and all Kali took from those words was that he loved her.

Kali imagines a bank of jellyfish underneath her now, diffusing the light like lanterns, looking up at her underside. If she let herself, she could feel them brushing against her skin – ghosts, reapers, a death that she didn't – doesn't – want.

The sun is strobe white through her closed eyelids. She flips over to her front and looks; the beach is farther than it might be. With the weight of the sky bearing down on her back – the sky with stars and rocks and universal mass on its shoulders – the weight like a harness – Kali swims back, legs moving like ribbons through the water.

37

She hadn't replied to his text. He had sent it last night, and waited, with his phone hot in his hand, for an answer. An answer did not come. No answer when he turned the lights off and lay in bed, thinking of all the reasons, and, in the morning – still no answer – a disappointment like a damp firework.

At midday – a phone call, from an unknown number – and a heave in Story's throat like a boat was being pulled up there, tugged through his windpipe. Up it came, drying his mouth and trawling his heart as it did.

'Hello?' said Story.

It was the Mitsubishi dealership. 'G'day, Story,' said a spry voice. His car, a month after the promised three weeks, was ready to collect.

In the cab on the way to the yard, Story remembers his test drive, the endlessly talking salesman, and the girls collecting for charity in bikinis. A fucking cliché, this city, at times.

Today, Story does not look out of the window. He looks at his phone. Reads his text again.

Hi Miranda, hope you don't mind me getting in touch. It was good to meet you at Vincent's wedding. If you fancy dinner sometime drop me a line. Story

Fuck.

What if Tree had given him the wrong number? He could call her, just to make sure.

'Thanks.' Story pays the driver, walks into the showroom and meets his salesman, same as before, but gleeful today, showing Story the dashboard and controls and alloys and keyless locking that he had chosen those weeks ago. He dangles the keys, as if they are a g-string, and Story takes them in his hand.

'Cheers,' he says.

'Enjoy it, Story,' says the salesman. 'That's one helluva car you got there, Story. Worth the wait, eh, Story?'

And still, she hasn't answered.

Story sits inside the chemical, new-car smell.

Still, she hasn't answered.

He will put his phone away. He will put it in the glove box, a landmine on top of the owner's manual and service log. And if it sounds he will not crash the car to find it, he will not take it up as if it were a drowning child, he will not look at it until he gets home.

Story adjusts the seat and mirrors, so that the car is his. The engine starts, and he drives, cautiously, away. Should he roll down his window and wave? Is this one of those kinds of moments?

He looks ahead and his phone trings and Story pulls the car over immediately. He lifts it from the glove box, cradles it in his hand — a baby bird, it is, this phone.

It is not her.

He puts the phone down, on the passenger seat, this time, and drives on. Breathes deeply of the air, the factory air, spray and sealant.

Dear car, he texts in his head. *If I move to London, I will have to sell you back to that man. Story*

And the stupidity of this whole thing strikes him. Why did he buy a car? He has never wanted a car before, and he doesn't want one now. How could he have allowed his boredom to drift so far that it arrived at this — this machine, built by men for hours and days, for no end but to sit in the shade of his underground car park, unneeded.

It seems like a decade ago he was in there with Cannie, looking at trucks and coupes and open-tops, signing papers and leaving deposits. It seems like a false memory — mis-appropriated from a television programme or somebody else's life.

And now it is his, this car, this thing, it belongs to him, every tonne of it.

And how long ago was the wedding? A week. A week and a few days. It, too, in this mist, seems like years. Vincent, JP, Mac, dressed up in their suits like pirates, same as fancy dress, same as school uniform. They could be standing against the mesh fence at Grammar. And Story remembers her there, like somebody from a different time, laughing at a thing Vincent Batty had said.

Story presses the entry code on the car park gates, unused for four years. He reverses his new car into its space. It is cool, down here, and dark, like a forest floor. There is a motorcycle parked in the opposite bay, a snazzy, muscled thing in red and white. The car and the motorcycle can become friends, growl at each other when no one else is about, mourn when one gets mangled up or sold on.

As he walks away from his car, to the lift that will take him back up to the light, Story looks at his phone.

38

'You should call him,' says Lise.

Miranda is in the salon, where she, Tree and Lise work. They are with a regular client, an old lady called Rita, with a magnificently wrinkled face, who comes in every week to have her finger- and toenails painted dark blue.

'Who is this you're talking about?' she asks.

'A friend of Teresa's husband, Vincent,' Lise explains. 'He's this really lovely guy called Story; he and Vincent were at school together.'

'*Story*, did you say?' Rita asks.

'Yep. Story.'

'Is that a nickname?'

'No, it's his actual name, isn't it?'

'I don't know,' says Miranda.

'Is he foreign?' asks Rita. 'I don't mean foreign like you two girls. Not English. I mean from somewhere funny.'

'He's Australian,' says Miranda, moving the nail file rapidly back and forth. Rita's nails are thick.

'And he's after you, this *Story*, is he, Miranda?'

'Ah, no. Not really. I just met him at Teresa's wedding. We were at the same table.'

'Teresa's had her wedding already, has she!' says Rita.

'Yes! You didn't know? Ten days ago.'

'Doesn't time fly. Crikey. Was it a nice wedding?'

'It was,' says Lise. 'It was very posh. At a golf club. Wasn't it, Mirry?'

'It was gorgeous,' smiles Miranda. 'Teresa looked beautiful.'

'I would have bought a present for her, if I'd remembered,' says Rita.

'Aah,' says Lise, 'that's lovely. She's on her honeymoon now, anyway.'

'Well, give her my love, won't you, when she's back?'

'Yes, of course,' says Miranda.

'So this young man, who's in love with you, you met at the wedding.'

'He's not in love with me!' objects Miranda. 'He's only texted me once.'

'He texted Teresa first,' says Lise, 'to ask for her number – while Teresa was leaving for her honeymoon! He's making a big effort.'

'Bet he is in love with you, dear,' says Rita. 'Weddings do that.'

Miranda taps the side of Rita's foot gently. 'Swap feet, please,' she says.

Lise's face is solemn, her mouth drops at its sides. 'I'd *love* it if a rich banker was trying to take me out somewhere nice.'

'He's a rich banker, is he?' Rita asks, her eyebrows lifting.

'I don't know,' says Miranda. 'You ask Lise. She seems to know a lot more about it than me.' She is running an orange stick under the nails, pushing dirt and soft skin out of their corners.

'You should call him,' Lise says again, reproachfully, as if

Miranda is somehow neglecting her duty, 'or at least text him back.'

'Oh, leave it,' says Miranda, lightly.

'Is he not your type, Miranda?' Rita asks.

'I don't know. I haven't really thought about it.'

'Is he handsome?'

Miranda pauses for a moment, and looks up at Rita.

'What? *Not* handsome?' Rita verifies.

'He's not *bad*-looking, or anything,' says Miranda. 'He's okay.'

'Is he *fat*, or something?' asks Rita.

'A bit,' concedes Miranda.

'My husband, Neddy, got fat before he died,' says Rita. 'It was *horrible*. He looked at least eight months pregnant.'

'He is not fat!' objects Lise. 'He's just not a bodybuilder. Makes a change, here.'

'She doesn't seem that enthusiastic to me, dear,' says Rita.

'She's crazy!' says Lise. 'Teresa says he's a really nice guy, and he's asking Mirry out to dinner, and she's not even replied to him!'

'Give me a break!' says Miranda. 'He only texted last night!'

'So you're going to reply,' says Lise.

'I don't know,' says Miranda.

Rita sighs. 'That length's good. Weddings always do this,' she decrees, 'put everybody in a tailspin. They're a bother, weddings. Funerals, too. But you're less likely to get picked up at one of those.'

Miranda and her flatmate, Peter, are standing in their kitchen in their small house in Alexandria. Lise is not home yet from the salon.

'I'm pretty pleased she's not here, actually,' says Miranda.

'She been moaning?' says Peter, without malice, as he goes to the fridge to retrieve more food. The walls of the house do breathe that much easier when Lise is not there, and Miranda and Peter regress – they're not always being told off for something, for not closing the fridge door properly, for leaving crumbs on the worktop and risking ants, for wasting electricity by putting too much water in the kettle to boil.

'No, she's not been moaning too much, today. She's just been on at me *all day* about this guy.'

'Oh yeah?' says Peter. 'What guy?'

Peter has settled on a packet of grated cheese to eat, and is taking pinches of it straight from the bag; rubbery, yellow snuff. He sips from his cup of tea, freshly made and boiling hot – as if his mouth is made from fibreglass.

'This guy I met at Teresa's wedding. He texted me last night to ask me out.'

'Cool,' says Peter. 'So what's Lise's problem? Did you sleep with him?'

'*No*, I didn't sleep with him! We just sat at the same table!'

He shrugs. 'So what's Lise's problem, then?'

It occurs to Peter that Miranda is like a fire, all these men coming to stand beside her – all of his mates, this bloke from the wedding. Even himself, for a while, when he first moved in. She has the face for it.

'She wants me to go out with him. On a date. She's been on at me about it literally all day.'

Peter is mulling this over, in between the sensations of cheese and tea. If he keeps some cheese in his mouth then drinks some tea, after a few seconds the cheese heats up and melts a little. 'So what?' he finally says.

'Well!' says Miranda. '*So what* is: I don't know if I want to go out with him!'

Peter puts the bag of grated cheese back in the fridge without sealing it — it's *his* cheese, and Lise is not watching him: freedom.

'Then don't,' he says to Miranda.

'But I can't not reply to his text! And I don't want to be rude' — she appeals to Peter, having not really absorbed what he has said to her — 'and what if I'm just being . . . *wrong*, or *nasty* . . . and what if he turns out to be the right guy for me? What if I *should* go out to dinner with him?'

'Well,' says Peter, sighing inwardly, 'if he's nice and you want to go out with him, then go out with him.'

'But I don't know if I do!' cries Miranda.

Peter tips his head back and finishes his tea. He clunks his cup unwashed in the sink — another satisfying act of insubordination.

'Then don't,' he says again.

'I'm going to answer him now,' Miranda says. He *had* been nice.

'Cool,' says Peter.

Story is, at his best: generous, humorous and loyal, idiosyncratic, curious, and kind. At his worst he is: insecure and shallow, fearful and propitiating. But all he really needs is the love of a good woman, and Miranda is certainly that.

The heavens watch. The gods argue. Nobody knows what is best.

Miranda picks up her phone, and presses *reply*.

39

Story is not a walker. He wishes he was. He wishes he could prefer to travel by one foot in front of another in front of another in front of another clip clip clop instead of favouring the fetid passenger seat of a taxi, as he does. He wishes he had the urge to propel himself forwards on his own limbs, as opposed to the forever triumphant desire to sit, like a yoghurt culture, absorbent and blubbery.

But the fact is, Story likes to get places. Be that home, work, bar, party, beach. Once he knows where he's headed, he wants to head there, no strolling or whistling or kicking leaves.

Unexpected, then, this. This plod plod plod, his ten toes and two soles continuing to impel him thataways – away from where the taxi had dropped him, away from his flat, the keys to which he rolls in his fingers, jittering and chiming.

Story is walking. He has been walking for over an hour. As Story paid the cab driver, he had only intended to walk around the block – for courage, before he walked into his flat for – what? – the three thousandth time in his life? The whole place like a theatre set, convincing at a distance, but the closer he got the more he saw that his bed was made of chipboard, his walls of polystyrene and the food in his fridge of painted clay. He would walk around the block, once, maybe to the convenience store to pick up a chocolate bar and a bottle of juice, and chocolate as sword and juice as shield he would walk back home and stand in silence as the lift whirred him upwards on its chains.

But the convenience store was closed, and Story had kept on walking. He had walked, without destination, although in his mind he kept the shoreline – the magnet of the sea pulling him like one little filing. The sea that breathed its salt into the city, rusting everything up and making everybody look more beautiful – far more beautiful – than they were.

He had walked through the shops of Double Bay, pastel and stout and named hideous things like *Fashion d'Amour*, and *L'Affaire Homewares and Linens*. Bald mannequins in dim windows – chemo dolls, Mac had always called them – wearing the muted layers of the middle-aged. Mum had never dressed like that. Whatever else she had become – Derek's coating of fat, a melanoma on his ear – she had never worn those kind of coordinated zip-and-hook costumes. If he had a wife – he, Story, this man walking, trot trot, stride stride – then his wife might one day wear these kinds of things. Blouses. Knee-length skirts. Jackets with one button in the middle. And if he – Story, step step, walk walk – died, then his wife might one day find someone like Derek to replace him, some grinning petty tyrant from Byron Bay who would eat from his plates and sit in his chair and talk about life as if Story had never been in it. As if he hadn't married her first; loved her first. As if she hadn't chosen *him*.

On Mum and Derek's wedding day, there had been no mention of Dad. Not from Mum, certainly not from Derek, and not from a single one of the assembled guests. Why is

300

that only occurring to him now? To Story, as he walks, a filing pulled to the sea.

Who knows, but it is occurring, with a billow of memories of lipstick on teeth, smiling ladies done up like cockatoos, all congratulating him with their champagne breath – as if he, Story, walking walking, were pleased, at all pleased, that his mother had gone away and through a stranger's front door.

But enough of that.

Story has walked through Rose Bay, looked up at Our Lady, the school on the hill where all the hottest girls had gone. But out of their league – one degree too rich and too fancy for the North Sydney boys, in this country of equals where everybody is the same. The roads around him are empty, and his breath is full, and Story can smell the sea, if he tries. Made from the same water as when you cry; although he never did. He'd been lucky in his life – he'd never had the need. Unlike Vincent Batty, who used to come round when his parents were at each other like dingoes, and he'd occasionally go quiet and sniff, and Story with embarrassment knew that Vinnie was holding in the tears. Story can't imagine Tree ever pissing on Vincent Batty's turkey.

He smiles to himself. And as his smile condenses in the air, Story feels he could put a hand up to his face and remove it like a mask, hold it up, and look at it. Underneath, what would there be?

Enough. Enough of that, too. There is a goriness in his thoughts, a maudlin asperity that is new, and unfamiliar. It has come into him on the seams of the salt air like a ghost; a spirit that has pressed into him, and taken his shape.

Soon Story will be in Vaucluse. He should check the time – it must be late. The taxi had dropped him at eleven, and he must have been walking for nearly two hours. He must wake up. Shake off the walking and the thinking and go home. He is thirsty, and out of breath, and tired.

But Story does not stop. His red shoes lead him on. His thoughts are pushing at the back of him, pushing him forwards, and he walks faster to avoid their hand in the small of his back. He takes his suit jacket off as he goes, and hangs it over a railing. He can collect it on the way back, or − who cares, if not.

Miranda. As pretty as one of the Our Lady girls, and probably nearly as young. Although not as cocksure or blasé − that, only wealth can bring. And, fuck, if he had just done something in his life to make her want him. Something to make her look at him as anything other than a podgy, harmless nobody. That's what he was − harmless. It's what he'd spent his whole life cultivating, and now − three cheers! − he had achieved it. *Story? He's harmless. He's pretty harmless. He's a harmless guy.* He was irrelevant next to JP's sour good looks, irrelevant next to Vincent's gangling good nature, irrelevant next to Mac's obedient certainty. He was not gentle and beautiful and blond like his sister. He was not macho like his friends, or learned and bright like his father, like a comet. He was just a harmless fucking nobody. And he would be lying if he said it hadn't occurred to him that he was a proposition − a step up − for a visiting Pommie beautician. But, even then, with his swanky flat and his expensive suits and the brainy status of his job − she said no. Even all that could not entice her to disregard the heart of him − which was sodden like a sponge, empty in its holes, pointless, saggy and dull. With his soft body and his stale cake of a soul, he was nothing more than harmless.

Story can feel, with spread fingers, the hand in his back.

And if he stopped walking, he would have to turn around and face the madness and cut the snakes from its hair, and so he will walk on.

What a wedding, what a wedding, what a day. A toast — a raised glass — to doing things by numbers, to small loves and predictable lives, to not being lonely so lonely that every night the flat was filled with white noise and electrical humming so that one's breath, recycled in the room a million times, became as noxious and throbbing as a rainforest.

Who the hell was he to want more? Who the hell was he to think that Vincent should have more than Tree, and Mac should have more than his biscuits, and Stavvo should have more than his suburban house and rack of babies? None of *them* wanted more, why should *he*?

A car drives past. Another person, going somewhere.

There is nothing more to say, about life and its pathways. They all lead to the same place — all rivers — to the sea. But Story had assumed, like his friends, that life just *happened*. It happened to you. You need do no more than sit and ride the current as it takes you. You just sat and waited. Life happened — life with all its magic and mystery — all its song lyrics and beating drums. You sat in your ring and floated.

And, who knew, as the river spat you out into the sea, that all there'd be at the other end was more water. Bigger and blanker and with no hope of anything but blue. Who'd've thought, that after thirty-five years of accepting and waiting and watching what others did and diligently copying, you'd just end up fucking here — water. The same water you'd been in your whole life.

What's the use in wishing he'd swum upstream? He hadn't. It hadn't occurred to him once, not even in the last months as the feelings of disquiet and fear and nausea grew.

Story keeps walking and the tiredness is too much to ignore, now. He has slowed down, and that hand that had been holding one thin finger in his small now has its palm outstretched over his back. It was keeping pace comfortably, and now that it was here, he didn't mind it. It was pushing him, in his weariness; a kindly sensation that made the stepping and the plodding, the walking and the clopping – easier.

If something was going to happen, it would have happened by now. Life had arrived, with slim luggage – it had packed light.

Fifty more years of this. Even the boredom was enough – forget the grief, and the anger, and the pain that is lynching Story as he walks these last few steps – jumping out from the dark and putting a hood over his head. Quite unexpected, this gang of feeling, brutal and thick as molasses, that ties his hands behind his back and pushes him on.

Story could have made something happen. He could've turned around and swum upstream with the salmon. Or, if he hadn't the muscle for that, he could have caught at a piece of river bank and pulled himself out. Before this – before now – before arriving here, at the mouth of the sea. The Gap – Watson's Bay – the edge of Australia, where the waves have teeth. Story stops walking.

He had passed two cars in the car park, with drunk, groping couples inside. Here by the wall, there is nobody else. The spray loops up vertically to look at him, this man, this nobody, this fat financial analyst with sweat over his skin. It retreats back down, and breathes for a second before crashing back up – Story's face is being coated in a fine mist. And with all the water on his face – the sweat, and the sea – Story begins to shiver.

He thinks, as his body shudders, of those kids poking and

jacking off in the car park behind. He thinks of himself, and the shivering, and the sweat. He thinks of his jacket, abandoned by the road. He thinks of his shoes, which have never done so much walking in their lives.

With an ungainly twist, he carries one leg, and then the other, over the barrier – despite practice, he has never been one of those people who could vault over things without thinking.

With his legs shaking and his heart beating and the self inside him as calm as oil, Story picks his way in the dark over to the rocks. Below, hundreds of metres below, the water curdles and shatters over slabs of stone, which hide with mouths wide. What is there to do, now? Strange as it is that he has brought himself here, here he yet is, and there is nowhere else to go. All he has to do now is stand at the edge, and wait, for something to slip.

From up here, the waves are tearing at the cliff with hands and claws, screaming and monstrous like a mad lady from a bad dream. Story is pinned to it – pinned to the sea like the rest of Sydney – pinned to it like a butterfly to a board.

40

Oliver was in late. Normally at his desk well before eight, today he was just coming out of the office shower at quarter past nine – a delayed flight back from Shanghai, then an hour at his laptop, meant he had only got to bed at 3 a.m. It had been two days of meetings with government officials and potential clients, and his head was still coiling with it – he had woken up cataloguing the phone calls he had to make before lunch, and paring his diary to find the most sensible time to make a return trip. The lists, the options, the layers of what might be best, were piling in on each other, and Oliver's brain kept slicing from one to the next. He couldn't settle.

Even after he'd run to the office – the sweat beginning to make his shirt cling, and his hair wet – the rings continued to spin disordered in his head – so he ran on, past the entrance to Redvale, and towards the Botanic Gardens. He jogged the edge of it, the sweat now dripping through his eyelashes, and his thumping heart filtering the air, making it feel cleaner in his lungs. He resisted the urge to close his eyes for a few steps at a time – he kept himself looking out, kept his thoughts from becoming sealed behind his skin.

By the time he had arrived again at the door of Redvale, he was feeling better – clearer, calmer. Coated in sweat and in his running gear, he went up to his office, where he kept a concise wardrobe of suits, shirts, underwear, socks and two pairs of shoes for the days like today, where his Trumper Oval circuits had to be sacrificed to a straight jog into the city. He took what he needed and went back down a floor to the showers.

It was proving uphill graft, more so than he had imagined, convincing the Chinese dragons – the companies of any prestige and interest – to get into bed with a law firm whose head office was in Sydney. A law firm without an international name. The only thing Oliver could push – and did push, until his blood was straining like horses underneath his concentrated tranquillity – was that Redvale would lay its entire self down, that each and every lawyer in the company would tie their fortune to their client, that they were not an Allen & Overy or a Freshfields, who had so many glitzy balls competing in the air. And, within three years – three years, he found himself saying, not four! – they would have offices open across Asia.

Oliver allows himself five extra, luxurious seconds under the water before turning the stream off. He pulls the curtain open, and reaches for his towel.

'JP,' says Oliver. 'Hi.'

'Oh.' Just out of the shower himself, JP had been running a towel over his face, and now ties it around his middle. Brawny, with a sinewy layer of fat over him, and hair close to his scalp, he looks like a soldier. 'Hi.'

'Been running?' Oliver asks.

'Yeah.'

Oliver smiles – at nothing, JP thinks; it grates.

'D'you run in every day?' Oliver is drying his upper body. His torso is completely hairless, and he's one of those guys who, if they didn't work out, would be scrappy-looking, pigeon-chested, JP reckons. As it is, he's got muscle over him, so looks half decent. He's not got a strand of fat — certainly no knob of hard flab stuck around his middle; it's irritating. But then he's only just into his thirties. Give it a few years.

'I have been, for the last coupla weeks.'

'Good for you.' Patronising git. 'You're not training for the triathlon, are you?'

'Er, yeah.' JP is putting his feet into his trousers. 'I am.'

'Good man,' says Oliver, nodding. 'How's it going?'

'All right,' says JP.

Oliver is fighting the urge to laugh. 'Good stuff,' he says. And then again, to entertain himself, 'Goood — sss-tuff.' Oliver, high on exercise, and thinking to himself that JP's complete lack of social nicety borders on art, beams at JP. A few minutes of silent dressing pass, after which Oliver breaks in again with 'Hey, where d'you swim?'

JP is slightly knocked by Oliver's cheerfulness — by the size of the smile that he wears as he ties his grey, polka-dot tie — a tie as unAustralian as its wearer — 'Down at the Icebergs. Bondi.'

'Where we met! You swim down there, too. Not just sing.' Oliver is smiling. 'How was your stag party?'

'Fine.'

'Has the wedding been yet?'

'Yep.'

'Hope it went well?'

'A wedding's a wedding,' JP says.

Oliver laughs. 'I suppose so.' His hair, towelled dry, is sticking up like a parakeet's. 'I swim there a bit, too, at Icebergs —

funny we haven't run into each other more. Do you live down there?'

'No.' JP does up his shirt, his straitjacket for the day. He watches his own fingers as they close the buttons – they look strangely large, like his dad's hands, too big and meaty for whatever they try to do. Oliver is still looking at him. 'I cycle,' JP adds.

'I should do that. I still haven't got round to getting a bike.'

'Tss,' says JP, through closed teeth. 'You're going to need one if you're running the triathlon.'

'I know. I've got to get on with it.' Oliver is lacing up his shoes, black leather with thin soles, they make JP's look like clogs. He was out of the shower after JP, has been doing all the talking, and yet has managed, without rush, to be ready first. Now fully dressed in his suit, Oliver scrubs his head with a towel a final time, and then runs a comb through his hair. Yellow mop. Yellow, even when wet. 'Well,' Oliver says to JP, as he pushes his towel and dirty clothes into a bag, 'back to it!'

'See ya later,' says JP, who is now tying his tie, red and navy.

Oliver hesitates; his hand is on the door, ready to push its way out – but he doesn't move.

'I read your brief for the Telecom Australia case, by the way.'

JP's insides stop. He pushes the knot of his tie up into his neck. 'What, this one?' he says.

'The current one. Off-peak tariffs.'

'Why? Why d'you read it?' JP is aware of an angry heat swelling around his temples.

'I was interested,' Oliver says simply. 'Michael said you were a good writer.'

JP looks incredulous.

'He's right. It was good. Excellent, actually – excellent.'

JP's skull is bubbling – alongside the anger, he doesn't know what he's feeling. 'It's just a brief,' he says. 'Pretty fucking run of the mill. Anyone could do it.'

'No,' says Oliver, 'no. I haven't got anyone who can write that well in my team. I've got a million and one pitches to get underway, and thus far I've had to rewrite most of them myself.'

'Who you pitching for?'

'Oh, just general new business. The usual.'

'Here? Or abroad?'

Oliver stays quiet. Shrugs. Smiles.

So. The office gossip has turned out true. Oliver Marchal is, indeed, the Messiah. He's taking Redvale global. And he's barely even passed puberty.

'I might come and talk to you about it sometime this week, JP,' says Oliver. JP finds there's something brutally intimate in hearing his name on Oliver's tongue. It feels ruthless, and close.

'What do you want to talk to *me* about?'

At that moment the door into the changing rooms is pulled open – Oliver moves with it for a second, and then rights himself backwards.

''Scuse me, mate.' Another sweating solicitor is coming in for a shower.

'Sorry,' says Oliver, moving aside. Then he nods, a virtually imperceptible nod, at JP. 'I'll set up a meeting,' he says, before walking out into the light.

'What do you need him *for*?' Michael Carrick is at his desk in reading glasses, three neat stacks of paper in front of him and his laptop closed.

'Two things. I want him to rewrite – edit – the Queens Dairy brief.'

'I don't need to tell you, Olly, that JP's not a tax lawyer.'

'No, you don't.'

'I didn't think so.'

'The legalese of the brief is written – the entire brief is written. Finished. The substance is there. It's just got no . . . style. No panache.'

'You're sounding like Cyrano de Bergerac. You do know, Oliver, that Cyrano de Bergerac was not a lawyer?'

'Yes, I do.'

'Good. Who's the barrister? Danny Peat?' Oliver nods. 'Danny'll add panache. He'll wear a feather in his hat.' Carrick is smiling to himself, half-moon glasses still perched midway down his nose.

'Barristers need to be led, Michael. I don't need to tell *you* that.'

'No, you don't.'

'We're inviting the media along to this case, Michael,' Oliver goes on. 'We need a bit of legal poetry that's going to look good in print. I don't trust Danny to wing it in court. And we need variations in tone, the thrust of the case needs to be quite . . . evocative. But all the back-tax stuff, all the stuff where we've got no precedent – needs to be direct, and chummy—'

'*Chummy*,' Carrick says, leaning back in his chair now. 'Can Danny do *chummy*? Can he even do *matey*? He can do evocative, I've no doubt. But, yes, he'll probably need a bit of leading with *chummy*.'

'I want JP to word it.' Oliver looks straight at Carrick, and then rapidly blinks at his watch – he has a call in fifteen minutes.

Carrick thinks for a minute. 'Do you want me to call him in here?'

'No. I'll see him separately.'

'We'll need to see what he's got on, and whether he's got the time. See what we can free him from. What's the second thing?'

'China. And eventually Singapore and India and Japan. I want him writing our pitches.'

Carrick breathes out through his mouth: ff-ff-ff-ff-ff. He raises his eyebrows. 'This is a whole different ball game, Olly.'

'He could stay in Corporate,' Oliver offers.

'Tk-tk.' Carrick shakes his head. 'You're going to have to do better than that, young man. Doesn't matter where his desk is – you're saying you want to poach him. Not borrow him. The Asian pitches will take years, three years on and off.'

'Four,' says Oliver.

'If I gave him to you for the pitches, I'd be down an Associate. And I don't reckon JP Fry would be too thrilled at being told he'd be writing pitches for the next four years of his career.'

'It's his strength.'

'Yes. Ffsh. It is. But he won't want to do it. And I don't want to lose a known lawyer from my floor.'

Oliver doesn't move. His instinct is to pull himself up in the chair, but he orders his muscles not to. He stays still. As he is. 'It's all very well having the offices, Michael, but if we don't have the clients, Redvale will flop in Asia. Without the clients, the whole exercise is pointless, a colossal waste of money – and a loss of face. And I'm not having us go in as some small high-street law firm. We need to be representing three, four – at least – of the big guns, when we open. These pitches are completely essential to Redvale's future. And you could give JP Partner in an Asian office, at the end of it. That'd make him keener.'

'No, no, no—' says Carrick, looking at Oliver with a smile growing, clearly entertained by the sheer foolishness of the idea 'No. JP would be a *disaster* in Asia. What do you think would happen if a single one of your Chinese, or Japanese, clients got him on the phone? Or in a meeting? Aussies can deal with his kind of bluntness – but JP'd kill us over there.' Imagining it, Carrick laughs.

'All right,' says Oliver. Carrick is right. 'Well, then, keep him here. But I need him.'

'Ah, Christ, Oliver. This is a pain in the backside.' Carrick takes his glasses off, finally, as if admitting defeat, and sighs.

'Do you really need him, Michael? I mean, what do *you* need him for? From what I can see, he's not heading up any of the accounts, or bringing in any new business – and I can use him somewhere where he'd make a crucial difference to the future of the entire company.'

'I'd have to hire someone else.'

Oliver shrugs with his face.

'Hm. How would you want to do it?' Carrick asks.

'Up to you. I can just borrow him for now – for Queens Dairy. That'd give you some time to think about it. I *will* need specific teams, Michael, to work on Hong Kong and Shanghai. As I've said, they'll be small at first, so if you want it to continue under the radar I can continue to minimise the external recruitment, and whoever I need can stay in their departments, do my work from their desk – for the time being. But, at some stage, soon, we'll need to call a spade a spade, and move people around, get them all on one floor.'

'Well, we knew that.'

'Yes.'

313

'It won't do anything for his career, being away from clients and courts for that long,' says Carrick.

'Michael, correct me if I'm wrong – but his career here is dead anyway. He can tread water with you for the rest of his life – or he can do something he's good at for a while, and make a potentially massive difference.'

Carrick dwells on it. He frowns slightly. 'You'll have to convince him, as well as me.'

'He can't be made a Partner? Even in a few years?'

Carrick shakes his head.

'Well, what can I go to him with, then? I can't offer anything without your approval, without senior approval.'

'New job title,' says Carrick: 'Writer in Residence. You want him, you're going to have to do the talking. I can't give you any carrots.'

'Fair enough. Do I have your go-ahead to approach him?'

Carrick dwells on it. He likes JP. He has always liked JP. Despite his bad manners, despite his absolute lack of passion as a lawyer. The act of affection that Michael Carrick on-goingly performs for JP is to keep him on as an Associate – to keep him on at all – where any other firm would have made him redundant years ago.

'Give me half an hour,' Carrick says. 'I'll call you.'

'JP Fry.'

'JP, hi, it's Oliver Marchal speaking. Are you training after work?'

JP is silent for a second. Oliver waits.

'I'm going for a swim.'

'At Bondi?'

'No. Icebergs shuts at six thirty.' JP's voice is utterly without welcome. His words sound like they come from a slingshot.

'Oh, does it? I only go there mornings. Where will you go, then?'

'Boy Charlton. In the Domain. Why?'

'I'd like a word. About work. I thought I could tie it in with a bit of exercise. What time are you heading there?'

JP hadn't thought about it. He hadn't even decided with certainty that he would swim, today. He looks at the time on his screen. 'Six thirty,' he says.

'That's the pool right on the harbour, right? Overlooking Woolloomooloo?'

'There's only one. In the Domain.'

'I ran past there this morning.'

Again JP is silent.

'I can be there at around six thirty, give or take – if that suits you,' says Oliver. 'I'll get in a few lengths, and then we can chat.'

'We can talk now,' says JP.

'No, let's leave it. I'll see you at the pool.'

Sydney did a line in spectacular swimming pools. All of them Olympic, all of them casually looking up at the Harbour Bridge, or out to the Opera House, or down over the crashing Tasman Sea. Boy Charlton was no exception. The pool seemed to grip the edge of the Domain, bridging the land and the water. The Finger Wharf, Woolloomooloo, reached out towards it, and behind were the banks of the Botanic Gardens, with cockatoos mawking and styling their hair. In front, today, was a liner the size of a small planet, a fearsome, eclipsing citadel.

And, like at all the other pools of Sydney – there was the Old Man. No younger than eighty, in a cap and goggles, titanic shoulders, the skin over his body only a fraction worn, carving up and down a lane like a plough. At home in England, he would be a marvel – famed and discussed, the BBC would pick up his story for a local feature. But here – normal. He and his brethren swam like saws through every pool in Sydney, and walked with bare, brown chests down every beach. Nobody even looked.

Oliver scanned and spotted JP in a central lane, wearing goggles, swimming front crawl – or freestyle, as it was called here. It amused him – freestyle should really be some interpretive stroke: *Today I'm going to swim in the style of a young penguin.* JP's legs were kicking up the most enormous amount of spume; it obscured the lower half of his body, and the water behind him was like a hurricane.

Oliver has left his suit and wallet in the office, and has jogged over with nothing but a towel around his neck, a credit card and twenty dollars in a pocket, and wearing only board shorts – swimming trunks – a T-shirt and trainers. His phone is at Redvale, being manned by his PA. A rare moment of liberation; although, of course, he has it in the back of his mind. Oliver takes his shoes off, hides the banknote and card in one toe, takes off his T-shirt and leaves it all in a pile with his towel, away from the edge. He waits for two swimmers to be farther away, into their lane, and lowers himself into the water.

After every four lengths, Oliver has been looking up to clock that JP is still in the water. This time – he's not. Oliver ducks under the ropes until he reaches the steps, and drips over to his towel. He puts it around his waist, and then discreetly takes his shorts off from underneath, wrings them into a drain, pulls on his T-shirt, sits, and waits, with no calls, no emails, no internet; a few moments of growing roots.

After five minutes, JP emerges from the changing rooms

wearing sunglasses and civvies, with a large sports bag over one shoulder. Oliver stands up.

'G'day,' says JP.

Oliver offers his hand. 'Good swim?'

'All right.'

'This is an amazing spot.'

'Compared to the puddles you get in London, I suppose it is.'

Oliver laughs. JP's face remains flint. 'You want to go up to the café?'

'If you like.'

The terrace is suspended over the pool, and there is a low-key brilliance in the swimmers disappearing and reappearing under them as they sit.

'Christ,' says Oliver, 'this is a proper menu. Makes me want to order a glass of wine.'

JP has not been here, up to the café, since its swankification.

'Do you mind if I eat?' Oliver asks.

'No,' says JP, his face scrunched, thrown by the question. Why would he *mind* if Oliver ate? He can do what the fuck he likes, surely.

'I suspect it'll be better than the office vending machine. Or some sandwich from a packet.'

'You're going back in? To the office?' JP asks.

Oliver nods. 'Just for a couple of hours,' he says.

JP frowns. Dissemblance is beyond him, at this moment.

'How long would the squid salad take?' Oliver asks the waitress, who has her pen poised – Oliver always warms to a place when they write his order down.

'Shouldn't take any more than ten minutes.'

'Great. I'll have that, then, the squid salad. And some still water.'

'Tap or mineral?'

'Tap is fine.'

JP tosses the menu on to the table as if it is useless. 'What beer have you got on tap?'

'James Boag Light and James Boag Premium.'

He has spent the last minute feeling angry with himself – at his inexplicable angst about whether to have a beer or not. He feels having a beer would be inappropriate, somehow, even though he's been at work all fucking day, and wants one.

'You've got enough takers for the Light to have it on tap?' he asks the waitress.

'Mm–hm,' she says, nods, smiles, pen ready.

'I'll have a Premium,' JP says, testily.

'Yep . . . Anything to eat?'

'Na.'

As the waitress walks away, JP glancing at her back view, Oliver sets himself and says, 'I need your help.' The warmth remains in his voice, but with it there is a downward inflection, an exactness.

'Right,' JP replies, wary. 'What with?'

'In the short term, I would like you to rewrite a brief for me. It goes to court in two weeks.'

Again, JP's face concertinas. 'What brief? A *tax* brief?'

'GST. For Queens Dairy. It's going to be a big deal.'

'Why? Why can't one of the tax guys do it?'

'We have done it. We've got it written already. I want you to look over it, change the tone, put in a bit of – pizzazz. The legalese is all there already, so you won't have to worry about that.'

'Right,' says JP. 'I still don't get why *I* need to do it. It's not my area.'

'I told you I read your Telecom Australia brief. You can write more clearly and more – eloquently – than anyone else at Redvale. Our barrister needs to be led through the different tones we need for each aspect of this case.'

JP's eyes widen. Something dips in his stomach, and he doesn't know why. He clears his throat.

'You'd want me to brief the barrister – I mean, verbally, too?'

'This is going to be a showcase, JP. An exhibition, of what Redvale can do. I need it like a piece of theatre. I'm asking you if you'll help.'

'Look, this is all a bit, ah, odd. Yeah, I'll help. If I've got time.'

'Michael Carrick is happy for you to do it.'

JP's head moves back into his neck. 'You've spoken to Carrick?'

'Yes. I mentioned it to him today.'

'James Boag,' says the waitress, brightly, 'and your water.' She puts down a large, frosted jug, with two water glasses.

JP looks at his beer as if it is a stranger. He watches it for a moment, more aware of a schooner on a table – a three-dimensional object, liquid and glass, separate from himself – than he ever has been before.

He's thirsty.

Oliver is pouring them both water.

'So what's the drama about this case?' says JP.

Oliver nods. 'Queens Dairy,' he says, 'their Cheezo line – d'you know it? Their spreadable cheese?'

' 'Course I know it, every Aussie kid was brought up with the stuff. It's like Vegemite.'

'Cheezo is currently classed by the Taxation Office as a Schedule 1 food – it's listed as a *savoury snack* – a non-basic food item – and as such it's subject to GST. Its classification as Schedule 1 was basically a hangover from the pre-Howard sales tax days – but even then spreadable cheese should hardly have been seen as space age' – Oliver raises an eyebrow – 'and the classification hasn't ever been questioned, or even thought of. It was just accepted.'

JP takes his first sip from the perfect top of his beer – it is like slicing a spade into the earth.

'We're arguing,' Oliver continues, 'that Cheezo is in fact not a non-basic item, it is a basic item, a cheese just like Cheddar or Parmesan, and so should be reclassified as Schedule 2, and be zero-rated.'

'I see,' says JP.

'We'll win the case,' says Oliver, with matter-of-fact mettle. 'They can't rule against us, as it would be discriminatory – Queens Dairy's competitors have several versions of spreadable cheeses that are listed as Schedule 2. Winning the case is not the issue. The issue is that this case needs to be our soap box.' Oliver takes a breath, looks quickly out at the view, and then towards JP again. 'Cheezo accounts for over fifty per cent of Queens Dairy's revenue. *Fifty per cent.* And arguably closer to ninety per cent of its reputation with consumers. With GST removed, and the retail cost of Cheezo coming down, it would be extremely likely that Queens Dairy saw a significant increase in their units sold. But what is crucial for us – for Redvale – is that we, holding hands with Queens Dairy, are seen as working for the Australian consumer. As saving them money. As—'

JP finds himself laughing. 'Championing the people,' he offers.

'Just so,' says Oliver, relaxing into a grin. 'But we can't beat our own drum too loudly. It has to be slipped in. You know, a quote here and there, which the media have no choice but to pick up on. A bit of prose poetry, about *removing the burden from the Australian taxpayer.* Or *providing relief.*' Oliver's whole being is animated. He seems to be creating – emitting – energy.

'Yeah,' JP says, engaged, now. 'Yeah, I get it. I don't reckon the Treasury is going to love you much, though. Losing GST off a nice little earner.'

'They'll be fine. As long as we make absolutely certain we don't use any blame language towards them. Not even a sniff of it. And as long as we don't open them up to any kind of back-payment – that's crucial. To keep everybody happy, we'll have to show them our language in advance, show them how watertight we are on the point of historical GST.'

'Right,' says JP, thinking, 'you'll need to present that to the court as an assumption.'

'*Exactly!*' says Oliver, feeling small triumph, vindication in his confidence in JP. 'Thanks!' he says to the waitress, with a disproportionate shine, as she puts his knife, fork and napkin down in front of him. 'We need our poetics on the Australian consumer' – Oliver is talking fast, it is as if there is not space enough or breath enough for his words – 'and Queens Dairy as, you know – a Great Australian Company . . .'

JP is silent as he drinks from his beer. It's not bad, actually, Boag. All of this – is a surprise. 'Do you have the brief, now?' he asks.

'No, in the office. I can have it biked to you tonight.'

'I can walk back and pick it up,' says JP, 'after this.'

'We'll do that,' says Oliver. They can walk. Walk and talk about the real work to come.

'So Carrick's all right with it,' JP says. 'He's going to have to divert some of my work, until this is done.'

'Michael's happy, JP. I spoke to him this afternoon.'

He says your name, Oliver. He holds your name in his mouth.

'I should talk to a mate a mine, who works at the Reserve Bank. He knows all the blokes at the Treasury.'

'Really?' says Oliver, raising a light eyebrow. 'What does he do there?'

'He's a research analyst. It's not his area, this, GST, but it's always worth a chat.'

'Definitely,' says Oliver, looking at JP with a different, pointed angle of curiosity.

JP, to his own surprise beginning to feel octopus vines of excitement, speaks his thoughts out loud—

'I can probably get the bulk of it done in a day or two.'

'Yes.' Oliver shifts again. He clears his throat. 'There's some other work, though. That will take longer.'

'Still Queens Dairy?'

'Completely unrelated. This work will be longer term.' Oliver does not waver, and JP is aware, with a discomfort in his brow, that they are looking at each other's eyes. 'But you'll have to be happy with it, too, obviously.'

'What,' says JP, flatly. 'What work?'

Without a splinter of uncertainty in his face – the future, to Oliver, is only a question of wingspan – he says: 'China.'

41

'Mum, isn't Uncle Story supposed to be here now?'
'Yes. I thought so. I've called him but he's not answering.'

'He should bloody grow up,' Guy says gruffly, his eyes on the television screen.

Kali looks at the back of her husband's head, hates him for a second, and then lets it go. The hatred has started to move to the left, recently, a graceful side step, to make way for a calmer, steadier, sadness.

Kali doesn't know when it was, exactly, that she stopped giving Guy her best stuff. Not in an existential sense – not, *the best of herself*, or any such thing. She meant, her best actual *stuff*.

Like the best slice of the lasagne, where the meat was thickest in the middle and the cheese was at its most concentrated. She had, for always, cut that bit for him. And if there was only so much Parmesan left in the bowl for the spaghetti, she'd say she didn't want any, so that Guy could take it.

Or the best pillow. There was one pillow in their bed that was the perfect firmness, and the perfect thickness. The others, you had to stack and align to get your head properly comfortable. But this one, alone, worked perfectly. Kali, getting into bed first, would swap the pillows around so that Guy had the good one, and for herself she would arrange two thinner pillows slightly overlapping. She never told him she was doing this, just inconspicuously put it to his side. But these days – she doesn't know when it started – she takes the best pillow for herself. Settles her head on it, happier for the night.

Was the day she took the pillow the day her love stopped?

Kali doesn't know. All she realises is that since this Christmas, since that one knock in a long line of knocks, she has not broken her silence. And Guy has given her no cause to. When he got back from South America, he had not asked her about the wedding – Tree and Vincent Batty's – and she had not told him. She had not told him about the un-expected talk of swimming, with JP. And she had not told him about the swim that came after – on her back like flotsam, her muscles waking up like those desert fish you read about that hibernate through a hundred dry summers and come to life again like magic when the floods finally come. Those few strokes she took, her muscles felt their weakness, and remembered back to their strength – and she told Guy none of it. It all remains inside her, like a stomach full of food.

Like everything else, as far as Kali could see – Guy didn't notice that she was withdrawing her care of him. That the gracious morsels – lasagne, Parmesan, pillow – and the innumerable other small joys Kali used to take in looking after him – had ceased.

She looks at Guy, across the kitchen, dispassionately. She is looking at him, without looking for anything in him. She no longer needs anything from him. He has nothing she needs. There is nothing left to search for in his face, because whatever she searches for is never there. He is simply a man.

This reality – that Guy is out of her reach, and she no longer wants to tow him back – overwhelms Kali with such sadness that she hears herself gasp, an awkward, loud pulling for breath.

'You all right, Crump?' Guy looks up at her from the television. Kali looks straight at him. At his eyes. She remembers with vivid nearness the way JP had looked at her at the wedding. He had looked at her as if he were looking at her by choice – as if looking at her was what he wanted to be doing – as if by looking at her he was feeding himself. Guy did not look at her like that. Guy's eyes tapped like a white cane over the simple fact of her. She existed, that's all.

'Just choked,' Kali said.

'Mum, your eyes are watering, you should drink something,' says Jacob, also swivelling round from the soccer, some European repeat.

Looking at Guy – the face of a far-away man, of a person she might see on a street, the face of a man who lives in this house with her – Kali feels like there is something being driven into her heart. How unbelievable, that life, and love, have left her here.

'What did you choke on, Crump?' Guy asks, looking mutedly amused.

'Oh. On myself. I choked. You know when you choke on yourself. Your own breath.'

'I do that sometimes,' says Jacob, loyally.

'Are we going to eat now?' Guy gets up from the sofa. 'We can't wait for your brother all day.'

Kali, looking away from her husband and towards that face of sweet solidarity, the beloved face of her son, wipes her cheeks with her fingers, and smiles.

42

Story's not answering JP's messages. It's fucking irritating. Story always answers messages, faster than anyone else – a retriever with tail eagerly wagging. But the one time, probably in their whole lives, that it's something remotely important, Story's gone bush. Not a peep.

JP has just swum, fifty lengths, at the Icebergs pool. With his sports bag over his shoulder and his hair still wet, without really thinking about it, he decides to walk round the cliffs to Tamarama. The day is at its best – neither evening nor afternoon, but the point at which the sun lingers, still hot, an old queen taking a long curtain call.

Answerphone *again*.

'Story, mate, JP. Look, I'm trying to get hold of you about this GST thing I mentioned. Give me a ring, will you? Tonight. I'm working on this thing now.'

Where the fuck is he? Incommunicado for two days. Tool. He's probably sunk off the radar after some coke bender, or shacked up with some unappealing, indiscriminate slapper for the weekend. Although, JP supposes, he's a one to talk. It's not like he publicises his own after-hours liaisons. He had only ever really had one actual, public *girlfriend* in his life.

They'd been together for a couple of months during his second year at Sydney Uni. Charlotte – Caz. Wonder what had happened to her. She'd had a nice face.

She'd probably thickened out now like Cannie – although maybe Cannie had already been a bit bottom-heavy at uni – JP doesn't quite remember. He and Cannie had never been close.

Caz – Caz – Caz – what? Sharp? Harp? Harper? Sharper? Something like that. She'd been in the year above him, they'd gone to the same series of art-history lectures. She'd even come to watch him play rugby once – that'd felt good at the time. He'd liked seeing her sitting there at half-time. He felt owned, or ownership, or something less than lonely. But afterwards – it struck him as a bit keen. A bit American cheerleader, boyfriend-girlfriend picket-fence-type thing. A bit desperate.

Why had they split up? Was it after that rugby thing? It had probably just run its course. He had liked her, though. She'd been funny. That old bullshit cliché, about women being attracted to men who made them laugh – well, she made him laugh, and he had liked it. She'd been a drinker; social. She'd always be out somewhere, and they'd meet afterwards. He'd ended up, for those few months, pretty much living with her in her houseshare. Once, she'd worn high heels with her jeans, which was unexpected, but he remembers liking that, too. She'd been suddenly eye level with him, which changed the way he touched her. She used to do this thing with her lips, sort of holding the air in her mouth and then puffing it out in little gusts – she did it when she was relaxed, in her own world, reading, getting dressed.

Funny, how he's thinking of her now. He'd forgotten she existed.

That's right – JP remembers. He remembers how they parted.

They'd been at the Thistle and Caz had been strange all evening. She'd hardly drunk, and she kept quietly looking at JP like there was something on his face. When they were walking back to hers, she'd said, 'I think I'm pregnant.'

JP had stopped. 'Fuck. You serious?'

'Yeah.' Caz was just standing there, too. Looking confused.

'Shit. You sure about this?'

'Not yet. I haven't done a test.'

'Oh, well, Christ. Do a fucking test. If you haven't done one, how do you even know?' JP had started walking again. He felt aware of – embarrassed by – all the people crossing their path.

'It's not fucking hard. I've not had my period for ages, and I feel like shit. Really fucking weird and shitty.'

'Did you have to talk about this now?' JP seemed suddenly angry. The people on the pavement kept coming and going, walking every way.

'What do you mean?'

'You could have waited until we were alone.'

'We are alone.'

'Until we were inside, private, I mean. You know what I mean.'

Later, she'd done that thing, of pretending they might have the baby – when they both knew not in a million years. She'd said to him, 'We'd have an eight-year-old when we were thirty.'

JP had blown out dismissively through his teeth.

And then she'd said, 'Would you want to have my baby? Would you want to have children with me?' She'd said it with her hand on his leg and the fantasy of it had irritated him.

'No,' he'd replied, 'of course not.'

There'd been an argument then – one JP hadn't understood, but it had ended up with him walking out and heading to a pub. Give it long enough, and she'd stop behaving like a mad bitch. He'd gone back some hours later and she'd screamed at him again, said some crap learnt off rote from a B-movie: *This is your baby, too, JP!*

He *had* felt sad in some small fold of himself, he supposed – but childish sadness, he knew that, even at the time. You do think – obviously, you think – of all those cells turning into a person, and what it'd be like. But, for fuck's sake, it was never going to be an actual baby.

'Have you got the money for it?' he'd asked her, when things had calmed down.

She'd nodded.

She said she wanted him to go with her, so he had. She'd been called from the waiting room and he hadn't known what to say so had said nothing. As she'd got up she said, 'You're going to wait for me here, right?' with fear all over her face, and he had felt a moment of closeness to her that felt like an ache. Closeness and yearning, but definitely not love – just two people, sitting in the same leaky old boat.

A few days later, they'd gone their separate ways. Whatever friendship they'd had was spoilt, and it was a relief to be shot of it. JP thinks of her face, doing that thing – puffing out air. She'd had a nice face. She'd been all right.

JP has been sitting on the sand for nearly an hour. The evening was beautiful, and as the light changed the beach cleared out – the muscle men and the topless chicks headed off like tumbleweed.

Before Christmas, as part of Sculpture by the Sea, there had been a huge mesh chicken on the beach, dark and sturdy, about where he was sitting now. The size of it had made all the people on Tamarama, from up on the cliff, look like eggs. Fried eggs. Scrambled eggs. Any kind of egg. There'd been a sign by the chicken, secured into the sand, saying, *Please do not enter the chicken*. That'd made him laugh. If she had been with him, Caz would've laughed at it, too.

Not Kali, though. JP can't claim to know Kali well, but he can't imagine her laughing at *Please do not enter the chicken*. He can't imagine her getting pregnant and standing in tears in an abortion clinic, either.

The only way he can imagine her is standing there with her thin arms, looking at him, by the bench at Vincent's wedding. What is life? A lifetime without her. What is love, but what you've lost. He could walk into the ocean, and keep swallowing water until he was sick.

JP stands and dusts himself off. His body is improving, he can feel it. Apart from losing fat and building muscle, his whole machine feels that much more biddable, even in an action as small as standing up. He has to walk back round to Bondi, to pick up his bike.

On a bench halfway up the cliff there are three boys drinking tinnies. They have the rest of their beer stash in a rucksack under the bench.

'She's a fucking skank,' one of them is saying.

'You seen her tits?' another says, after a swig. 'They're like your mum's.'

There's laughter at this.

It occurs to JP as he passes them that, with relative ease – with one smooth movement – he could take two of these boys and crack their skulls together. Crack. They'd bleed.

But of all the things in the wide world he could choose to do – why would he choose to do that?

43

Cannie is giving a presentation to Sydney University students – as an alumnus it was something she did every year – about a career at Onestar, where she had worked since graduating. Afterwards, as always, there were drinks: *an informal opportunity for questions to be raised*. In reality, a mash-up. A percentage – if not a majority – of the students only came for the grog.

Cannie normally stayed for an hour, while things were pretty sedate, then left one of the other Onestar boys to evacuate and shut down later – normally when the wine had run out. She would stand, and do her duty, and amiably notice how arrogant and ignorant all these children were. She must have been the same at that age, albeit in her own, sober way.

'Are there ways,' a girl is asking Cannie, 'as a member of staff, of having your input – your ideas, I mean – heard by the company?'

These kids have no clue.

'Of course,' says Cannie, an old pro by now, finding the right piece of truth to fit this particular nonsense. 'One of the great things that Onestar has going for it, especially for such a big company, is that its teams are really small. Each department is deliberately kept intimate. So it's a work environment in which your voice can automatically be heard, no matter what your position is—'

'G'day,' says an interrupting voice.

Cannie is taken aback.

'I'm Ben,' the young man says. 'I'm an architecture student.' He smiles, a broad, capricious, happy smile.

The girl who had been talking to Cannie, earnest and ambitious, is annoyed by this interloper.

'Architecture?' she says, unconvinced.

'Yeah,' explains Ben, 'I'm only here for the free booze.' He lifts his glass to demonstrate. He turns back to Cannie. 'I hoped you'd be here,' he says, 'although I didn't really think you would.'

'Sorry,' says Cannie, 'hi.'

'It says there' – Ben points to her name badge with his wine glass – 'your name is Abigail.'

'It is.' This is an ambush. Unexpected and discomfiting. Cannie wishes she were in a dress, instead of a skirt and jacket – and that she were in better shoes. His eyes are on her.

'You said you were called Cannie.'

'It's a nickname.'

Not to be excluded, the girl says, disapproving, 'Do you two know each other?'

'No—' says Cannie.

'Yes—' says Ben.

'Yes,' concedes Cannie, 'but not really.'

'Ha!' Ben laughs. 'Tell me then, *Abigail*, if you don't really *know* me, then who, exactly, *do* you really know? My mind races thinking of what you get up to with people you

334

do really know. I'd like to see that. That'd be something.'

Cannie feels herself blushing. She gathers herself; a warhorse.

'Ben, could we continue this conversation a little later? Lindsay, here, was—' She stumbles. 'Had a few questions for me.'

'Sure.' Ben's answer comes fast. It is hard to tell what he is thinking. He empties his glass into his mouth. 'Yeah, sure,' he says. 'You don't know me.'

He walks away. He is very thin – a narrow, straight line from behind, so unlike anyone Cannie has ever been with. His hands are big – paws – at gawky, not un-charming odds with the slight rest of him.

Cannie stops watching him, takes her eyes away. He is leaving, and she does not need to follow him until he is through the door. This is the kind of thing she has never done – nor wanted to. Friends have told of awkward moments, the ghosts of one-night stands coming to haunt them at the worst imaginable moments, and Cannie would listen in entertained incredulity – how could someone ever get themselves into such a puddle? And yet here she is. Ankle deep, water in her shoes.

Cannie apologises to the girl, and mechanically answers the rest of her questions: *Under the graduate scheme, is there any opportunity to meet or work with senior staff? How much control would you have in deciding the projects you work on?* But, as Cannie responds, her disappointment grows. She had not known what she felt when he was here, looking at her, but now that he is gone – she feels sad.

He had turned up – as if conjured by a snake charmer from between the carpet tiles – and when it had dawned on Cannie who he actually was, the curtain of grey seemed to part for a small ray of light. It had been exciting – Cannie was not used to the uncertainty of that feeling. Ben's bright arrival – and his departure – had made the rest of the evening feel dreary.

She retrieves her case from the lecture hall, inside it her small computer, her papers, a selection of pens, a slim box of business cards, a packet of tissues, a roll of breath mints and a spare pair of tights. She may have hurt him, she thinks. He had landed near her, and all she had done was throw stones. She remembers the morning she sat by the cemetery wall, remembers the joy she felt, the perfect warmth of the sun, before it ripped open and let out its locusts of heat. Her feet, unpedicured, untended, but not ugly – bare on the grass, heedless of ants, heedless of dog pee, heedless of cigarette butts. There is no shame in the memory. The shame was in the night before, at the wedding, with that stupid flower in her hair.

With her bag on her shoulder, Cannie walks through the cool lobby and out into the bubbling heat. Her bag is unwieldy – in addition to her laptop and work papers, it has inside it the owl, the scarecrow she had ordered to exorcise Max. It is in a box, inside a padded envelope – she had hastily put it into her bag as she left the office, without unwrapping it.

Cannie stops at the bottom of the steps, by a dustbin, and takes the large envelope from her bag. She pulls the tab to open it, and takes the box out. Then, slicing her fingernail through the tape, she takes the deflated plastic owl from inside, and throws the packaging away.

'What the fuck is that?' says a voice.

Cannie's heart, in its cage, sweeps high in a helium circle and grazes against the bars.

'It's an inflatable owl,' she says. Ben is sitting on the steps above her – busy freeing the owl from its layers, she had walked straight past him,

'You are kinkier than I had ever imagined,' Ben says, dragging on a cigarette.

Cannie laughs. There is air around her heart. 'It's a scarecrow,' she says.

'What, to scare away pissed students?'

'No. To scare away this bird that keeps crapping on my window sill.'

'An inflatable owl.'

'Yes,' says Cannie. 'Although I don't actually need it, now. The bird's already gone.'

'What did you do?'

'I drew an owl myself, and stuck it up on the window.'

'Seriously?' Ben is looking right at Cannie's face, and the facts – the physical memories – of her night with him are flooding into her cheeks.

'Yep.'

'Good onya,' says Ben.

Cannie had also put mustard powder on the window ledge, but she cannot tell him that. Colman's mustard powder in a tin, taken from the shelves of the deli on an impulse. Cannie had imagined Max's burning tongue, curling in his mouth like frying bacon as he pecked at it, and it is the thing in her life that she is most ashamed of. Apart from that kiss – that kiss with JP when they were kids – at the party. Apart from the look on JP's face.

'Do you wish I'd left?' Ben asks, breathing out smoke as he talks. 'I didn't mean to stalk you. You didn't leave a number, or anything.'

'No. Well, I thought it was just . . .'

'Yeah, I get it,' he says. 'A wedding shag.'

Cannie clears her throat.

'So,' Ben stubs his cigarette out on the step, 'you want to come back to mine and root? You can bring the owl.'

Cannie opens her mouth, and closes it again. 'Just joking. You said you worked for Onestar, so I thought I'd come along, in case you were here. But I didn't actually reckon you *would* be here.'

Cannie doesn't understand it, but she's laughing. He's so implausibly young, like he has a potion of light, and space, and newness inside him. Like he is a cartoon, outlines filled in with perfect block colour.

'D'you fancy having some dinner? There's a good Thai place a minute away. Or do you just want me to piss off?'

'Look,' says Cannie, talking from within her box of responsibility, of fear, of four square corners, 'about the other night.'

'Don't worry,' says Ben, 'I know we're not going to get married and have kids and live happily ever after. I had a laugh, is all. And I like a woman who's unavailable. Who leaves in the middle of the night.'

It is the most glamorous description of herself that Cannie has heard.

'So, dinner? Or not? You're probably busy. With your mates in suits. I'm going to go anyway. I've got to eat something before I chunder two litres of Sauvignon Blanc.'

Cannie thinks of the noise she made when Max would come, to sit and shit on her window. *Chaaa!* Chaaa. Get away.

'We can have dinner,' Cannie says. She and Story had made tentative plans a week ago, but she hadn't heard from him since, and she won't text, now.

Ben springs up from the steps as if he is a spaniel – not like

JP, with all his Rottweiler heaviness; not like JP at all.

'Fuck, it's hot,' he says. He puts his arm around Cannie's shoulder, a sloppy, happy sling – as if she is the same as him, as if he has not noticed that she is separated by years, and clothes, and work, and money, and liability, and circumstance. As if she is just another person, whom he likes.

They walk, Ben's arm bearing down on the strap of Cannie's bag, with the owl inside, and Cannie feeling light as a dancer. And, as they walk, the jacaranda trees bend down their branches, to touch their heads. The pavement holds its breath, puffs out its chest, up, up, to meet their toes.

44

*D*ude, *sorry not to return your call, was on an aeroplane. In
London until Fri. Call when you wake up. Happy to help if
I can. Story*

And, when that is sent: *So sorry Kali not to turn up. Had to
get on a plane to London at the last minute. Job interview! Will
explain when I'm back on Fri. Sorry again. Sorry to Jacob. Story x*

He had landed in the dark, six in the morning, wet,
February. The taxi had taken him through the grey dawn, to
a hotel in Covent Garden, where he had showered, eaten,
and in a state of vulnerable, nervous discomposure, got into
another taxi to Fleet Street, to Goldman Sachs.

The smell in London was metallic and dry, you tasted it in
the back of your throat. And the noise was overwhelming. A
rumble, like an old lion was asleep under the streets – his
breath, the sound of his lungs drawing in and out – rising
through the pavement. Too loud, too constant, too frightening, to let your own sounds swell. No yeast, here, for your
own, small monsters.

Not like the garden sound of Sydney, feathers, beaks,
scales, tongues, fur, teeth, branches, leaves – a sound that your
sweat became a part of, and that your voice rang clear above.

Here, in London, the sound swallows you up, blessed release.

Story had had three meetings throughout the day, and even though the walk was short, had taken the tube back to his hotel – another roaring monster, nightmare noises, as if the metal braces of the trains were about to snap. He had slept, as if suffocated, and now wakes in the padded, hotel dark, the only light the red glow from the alarm clock. 4:04 in the morning. The streets are dim and empty outside.

Twenty-three emails have amassed within his BlackBerry, which he leaves switched on and silent overnight. Story scrolls cursorily through, with one eye, his face still on the pillow. He fumbles for the light switch – in an unfamiliar place – and sits up, stiff in his lower back. When he stands – it will be his knees. It was a shock when Story first heard his knees creaking – they were actually producing a sound, that any passer-by might hear; a squeak, as if they were aged, unloved doors, rubbing at their hinges.

At first Story thought that he had a *problem*, with his *knees*. But then he realised, as his lower back joined in the chorus, that there was no problem. It was just stiffness – loss of elasticity. Was youth – the period of time when you woke up supple and lived your day oiled and noiseless – really so concise? Did it really only last until thirty, when you were still painting the town and sleeping around and part of that sacred demographic that every marketer wants a piece of? Is that what gravity did? As well as pushing you down, round, down into the earth like a corkscrew, did it compress your bones and chew up your ligaments and dry out the jelly in your back?

Apparently so. Because Story – skirting the fact of his maturity like a terrified child at the edge of the ocean – wakes in the morning to the rattle of his body.

Story sends his texts, to his sister and to JP. If JP calls, to talk about whatever GST thing he needs to talk about, it will be strange hearing his voice. He could say, *Do you want to meet after work for a drink at the Green Man?*, and it would sound reasonable, to eardrum and jetlagged logic, to the part of his head catching up with the flight. But of course he can't, because he is here, and with hammering relief Story feels that here is where he wants to be. Where the only familiar things in the room are his open suitcase, his phone on the bedside table and his wash bag in the bathroom. Nothing else. The room is neutral, made for passing in and out of, like water, like leaves, like a bird flying through.

Story gets up, and walks to the bathroom. He opens the shower and turns the water on, and as it heats he removes his boxers and singlet, and tosses them back out into the bedroom. Testing the water first with his foot, Story steps under, into what may be his favourite ten minutes of the day. There is nothing, yet, in his stomach, no food making his muscles grind and depositing itself like grit around his arteries and weighing him down like sand. There have been no conversations had, no websites browsed, no news ingested, no information configured, no desires felt or reflections seen. With the water on him, feeling empty, only his blood in his veins for company, this is Story's ten minutes of purity. Before it all begins, gram by gram, collecting on his shoulders.

Story pees a dark stream into the shower, at the same time as tipping his head back and allowing the hot water to rinse out his mouth. He gives himself time before washing, and time after, the water just falling at the back of his neck, his head down, the rush of it obscuring everything else like the sound of a jet engine.

Once dry, Story brushes his teeth and shaves, with the towel around his waist, tied high just above his navel. He has never enjoyed shaving, but has to do it each day – for work, and for the fact that if he grew a beard, he'd look like a child in a Nativity – his skin is too soft, too silk-worm smooth, to carry off any shadow with style. It was one of the few things he did, yesterday, before going to Fleet Street: get rid of the twenty-four hours of growth.

Story puts the hotel dressing gown on over his towel, and tightens the belt. It is still not yet five. His phone shudders.

I'll call in an hour. Have you seen what's going on in Sydney? Fucking weird day. JP.

Story reads the text again. And again. With illogical panic, he thinks that maybe JP – knows. About the Gap. About him having gone up there.

How could he know? Who could have told him?

Story had walked back, that night, and found his jacket hanging, like a snake's shed skin, on the railing where he had left it. Nobody had touched it. It was there, shapeless and lifeless, shoulder pads sagging, a shroud. He had picked it up, marvelling at the fact that it had ever been his.

For years Story had filled up his diary with events to haul and distract him – weddings, cars, dinners and parties. Since Dad's funeral – the glitter and the calamity of it – Story had needed more occasions and happenings to lead him on, Monday to Friday, Saturday to Sunday. The organ had blared, that day, like deafening bagpipes – Story had wanted to walk round the altar to the organist, and shoot him in the face. Punch him, with both hands. Bite and kick and spit on him.

There had been Christmas. And then Vincent's wedding. And then: Miranda. The idea of being in love with a stranger, to help him through the week. He needed something,

343

because a circus was not going to knock on Story's door, and ask him to join. He should have trained in tightrope, had he wanted that. And seeing as he needed a next thing, a new next thing, and a new next thing, to get him to the end, then he might as well choose well. And London was better than a crush as humiliating as a whoopee cushion. Story couldn't sit in Sydney any more, in that place – that flat – watching them all live out their cheerful choice to do nothing under the sun.

Story reads JP's text again.

Have you seen what's going on in Sydney? Fucking weird day.

The message is not about him.

He opens his laptop, and goes to the *Herald* webpage to discover what strange thing JP means.

'Fuck me,' Story says.

On his screen, he sees Sydney suspended in red dust.

Dust coats the street; strange, red snow. It covers the pavements, the cars, every edge of every building. It sits on top of the bus shelter, an opaque ceiling. It blankets the city. Red dust fills the air, as if the whole of Sydney has been eaten, and is sitting inside the stomach of a ghost. The dust hangs, colouring what was colourless, filling empty space, clinging to oxygen, hydrogen, carbon, wrapping each atom with its hands. There are no cars, no buses, no movement at all. The light struggles through the powder, an eerie, suffocated orange.

The voice of the reporter is saying:

. . . scenes from early this morning that have had Sydney on front pages all over the world. Sydney is slowly returning to normal, but as you can see, some of us are making the most of this striking phenomenon . . .

There are clips of people outside now. Children on their

backs making angels in the dust. Somebody has drawn a suicide shape, the police outline of a man, underneath a city skyscraper.

. . . it is still advised that if you suffer from asthma, or respiratory conditions of any kind, to stay indoors until tomorrow, when most of the dust is expected to have cleared . . .

Story closes the screen – *phtt* – and he is back. Here, in this room, in London. Suitcase on the floor. Room service menu open on the desk. The dawn still not arrived outside.

If Story had been in Sydney, and walked out into that dust, it would have eaten him alive. That dust had come – for him. It had been waiting, since the first page.

But when it came, he wasn't there. Story knows he has escaped.

Story – inside, hermetic, pristine, his lines clear and his carpet clean – thinks of the dust, hurled up from the ancient guts of Australia, sitting over Sydney like a crown. His *life*, was underneath that stuff. Pushing through the membrane of each slow second into the next.

Story has the feeling that it will rain. And when it does – when the red dust is washed away and he returns – everything will be different.

It will be older, and it will be sadder, and it will be worse. But hopefully, in its heart, it will remain the same.

ACKNOWLEDGEMENTS

Thank you:

Jane Lawson, the backbone of this book.

Peter Straus.

Andrew O'Hagan, generous, brilliant and kind.

Will Self.

Jeremy Langmead, one of the world's best people. And one of mine.

Nancy D'Souza, without whose love, patience and hard work I couldn't write even a postcard.

My little A&I, the two most delightful people on earth.

Rupert, Lion.

SRM and ASBK, for everything, always.

ABOUT THE AUTHOR

Afsaneh Knight lives in London with her husband and their two children. *The Sunshine Years* is her second novel.